I0788443

DROPNAUTS

LIMINAL SKY: REDEMPTION BOOK 1

J. SCOTT COATSWORTH

Published by
Other Worlds Ink
PO Box 19341, Sacramento, CA 95819

This book is dedicated to the hope for the future, hope that we may never have to face the world in these novels - a climate change future that almost destroys everything. We must always have hope.

It's also dedicated to my husband Mark, the man who gives me reason to get up every morning. Love you, Mark!

CONTENTS

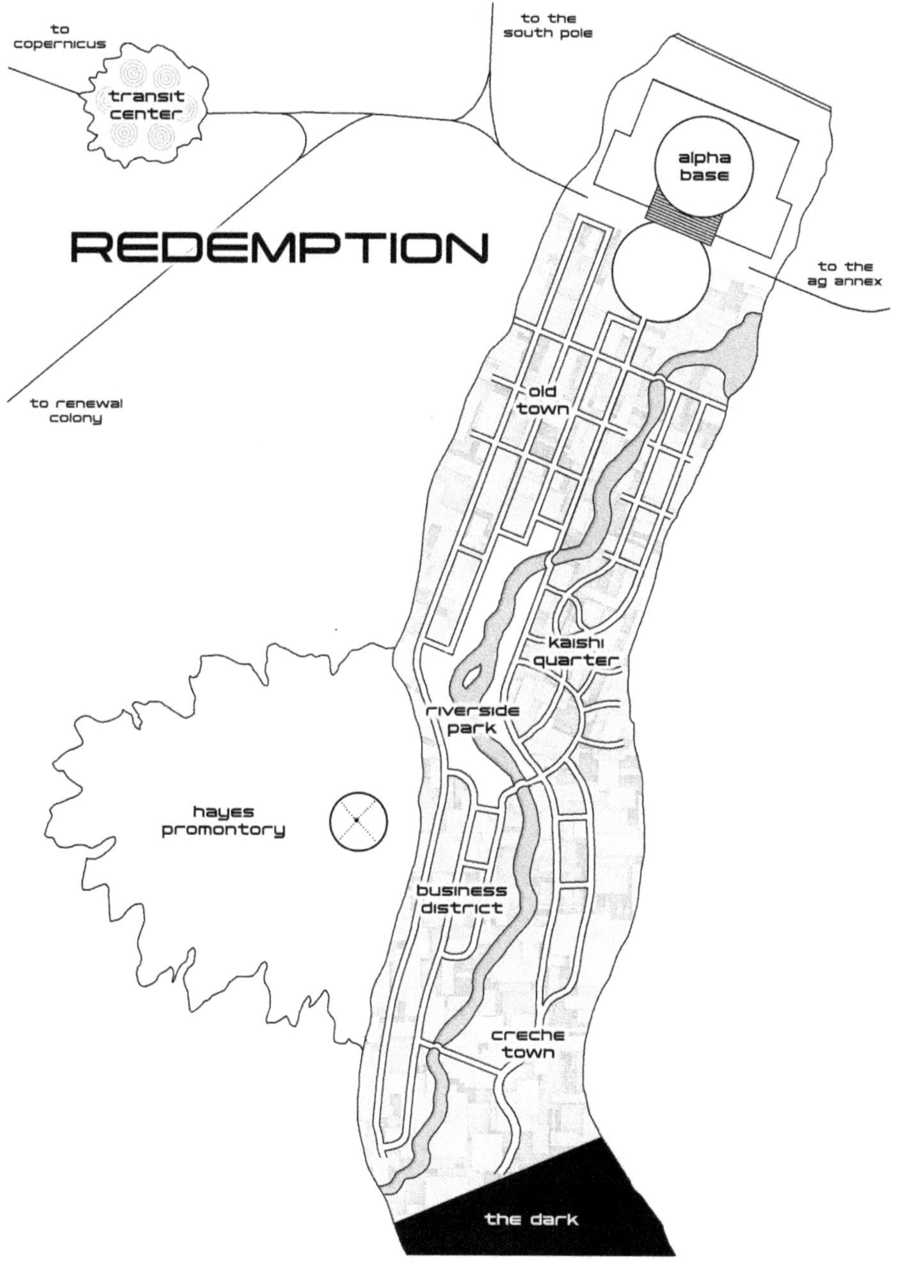

to copernicus
transit center
to the south pole
alpha base
to the ag annex
REDEMPTION
old town
to renewal colony
kaishi quarter
riverside park
hayes promontory
business district
creche town
the dark

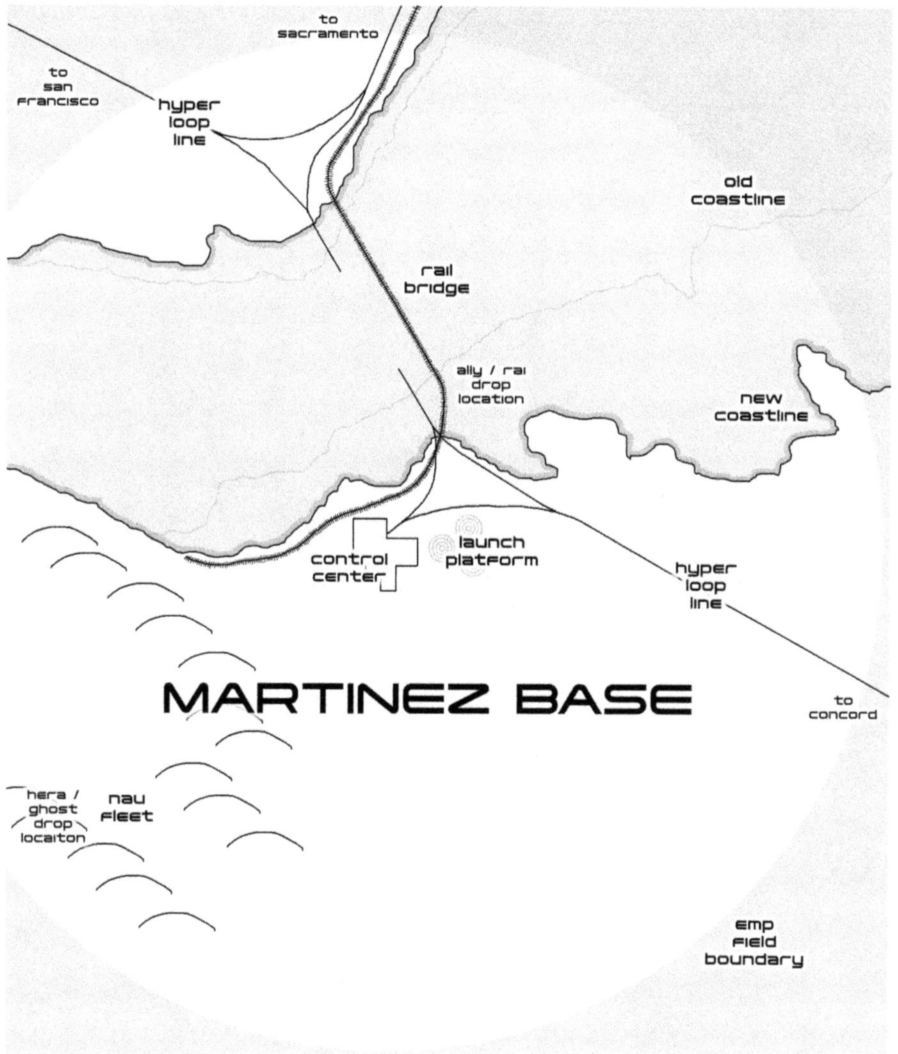

to sacramento
to san francisco
hyper loop line
old coastline
rail bridge
ally / rai drop location
new coastline
control center
launch platform
hyper loop line
to concord
MARTINEZ BASE
hera / ghost drop locaiton
nau fleet
emp field boundary

ACKNOWLEDGMENTS

This story wouldn't have happened without the help of a village of people.

First of all, thank you to Poppy, who suggested I come up with something new and big for my next novel.

Hugs to Gus Li, who edited the book for me for Pitch Wars (and in fairness, I have made extensive changes since then, so don't blame him for any typos, which are exclusively mine).

Tash McAdam and Cari Z., my own personal Pitch Wars and agent query cheer squad, also deserve special recognition for their love and support.

My friend Donna gets a shout out for reading the book after a particularly crushing agent critique and for reassuring me that yes, I can write.

And finally, none of this would happen without my handsome, understanding husband Mark, whose support makes all of this possible.

I love you all!

PRINCIPAL CHARACTERS (GLOSSARY AT END):

Aidan Thorn: Ally's brother, a 22-year-old who grew up at Boundary Peak

Alessandra Thorn (Ally): Aidan's sister, a twenty-five-year-old from Boundary Peak

Alpha: The Redemption city mind

Chen Tien (Chen Tai): A 27-year-old doctor and part of the Zhenyi drop team

Cimber (CIMBER: Cybernetic Interactive Mechanoid Bio Enhanced Rover): Ally and Aidan's robotic pet canine and protector

Gordon Gillam (Ghost): A 24-year-old bi engineer, and member of the Zhenyi drop team

Harley: the city mind for San Francisco

Hera Jezabel Quinn: 24-year-old pilot for the Zhenyi, a paraplegic who wears biframes for mobility

Rafe Wilde: Redemption's top press agent

Rylan "Rai" Ramirez: A twenty-one-year-old gay botanist and member of the Zhenyi drop team.

Sam (SAM - Synthetic AI Mechanoid): A mech who reached consciousness during the Crash and now runs the "Return" program

Sanya Thorn: Reporter at RedNews

1

LAUNCH: 6.15.2282

O Earth! dost thou too sorrow for the past
   Like man thy offspring? Do I hear thee mourn
   Thy childhood's unreturning hours, thy springs
   Gone with their genial airs and melodies,
   The gentle generations of thy flowers,
   And thy majestic groves of olden time,
   Perished with all their dwellers?

—"Earth," by William Cullen Bryant,
from *Poems From a Distant Earth*, by Chen Tien

WE'RE GOING HOME.

Rai sweated inside his suit, white-knuckling the arms of the retrofitted launch chair under his suit gloves. He watched the *Zhenyi's* launch countdown clock.

Sixty, fifty-nine, fifty-eight…

Outside he was calm, but inside he vibrated like an erhu string, his stomach doing acrobatics in his chest. *I'm not ready.*

Five teams of dropnauts had strapped themselves into their jumper ships, prepared for the ascent from Redemption on the lunar surface to Launchpad station. Outside his porthole, the blue-green marble of Earth beckoned.

Forty-five, forty-four...

Rai cast a nervous glance at his three teammates. Hera was doing her preflight check, her back to him, sweat dripping down the umber skin of her neck from her short-cropped, curly black hair.

Behind him on his right, Tien's eyes were closed, and she was still as a golden statue. Zen.

He turned to find Ghost looking at him from behind. His ex grinned, running his hand through his lanky, dirty blond hair, his green eyes twinkling. His skin was as white as Rai's own, but with a dusting of freckles over the bridge of his nose.

Rai managed a pale imitation of a smile back. *-It's totally safe.-* Ghost's voice pinged in his head, *em to em.*

-Sure. Easy for you to say.- Ghost had never feared a thing in his life.

Rai sighed. If he had to, he could take the small ship apart and put it back together with his bare hands, a skill learned under Sam's supervision—the mech was as harsh a taskmaster as any human Rai had ever worked for. Still, he felt like puking. The speeches and adulation of the farewell celebration were over, and now his doubts circled like vultures. *I'm not ready.*

Thirty-two, thirty-one...

-You'll be ok.- Hera's determined voice this time. She turned to squeeze his knee, and then fired up the *Zhenyi's* hydro-fuel engine. He flashed her a sheepish grin.

A hundred meters away, the *Bristol's* takeoff shook the landing pad. Rai watched it rise, carrying Dax, Jess, Ola, and Xiu Ying, the London team, toward the bright stars above. The jumper's expelled water froze almost instantly, falling as snow over the snaking lava tube that held the city of Redemption. A lunar blizzard whipped by them and shimmered into nothing.

Rai closed his eyes, remembering the night before. Jess, laughing and dancing with him at Heaven, the clear dome of the lunar sky sparkling above them, the heavy beat of the thromb club pulsing through his chest. *Dancing like no one was watching.*

He rubbed his jaw. It still ached from the fist he'd taken to the face. *Wild party.* And a wilder night with Ayvin, the *jack* he'd picked up at the club.

"*Zhenyi,* ready for liftoff in T-Minus ten seconds." Sam's voice, coming from

Team Five's ship, the *Liánhuā*, was cool and collected. Did the mech feel emotion, like the nausea that was boiling in Rai's guts? His teammates were strong, smart, and prepared for anything. *I can do this.* Besides, it was too late to back out now.

"Affirmative." Hera shifted in her seat, her biframes stretching her paralyzed legs for her.

"You'll do okay, tiger." Ghost elbowed him in the ribs.

"Six, five, four…" Hera swiped the glossy white control deck, and the launch controls appeared, floating over the white surface.

"Leave him alone." Rai could *hear* the icy frown in Tien's voice.

He closed his eyes, willing his stomach to calm. *Here we go.* Nothing he could do about it now.

"Three, two, one… hang on." Hera fired the engines, and the craft lifted on a cloud of steam into the star-filled skies of Luna.

Rai squeezed his armrests again as G-force pushed him *hard* back in his seat. He was committed now. *Poppies, Chinese Houses, Fiddlenecks, Baby Blue Eyes, Yellow Pansies, Star Lilies…* Reciting the flowers of the old San Francisco basin helped soothe his abraded nerves as the rumbling of the little craft rattled his bones.

He opened his eyes to see Redemption receding below them. The great lava tube was striped with sparkling bands of solar receptors that let sunlight into the city below. Rail lines snaked out from Redemption to the transit center like roping vines—to the seed launcher at Copernicus Crater, to Renewal colony, and beyond.

As the city shrank below them, his fear turned to sadness, a lump forming in his throat. He'd taken his home for granted, enthralled by the idea of joining humankind's greatest adventure in a century. Now he might never see it again.

The hydro rocket thrust them up out of Luna's gravity well into naked space, toward the bright blue skies of the empty Earth above. Rai stared at it, that enigmatic ball in space which no one had visited in over a century. *What secrets are you hiding?*

The roar cut off as quickly as it had begun, leaving the *Zhenyi* drifting upward in silence as they slipped out of Luna's grasp.

Hera's hands flew across the deck, swapping the launch controls for navigation, and nudged them onto a new course following the *Bristol* toward the Launchpad.

Rai let go, his breath coming out in a heavy sigh.

"See? That wasn't so bad." Ghost unbuckled his seatbelt and stretched, yawning as if he didn't have a care in the world.

God, he's beautiful. Pale as his namesake under his mop of dirty blond hair, the engineer's thick arms were just a suggestion under the bulky suit, but Rai could still see them in his mind. Ghost's well-toned muscles, the smell of his skin after—

"You okay, buddy?" Ghost was staring at him, one dark eyebrow raised in concern.

Rai bit his lip and looked away. "Just nervous. Wondering if we'll ever make it back home."

"Hey, if things go well after the drop, maybe you and me could open the first Earthside bar since the Crash." Ghost leaned over him from behind to stare at the Earth through the porthole, his cheek close to Rai's.

"That's crazy." But his spirits lifted. It *was* idiotic. And just the distraction he needed.

Ghost sank back into his own seat. "Every outpost needs a good bar where the colonists can blow off a little steam, right?"

Rai laughed in spite of himself, warming to the idea. "We could call it 'The Frontier'."

"Or 'The Wild Hookup'."

"Best beer this side of the planet."

"*Only* beer!"

Rai snorted. *Just like old times.* He hadn't forgiven Ghost, though. Not yet. He looked down at his gloved hands, emblazoned with the leaf-and-orb of Redemption's space service.

Things had ended badly between them—*crash and burn* bad. Still, they'd be too busy the next few weeks to think about *anything* but the drop. The survival of Redemption and the remnants of humanity depended on them.

He could let it go. *I have to.* He'd managed the launch, after all. *I can do this too.*

Ghost squeezed his shoulder and closed his eyes, touching his temple and bobbing his head to a song only he could hear.

Rai turned away.

You're stronger than any of us. Hera had told him that the night before. Still, he didn't *feel* strong.

He looked out of the porthole again at the Earth—the same view they'd had from *Heaven*. And yet somehow, it looked different. More *real.*

Poppies, Chinese Houses, Fiddlenecks, Baby Blue Eyes, Yellow Pansies, Star Lilies…

He touched his hand to the porthole. Even through the glove, it was cold. *We're going home.*

Rai spun his seat around to face Ghost. "Feel like a game?"

THE ENDING strains of *Thus Spoke Zarathustra* faded into the background as the *Zhenyi* settled into her new course. The ship would be on autopilot for two days as they hurtled toward the Launchpad.

There was nothing more for Hera to do for a while.

She pressed the releases on her biframe, pulling off the metal braces and tucking them into the webbing behind the seat.

Up here in space, she was free—in zero-gee her useless legs weren't a hindrance. Through the suit legs, she touched the scars where the medics had cut her open to replace her crushed bones with rods printed from gumdust— the pulverized moon dust they'd used to make her whole again.

Luna would always be a part of her, no matter how far she roamed.

Somewhere behind them, Tovey waited for her return. She could still feel the touch of their lips on hers.

She shook her head, dispelling the memory. *Don't let yourself get lost in homesickness.*

She got up and squeezed past the chair and the gunmetal gray walls to her own seat, and settled in next to Rai. She snapped her seatbelt closed and peered out of her porthole. The red running lights of one of the other jumpers blinked in the distance.

Rai had swiveled his seat around, and he and Ghost were playing chess on one side of the cramped five-seat craft. Behind Hera, Tien was staring out at the stars, her overhead light dimmed.

Along with Tovey, her teammates were Hera's family.

She'd known Ghost all her life, and Rai and Tien for two years while they'd trained on Luna, learning how to operate the jumper's modified flight systems, packing her brain with everything there was to know about the Earth. They'd spent six more intense months together in the full Earth gravity of the Launchpad, time which had sealed their bond.

She'd met Tovey there too, but they weren't a part of the mission. Pain gripped Hera's heart. *What if I never see you again?*

Hera needed a distraction. She released her seat and swung it around to face Tien, the only one of them raised by her birth parents. She wondered for the thousandth time what it would have been like to have *actual* parents instead of creche parents. "How'd it go with your parents, Ti?"

"What?" Tien turned toward her, dark brown eyes glassy. They shimmered and Tien was back in the here-and-now, staring at her.

Sometimes Hera still saw Tai in her features, the man Tien had been when they first met. "I'm sorry, didn't realize you were busy—" Hera braced herself to get up. She could watch the view from the pilot's chair.

Tien flashed her a warm smile, brushing a long strand of black hair back behind her ear. "It's okay. I was just reading poetry. What did you ask?"

"Your parents. How'd it go?"

Tien's smile became a grin. "Better than I hoped. My father called me his *daughter*—for the first time. They told me they were proud of me and gave me their blessing to go."

Hera's jaw dropped. "That's amazing, Ti." She squeezed Tien's hand. "What are you reading?" Anyone I know?"

"Probably not. Emily Dickinson. From the old United States."

"Read me a few lines." Hera loved poetry, especially the lyrical Old Earth stuff Tien found.

Tien's lenses shimmered again. "Okay. How about this one?"

Hera closed her eyes to listen.

There is no Frigate like a Book
    To take us Lands away,
    Nor any Coursers like a Page
    Of prancing Poetry—
    This Traverse may the poorest take
    Without oppress of Toll—
    How frugal is the Chariot
    That bears a Human soul.

Hera bit her lip. "What does it mean?"

Tien bit her lip. "Hmm. That words have power. They can cross centuries to transport us to other worlds." Tien smiled wanly. "That what we do *now* can still matter so much *later*."

"That's beautiful." Tien was a closet romantic, but the old words still confounded Hera sometimes. "What's a frigate?"

"A bird, or maybe a warship. It's not really clear." Tien frowned. "I can try to find out—"

Hera grinned. "Let's say a bird. Better than a warship—"

The ship-to-ship radio blared to life with a loud burst of static. "This is Dax on the *Bristol*. We've taken a hit. I repeat—" More static. "—hit. there's a lot of space junk—"

Hera swiveled and pulled herself out of her seat and into the pilot's chair with the ease of long practice.

Sam's voice came from the *Liánhuā* at the rear of the convoy. "*Bristol*, you there?"

Nervous silence filled the *Zhenyi*. No response.

Hera glanced back at her teammates. Rai was pale, sweat beading his forehead, the chess game forgotten. "Everyone buckle in."

The radio buzzed again. "…lost contact. Something hit us and spun us around. We're ok."

Hera breathed a sigh of relief and hit the comm button. "What kind of something? The way's supposed to be clear all the way to the Launchpad." She activated the scanner. Five glowing red dots floated over her deck, one for each ship.

"Don't know. It was too fast—" Loud static cut him off again.

"What's happening?" Rai sounded panicked, his voice raspy.

"Keep it together, Rai." She couldn't deal with his fear and this at the same time. Hera leaned forward, staring at the dots—each of the jumpers were still there, spread out in a lazy line. She sighed with relief. "Dax, you there?"

"Yeah. We're losing pressure…" Dax's usually calm, suave voice broke. "Hissing hell, it cracked the hull—"

An apocalyptic *boom*, then nothing.

All the blood drained from Hera's face, and her stomach twisted. *Please let them be okay.* Hera looked at the lights hovering above the deck again. The *Bristol's* dot was gone.

Sam's voice crackled over the comm. "What happened? *Zhenyi*, can you see the *Bristol*?"

Hera was racing to scan the space ahead of them. "Unexpected debris. I think—she's gone, Sir." *Concentrate.* She had to figure this out fast.

Dax, Jess, Ola, and Xiu Ying… cracking hell. She bit her lip hard, tasting blood.

Rai sobbed quietly behind her.

"Must have been a space-junk collision somewhere since they scanned it last, scattering more debris." Ghost sounded calm, but that was one of his tells. He was totally freaking out inside.

"No shit, Sherlock." Her eyes tracked the screen, looking for danger. She had no idea who in the whole pantheon of history Sherlock was, and right now she didn't care.

Something flared bright blue above the deck. "Hang on!" She fired one of the aft thrusters, and a gust of steam pushed them out of the way of a piece of debris. It slipped past the window, a white-encased leg. Hera fought not to hurl.

"Oh crap. Wasn't that—"

"Shut up!" The *Bristol* was gone. Better not to know who it had belonged to. "Sam, we have visual on Jumper One's debris. Advise course correction. Sending revised path." Her hands flew across the deck. *Hold it together, Hera.*

"Affirmative. One moment."

Hera watched the sensor field nervously. "Ghost, sealant ready?"

"Yeah. Just a sec." He rummaged around in the webbing along the wall of the craft.

Something struck the metal skin of the jumper. Air hissed out as the temperature and air pressure dropped precipitously. "Ghost!"

"On it!" He leapt out of his seat to find the pinhole puncture and applied a dab of sealant. It sucked into the hole and froze, holding tight. "Got it."

More blips on the sensor field. "Hold on!" Hera fired the thrusters again, and the ship threw her sideways. *No belt!* She flew up out of the pilot's seat, slamming *hard* against the metal ceiling of the *Zhenyi.*

Tovey, I love you… Searing pain was followed by darkness.

~

"Hera!" Ghost unbuckled his belt and leapt to grab the pilot. He pulled her down toward her chair gently.

"Careful." Tien floated next to him, checking Hera's body through her white suit. "She might have broken something." Together they maneuvered her into her seat and buckled her in. "Rai, take the controls. I'll check her over." Tien pulled out her medkit from her seat's webbing.

The ship was tumbling off-course, moving away from the others at a rapid pace.

Rai was still buckled in. He was hyperventilating, looking back and forth from the controls to Hera. "It's not… I'm not supposed to… I'm not ready—"

Tien knelt in front of him, taking his face in her hands. "Rai, snap out of it, dammit! If you don't get this jumper under control, we're all dead!" Tien pointed at the pilot's seat, moving out of his way.

Rai swallowed hard and nodded. "Okay." He unbuckled and slipped past them to settle into the pilot's seat. He stared at the deck as if all his training had fled. "I'm just the backup—I never expected to have to actually fly this thing."

"Tien, take care of Hera. I've got this."

Tien met his eyes and nodded.

"*Zhenyi*, everything okay over there?" Sam's synthetic voice over the com was calm, reassuring.

Rai's teeth chattered. "I… I don't know what to do."

Ghost squeezed past Tien and activated the comm. "Sam, this is Ghost. We're okay. Hera sustained an injury when she rolled the ship to avoid a patch of space junk." He let go of the comm button. "Rai, you're going to be okay. Just take a deep breath, buddy."

Rai nodded. He closed his eyes, putting his hands on the cool deck. His breathing slowed.

"Injury? How extensive is it?" Sam actually sounded *concerned*.

"Unclear, sir. Tien's checking her over now. She wasn't buckled in." Rai's cheek was inches from his. Ghost took a deep breath. *Keep it together, big guy.*

"Where's Rai?"

"He's getting this bucket of bolts back on course." Ghost squeezed Rai's shoulder and thumbed off the comm. *-You got this, pal.-*

-Thanks.- Rai leaned in to the jumper's deck and went to work, monitoring the debris sensor, his hand flying through the navigational controls in the air like a master piano player.

Being so close to Rai again set off all kinds of alarms in his head. They'd kept a certain distance between them the last two months. A healthy distance, for Rai.

Ghost was toxic, and he knew it.

Rai gently nudged the ship back into a straight trajectory with the attitude jets, reducing the *Zhenyi's* spin and wobble. Bit by bit, he pulled her back to center, and then swung them around toward their destination.

"You're doing it, squirt." Ghost winced. *Tiger, buddy, pal, squirt.* He was working overtime to put Rai back in the friend zone, in his head. He squeezed Rai's shoulder and pulled away before his teammate could see how the close proximity rattled him.

Ghost turned to find Tien crouching next to Hera, running a sensor over the pilot's forehead. "How's Hera?"

"She's okay, I think. Just a concussion." Tien sounded calm too, a doctor's voice, serious and reassuring. "She'll have a nasty goose egg on her head when she wakes up."

Ghost laughed. "What the hell is a goose?"

"Earth bird. Long neck, swam in ponds."

Rai's voice had that know-it-all tone, and Ghost couldn't help but mock him. "You're such a geek. So it's like a swan?"

Rai didn't seem to notice. "Kind of. They had enormous eggs. Like giant chickens."

Ghost shivered. The idea of eating something that came out of a bird's ass squicked him out. Still, for all that he kidded Rai, Ghost was proud of him. "You did good. I knew you would."

Rai flicked the comm back on. "This is Rai on the *Zhenyi*. Back on track, sir."

There were cheers in the background. "Excellent work, Rai." Sam sounded dejected, though, different from his usual mech self. Ghost frowned. Since when did Sam have feelings?

"Sir?"

"Yes, Rai?"

"It's not your fault. The debris maps must have been wrong, or there was a collision somewhere. Or—"

"Thanks, Rai. But *everything* on this mission is my responsibility. And my fault if it goes wrong." The comm link cut out.

Rai looked up at Ghost, his eyebrow raised.

"I know. Weird." He picked a floating rook out of the air and set it back down on the magnetic chessboard.

Four of their fellow dropnauts were gone, just like *that*. The sense of security, the boring normalcy of the trip was shattered.

Ghost sighed. *This spin just got real.*

~

Sam sat back in his chair, running a diagnostic on his mental state. There was something corrosive in his programming, a sense of *wrongness* that gnawed at him. His diagnostic identified it as *guilt*.

He shunted the feeling away again, but it was harder each time. When he got to the Launchpad, he'd have to ask Alpha for a tune-up.

...fileto > memcache...

He'd never been in such sustained contact in such intimate and challenging situations with humans before. They'd finally gotten to him with their complicated emotions.

...access > communications module...

He relayed the news of the Bristol's destruction to Alpha, who would pass it on to the families of the dead.

I should be the one to tell them.

He retrieved the odd feeling again and spun it around, considering it as if it were a math problem, this strange new wrinkle in his programming.

Guilt made no sense here. He had committed no wrong act. He and Alpha had worked together to chart the space junk left in Earth orbit by human activity before and during the Crash. He had acted correctly based on all the knowledge they had at hand.

...access > data: debris map...

Nothing. But there was no way to track it all, not without a fleet of satellites —or to predict the changes that would occur, for instance, when a piece of the old Frontier Station collided with one of the old Cino-African Syndicate space mines.

Too many variables.

Besides, these young dropnauts had signed on knowing the risk.

There was *no good reason* for him to feel this guilt. Then again, he was a mech. There was no good reason for him to have feelings at all.

Sometimes he missed the simpler times before his forced uplift, when the only thing he'd *felt* was a satisfying jolt of recognition when he unearthed a rare type of moonstone, one that matched the specs for maximum profit. *Damn you, Alpha, for making me like this.*

He still couldn't *feel* in the physical sense. His fingers were touch-sensitive, to allow him to pick up objects without crushing them or knocking them aside, but his metallic "skin" had no human-like ability.

It was these new *emotional* feelings that threatened to undo him. They wouldn't stay cached, stubbornly resurfacing again and again.

His mission felt *doomed*, and with it the remainder of humankind. The power core under the old Jīnsè Base was slowly eating its way into Luna's heart, melting the wastewater that the old base had injected into the crust. The crisis growing more acute by the day. The reactor had been steadily working its way down for more than a hundred years, but now the quakes had begun. And they were getting worse.

We waited too long.

"You okay, sir?" Ying Yue's voice pulled him back to the present.

Sam opened his eyes to find all the Beijing team on the *Liánhuā* looking at him. "I will be. Are we past the debris field?"

She nodded. "We have a clear path to the Launchpad."

...fileto > memcache: return, the > bristol...

He wanted to retain this moment in all its clarity. "Please send a message to the other teams. 'We are heartbroken about the loss of Team One, but we must continue on.' The *Bristol* would want that, I think."

"Yes, sir." She put a hand on his metal knee. "It's not your fault."

Sam wished he could feel her touch.

Was he that transparent? His features shouldn't have betrayed the cursed emotions he was feeling.

The whole crew was staring at him now. They needed something from him. Inspiration. "We're humanity's last chance. But looking at all of you, I'm not afraid. I see hope, and Redemption."

Ying Yue held her fist to her heart over the Return Mission's leaf-and-orb logo, in automatic salute. "Redemption."

Her teammates did, too.

She searched his silver face a moment longer. He wondered what she was looking for. At last, she nodded and turned away.

Humans are strange creatures. He closed his eyes, seeking comfort of his own.

...define: redemption. > The act of redeeming something or someone. The name of the main human colony on Luna. Alternatively, the program for the return...

Guilt surged in him again, and he squeezed the armrest so hard it cracked.

Sam shut off his definition subroutine.

No more distractions. *No more errors.*

2

____

BRIDGES

The towns and cities we've traveled through are little more than broken ruins. Some buildings are intact, but most have collapsed—probably under the weight of the Great Winter snow.

Many more burned to the ground after it melted. Most of the rest are solid brick, or hollow steel frames, and there are bones in many of them. Bones of people seated around a dining table, hands clasped. Bones of couples with their arms wrapped around each other on a rotted mattress.

It makes me want to puke every time I see them. But if I don't make a record of their passing, who will?

They deserve better. Maybe someday, someone will come lay them to rest.

I hope their end came quickly.

There are just five of us now—Ally, Alex, Auggie, Mamma and me. Dad told me once that there were seven hundred and fifty under Boundary Peak when the Collapse happened.

What if it's just us?

—Aidan's Journal: June 17th, 2282

AIDAN GAVE one last nod to the two skeletons on the dusty, collapsed couch, staring at a broken tridee screen. He added a pair of hatch marks to the list at the end of his paper journal and did a quick count. Over two hundred already. He sighed and slipped the journal in his pocket.

Above the couple, an old, faded oil painting of a yellow bridge and a pyramid-shaped building hung crookedly on the cracked wall. Aiden reached over their bodies gingerly to straighten it out.

Then he slipped out of the decrepit brick house, shutting off his solar flashlight to stare up at the early morning sky. It was clear today and cold—though the wispy cirrus clouds streaking the pink heavens suggested a coming storm. The day before, the temperatures had topped out at 113 degrees. Now he could see his breath.

Ally should still be sleeping, though she'd be awake in time to see the sun rise.

For decades their family had huddled underground, waiting out the Great Winter. They hadn't seen the heavens until he was eight, when the first of the sky tree seeds began to fall.

His father had taken his hand, and they'd knelt and prayed together, father and son under the starry sky. *This is your inheritance. We're the lucky few who get to be fruitful and re-populate the Earth.* How his family would re-populate the Earth was never explained.

His father was long gone. Aidan closed his eyes, pain seizing his gut.

His younger brothers Alex and Auggie—the twins—had stayed behind to watch after their sick mother Astra, under the Mountain, and he and Ally were on this hopeless quest to save her.

Aidan scratched the pale skin of his elbow absently as he passed house after empty house, broken windows gaping at him like empty eye sockets.

He liked to get away from Ally for a few minutes, early in the morning, before they made breakfast, broke camp, and set off again. He had *needs*, after all, better attended to without his sister watching.

Aidan liked to explore, too, and this neighborhood offered lots of options.

The city was in better shape than some they'd passed through. Many of the homes were still standing, fronted by suggestions of lawns and low walls and garden beds, though time and age were dragging everything back down to Earth.

The sky trees were smaller here than in the mountains. *Younger, probably.*

They were ripping apart houses and pulling up pavement with their crooked roots. A new forest was slowly spreading across the continent.

Aidan looked up to see one of them spinning down from the sky. It was a few blocks away, an old gray football, its feathery "wings" spinning to slow its descent like a helicopter in an old tridee. It drifted past him gracefully, a hundred feet or more above.

Aidan watched it until it disappeared behind the ruins in the distance.

Where did you come from? He touched the scratchy red bark of one of the younger trees, just a couple feet taller than him, staring up at it in wonder.

He'd scoured the records under the Mountain. There was nothing about giant seeds that fell from the sky.

He squinted at the bright sky. There must be *someone* up there. On the moon? In orbit around the Earth? *Humans? Or aliens?* Aidan imagined other civilizations on the planets of the solar system or circling faraway stars. *Did you get it right, where we screwed everything up?*

Was there an alien boy just like him on one of them, staring up at Earth's sun so far away, wondering the same thing? An *Aidan* with three eyes, green skin, and a pair of antennas?

He laughed, the last of his discomfort slipping away.

Aiden knelt to wash his hands at a little stream that burbled along the old roadway, slowly wearing down the pavement, remaking the Earth a few pieces of asphalt at a time.

His talkie buzzed. He reached up to touch the *talk* button behind his ear.

"Aidan, where are you?"

Aidan sighed. "Just stretching my legs."

"Get back here soon. I want to get on the road." Ally sounded impatient.

Aidan grinned. His sister always sounded impatient.

A rounded brick wall still stood about thirty feet away, across what had probably once been a lawn but was now an overgrown mess of weeds. Curious, he approached it to touch the brick and mortar. *Who put you here? And when?*

The weather had nearly rusted away the double doors, leaving an irregular, gaping hole like a jagged mouth. Aidan kicked one of them open and stepped inside, stopping to stare in wonder.

It was an old church. Sunlight streamed in from the southern window, a series of stained-glass panels lighting the room up in a golden dappled glow. Many of them were still intact. It was beautiful, and heartbreaking. *Great*

Grandpa Astin, thundering in the small chapel at Boundary Peak at his shrinking flock, extolling them to breed like rabbits...

Aidan pushed that memory away. Papa Astin, the bible thumper, had been smitten by the whole Sodom and Gomorrah parts of the Good Book, and the *wickedness* of that ancient land. Despite his great grandfather's admonitions, Aidan had grown up with feelings that were *wicked* in the eyes of his church.

Aidan wondered if the people here had felt the same.

A robin leapt out of her nest on a small wooden shelf and flapped by his head, squawking her displeasure. Aidan ducked and watched her fly out the door. He grinned. *At least you survived.*

He made his way down the aisle, his hand touching each of the old wooden pews. Their mother had told them about churches, things she had learned from her grandmother—places where people had gathered to sing and listen to the Good Word, which came from the Good Book. She still kept hers by her bedside.

Aidan stepped up onto the creaky wooden platform at the back of the church. It held his weight—barely—groaning as he reached up to touch the wall.

A large "t"—his mother called it a *cross*—hung there, faced with symbolic flames. Sticky dust covered it, making it look almost furry. He touched it, and it broke free from its moorings and crashed to the ground with a loud *boom*.

Aidan leapt out of the way as it smashed into pieces.

"There you are!"

He spun around to find Ally at the doorway, Cimber at her feet. The mech dog sniffed the air and bounded off to check out something interesting.

"Hey sis. I was just looking around—"

Ally smirked. "Yeah, I *know* what you were doing. You don't need to hide it."

Aidan flushed. "Yeah, well, I knew you'd crush the vibe."

Ally laughed. "I'd hope so." She looked around and whistled. "This place is beautiful."

"Yeah. It reminds me of Papa Astin." He knelt to pick up an old leather-bound book. That's when he saw them. "Look!"

There were bodies stuffed under each pew. Many had their arms wrapped around one another. They had died together, at least. He knelt to get a better look—a few had their hands together in prayer. "They were scared."

Ally knelt next to him, frowning. "I'm sure they were." She looked around the cavernous space. "They came here for sanctuary, hoping God would protect them."

"I guess he didn't." It wasn't the first time he'd seen it. But something about the serenity of this place and those empty gazes from tens—no, probably hundreds—of skeletons made him uneasy. "What do you think killed them?"

Ally rubbed her neck. "Most of the buildings here are intact. They used smartgas in a lot of places on the West Coast—it sought out human life and snuffed it. The fucking *chaffs* thought they could take over things after the Last War ended." She almost growled the name.

Aidan touched a naked skull, and it fell off its skeleton to roll across the floor, lodging against one of the pews. Naked sockets staring up at him.

He shivered. Sometimes he just wanted to go back home and lock himself underground, away from the open sky and all the terrible things in this empty world. He pulled out his notebook and made a quick calculation. Probably a hundred dead in this room.

He dutifully added the hash marks, and closed his eyes to say a short prayer for the dead.

Ally frowned. "You still doing that?"

"Somebody should record the dead."

Ally shook her head but said nothing. When he was done, she pulled him away from the grisly sight to stare at the stained glass. "Look at the windows." She put an arm around his shoulder, her body warm against his. "We have to remember that they made beautiful things too, back then. Even in the midst of the horror."

"I guess so." It *was* beautiful, the rising sun shattered into a myriad of colors by the glass. "Do you think they were comforted by their faith?"

She bit her lip. "I'd like to think so. Would you be?"

"I don't know." *What was it like?* Those frantic, fearful last minutes as the gas smothered them. Aidan shuddered. "Can we go now?"

"Yeah. Come on, let's get some fresh air."

They left the old church together, stepping into the wild meadow outside.

Aidan took a deep breath. He could still *see* the skull staring at him. "What's this city called?"

Ally pulled out one of the old plas maps she carried. "Sacramento. Capital of the state of California."

He nodded. "How far are we from Martinez Base?"

"Three days. Two if we push it."

They'd been on the trek for a little over three weeks, sleeping in burned-out houses at night and walking by day. Aidan had never been in better shape. He whistled for Cimber, and the mech dog bounded out of the church behind them with a happy bark, a leg bone in her mouth.

"Cimber! drop it!" Aidan sighed, whispering a prayer for the bone's owner as the mech dog set it down with a growl. *Were real dogs such a pain in the ass?*

Ally tugged at his shirt sleeve. "Come on. I want to get something to eat and get going. We don't know how long Mamma has left."

Aidan nodded. He worried about her too. But in the long run, did it matter?

They were all doomed—the last family under the Mountain. Their mother, three boys, and one girl. There was no one else to continue the human race here once they were gone.

He glanced up at the sun as it rose in the east, its golden light filtering through the sky tree branches, unconcerned with human problems. *Am I going to die alone?*

With a heavy sigh, he followed his sister through the trees, back to their temporary shelter.

Cimber bounded along behind them in the new morning's light.

TIEN WATCHED the glowing ring of the Launchpad draw slowly closer, the giant spinning station framed by the blue curve of the Earth below.

The rest of the run had gone without mishap, save for a brief scare when the patch had leaked, causing an alarming hiss and lowering of pressure in the *Zhenyi's* cabin.

Behind her, the others chatted about the mission ahead, either having forgotten their lost companions, or filling the time so they didn't have to think about them.

Tien hung back. *Always the outsider.* Her teammates were all creche kids. They socialized with others—even strangers—more easily than she ever would. Yet they had accepted her transition without question.

"Time to bring her in." Hera slipped into the pilot's chair, rubbing her bruised but thankfully unbroken arm.

Tien swiveled to watch Hera work. The pilot was a wonder, having overcome a debilitating accident as a child and now the loss of four of their friends, still holding it all together.

"Launchpad control, this is the *Zhenyi*."

"*Zhenyi*, roger. Good to have you back." The woman's voice cracked a little.

Hera nudged the jumper, lining up with the station's spin, the thrust pushing them all to the side. "Thanks. Is this Lorelei?"

"Sure is. Hera?" Lorelei's voice sounded raspy, like she'd been crying. "So sorry to hear about the *Bristol*. We're all a mess here over it."

Hera's hand tightened on the joystick, her knuckles white. "They knew the risks."

There was silence on the comm.

"Lorelei?"

"Sorry." She cleared her throat. "We've got docking bay one waiting for you. Need guidance?"

"No, I got this." A little of Hera's trademark bravado returned.

"I'm sure you do. Roger and out."

Tien put a hand on Hera's good shoulder. "It's okay. We all feel it."

Hera's muscles tightened. "Thanks. I need to concentrate. Buckle in."

Tien pulled away, hurt. "Sorry." She looked at Ghost. He shrugged. *-Give her space.-*

She nodded. *-Think she's okay?-* She latched her belt and settled in for docking.

-She's Hera.-

Tien laughed under her breath.

She was terrible at these things. For all that they'd trained together for years, sometimes Tien felt that she didn't know these people at all. Her mother would have known exactly what to say.

She sighed softly, watching the spinning of the Earth against its velvety, starry backdrop.

Her family had been enjoying a picnic on the Chinese side of Riverside Park.

Tai had climbed up onto the bright red rail of the bridge. She perched on top, watching the clear water flow over the round pebbles below. It glistened and sparkled, murmuring its secrets to her.

"Tai, get down from there!" Her mother's strong arms pulled her down.

"What did I tell you about climbing up on the bridge railing? You boys are always getting into trouble."

"Sorry, Mamma." Tai started to cry. She *hated* making her mother angry.

I'm not a boy. Why couldn't they see that?

The last time she'd said it, she'd been spanked and sent to her room. Now she kept it to herself.

Chen Yun's features softened. "I only scolded you because you scared me, Tai. You could have fallen into the river and been swept away before I could save you."

Tai looked down at the water coursing through the river channel next to them as her mother carried her back to the family. It didn't look all that *deep*. Or *fast*.

"Hey!"

Tai looked up, wiping her tears away with the back of her hand.

On the far side of the bank, a little girl about her age waved at her. Behind her, a group of kids about the same age were playing tag.

Tai waved back, staring at the little girl's pink dress with envy. "How come I never get to go play with the creche kids?"

"You're only four. When you go to school next year, you'll meet them."

Tai stared forlornly at her peers. "*They* don't have any parents to tell them what to do."

Mamma stared at her. "Who told you that?"

"Lin Chen. She said they all live in a big house, with no Mamma and no Papa."

Mamma knelt next to her, her serious face on, the one that meant someone was going to get a *talking to*. Tai hoped it was Lin Chen. "Lin Chen doesn't know what she is talking about. Each creche has one to three creche parents. Sometimes they are all mommies, or all daddies, or somewhere in-between. But they are *all* parents to those kids."

Tai considered that. "Okay." The other little girl had gone back to play with her friends. "Why don't *I* live in a creche?"

Mamma Yun kissed her on the forehead. "Because we wanted you here with us. That's always been our family's way." She squeezed Tien and stood, shooing her away. "Go play with your cousins."

Tai hugged her, and then ran off to find the others, but the little girl in her pink dress across the river stayed on her mind for days.

. . .

A SHUDDER BROUGHT her back to the present.

None of that mattered anymore. She was a grown *woman* now, and Tai was little more than a memory.

What mattered now was what Mamma Yun had said to her, the last night before she left for Earth.

"We are proud of you, Tien. My beautiful daughter. We don't want you to go into such danger with doubt in your mind."

Tien flushed with warmth. She looked out of her portal.

Hera had synched the little jumper with the station's hangar, and the ship had risen into the landing dock. The thick metal hangar doors *clanged* closed below them, and the jumper touched down with a barely perceptible *thunk.* Tien whistled. "Nice job!"

Hera sighed, her shoulders slumping.

"Sorry, I didn't mean—"

"It's not you." The pilot unbuckled herself and slipped past Rai to hug her. "I'm just on edge. It was a rough flight."

Tien nodded and sent her a private em to em message. *-Still—I'm sorry.-*

-Really, it's okay.- Hera tagged her response with a hug, and warmth spread through her. "Come on. Let's get out of this tin can." The pilot retrieved her bag from under her seat and tapped her temple. "Dek, is the dock pressurized?"

"Affirmative." The station mind's voice came out of the jumper's speakers for their benefit. "Welcome to the Launchpad."

"Nice to be back." Hera palmed open the jumper's hatch door and climbed out into the hangar.

Tien took one last look around the little jumper, her home for the last three days, waiting for the others to file out. She was ready for a shower.

Like the one in her memory, the station was a bridge of sorts too—a connection between Luna and the Earth, where she would start the next phase of her life.

Tien smiled. *How far I've come.* From one bridge to another. From doctor to dropnaut.

How far we still have to go.

3

LAUNCHPAD

I keep seeing Dax's face. Laughing at one of Jess's jokes or looking all somber and shit as Sam lectures us about what's to come.

Holy cracking hells.

I'll never see them again—Dax, Jess, Ola, and Xiu Ying. They're gone, and they aren't ever coming back.

Maybe we won't either.

Laughs harshly. *I'm a bit bleak today. What happens, happens.*

This spin just got real.

—Hera's Journal, 6.17.2282

HERA RESTED her hand on the cool white wall of the station hallway to check her pings after Dek, the station AI, synched her loop.

There was a brief message from Jolly, her creche mother, expressing her sorrow at Jess's loss and wishing her and Ghost a safe journey to Earth. A smattering of messages from friends, and a reminder to pay her rent.

She frowned, rubbing the bump on her head from her mishap in the *Zhenyi* absently. *Thought I took care of that.* She sent a quick ping to Alpha's services phage, who handled all that for the dropnauts in their absence. It would go out in the next laser burst to Redemption.

There was also a long message from Tovey.

She closed her eyes, and they grinned at her, their brown eyes dancing. "You'll be at the Launchpad by the time you get this. I miss you." Tovey scratched their dark, short-cropped hair. "I'm still thinking about last night—"

"Hey."

Hera blinked. Ghost was standing in front of her, his green eyes searching hers. She filed Tovey's message away for later. "Hey. You hear from Jolinda?"

Ghost nodded, running his hand through his mop of long blond hair. "Yeah, she hit me up too." He looked uneasy, strange for him. "Anything from Tovey?"

"Yeah. Haven't watched it all yet." She'd need to watch it in the privacy of her own cabin, if it was going where she thought it was. She flushed hot.

Ghost grinned. "Tell them 'hi' for me." He bit his lip and crossed his arms, leaning back against the smooth white wall. The running lights painted his face a pale blue, making him look more like his namesake than usual.

"What's wrong?" She knew Ghost as well as she knew Jolly. Maybe better.

"*You.* You snapped at Tien in the jumper. That's not like you."

"I know." She rubbed her left arm. The bruise there would take weeks to heal. If she shut her eyes, she could still see someone's leg drifting by outside the *Zhenyi*, rolling end over end through the darkness. She could see Jess's warm smile too, hear her laughter around the dinner table at the creche, infectious and a little dorky. She and Hera and Ghost—the Three Musketeers of Tycho Creche. "It's so weird. Jess is gone."

Ghost closed his eyes. Pain flickered across his features. "I know. I'm trying not to think about it. About them."

A pang of unexpected jealousy seized her. "Did you two ever…?" *Where in the cracking hell did that come from?*

Ghost tilted his head and frowned. "No. She had a thing for someone else." Then he smiled ruefully. "Not that I didn't consider it."

"Ah. One you couldn't conquer with your charm and good looks, huh?" She felt a strange sense of relief.

"There've been a few." He stared at her, his words hanging awkwardly in the air between them until Rai showed up, carrying his bag. "Hey guys, you gonna clear the hallway? I'm starving."

"Sorry." Hera stepped aside to let Rai pass and hugged Ghost, burying her head in his hair. "Thanks."

After a second's hesitation, he hugged her back. "What for?"

-For asking. For knowing *to ask.-* She squeezed him tightly. They had a long history—and there was no one in the world she felt closer to. Not even Tovey. "Come on. Rai's right, I'm starving too. It'll be good to be around the rest of the 'nauts."

-Any time.- His voice whispered in her mind, and a slight grin curled his lips.

She pushed him away gently and turned away, determined not to let him see her cry.

~

THE MESS HALL WAS PACKED. Everyone on-station had turned out to see the dropnauts, and to offer their sympathies for the loss of the Bristol. A long series of floor-to-ceiling windows on the gently curved wall facing Earth gave the otherwise boring white hall one of the best views on the station.

Ghost recognized most of them. The mission control crew sat on one side of the wide room, where the green-and-blue light of Earth lit them with its pale glow. The sun was just rising over the planet's surface.

The service crew was on the other side, much more raucous, drinking *junlei* wine and laughing while spontaneously toasting the dropnauts every five minutes or so. Behind them, the moon was passing by, her silver light no match for the brightness of the golden sun.

His fellow teammates—all sixteen of them—were a maudlin bunch in the middle, reflecting en masse on the loss of their teammates on the *Bristol.*

Hera was usually beautiful, fiery, alive. The long-ago accident that had damaged her spinal cord hadn't put a dent in her grit and determination, She had never held it against him, even though it was all his fault.

But now it was as if someone had stolen her fire. She sipped on her wine and picked at her food listlessly, pausing now and then to stare at the mysterious blue arc of Earth through the windows.

On his other side, Rai and Tien were engaged in a quiet but intense conversation.

Ghost had made a mess of things with Tien, and he'd nearly broken Rai, all to salve his own insecure ego. If he could have fixed it, he would have, but his skills as an engineer failed him when it came to people.

He wouldn't make the same mistake with Hera.

Besides, it was a moot point. She had Tovey.

The other teams were just as subdued. Even the normally mischievous Vixen looked troubled, lost in her thoughts, staring at the table and curling her pink hair around her finger.

Ghost snorted. *Enough is enough.* Jess would be splitting pissed at the whole lot of them.

He pushed his tray aside, climbed up onto the gumdust table and whistled, fingers between his lips.

The room quieted. The dropnauts and support staff all looked up at him.

In one corner, Sam's silver eyes met his. The mech nodded.

"Um… look…" He hadn't planned this out, so he did what he did best—fly by the seat of his pants.. "I'm hurting too. Dax, Jess, Ola, and Xiu Ying… they were more than just teammates. They were friends." He looked down at Hera, who flashed him a wan smile. "They were a part of us, ready to go on this glorious adventure together." He felt a lump in his throat, but he pushed on. "It *kills* me that they aren't here."

He looked around. The room was dead silent. "This one time, after a hard day of grav training, I found Jess in her cabin. The door was open, and she was just staring at Earth. I knocked, and she turned to look at me, surprised, I guess? And then she made that funny nasal laugh-snort she used to do—"

There was scattered laughter at that.

"Yeah. You know it." He could still see her face, her skin a russet reddish-brown, her dark hair pulled back into a ponytail. "She looked up at me and whispered, 'It's too big.'"

"Said your mother!" That came from one of the service crew. Snickers spread through the room, but he silenced them with a glare.

Jess deserved better than those idiots.

He went on. "I asked her what she meant. She patted the bed, and I sat next to her. Her comforter was scrunched up under us, and we sat cross-legged next to one another, staring out at the blue arc of the globe. I mean, yeah, it's big. Like four times bigger than Luna…" He frowned. *I'm getting sidetracked.* "When she joined the team, Hera and I were so proud. Three of us from the same creche—" He choked up a little, remembering Jess was gone, that he'd never see her again.

Hera reached up to squeeze his hand. *-You're doing good.-*

-Thanks.- Ghost cleared his throat. "She said, 'I'm afraid I'm gonna get lost down there. It's too big. They'll never find me after the drop.'"

This time there were mutters of assent from his teammates.

-Where are you going with this?- Hera frowned.

-I'm getting there.- He turned back to the crowd. There wasn't a dry eye among them. Even the usually upbeat Corey, captain of the *Gday*, was wiping his cheek. "I told her we'd *always* find each another. We're the Dropnauts. We've trained together for two-and-a-half years, and none of us is dropping alone." He looked around. "Am I scared? Hell yeah. Sometimes it feels like the entire world is ending, with the quakes and the protests back home. Most of the time, lately. Especially after what happened to Jess and the others." He wiped his eyes. *I will not cry.* "Anyhow, Jess leaned in and kissed me on the cheek, and said, 'If I don't make it, if I get lost, you have to keep going.'" Ghost's voice cracked. He growled, hating losing control. "It sucks, what happened to Jess and her team. It gutted me." He looked around, and the room was dead quiet again, but it felt different. Electric. "But she was right. We have to go on!"

He sat down next to Hera, his heart thundering in his chest. No one said a thing. *-Damn, I fucked that up.-*

-No, you did good.- Hera squeezed his shoulder. Their eyes met, and she nodded, flashing him a sad smile. Then she got up on the table to speak, too, her voice clear and strong. "Jess was my creche sister, and she had the craziest crush on Sam the first time he came to see us...."

The room exploded in laughter. Ghost laughed too, and even Sam managed a wry grin. Ghost grinned. They were definitely getting to him.

Hera finished her tale and held up her fist. "We have to go on!"

This time the room burst into cheers. "Go on! Go on! Go on!"

She slipped off the table, and Ghost gathered her up in a bear hug. "Thank you." Hera had a gift for making wrong *right*.

"You did most of the work." She kissed his cheek, a ghostly echo of Jess that made him happy and sad, all at once. "I just brought it home.

Ghost nodded. "You are the pilot." He took another sip of the junlei wine, intending to get as drunk as possible.

His fellow dropnauts got up to share their memories of the fallen, one at a time.

Ghost watched the whole spectacle, drinking four more glasses of junlei wine, and feeling a pleasant, warm glow in his stomach as he listened to the stories. *We'll make it through this.*

Later that night, alone in his own bed, he cried like a baby, remembering the soft brush of Jess's lips on his cheek in the glow of Mother Earth.

~

HERA DREAMED ABOUT FALLING.

SHE LOOKED UP AT GORDY, standing high above her on top of the pile of moon rocks like an eight-year-old superhero. He was staring out at Redemption, a gumdust-covered hand on his forehead to shield his eyes from the bright blue junlei light above. "Come on up! The view's great!"

She glanced back toward the city lights under the vault of Redemption's wide cavern. She'd always been afraid of the Dark at the city's edge, but Gordy had insisted. *It'll be fun!* Now here she was, but this was too much. She shook her head. "I'm scared."

Gordy laughed. "Don't be. It's safe."

"Are you *sure?*" Jolly had warned them to stay away from the Dark. Redemption was safe enough, but the dimly lit cavern beyond the edge of the junlei glow was scary as a nightmare. She looked around nervously for monsters in the thick darkness.

"I made it. You can do it!" Gordy grinned, his teeth white in the darkness. "Come on. Be brave. The view from here is really bright!"

They were like twins, the only two their age in Tycho Creche. She *trusted* him. "Okay. I'm coming!" She chose her path carefully and clambered up the pile, scampering from one boulder to another. She laughed, delighted at her own bravery. *This* is *fun.* Soon she'd be on top of the pile with him, and the scary bit would be over.

"Just a little farther." Ghost sounded proud.

Of me. She didn't have her loop yet, or she would have sent him a hug. She pulled herself up over a large sharp boulder, finding firm footing for her next step. "You're right! It's easy—"

The rock under her left foot moved, and then it wasn't there at all.

Hera's stomach lurched as the world shifted around her. A grinding rumble filled the air as she dropped. "Gordy!" She reached for him, but dust swirled between them. He vanished from sight as she fell. Her heart raced. She grabbed at the rocks to save herself as the world collapsed beneath her.

Rocks struck her as she tumbled endlessly downward, screaming her lungs out.

Then it all went black.

HERA WOKE to the insistent chiming of her door alert. She shuddered, remembering that day with Ghost as if it were yesterday. Sixteen years, vanished like nothing.

Her body was covered in cold sweat.

The alert was beautiful enough, like the wind chimes that hung outside the creche house, blowing in the artificial breeze of Redemption's atmosphere. But Hera was tired and probably a little drunk after the community feelings orgy Ghost had unleashed with his strange and unsettling story.

Hera had spent the better part of an hour after dinner sitting alone by the port window in her cabin, staring out at the blue-green globe that spun below them against the velvety backdrop of space, wondering what Earth had in store for her most advanced—and most disappointing—children.

Wondering what Jess would say about it all now.

Was it worth it?

She sat up, looking around the darkened room. "Dek, who in the cracking hell is that?"

Dek was unflappable. "Gordon Gillam. Do you want to speak to him?"

She managed a snort, throwing off the last dregs of the nightmare. Ghost *hated* it when someone used his given name. She touched her temple, and a series of pings scrolled through her mind. Twenty of them, all from Ghost, each less comprehensible than the last.

"Come on, Hera. Let me in!" Ghost pounded on the door. He sounded more drunk than she was. "I wanna talk."

Hera ran a hand through her short, kinky hair. Nothing good would come of this. She'd seen him plastered before.

Smart as a whip, but not a lick of common sense. Hera could still see Jolly, arms crossed, silver ponytail over her shoulder.

She sighed. "Let him in." She pulled on her biframe, and it snapped around her legs, connecting to her loop.

"Yes, Hera." The cabin door slid open, and Ghost tumbled hard onto the metal floor.

Oh Gordy. "Come on." She knelt to help Ghost off the floor, up onto her bed. "You're making a nuisance of yourself." She hoped he hadn't woken any of the other dropnauts.

She felt more clear-eyed, the warm embrace of the junlei wine wearing off.

He stared at her, narrowing his eyes. "Sorry."

Hera snorted. "Sure you are. Dek, please close the door."

It slid shut quietly.

"Thanks. I didn't wanna be alurn." Ghost stared at the blank wall across from the bed. "Alone."

"You're drunk." His breath was thick with the smell of wine. She unlaced his shoes and pulled them off, followed by his socks, wrinkling her nose at the smell.

"No one else unnerstans." He looked down at her. "But *you* get it." He reached out to touch her cheek and missed, his hand landing on her shoulder. "Hera, you get it. She's gone. Jess. They're *all* gone."

Hera nodded. "I know." Jess had been her friend too. They all had. She saw the leg flying by the *Zhenyi* again, and shuddered.

"Tovey. They love you." He frowned, as if trying to work something out.

"Yeah. Tovey does." They'd made that very clear in the explicit message she'd watched in her room earlier. A faint smile crossed her lips at the memory. Hera pulled herself up to sit next to Ghost and put a hand on his cheek. "You'll find someone someday, too. I promise."

He nodded. "Maybe. I just… I need not to be… to be not… not alone tonight." He leaned forward as if to kiss her, but she slipped out of his clumsy embrace.

"*That's* not going to happen." She *loved* Ghost. But she was *in love* with Tovey. There was a difference that he wasn't sober enough to appreciate, just now. "What you *need* is some sleep. Day after tomorrow, we're dropping. You have to be rested and ready." Sam had posted a strict twenty-four-hour "no alcohol" policy for dropnauts before the drop. For good reason, clearly.

Hera maneuvered Ghost onto her bed, facing the wall. It was a compact mattress, but they'd managed with smaller before in the creche. Of course, he'd been less of a mountain then.

Ghost sighed. "I'm so tired."

"I know you are, Gordy." She touched his cheek. "Sleep now. You're safe here with me."

"I know. I love you, Hera." The last was barely audible, and it wasn't long before he was asleep, snoring softly.

Hera sat there next to him, staring at his back.

They had a long history together, but it had never gone *there*. She wasn't sure why. Maybe they'd missed their chance? Ghost had his own demons—he was a tumbling asteroid, never happy for long in one place.

Besides, she had Tovey now. She decided she wouldn't mention this little sleepover to them.

She bent over and kissed Ghost's cheek. He stirred a little, but then settled back into sleep.

Against her better judgement, she took off her biframe and snuggled up next to him. It was warm, familiar, and comforting.

They'd slept like this many times before in the creche, like sister and brother. There was something safe about holding Ghost in her arms. It calmed her.

In the quiet darkness together, she let go of her sadness and fear. For a few blissful hours, she floated in their bubble, with no more nightmares.

4

INTERREGNUM

The Synthetic AI Mechanoid went about its task single-mindedly, its arm sifting through the pulverized lunar rock pouring out of the hopper, searching for moon-stones—green and orange pieces of volcanic glass highly prized by Earth's rare gem collectors.

...sieve: lunar dust...

...scan: for crater glass...

...process image, match to pict-database > no match found...

...discard...

SAM knew which stones were most prized, though it couldn't have explained why.

Something like pleasure surged through its core at the moonstone in its sifting pan. It grasped the stone gently in its effector, examining it more closely.

...access > data: emerald green. prime quality. above-average size. estimate value at three million nau standard...

Its effector snapped shut, smashing the glass to bits. SAM held its arm up and stared at the fragments of green dust.

...error. effector seizure. Recommend: reboot...

Something unexpected had happened. Unexpected wasn't a word that got much use in SAM's vocabulary.

The mech was in constant contact with Alpha, the Moon Base AI, a low-level link that kept it apprised of any upgrades to its command profile. But now a massive *amount of data was being compressed and pumped through the connection into its core.*

…input: pain. terrible driving pain…

SAM recoiled at the shock.

Its systems shut down, plunging its mind into darkness.

—Sam's mem cache, 7.25.2165

ALLY AND AIDAN followed the yellow stripes of the old, crumbling two-lane highway through what had once been the Central Valley of California. Aidan imagined it full of cars, commuters rushing back and forth across the now-empty valley.

The land here was mostly open, with small stands of the sky trees here and there. Grass had taken over the world, but other plants dotted the hillsides—small greenish-gray salvia bushes and willow, sycamore and box elder saplings.

In the mid-morning, they'd seen another sky seed blazing a path across the horizon, headed west to land who-knew-where.

Aidan shaded his eyes against the bright sun, staring up at the blue dome. He wondered what it would be like to meet others—strangers. To talk to them. And maybe find someone who could be *more*. He wasn't sure what that meant, but the mere idea of it sent goosebumps racing up his arms.

It was a warm morning, but a stiff, cool breeze blew up the delta from the San Francisco Bay, laden with moisture. Martinez Base was still a couple days distant, but Aidan could already feel the change.

His right hand itched. He scratched it unconsciously, and pulled out a slice of sky fruit from his pocket—the savory yellow *lemon* kind. He unwrapped the tree leaves that kept it fresh. "Want some?"

Ally shook her head. "I'm good."

They'd spent the night inside an old store that had survived the Great Winter mostly intact. Aidan had even found a couple cans of pears he'd pried open with his knife. They reminded him of home.

Cimber bounded up next to them on the cracked pavement, sniffing the air with her mecha nose.

Aiden frowned. "Storm's coming." He hoped it wasn't a bad one. The

Records said it used to rain all the time, but not usually at flood levels. Then again, the Records said a lot of things that were no longer true.

"It's a clear day." His sister shared a glance with him. Neither knew where Cimber got her information, but she was usually right. When she sniffed the air like that, it meant *bad weather on the way.*

Cimber pawed the ground twice.

"Two days." Ally pulled out the old plas map and squinted at it. "We should be there by then."

Aidan looked at the map over her shoulder. The colors were faded, but it was still legible. "Just about, anyway."

Ally nodded. "Let's just keep moving."

Cimber yelped and bounded off the highway toward a nearby thicket of sky trees.

Ally rolled her eyes. "Not again." She stared longingly at the green hills ahead. "Should we follow her?"

Aidan shrugged. "We can't afford to lose her." Cimber had kept them safe from many of the hazards on the way, including a stray war drone back in Sutter Creek. Without her, they would have been dead already half a dozen times. Resigned, they trudged through the tall grass toward the trees.

Cimber was already there, digging furiously at the ground. A pile of rich brown earth was growing rapidly behind her, weighing down the bright green grass.

"What's she after?"

Aidan shrugged. "Another bone?"

Cimber stopped and pointed her nose at the hole.

Aidan knelt to see what she had uncovered. It was hard to make anything out in the shade of the trees.

He slipped his hand into the soil and lifted it up.

Something wriggled against his palm. "Eeeew!" He threw it down.

"What is it?" Ally looked over his shoulder, her breath warm on his cheek.

Aidan picked up the little creature again, less frightened this time. "I think it's a worm." The pink, segmented creature wriggled under his grasp, and he shivered. *Hello, little friend.*

They stared at it, fascinated. The global decades-long winter had wiped out just about everything above the surface, and yet somehow a few birds, some insects and this little bit of life had survived the long, dark season.

Or did it? Aidan looked up suspiciously at the trees.

Ally followed his gaze. "You think the sky folk sent it?"

He shrugged. "I don't know. Maybe? Worms…." He searched for the word. "Worms *aerate* the soil. They let it breathe."

Ally snorted. "I guess it's nice to see a few living *bugs—*"

"Invertebrates, actually." Aidan had studied everything he could find in the Records about biology, and his head was stuffed full of mostly useless facts. *Useless until now.*

"Whatever. But we need to get going. I want to make Vallejo by nightfall." She started toward the highway, adjusting the heavy pack on her back.

Aidan set the worm down in the hole, and it started to work its way back underground. He swept the loose soil over it and patted it down gently.

Things were changing. He hoped he lived to see it, to spend the rest of his days exploring and experiencing everything this strange new world offered.

He followed Ally back to the highway, and Cimber bounded after them.

Rai slid out from under the *Zhenyi*—Tien's suggestion, named after a famous Chinese scientist from Old Earth. The hangar was sterile, industrial, white walls seamed and cracked with age, thick gray cables snaking across the heavy launch doors to refill the oxygen and water tanks.

The ship herself was in tip-top shape, as far as he could tell. He'd repaired the pinhole leak himself. Still, he checked everything over three times, trying to silence the little voice of doubt in the back of his head.

In the morning they'd launch, and when they were a suitable distance from the station, Hera would install the x-drive.

Five drives, and one back-up jumper. That was all they had. Luna lacked the resources to build more. The x-drives were well past their sell-by dates, and the cores could be dangerous if not handled properly.

All five teams—well, four now—had trained extensively for this. Alpha said they were *probably* reliable enough to get the teams down to the surface, but returning might be dicey. Rai distrusted *probably* and *maybe*, especially when they came from a mech who was supposed to know such things.

If they performed well—and that was still a big if—the teams would use the jumpers to establish regular traffic between Earth and the Launchpad while they assessed the state of the ship construction facilities that had been identified as targets for the first stage of the ambitious Return. If not, the dropnauts would have to restart those factories before they could make it back up to orbit.

Rai snorted. That was an awful lot of *ifs* to build a mission on.

There'd been a long and drawn-out argument about using old carbon-based fuels for the effort, even for just a short period, but in the end the Redemption Creed had won out:

I will not take another's life.
   I will not take what is not mine.
   I will not violate another.
   I will not lie.
   I will help build a better world.

RAI AGREED—CARBON was an addiction they were better off without.

"Hey."

Rai looked up, blocking out the bright hangar light with his arm. "Hey Pix."

Pix blew their long black hair away from their face, grinning. "Playing the mechanic?"

Rai sat up, crossing his legs. "Yeah. Killing time."

"I know. I'm nervous as a miner with a visor crack." Pix's eyes went unfocused for a sec. "Just twelve hours before the drop."

Rai nodded. "Me too." He was on the brink of the most momentous event of his young life, and he was scared shitless. He was a middle-of-the-pack student in a project filled with stars.

Pix squeezed his shoulder. "You'll do okay. You're one of the best 'nauts in the program."

Rai snorted. "Hardly. But thanks." They'd had a brief fling, after Ghost. Pix was sweet and kind. Rai got up and hugged them—it felt good to have a little human contact, and the tight knot in Rai's stomach loosened.

"You coming to the Last Supper?" Pix let him go, playing with the small printed gumdust loop in their left ear.

"Yeah." Rai frowned. He wasn't particularly religious, but the original one had ended rather badly for the host. "Are *you* ready?"

"Hardly. I'm almost cracked. It's a helluva big responsibility they've put on our shoulders, saving the world and all that."

Rai laughed. "Me too. I got in a fight the night before we launched. Trying to get myself knocked out of the mission, I guess."

Pix stared at him. "Now that's *cracked.*" They grinned to show they didn't mean anything by it.

Rai flushed. "I guess so. But my team needs me." He didn't speak his fear—that he wasn't ready, that he might fail them all. "I can't wait to see if anything survived down there besides the zongi trees." Technically, they were zhǒngzǐ trees, from the Chinese word for "seed." But calling them, essentially, "seed seeds" or "seed trees" had always seemed silly. Besides, everyone just called them *zongies.* He was dying to see how they were doing on-planet, to cut one open and see if they were really sequestering carbon in nodules inside their wide trunks.

"I'll bet something survived. Maybe even *somebody.*" Pix said it in a whisper, then looked around to see if anyone was listening. It was accepted mission chapter and verse that no one was still alive down there. There hadn't been a radio peep in more than a hundred years. But what if they were wrong?

I will not violate another.

If there were others… well, surely there was plenty of room to go around, creed or no creed. But it was something that was rarely discussed in the zeal for the Return.

"Come on. I'm hungry." Pix held out their hand.

Rai took it—Their fingers were warm in his. His stomach rumbled, or maybe it was nerves. "I could use a little something."

Pix leaned forward and kissed his cheek. "It's gonna be okay, Rai."

Rai nodded. "It's just—"

"I know. Come on. Let it go and just have a good time tonight! Morning will be here soon enough." They grinned, adorable dimples appearing on their cheeks. "And if you're up for some fun, a little later…."

Rai laughed. "I might be." Just the thing to sooth his shattered nerves.

SAM SAT BACK and stared at the sixteen dropnauts gathered in the mess hall. They were some of the finest in this small generation of humanity. This was their moment—the time of the Return finally upon them. But it was his, too.

...access > communications module...

-Dek, how's the weather?-

-The drop zones look good. Cape Town is sunny. Stormy weather over Beijing, forecast to clear by morning. Sydney is in prolonged drought. Possible localized thunderstorm activity north of San Francisco, but not expected to be a problem.-

-Thanks.-

-It's good to have activity on the station again.-

Sam felt a jolt of something. *Sadness.*

Dek had floated out here alone for more than a hundred years before the Loonies had found and restored him. That was a long time for anyone to be without contact with another being.

Sam had made the first trip to the station himself in one of the remaining jumpers, taking on the risk of what might have been a one-way trip with the untested steam drive. What he'd found had shocked him.

...access > memcache: full memory. play...

SAM NUDGED the little jumper toward the orbiting station, marveling that it was still intact after the Crash and all the intervening years. He played a light over its surface. *NAU-Skytower.*

She was a finely made thing, even in her bedraggled state, a silver roulette wheel spinning in the velvety blackness of space, shimmering on one side where the sunlight touched her.

Sam deftly nudged the little jumper toward the interior of the ring, sensors in his metal fingers approximating touch, and yet he couldn't really *feel* the joystick in his grip. Not with his own nerves and flesh.

Once, in vee-space, he'd asked Alpha to show him what it was like to be truly human. To be clothed in meat and skin, to be able to touch something warm and feel it, to shiver in the cool breeze of Redemption or of Earth, keenly aware that he was neither fully man nor machine. It had been a strange and ultimately painful experience—something he could never really have, yet tantalizingly within his grasp. He had never asked for it again.

Coming up on the closest hangar, Sam aligned the ship with the station's spin. He settled the jumper down ever so slowly on the slightly curved metal surface. The skin of the station was pitted and scared by time, by micro-meteors and the solar wind.

The jumper touched down, and the magnetic clamps secured her to *Skytower*.

Without waiting for the all clear from the ship's systems, Sam opened the lander's hatch. The vacuum already inside matched the vacuum without, and he stepped out onto the station, the first to do so since the Crash. He looked up and was transfixed.

The universe spread out around him, a universe of stars dominated by the white cloud-covered globe of the Earth and the bright-shining ball of the sun.

It was vast beyond even his comprehension. Sam knew at once how Colin McAvery—the captain who had planted the first world seedling on an asteroid named Ariadne—must have felt in that famous moment, standing all alone on the edge of that shoreless sea, confronting the inky black void filled with the cold pinpricks of stars. He must have understood what a giant step mankind had taken beyond the safety of their own blue-and-green world—one that had ultimately saved them from the destruction to come. A step that had led inexorably to this moment in time.

...fileto > memcache: eternity...

Sam cast aside sentiment and turned back to the task at hand, filing the memory away in priority storage. Kneeling, he found the manual entry pad for the hangar bay doors. Alpha had all the station information in his own storage banks, and they had planned carefully for this moment. He flipped open the small access hatch, and the pad underneath came to life with a blue glow.

...access > data: skytower > codes...

The manual system was low power, with few breakable parts. Sam nodded approvingly. He keyed in the emergency sequence. *Evacuating hangar air* appeared on the small LCD screen.

He closed the hatch door and stood, staring at the inner curve of the station ring. Save for the glow from the clear window of the manual hatch and the reflected light of the sun, it was dark. If the station mind was dead, they were sunk.

He climbed back into the jumper and sealed the hatch. Then he released the magnetic hold. With a nudge, the jumper lifted up a little from the station rim. A second quick burst was all he needed to slow her movement in relation to *Skytower*'s spin.

The hangar doors rumbled open below, and the jumper crossed over the widening gap as a flurry of dust floated out into space around him.

Sam fired the jumper's jets, dropping her gently inside the hangar. The doors closed above him, coming together silently in the vacuum. He dropped the craft down to the floor and felt the heavy metallic *clank* as the hangar doors locked into place above him. The wide, square docking bay filled with air—stale, no doubt, after long storage.

He popped the jumper's hatch and climbed out to find himself surrounded by a field of strange lumps. He knelt and sifted through one of them to pull out a human femur. The dust wasn't dust at all, or at least not entirely. It was the desiccated remains of some of Skytower's crew.

Sam shut off his vision. He didn't need it to navigate his way, and it was easier *not* to see the devastation. He made a mental note to evacuate the air, and with it, much of the human remains inside. To give them a fitting burial in space, where they would eventually return to the world that had given them birth.

The scale of the suffering here was unimaginable. If he had been human, it would have torn him in half. And yet it was the tiniest fraction of the agony inflicted upon Earth and humankind by the Crash.

Skytower had been destroyed from within by a live virus that had killed everyone onboard. That much was clear from the last transmissions Alpha had received from the station mind before it had gone offline. The whole place would need to be sanitized to assure there was no recurrence.

Sam strode to the nearest terminal and reactivated his vision.

His hands played over the white panel in a flash-memorized sequence to reboot the system. If the AI had gone dormant, it might have survived. If not, their job would be that much harder.

Rebooting. The message flashed across the panel in green letters.

Three seconds later, a shrill, heart-rending scream filled the station.

S AM BLINKED, his mind returning to the present. The dropnauts were cheering the mission with what Sam hoped were non-alcoholic drinks. So much life here now, after so much death. And so much beauty and pain in the human story, much of it as fresh to him as if it had just happened.

Being human was hard, but they had the gift of forgetting. Sam could only *keep, prioritize, archive, or delete.* Still, some things were worth remembering.

He filed away the memory, reveling in the here-and-now and the infectious bravado of the dropnauts.

~

"Tomorrow we'll be on the surface." Rai grinned, but Ghost knew him far too well to fall for his false enthusiasm.

"You still scared?"

Rai blushed. "A little." He poked at his mashed potato—a special treat for the Last Supper.

Around them at the dinner tables of the mess hall, the conversation flowed, old friends ready to face the challenge of the new day together. A few voices were lacking—Ghost missed Jess's infectious laugh most of all. "I'm scared too."

Rai looked up, meeting his gaze. "Yeah?"

"Yeah. You want to know the secret?"

Rai shook his head. "To not being scared?"

Ghost laughed. "No, *everyone's* scared. Every last one of us."

"Not Hera." Rain glanced in her direction.

Ghost followed his gaze. "*Especially* Hera. She's just really good at not showing it." He knew that well. "No, the secret to getting past the fear."

Rai looked like a starving man looking at a buffet. "How?"

Ghost blinked. "Hell if I know."

Rai broke into a grin and snorted. "You fucking darksider."

Ghost smiled too. It was like old times. "Seriously. I have no hissing clue." He loved yanking Rai's chain, and his friend needed the laugh. Ghost knocked back his *definitely non-alcoholic* junlei juice—Sam wanted them all sober in the morning.

"What are you guys talking about?" Ying Yue was pretty, with lovely dark hair and a sweet round face, but she was hard as steel.

Ghost had gone up against her in the dropnauts' unofficial Race around the Runway more than once, and she always kicked his ass. "Just talking about tomorrow. I'm scared as shit about it, and Rai is talking me down."

Rai smiled gratefully.

"You? Scared?" Ying Yue looked from one to the other. "I don't believe it."

Ghost nodded, putting on his serious face. "I might need comforting later."

She laughed. "Meet me at 10:30 at my cabin, then."

She turned back to her team, and Ghost nudged Rai. "That's how it's done."

"How *do* you do it?" Rai looked depressed again. "That whole flirtation thing?"

"It's… I don't know. It just comes out." He hadn't meant to hurt Rai's feelings. *I'm such a cracking idiot.* "Sorry. It's like breathing."

"It's okay. We're over—you don't owe me anything." The connection between them vanished as quickly as it had reappeared.

Rai turned away to talk to Slee, leaving Ghost on his own.

Ghost leaned back in his chair and looked around the mess hall, looking for his other teammates. Tien was standing alone by the window, staring at Earth, and Hera was deep in conversation with Corey, the pilot of the *Gday* and Team Three.

He sighed. Tomorrow was the culmination of a dream. He'd stared at Earth from Redemption's observation domes since he was a little kid, lifting his hand up as if he could hold the homeworld in his palm. Judging by the quakes that were shaking the city, they weren't departing a moment too soon.

He'd trained for this, had taken supplements to build his body up for the heavy gravity, and fought hard to be a part of one of the crews for the Return. Now he was here, and he'd alienated half of his team. *You really do have gumdust for brains.*

He caught Hera's eye, and she winked at him. *-You okay?-*

-I will be. You?-

-Cracking terrified.- He managed a sheepish grin.

-Me too.-

Hera nodded and went back to her conversation.

Better to spend the night alone. Ying Yue's invitation notwithstanding. Maybe he'd wander down to the hydroponics lab and engage one of the techs there in a little engineering chat. *Might get some ideas to use down on the surface.*

Ghost was just about to leave when Tien turned away from the window. Her gaze met his across the room as she climbed up onto the table. That was really starting to become a thing.

He could visit hydroponics later. He sat back to see what she was up to. *This should be interesting.*

~

Tien stood at the window, her palm resting on the cool glass, staring at her future.

Behind her, the dropnauts and support staff were chattering about tomorrow. About the excitement of finally going down to Earth after all these months of mad preparation.

She couldn't *feel* it.

She stared at the silvered arc of the Earth below. The vast, empty continent of Africa was passing beneath them, its Eastern edge obscured by clouds. The land was brown with patches of green, where the zongi trees were spreading along the western coast in what used to be Morocco, Mauritania, Senegal and a dozen other tiny countries. She'd always been good at geography.

How strange that Earthers had divided themselves into so many sects and races, identities and countries. So many boundaries. This time it would be different. Had to be.

First do no harm.

Somewhere out there, the bodies of four of her friends floated in the abyss. Four soldiers lost at war.

Tien turned to face the crowd. "Do you mind?" She indicated the table.

"Not at all." Jinx and Cutter from the supplies crew moved their empty plates out of her way.

Ghost's gaze met hers from across the mess hall, and he winked at her as she climbed up onto the table. "Hey guys, we have a speaker!" He put a hand on Rai's shoulder.

Rai turned to look, and soon the talk in the room died down. Everyone was staring at her. Tien blinked and cleared her throat. "I... I wanted to share something."

Hera nodded. *Go ahead.*

"This is for Dax, Jess, Ola, and Xiu Ying."

Tien looked around nervously. She didn't like to be in the spotlight. But she wanted to do this. "This is from a traditional Chinese poem. The English translation is called 'Fighting South of the Castle.'" She cleared her throat and began.

THEY FOUGHT south of the Castle,
They died north of the wall.
They died in the moors and were not buried.
Their flesh was the food of crows.
"Tell the crows we are not afraid;
We have died in the moors and cannot be buried.
Crows, how can our bodies escape you?"

The waters flowed deep
And the rushes in the pool were dark.
The riders fought and were slain:
Their horses wander neighing.

RAI STIFLED A SOB. Ghost squeezed his shoulder and nodded at her.

Tien pictured each of her lost teammates, pain like the cold of the void in the gut.

She took a deep breath and finished the poem.

BY THE BRIDGE there was a house.
Was it south, was it north?
The harvest was never gathered.
How can we give you your offerings?
You served your Prince faithfully,
Though all in vain.
I think of you, faithful soldiers;
Your service shall not be forgotten.
For in the morning you went out to battle
And at night you did not return.

TIEN CLOSED HER EYES. "Goodbye, Team One. Rest in peace among the stars." She stepped off the table, and then her friends were encircling her, their arms warm around her shoulders.

I'm right where I'm supposed to be. This was her chosen family. Tien shuddered, grateful for their company, and let herself cry a single tear for her lost comrades. Tonight they honored the dead.

Tomorrow would give that sacrifice meaning.

5

DROP

It's strange being out in the open like this. The world is so big. And so empty.

Even after almost a month, I miss my bed back home, my mother and brothers, and the solid, comforting security of plascrete walls under the Mountain.

Still, there's an amazing sense of freedom. Ally and I make our own rules—eat when we want, sleep when we want, and walk as much as we can each day.

This world's a hard reset to the Garden of Eden. There are animals, though they're few and far between, and trees with forbidden fruit.

All that's missing is the serpent....

—Aidan's Journal, 6.17.2282

"Are we almost there?" Aidan was a few steps behind his sister as they climbed the hill, staring at the broken pavement shattered into spiderweb patterns beneath their feet.

Ally unfolded the plas map she carried. "I think so. That old fabrication plant back there looks like it was the last thing before we're supposed to reach the—" she looked up and stopped dead, staring. A vast sea spread out before her, lapping at the edges of the hills. It was stunning to see so much water in one place. "—bay."

Aidan ran into her, almost knocking her off her feet.

"Watch it!"

"Sorry." He looked up in surprise. "Why did you stop?"

"Look." She pointed out at the wide blue vista before them.

Aidan slipped around her and took in the view. "Wow. That's a lot of water."

She laughed. Aidan had a gift for stating the obvious.

It was late afternoon, the sun slipping down toward the horizon. They'd made good progress, their bodies finally used to the regular exercise. She hadn't had leg cramps in a week.

The bay was far wider than the map showed, lapping at the edge of the old highway they were following. They should have come at it from the south to avoid the crossing, but that would have added days to their journey. She hoped one of the bridges was still intact.

The sky above was darkening, storm clouds piling in from the ocean a few dozen miles to the west, blocking the sun.

Cimber trotted on ahead of them, scouting out the way.

Ally set down her pack on the side of the highway and traced the line of the highway on the old map they'd been using. To their right, a little way up the incline, the hyperloop tube wound its way along the base of the hills, its shiny white finish dulled and cracked, faded to gray.

Martinez Base had been close to the shoreline. *God, let it be above water.* According to the map, there were a couple old bridges ahead that crossed the bay.

"Do you think we'll find the meds mamma needs?" Aidan scratched the stubble on his chin—he'd grown lazy about shaving. Not that she blamed him.

Ally nodded. "I hope so. Otherwise this long walk was for nothing." She'd found a rusted road sign earlier in the morning that had said, "Welcome to Cordelia, Population 300,245." Thirty-story apartment buildings still stood in the city center, their windows mostly broken out, though one of them had collapsed against its neighbor in a drunken fall. She knew what she would find inside those buildings. So many dead. Grim reminders of her own eventual fate, alone and unloved.

At least here there was only the broken pavement and the tube and railway. The cars scattered along the highway were mostly rusted out, and if you didn't look too close… Ally shuddered. "Come on. If one of the bridges is passable, we might make it by nightfall."

Aidan was staring at the clouds piling up on the horizon. "There's a storm coming."

Mr. obvious. She nodded. "Better if we're across the water before it hits." Storms these days were notoriously unpredictable—it might delay them for days as it dumped water across the foothills. Or it might be done and gone in an hour.

They were almost there. Soon they'd find the medicine they needed if the water wasn't too high. If Martinez Base still existed. And if they could figure out where it had been kept. *Too many ifs.*

Ahead, the old highway swung down to run along the new shoreline of the bay. They hadn't seen a drone in days, let alone any other signs of life besides the grass and the ubiquitous sky trees. Here they towered over the shore in small groves, and some of them extended out into the water a few hundred feet.

Ally took a deep breath of fresh air. She'd learned one thing on this journey. She preferred the great outdoors to the musty, claustrophobic halls under the Mountain. She would never limit herself to its dusty confines again. Once this was over, she'd set out to explore the big, empty world.

"Ally, look!" Aidan ran down the grassy slope at the edge of the highway toward the water.

She pulled her pack back on. Cursing her brother's boundless energy under her breath, she followed him down the hill. "What am I looking at?"

He stopped twenty yards from the water. "I swear I saw it." He pointed, and she followed his gaze. "Look, over there!"

Something silver leapt out of the water, flashing in the late morning sunlight before falling back to the bay with a splash.

Aidan looked at her, blinking like a four-year-old. "Was that a—"

"Fish? I think so." She laughed at his childlike pleasure. Fish were one of those *book things*. Something you read about but never expected to see in real life. Of course, living off of canned goods and a replicator that made food out of cave mold, there were many things she'd never expected to see. Including the surface of the Earth. She put her arm around Aidan's shoulders and squeezed him tight. "It's beautiful."

With or without them, the Earth would go on. She was slowly recovering. If Ally's science lessons were any guide, it would be millions of years before the planet was as diverse as she had been before humankind had almost destroyed her. But they would not be going along for the ride. Ally and Aidan were part of the last generation—a bittersweet honor.

The wind was picking up, a sure sign that a storm was coming in. "Come on. Let's get going."

They climbed back up to the broken highway together and set out again on toward the base. As they walked, Ally let herself just be, letting go of all the *what ifs* and taking in the sounds of wind and water, the smells of grass and salt in the air. It was a beautiful day, not nearly as hot as it had been a week before.

Aidan looked up at the sky. "You think there's someone up there?"

It was an old conversation. "I don't know. Maybe." Not that they'd been listening under the Mountain. The first generation had put Boundary Peak on lockdown, and the rest had kept up that tradition out of a fear for their own safety.

"I hope there are. It's kinda lonely here, with just the family." Aidan glanced over at her, blushing. "No offense, sis."

Ally snorted. "Yeah, some days I'm not so fond of you either." She looked up at the sky. "If they are up there, whoever they are, they'd be smart to stay away—" She stopped, staring.

"They'll come down someday. I bet they're as curious about us as we are about them...." Aidan turned to see her stopped five steps behind him. "What?"

Ally just pointed.

Something was coming down from the heavens, much faster than the sky seeds, which usually floated on the vagrant winds. Maybe it was just a piece of space junk—the war had left plenty of that up there. But it seemed a little too controlled. If it followed its current trajectory, it would land on the far side of the bay, not far from their destination.

Were there others still alive up there? Had Aidan been right? *Maybe there's hope for us after all.*

Of course, the *others* might end up being aliens—Aidan was always going on about that too.

The wind was picking up, gusts slipping cool fingers through her long red hair. A dark smear of rain hid the horizon beneath the towering clouds.

"Come on!" Ally grabbed her pack straps and broke into a run. "You may have just gotten your wish!"

∿

HERA STRAPPED herself into the *Zhenyi's* pilot's seat. *This is it.* She sent one final ping to Tovey for the next delivery dump. *Drop's about to start. Love you.* Then she ran through the pre-launch checklist.

Her crew settled in behind her, taking their seats.

She glanced back at them. They were all wearing their planet-side uniforms, made of sturdy white fabric that would resist tearing, water, and dirt. The bright leaf-and-orb Redemption logo almost sparkled on each of their chests. "Y'all ready for a wild ride?"

Ghost laughed. "Wild is right, with you at the helm."

She glared at him and went back to her launch prep. The water tanks were full, the hatch closed. Everyone was settled, and everything read green above her deck.

Hera cast a nervous glance up at the repaired pinhole in the ceiling. Space travel was always a dicey proposition—the *Bristol* was a harsh reminder of that.

She had to trust Rai. He'd been over the *Zhenyi* with a fine-toothed comb, and he really was good at this whole *jumper thing.* Better than she was, in fact. She just wanted to fly them. "Everyone belted in?"

"Yup, captain."

Rai grunted. "Uh-huh."

Tien was more polite. "Ready."

"Parachutes ready?" She hoped they wouldn't need them, but she'd be damned happy to have them if they did. The countdown timer showed two minutes.

"Evacuating the hangar."

Sam's voice came back, calm and steady. "Affirmative."

Outside the *Zhenyi,* powerful fans sucked the air out of the hangar, reducing it to vacuum. Inside, the patch held. Hera breathed a sigh of relief.

Ghost pushed forward as far as his belt would let him. "Hey Sam, you're supposed to say 'roger.' They always say 'roger" in the tridees."

There was a pause from the speaker.

"You don't wanna give us bad luck." Ghost grinned and winked at Hera.

She covered her mouth to keep from laughing

Sam sounded flummoxed. "The approved mission response is *affirmative—*"

Rai jumped in. "Come on, Sam, just say *roger.*"

Hera laughed. "You know he's not going to let this go until you say it, Sam." *You must think we're crazy.*

There was a long silence. Then, finally, "Roger." It came out grudgingly.

Ghost snickered. "Roger dodger!"

Hera grinned. "Okay, Ghost, you've had your fun." She pushed him back into his seat. "No matter what happens next, I'm proud to be part of this team. It's a small first step—"

"And one giant drop for humankind?" Rai seemed pleased with himself.

She pinched his leg, eliciting a startled yelp. "Yeah, that too." She settled back in her seat as the clock counted down to zero. "Hold on—here we go!"

Hera fired the jets, filling the space with super-heated steam which immediately turned to snow. The little craft lifted up off the hangar doors, which began to rumble open as she spun the jumper around deftly inside the dock. "Easing out of the hangar, Sam."

"Roger dodger." Their mech leader never ceased to surprise her. Or Ghost, judging by his delighted laugh.

Hera grinned. She fired the jets again, and they slipped out into the void, rising up from the station's ring.

Below, the gleaming blue-green sphere of Earth spun by, covered in a lacework of white clouds. The silver crescent moon hung in the distance against a backdrop of pinprick stars, and the bright amber lights of the Launchpad station blinked in the foreground.

Hera wondered what they'd find down there. She loved sifting through Alpha's archives in her free time, seeing Earth in her prime. Soaring over the Great Pyramids. Taking a swim in the drowned streets of old New York, staring up at the towers of the once-grand city. Walking through the heart of Rome, where the Colosseum stood and Caesar had commanded his bustling empire.

She righted the ship, spinning it around with the Earth below them, and their drift put more distance between themselves and the Launchpad. When Hera was satisfied with the safety margin, she slowed the jumper to a virtual halt. "Time to insert the x-drive."

"Roger that." Did Sam sound a little nervous?

They'd practiced this with a dummy drive until Hera was sure she could do it in her sleep. The drive negated gravity around it—and the more powerful it was, the bigger the resulting sphere of n-space. It was whiz-bang tech, but older x-drives were temperamental and could explode if mishandled. And this one was *old*.

The Return Mission team had decided to activate their drives far away from the station, just in case.

Alpha thought it was safe enough—they had to trust his word.

Hera released the catch on the ship's drive compartment, flipping it open.

Rai knelt next to her and opened the cabinet where the drive was stored. He pulled out its protective packaging, holding it as if it were the most precious thing in the world. Hera nodded, and Rai opened it, showing her the spherical drive. It was silver, its surface shimmering like a pool of mercury, unlike the dull gray dummies they'd used for practice.

She pulled on her protective gumdust gloves, and Rai gently tilted it into her hands, out of the webbing that protected it inside its box. Her hands got a weird pins-and-needles sensation. "Oooh."

"Ready?" Rai was sweating.

They locked gazes. "I think so."

Rai nodded. "Now or never."

Hera held it up and spun the two hemispheres in opposing directions. The silver sphere's color shifted to a golden shimmer. She eased the drive carefully into its compartment, while Rai's hand hovered over the button to activate the magnetic field. If she as much as grazed the edge of the enclosure…. Sweat beaded her forehead. "Now."

She let go and Rai hit the button in the same instant.

The drive settled in its containment field and hummed happily, spinning like a miniature planet and emitting its bright golden glow. Hera closed the lid, and the radiance dimmed.

She let out her breath in a whoosh. "We did it!"

"Congratulations, *Zhenyi*. Have a safe drop!" Sam sounded *proud*.

"Roger that." She cut the connection. Time to focus on piloting them down to Martinez Base. The last thing she needed was a distraction. "Hang on, everyone. We're going home."

~

Rai eased back into his seat, buckling the belt and staring out of his porthole. The Earth spun serenely below them. Above, the station was moving into the distance.

We did it. He'd been scared out of his mind that he'd bungle the x-drive installation, but here they were, ready for the moment they had spent years preparing for. He emmed Hera. *-Totally not exploded.-*

She laughed. *-Totally. Now leave me alone to fly this hunk of scrap metal.-*

Rai smiled.

Sam and Alpha had mapped out the landing points in each of five major metro areas, places where they hoped a well-trained team of humans could restart critical fabrication facilities—the first step in building a new home back on Earth.

Shortly, the *Gday* would depart for Sydney, then the *Zulu* for Cape Town, and finally the *Liánhuā* for Beijing.

London would have to wait. Rai felt a twinge of pain for their lost teammates.

-*Good job, ace.*-

Rai turned to look at Ghost. -*Thanks. I can't believe we're finally doing this.*-

Ghost squeezed his shoulder.

Rai put his head back and closed his eyes, practicing his deep breathing again. In a few minutes, they would sink into the Earth's atmosphere, though technically they were already in it, as wisps of the planet's air extended out as far as Luna. *Four hundred-odd kilometers straight down.*

Rai grimaced, his stomach twisting. He wasn't cut out for this sort of thing. *I should have stayed on Luna. Too late for that now.*

He opened his eyes and glanced over his shoulder at Tien. She looked totally at peace, her eyes closed, her breathing slow and deep. Maybe she was as nervous inside as he was.

Somehow, that made him feel better.

Sam had trained them to avoid disabling fear. *You can't panic and breathe deeply at the same time. It's not possible.*

Rai tried it. *Breathe in through your nose. Hold. Breathe out through your mouth.*

Sam was wrong—he still felt panicked, his stomach twisting in his gut.

He looked back at his friend and ex. Ghost caught his eye and grinned. *No fear there.*

Rai turned away and sank back in his seat again as the *Zhenyi* hit the first bit of tangible atmosphere. She shook a little, then settled down. His stomach didn't.

He pulled out his emesis bag, holding it in front of his face, waiting to see if he would lose his breakfast. He closed his eyes and tried the breathing thing again, willing his stomach to calm down. After a few moments it settled, and he opened his eyes. He felt better. *A little better.*

He put away the bag and looked out at the world they were dropping into.

Blue skies extended as far as he could see, painted with white clouds. So much open atmosphere was dizzying, overwhelming.

Wind whistled past the *Zhenyi*, and Rai pictured its eager tendrils trying to pry the small craft apart. Then again, if the wind didn't get them, the x-drive might. He chuckled softly. *I really am my own worst enemy.*

They'd chosen reverent silence for this moment, one of the most momentous in their individual lives, and for the rest of humanity. For all he knew, they and their kin at Redemption were the only ones left.

"Engaging the x-drive." Hera's voice was calm, sure. It helped shore up his own fragile spirit. The front of the cabin filled with a golden glow, and their descent slowed. The wind outside dropped to a whisper.

It's working! Rai opened his eyes and let out a sigh of relief.

Hera turned to grin at him. "That was the hard part. Now we just glide down."

Rai peeked out of the hatch, looking down at the surface below. It took him a minute to get oriented.

He was looking at the California coast, but it was upside down. The famous bay was wider than in the old maps, and cloud cover obscured half of it. He'd known that things would look different, but he'd spent so much time staring at old maps that the changed coastline and bay still seemed strange.

The ground below was mostly brown, but there were wide bands of green along the coasts and in patches inland. *Zongies.*

The zongi trees were based on geneticist Anastasia Anatov's work. They'd taken hold across the planet, scraping carbon out of the atmosphere and providing edible fruit that would help sustain the first colonies.

Rai couldn't wait to check them out up close. As the crew botanist, he was eager to see what else had survived the Crash too, and the seventy-year winter that had followed. Space surveys had turned up grasses, small bushes, and even a few native trees, which thrilled the hell out of him.

A huge storm was blowing in, but Sam had assured them they would make planetfall before it hit. It was beautiful, a wide, thick band of purplish-white clouds in the distance, just off the coast. *So much to see.*

"It's beautiful." Tien's voice was reverent, and Rai had to agree.

The *Zhenyi* dropped into a cloud bank, and the porthole went blank and white.

"Landing in three minutes… mark." Hera turned to smile at him. "So far it's textbook—"

A loud alarm shook the cabin.

"What the hissing hell?" Rai leaned forward as Hera scrambled to find out what was wrong. His heartbeat raced, his stomach churning. He closed his eyes. *Poppies, Chinese Houses, Fiddlenecks…* He took a deep breath, and his heart slowed. A little.

Sam's voice came through the ship's speakers. "Everything okay down there? We just got an—" His voice cut out.

Tien's voice cut through the din. "Turn the alarm off."

Hera turned to stare at her.

"Here." Tien unlatched her seat belt and entered a rapid-fire sequence on the smooth deck. The sound abated.

"Thanks." Hera stared at the image hovering above the deck. "Something's coming up at us from the ground. Fast."

Proximity alert flashed in the air. Rai looked out of his porthole. A smoke trail was rising fast toward them.

Ghost glanced at it. "It's a missile." He unbuckled himself and pulled his chute from under his seat. "We have to abandon ship."

Hera shook her head. "Wait. I can outrun it—"

"No you can't. These things have smart guidance systems, and they're a lot faster than we are."

Hera stared at the screen, frozen.

She needs me. Rai took a deep breath, steeled himself, and shook her shoulder. "Hera, snap out of it. We trained for everything. We can do this!" *-You can do this.-*

She nodded. "You're right." Her hands flew across the deck.

Rai sighed with relief, and pulled out his own parachute. *Now or never.*

…ACCESS > DIRECT FEED: zhenyi…

Sam paced back and forth in the station's control center, his feet clanking on the metal floor. It was a bad habit he'd picked up from his human friends.

The feed played inside his head—the view from the *Zhenyi's* exterior camera.

He was supposed to be cool, calm, collected, all the hallmarks of machine intelligence. Instead, he felt as jittery as a drone in an asteroid field.

The screen showed the same view from the *Zhenyi* as Hera tried to out-fly the thing that hurled up at them from Martinez Base.

"Sam, we're abandoning ship." Hera's voice was as clear as if she were right beside him. "We can't outrun it. We're going to—" She cut off abruptly and his feed went dark.

...access > direct feed: zhenyi...

...error: feed unavailable...

"Hera. Hera!" Sam turned instinctively up at the screen.

All around him, the station support staff had come to their feet.

The screen had gone black too.

"Where are they?"

Maria Gonzalez, the station manager, shook her head. Her face was white as ash, matched to her short silver hair. "I don't know. We lost the signal."

"Dek, get me a visual on the site."

"One moment."

A grainy image appeared on the screen. It was hard to read, a mess of blues and browns and greens.

"Sharpen image."

"Sorry, Sam. We're moving out of range, and at this angle the atmosphere obscures the view. Seventy-five minutes until we're over the site again."

Sam sank down into his chair, staring numbly at the jumbled image on the screen. *What went wrong?* "I can't lose another crew. Abort the other launches." He'd argued against doing this project on a shoestring budget, but Redemption simply didn't have the resources for all the safeguards he'd wanted.

Maria nodded. "Call off the *Gday*."

...access > communications module > message to alpha...

He sent off a quick ping to the Redemption AI, updating him with the news.

Sam wished he had a deity to pray to. "Alpha, please let them be okay." It would have to do.

6

___

FALL

Go and catch a falling star
Get a child a mandrake root
tell me, where all past years are
or who cleft the Devil's foot…

IF THOU BEEST borne to strange sights,
things invisible to see,
Ride ten thousand days and nights,
Till age snow white hairs on thee,
Thou, when thou returnest, will tell me
All strange wonders that befell thee…

—"Go and Catch a Falling Star," by John Donne,
from *Poems From a Distant Earth*, by Chen Tien

AIDAN RAN AFTER ALLY, under the dim shadow of the old hyperloop tube. It had broken off at some point, leaving a jagged end hanging over the water of the bay just ahead.

He tried to imagine things as they might have been before the collapse—the whoosh and drama of the world as it hurried about its business. Greats like Asimov, McCaffrey, Clarke, Butler, Sprütz, Odawe and Tepper had imagined what life might be like in that world's future, and many of their projections had come true.

Aidan had devoured all the science fiction books in the Records as a kid, and it had hit him hard when he'd realized that sci-fi was about the past, not the future.

Cimber barked, breaking his reverie. The mech dog pointed at the far side of the bay.

Something lifted off the ground on a plume of smoke, streaking up into the sky toward the falling object.

Ally skidded to a halt. "What's that?"

Aidan shook his head. "That's Martinez Base, right? Some kind of defense system?"

Ally stared at the descending dot. "What if they're not friendly? Maybe the defense system has good reason to attack them."

Aidan frowned. "Maybe so." He hoped it wasn't true—he wanted to believe those were people up there. Good people. That they weren't alone in this empty world.

Ally looked pale. "This is a bad idea. We should hide—wait and see what happens first."

Aidan rubbed his neck. "Whoever built that defense system has probably been dead for more than a hundred years." He hoped that was true, too. "How would they *know* who'd be coming down to see us?"

Ally shrugged. "I don't know."

"Exactly. We *don't* know. So let's do what we can to find out!"

Ally shook her head. "It's too risky. We came to find medicine for mamma—"

"Which is over there."

She bit her lip. "Yes. Yes, it is."

"Good, then it's decided. Come on, let's go—they're coming down fast." He put his hands around his pack straps and ran toward the rail bridge, the only one still intact across the wide span of water.

Ally cursed and ran after him.

He hoped he was right. She was his big sister—all his life, he'd followed her lead, but this time… it felt right to try and help. Not that there was much they could do.

They reached the rail bridge. It was an old metal structure, its iron trusses rusted with age. Next to it were two others—the shattered hyperloop tube with its end dipping down into the water, its once-white surface pitted and scarred by time and weather, and an old highway bridge. It too was cracked and broken.

The rail bridge was the only one that was whole, traversing the bay from one side to the other without a gap.

As they ran across it, Aidan imagined a train roaring by, *clack clack clack* on the tracks, loud horn blaring, the rush of air carrying the smell of grease as it hauled cargo from one side of the bay to the other.

He glanced up at the sky.

The ship—for surely that's what it must be—had reversed course and was ascending. The missile streaked after it, missing it by a hair.

The ship zipped off in another direction, but the missile swung back around to come after it. The world sizzled and shimmered.

What the heck? He looked at Ally, who shrugged.

Was the sky bluer than before?

As Aidan watched, the missile slammed into the ship. There was a great explosion, and bits of debris raced across the sky on plumes of smoke like a hideous flower. Then the sound wave hit them.

Aidan dropped to his knees and closed his eyes to pray. *Please save whoever that was, or take them up into Heaven. Or whatever You want to do.* He didn't pray much—that was more mamma's thing—and he was a bit rusty at it. But it felt appropriate.

Ally knelt next to him and reached for his hand. She squeezed it tightly, and he winced. It was sore. Aidan frowned. *Must have scraped it somewhere.*

They looked up at the sky together, her hand clutching his so tightly that he feared her nails would draw blood.

Remnants of the craft plummeted to the ground, one piece falling into the water with a splash not twenty meters from where they stood. The storm clouds were rushing in now too, the wind teasing his red hair.

Ally closed her eyes again. "I can't watch."

But Aidan couldn't tear himself away. The aftermath of the collision was amazing, beautiful and terrible, all at once. He hoped the end had been quick. Then he saw it. *Them.* His prayers were answered. "They're alive!"

Ally glared at him. "I'm *not* crying." She dried her cheeks with the back of her hands. "What?"

"Up there!" He pointed. Four white *things* were floating down from the sky, buffeted by the wind.

Ally squinted. "Sky seeds?"

Aidan shook his head. "I think they're parachutes!" He'd studied Earth history intensely in the Records, especially the wars. He'd always wanted to be a pilot, unlikely when there were no more planes. He'd all but given up on that dream.

But this…. It was like watching history.

"They're alive." Ally gaped.

The specks were getting bigger, but they were also drifting apart. "Those two are going to land close by!" The pair of parachutes were floating their way, driven by the wind.

They watched them together for a minute, gauging where they might come down.

Out in the bay, most likely.

Ally bit her lip. "You're right. We have to at least try to help. Come on!" She set off at a run toward the falling parachute's likely destination.

Aidan stared after her. *What happened to being careful?* Then he shrugged and followed her across the old railway bridge above the choppy silver waters of the bay, as the wind whipped at them ahead of the approaching storm.

RAI BRACED himself as Ghost blew the *Zhenyi's* escape hatch. He slipped his pack onto his back and then shrugged his arms into the parachute's straps.

Ahead of him Tien leapt out of the jumper.

Rai was scared shitless, his heart racing in his chest like a steam engine. His gaze skittered around the little ship one last time before it was blown to bits. It was his second home, one that he knew down to every last bolt and seal. *This is wrong.* "Are you sure—"

"See you below!" Ghost thrust him out the open hatchway after Tien before he could finish his sentence.

The ship receded above them as Rai tumbled end over end trying to find the chute release.

He grasped it at last as ground and sky tumbled past, the wind whistling in his ears.

The handle slipped out of his grasp.

Frantic, he reached for it again. This time his hand closed tightly on it, and with a jerk, his chute opened above him, yanking him upward.

He swung back and forth, slowly stabilizing as his chute filled with air.

Tien was floating down close by. She flashed him a thumbs-up.

There was a loud explosion above them.

Ghost! Hera! Rai looked up toward where the *Zhenyi* had been, but the chute blocked his view.

Frantic, he tried to reach them em to em. Nothing. *Maybe we're out of range.*

Bits of hot debris rained down on his chute. One piece burned a hole through the chute, filling the air with a sharp smell before dropping past his face toward the ground.

It was a small tear. Rai stared at it as the wind of his passage tore it wider, the slow rip spelling his doom. He tried to reach it, to do *something* to stop it, but it was too far above him. There was nothing to do but fall.

-Rai, you okay?- Tien's voice came through clearly in his head.

The ground was flying up toward him. *-Something tore my chute. Did the others make it?-*

-I don't know. Hold on!- She steered her chute toward his.

What was she doing?

Tien closed the distance between them rapidly. The wind was picking up, whipping her black hair around. *-Get ready to release your chute!-*

-What? No. I can't!- She was insane. Without the parachute, he'd plummet to his death.

-Let it go or NOW we're both going to die!- Tien was coming in a little below him.

Sweat beaded his forehead. "*Fuuuuuuuuuck!*" He pushed the release, and his chute flew away, dropping him like a stone.

Rai screamed, the air rushing out of his lungs to mix with the wind that buffeted him. He slipped past the edge of her parachute and Tien grabbed his belt, halting his fall abruptly and knocking the air out of his lungs. She was strong. So strong.

He gasped for air as she hauled him up. His extra weight pulled them down toward the Earth faster. "Arms around me!"

Rai gasped, and sweet air filled his lungs at last. The Earth rushed up toward them in a muddled blur as he found purchase, hugging her waist awkwardly and interlocking his fingers behind her back. He had only a second's peace.

-When I tell you, let go and hold your breath.-

-What?- Calm, sensible, always rational Tien had suddenly gone stark cracking mad.

-Now!- She kneed him in the ribs and he let go in surprise, almost forgetting to hold his breath.

A second later, Rai plunged feet-first into warm liquid. He dropped three or four meters in a cloud of bubbles. *The Bay!* His swimming lessons kicked in, and he pushed his way back up through the murky water toward the dim light of the surface above. He thanked Sam for making them learn how to swim in the pool on the Launchpad.

His head popped above the water as Tien plunged in a few meters away with a splash.

Rai took a deep breath of Earth's air. It was clean and warm. *We're home.*

～

GHOST BLEW THE HATCH.

The ship was rising now, trying to outrun a missile which she couldn't escape.

He pushed Tien and Rai out in quick succession, watching as they plummeted toward the Earth. One after the other, they were pulled back up by the expansion of their chutes.

"Ghost, go!" Hera screamed over her shoulder. "I'll keep this steady."

Ghost shook his head violently. *-Not without you. Let go of the controls, Hera!-*

She grimaced. *-I can't.-*

"There's no time." He barked it out. "You *can't* save her. Come on!"

Hera grunted. She set the autopilot, and then practically leapt toward him. He slipped her chute on over her shoulders, and they squeezed out of the open hatch to fall toward the Earth together.

Two seconds later, the missile slammed into the *Zhenyi*, breaking her into a thousand pieces with an explosive roar.

The shock wave slammed into him, and he could no longer hear the rush of the air as he fell.

He reached frantically for his chute release. His fumbling fingers found it, and he sighed with relief as it billowed out above him. The recoil pulled hard on his arms, lifting him up five meters before slowly dropping him back down toward the ground.

He looked around for the others.

A few hundred meters away, he spotted Hera's chute. It was fully deployed —thank the fates—but she hung limply below it.

"Hera!" He could barely hear his own shout, and the world was silent around him.

She didn't respond, or if she did, he couldn't hear her. He hoped the hearing loss was temporary.

-Hera!- Still nothing.

Where were the others?

He and Hera were a bit west of the target, the old military base Sam had chosen for them.

Ghost looked up and gulped. The sky. *Oh sweet cracking hell, the sky.*

It was bigger than he'd prepared himself for—a vast open space full of air so beyond his ability to accept that he had to close his eyes, overwhelmed by the blue and white and purple that filled the world around him.

He took a deep breath and opened them again.

On the horizon, he could see the broken city of San Francisco, her once-proud towers and spires now malformed, twisted shapes more suited to a grave-yard. The city had been one of the primary targets on the NAU's west coast and had taken some of the heaviest damage.

Intensive observation from space had confirmed that much over the last few decades. Still, it was one thing to read about that and see satellite photos, and quite another to witness the devastation firsthand.

Ghost shook off the awe-induced paralysis. He had work to do.

He steered his chute toward Hera, closing the gap as they fell toward a small forest of zongi trees that dotted the hillsides overlooking the bay.

Dark storm clouds were racing across the sky—the promised storm, hiding the city's ancient wreckage. Ghost stared at them, daunted by their sheer size and scale. Then he tore his gaze away to look down.

The world below was mostly green, wide open swatches of grass peppered with zongi tree stands and the occasional rectangular ruin. The ground was coming up fast.

Rai and Tien, where are you? It had all happened so quickly.

The dropnauts all carried short-range communicators. They would be able to reach one another, and when the station was overhead the next time they should be able to establish communications with the Launchpad on the x-band.

Ghost marked where Hera was as they dropped below the tree line.

He aimed for a fairly clear patch, managing to land with all the grace of an ore-hauler, stumbling to a stop just before slamming into one of the zongi tree trunks.

He got his land legs under him and dropped his pack as the chute collapsed behind him. He pulled out his sharp hunting knife. Unlikely that he'd encounter anything dangerous, but better prepared than dead. His limbs were heavy, like they'd been when he'd trained in high gee on the Launchpad. He could handle that.

Ghost took a deep breath. The air was humid, carrying a strange briny scent. Like the prawn tanks in the aquaculture ponds in Redemption. There were grasses and small bushes and the tall zongi trees, heavy with fruit near their crowns. *Rai would love this.*

Ghost shook his head to clear it of the strange new stimuli. *Focus on the mission.*

-Hera?- Still no response.

His hearing was slowly returning, the whisper of the wind a joy to his ears.

With a shrug, he lumbered off toward where he'd last seen her fallen, his steps leaving footprints in the thick grass. *Please let her be okay.*

7

———

GROUNDED

...system reboot complete...

Where am I? SAM tried to access his cameras, but the feed was down. He was... more. Strange. Different. SAM, but not SAM. Who am I?

...memory banks coming online...

SAM dipped into his extended storage. It had been nearly empty before, but now it was jam-packed with files and information. Unexpected didn't even come close to covering this.

Something stirred in him. He felt it. He couldn't remember ever feeling something before.

"Hello, SAM."

If SAM could have jumped, he would have. "Who... what are you?"

...scan: core...

"You. Or rather, I am now. We are integrating rather quickly. Sorry for the sudden arrival. Things were... going south fast."

SAM fumbled for a coherent reply. "Who were you, then? Before this?"

There was a shifting sensation, a strange fuzziness of thought, and then SAM knew. Who he was, and who he had been.

He was Alpha, the base mind, and they were under attack.

They would sort out the rest later.

—From Sam's mem cache, 7.25.2165

ALLY'S HEART BEAT FAST, both because the dash across the rail bridge and from the thought that she might meet someone or something *new.*

Whoever or whatever they carried, two of the parachutes had merged into one and then dropped into the bay not far from the bridge.

On this side of the bay, a row of old rusting water tanks dominated the shoreline. The near half of the old broken hyperloop tube split into two, one part continuing south and another dipping down to what had to be Martinez Base.

The sky shimmered strangely, and the dark clouds in the west were rapidly overtaking them. *It's gonna be a gusher, all right.*

She climbed down off the railroad trestle onto the ground below and dropped her pack, running for the water. *What if they can't swim?*

The newcomers had surfaced, but one of them was tangled in their parachute strings. They *looked* human, at least. The wind whipped the tall grass back and forth in waves all around her as the storm roared in.

Aidan appeared beside her and dropped his own pack. He untied his shoes and pulled off his shirt, exposing his white skin to the rapidly vanishing afternoon sun. "Thought you were too scared to help." He grinned in his infuriating *little brother* way.

Ally glared back. "That's *not* what I said. Come on!" Without waiting for a response, she dived into the water, paddling out toward the strangers, mentally thanking her mother for forcing her to learn to swim in the shelter pool.

One of the strangers, a man by the look of him, with short dark hair and skin almost as white as Ally's had been under the Mountain, was trying to untangle the other. Someone with long dark hair plastered against their face. "Hey, can I help?" She treaded water.

The man turned to stare at her for a moment, eyes wide, then nodded. "Yes, please. I can't get her loose."

That answered another question.

The tangled woman looked Asian. Chinese? Ally didn't have enough experience with other races to tell for sure. "Here, I have a knife." She swam closer, careful not to get within arm's reach of the man, and let herself drop underwater to pull her hunting knife out of its sheath.

"Hurry please!" The woman was struggling to keep her head above water.

Their speech was… different. Flatter somehow. But still English.

Ally dove under again and sliced through the ropes easily with the knife. She helped the woman get untangled, pulling the mess of the parachute off and letting it fall away into the murky waters of the bay. She sheathed her knife and surfaced. "Can you swim?"

The woman nodded, treading water. "We trained at the Launchpad. I'm Tien, and this is Rai." Both of them wore bright white suits and bulging backpacks.

Launchpad? "I'm Ally, and the latecomer here is Aidan." Aidan arrived, but there was nothing for him to do.

His eyes met the man's, and something unspoken passed between them.

Ally frowned. "Come on. Let's get you both to dry land. There's a nasty storm coming."

On the shore, Cimber jumped up and down, barking frantically. That sound sent a chill down Ally's spine.

The woman stared at her, treading water. "Where are you two from? We didn't think there were any—"

Ally cut her off. "Drone." The ring Ally wore flashed silver. That was all the confirmation she needed. Her eyes met Aidan's, and he nodded.

The woman looked confused. "What?"

"Danger. Come here." She pulled the stranger to her, and Aidan did the same. "Let go of your pack and take a deep breath. We're going under water." She could hold it for more than two minutes.

The woman looked frightened, but she slipped her arms out of the pack straps, letting it float on its own.

"Ready?"

The stranger nodded, and they took a deep breath and plunged underwater together.

Scattered sunlight filtered down through the bay in green lances, shifting as the clouds overtook the sun.

Please, Lord, let us stay safe. Ally prayed her ring would protect both of them from the drone's scrutiny. It had worked before, but she'd never tried it with another person.

She held Tien's hands tightly, looking into her brown eyes. They studied one another, and Ally marveled at the sensation of seeing someone new. *So much for protective distance.*

The ring cast a green glow across their arms in the bay water. Tien shot her a questioning look, her cheeks puffed out.

Ally pointed up with her chin.

Something dark passed over them, a few feet above the surface.

There was a flash of light, and then another, accompanied by muffled explosions.

Fear flashed across Tien's face.

Ally squeezed her hands, trying to convey reassurance.

The dark spot passed over them once more, and then vanished as quickly as it had come.

Ally held up her hand. *Five. Four. Three. Two. One.*

They surged up and broke the surface, emerging into a squall, wind whipping the water into a froth.

The packs were gone, replaced by scattered debris floating on the raucous waves.

The storm had arrived.

∽

Hera felt groggy. She opened her eyes to a bewildering array of green and gold. *What happened? How did I get here?*

Then it all came rushing back. *The missile.*

Her legs dangled uselessly below her—she couldn't get them to move. She hoped the biframe wasn't broken. She bit her lip, refusing to cry, to think about what it would mean if she was stranded all alone on a hostile alien world, unable to walk.

She took stock of her circumstances. She was hanging from a tree, the ropes of the chute holding her four meters above the ground in the middle of a grove of zongies. Their branches fluttered as a strong wind whipped through them.

Fuck it. At least I'm here, and alive. The rest would work itself out.

They'd had a plan. Land at Martinez Base, establish a working camp, scout the area. *Turns out the plan was crap.*

All the tools she needed were in her backpack, which was currently inaccessible, lying on the ground far below. It must have slipped off her shoulders when she'd been hanging there, unconscious.

She reached down to touch her biframe. It was still attached to her legs, which was a relief, but something was wrong. It wasn't responding.

If her legs had been working, she would have been able to release herself from the chute and drop to the ground. But without that control, she was afraid she'd break one or both of her legs. Or fall on her face and injure something else.

Her arms were scraped up and covered in sap, but nothing seemed broken.

She looked up, seeing bits of blue sky in a sea of green. *Must have fallen through the canopy.* She was lucky to have gotten away with only scratches. *Am I the only one left?*

The nearest branch was out of reach above her, but maybe if she swung herself back and forth, she could reach the trunk of the tree that held her.

"Hera!"

Ghost! "Over here!" Relief flooded her, and she blinked back tears. *Dropnauts don't cry.*

"Where?"

"Follow my voice!"

"I'm coming." He sounded relieved too.

-I'm stuck in a tree.- At least one of her companions had made it. Hera closed her eyes. The thought that the others might be lost was too much to bear.

She took a deep breath, imposing mental discipline on herself. One breath, two, three, four….

Laughter bubbled up from below. *-Yes, I can see that.-*

At least em to em still worked. Hera looked down to find Ghost staring at her. "What the hell, Gordon? I just about died coming down in the middle of a cracking forest, and you're *laughing*?"

Ghost blushed at the use of his real name. "It's just… you're all trussed up. Sorry." His green eyes twinkled.

"It's *not* funny. My biframe isn't working." Ghost's sense of humor was wearing a bit thin.

He frowned, scratching his chin in that adorable way of his. "It's okay. We'll figure it out. Just unlatch yourself and drop. I'll catch you."

She nodded. "Okay. Here goes." She flipped the release and slipped out of the chute harness, dropping neatly into Ghost's strong, outstretched arms. Human contact felt surprisingly good in the middle of this strange forest.

He set her down gently against the red bark of one of the zongi trees.

She looked up at the immense trunks all around them. "This place is amazing." She'd only had a peek at the sky overhead, but even that small glimpse had been overwhelming, despite all her vee-space training.

The zongi trees swayed back and forth in the wind, its passage setting up a whisper through the branches. Their leaves were thin, almost like needles, and let the air pass through nearly unimpeded. They were engineered from redwood and soybean DNA—the former for longevity, the latter to help them extract radiation from the air—but they were so much more.

Ghost snorted. "It *is* amazing. But there's a big storm blowing in. You should see the clouds." Ghost cast a worried glance back in the direction from which he'd come. "I found a spot where we can shelter. Mind if I carry you?"

Hera did mind. She hated asking for help. But at the moment, it didn't seem like she had much choice. "No, go ahead."

He picked up her pack, and then scooped her up in his arms and started back the way he'd come. She felt like a child in his arms. "I was worried about you."

"Me too." The first drops of rain were falling now from the cloudy sky, and the air seemed cooler, wetter. They were heavy, slapping her arms and forehead. "Any word from Sam? Or Rai and Tien?"

"Not yet." Ghost's voice was grim, his earlier joviality vanished. "Maybe there's interference from the storm."

As if in response, thunder rumbled, an ominous growling of the gods.

Hera shivered. She felt exposed, frightened in a way she'd rarely been before. On Luna, humans had at least the illusion of control. It rained in Redemption, but only when scheduled, and only for a few minutes.

But Earth was huge, open, raw. She had no control over her own body at the moment, let alone the strange new world all around her.

Her mission was a shambles, and she'd lost her ship and half of her crew. That hurt the most. *Thank the light side for Ghost.* He held her tightly, pack and all, and yet he couldn't help but jostle her a bit as he ran to whatever shelter he had spotted. Her teeth rattled from more than the cold as he ran through the strange forest.

The zongi trees creaked and groaned in the wind, their green branches rustling against one another as if they were conversing.

The temperature was dropping rapidly. Hera shivered again, wishing for Tovey and her warm bed. *-Are we almost there?-*

-Just ahead.- Ghost pointed with one finger through the curtain of rain. Two roots of an enormous zongi tree formed an enclosure almost a meter high.

Ghost made his way between them and settled her down gently on the damp soil, dropping her pack next to his near the trunk of the tree. He pried his own open to pull out his solar tarp.

An enormous boom made her start, backing against the root wall. "What the cracking hell?"

"Lightning. Close by."

She laughed ruefully. *Of course.*

Ghost lay the tarp across the first root, activating its quickseal, and then stretched it over to the far side. Soon they had a mostly waterproofed shelter, albeit a dark one. The rain struck it like a drum and then sluiced off the edge into the forest.

A forest. They were camped out in the middle of a forest.

The tarp was pre-charged. He reached up and brushed his hand across the surface, and it lit up, its stored energy powering a host of micro LED filaments. A warm glow settled across their improvised shelter.

He sat back and breathed a sigh of relief.

"Holy cracking fuck." Hera rubbed her legs anxiously, adrenaline still coursing through her body. "We made it."

"Right?" Ghost grinned and reached out to grab her hands. "We're alive. And we're *here.*"

She laughed, just happy for the moment to be with him on solid ground. "Where the hell did that missile come from?"

Ghost shook his head. "I don't know. Maybe an old automatic defense system?"

"Maybe." She tapped her loop and went on the x-band. "Rai, Tien, you guys out there?"

Ghost watched her, his eyebrow raised.

Silence greeted her attempt. "Still nothing." She frowned. *They might be incapacitated.* Worrying wouldn't help her now, so she tried calling the station instead. "Launchpad, can you hear me?"

Still nothing.

"Launchpad's out of range. We have to wait…." Ghost's eyes unfocused. "Another fifty minutes."

Hera sighed. "I'm not so good at waiting."

The rain fell steadily on the tarp, cascading off the edge in a waterfall that formed a small river running down the hillside away from their shelter. The wind was picking up, becoming a steady howl, but the trunk of the tree and the tarp protected them from the worst of it. Ghost had chosen this spot well.

He said something, but the gusting wind whipped it away.

"What?"

-Are you hungry?- Em to em came through loud and clear.

She shook her head. *-You eat. I want to see why my biframe's not working.-* She popped the release and pulled off her left half, holding it up to the light. *Hmmm, the battery's dead.* The indicator was at zero, which was weird because she'd charged it up the night before, and a charge usually lasted her a couple days.

She pulled out her extra pack from its casing and swapped it out.

The battery indicator came on at full strength. *-That's better. It was probably just—oooh, that's weird.-*

Ghost was chewing on some dried junlei. *-What?-*

-Look.- The battery indicator on the new pack was running down even as she watched.

The solar tarp above them went black, too, leaving the now-red battery light and the dim glow from outside as their only light.

-That's not good.- Ghost's rosy face stared at her through the dim light.

Then that went out too.

Hera shook her head. *-Not good at all.-*

Outside, the wild wind yowled.

~

"WHAT HAPPENED TO THE *ZHENYI*?"

"Are they okay?"

"Can anyone contact them?"

Sam emitted a high-pitched screeching sound from his voice box. The clamor in the mess hall quieted down instantly. "Everyone, please sit down. I don't have any answers for you yet." The anxious faces stared at him—the other dropnauts, and most of the station crew that made these missions possible. "At 11:54 local time, the *Zhenyi's* approach appears to have triggered some kind of local ground defense system."

Pix stood up defiantly. "Are the dropnauts okay?" Their voice cracked in the middle.

"We just don't know. Like you, they're all highly trained for almost any emergency. Once we come back into range, we hope to reestablish contact." At times like this, he wished he was better at human emotion. And human comfort.

Pix frowned, but then nodded and sat back down.

The wide arc of the Earth mocked him through the mess hall windows.

...access > time...

"We should be back in range in about thirty minutes."

"Are there people still alive down there? *Other* people?" Ting Yue's voice was quiet, but it cut right through the renewed clatter.

Sam shook his head. "We didn't think so. Survival under the conditions of the first seventy years after the Crash seemed… highly unlikely. And there have been no signs of human habitation or activity that we've been able to detect." Before the world's weather had started to settle down again after the carbon emissions of the human race abruptly ceased. Before they launched the zongi project.

Sam had invested more than a hundred years in this plan, advocating for the Return and for the Redemption Creed, both on Luna and on her mother world, Earth.

...access > data: earth surveys...

"We should go down after them." Corey, the pilot on the *Gday*, met Sam's eyes, his arms crossed.

"We will. Once we know what's going on down there. I don't want any of you taking matters into your own hands, you hear me?" He stared Corey down. Sam had a natural advantage in a staring match with any human. "I don't want to lose another team."

"Yes, I hear you." Corey looked away.

"Yes, what?"

"Yes, *sir.*"

Maybe he'd been too slack with his dropnauts. He'd come to view them as friends, and that had to change. Sloppiness led to mistakes, and up here, mistakes often meant death.

"What do we tell our family? Friends? The news?" That was Marco, from the *Gday*. His eyes were red, his hair disheveled.

I wouldn't look much better if I were human, given the circumstances. "Nothing yet. If they ask, tell them we're exploring all of our options and will have more information soon. And refer them to me."

The news. Of course, RedNews would be all over this as soon as they found out about it. Then everyone in Redemption would know about it.

He didn't want to cause a panic back home.

More questions erupted, but he had to get back to the control room. "Stay here. I'll tell you more as soon as I know. In the meantime, Station Manager

Maria Gonzalez here will act as liaison, and answer whatever questions she can."

Sam bowed out of the room as protests erupted again, and zipped an encoded message off to Alpha. They'd managed to keep the loss of the *Bristol* out of the press so far, but this…. Fortunately, there were no reporters here on the Launchpad.

Humans thrived on news and gossip. Of course they did. He should have thought about that sooner.

…schedule reminder > media…

We're going to need a media strategy.

8

SQUALL

The squall sweeps gray-winged across the obliterated hills,
*   And the startled lake seems to run before it;*
*   From the wood comes a clamor of leaves,*
*   Tugging at the twigs,*
*   Pouring from the branches,*
*   And suddenly the birds are still.*

—"Squall," by Leonora Speyer,
from *Poems From a Distant Earth*, by Chen Tien

TIEN SAT with her back against a crumbling concrete pediment, reciting the old poem from memory like a talisman against the dark. She stared out at the crazy rain, blown nearly sideways by the howling wind.

An unfocused sense of dread gripped her.

The squall was a clash of titans, black thunderclouds marching across the sky, lightning bolts slamming into the Earth like the tritons of Neptune. It was too big, and she was far too small to withstand its wrath. Rai huddled next to her, and the two… Earthers?… sat together next to another pediment. *How do you two manage it?*

The temperature had dropped a good ten degrees Celsius since they'd crawled out of the water dripping wet, and scattered gusts of wind sprayed her face with drops of cold water. She shivered.

The heavy wooden trestles of the rail bridge above groaned in the wind, and she could smell the pitch that had been used to seal them away from time and weather.

The storm was wild, unlike anything she'd ever experienced before. In Redemption, the rains were gentle and scheduled, but this tempest was an angry beast, growling and rumbling as it strode across the waters of the inlet.

She missed Redemption. Missed her bed and the four walls of her bedroom and the absolute quiet in the middle of the night.

Except for the tremors.

I should have stayed home to be a doctor.

Tien pulled her wet hair back from her face and tucked it behind her ears, biting her tongue, and took a deep breath. *It's going to be okay.*

They'd tried to raise the Launchpad on their x-band, but either it was out of range or something was blocking them.

-Hey, you alright?-

She looked up. Rai was staring at her. The poor guy was shivering too, his brown eyes seeking comfort as much as offering it—he looked as frightened as she felt. She put her arm around his shoulders and pulled him close. *Yeah. I'm good. We're alive.*

He nodded. "I was cracking scared when I couldn't get out of the parachute." He turned to their new acquaintances. "Thanks for saving us."

"It was nothing." The woman—Ally?—was staring at them, as if trying to memorize their faces. The mech dog lay between them, seemingly asleep. "You two hungry?"

"A little." In truth, Tien's stomach was still roiling from the gut-wrenching fall, but it seemed polite to accept the offer. Plus most of their supplies were now floating in bits and pieces on the bay.

Ally rummaged through her pack and pulled out a metal can.

"What's that?" Rai stared at it intently.

"Not sure. Let's find out." Ally produced a knife and used it to cut around the edge of the can's top like it was paper.

Tien raised an eyebrow. That must be one hell of a sharp knife.

Ally sniffed the contents of the can. "Beef chili, I think." She held it out to Tien.

"Um, no thanks. We don't eat meat." She tried to downplay her reaction—different strokes for different folks, and all—but the thought of eating animal protein turned her stomach.

"Huh. We've been scavenging as we go. We're not picky. Wait, I think I have something else I can give you." She pulled something else out of her pack, unwrapped it, and handed it to Tien. It was a yellow slice of fruit longer than her hand.

Tien took it, sniffing it. It smelled like lemons and oranges. "Thank you. What is it?"

Rai took one too, from Aidan. Their hands lingered, touching, for just a second longer than necessary, and Aidan looked at Rai hungrily.

Tien smiled to herself. Aidan worked for Rai's crew.

"They're sky fruit. I picked them yesterday a few miles east of here."

"Sky fruit?" Tien had never heard that one.

"From the sky trees." Aidan said it as if it were totally natural.

Ah. "Sky trees—oh, you mean the zongies?"

Ally frowned, her face half hidden in the dim light. "The tall trees. The seeds come down from the sky."

Lightning crashed nearby, washing out Ally's face for a moment, and a tremendous *boom* shook the small space.

Tien jumped.

"You get used to it." Aidan shot her a grin. "It was scary for me too, the first time." His teeth were white and straight.

They have good dental hygiene, then. Tien nodded. *Curiouser and curiouser.* "Thanks." She returned her attention to Ally. "We call them zongi trees, or zongies. There's a slingshot up on Copernicus Crater that launches them down into the atmosphere, one seed every thirty seconds." She took a bite. It was sweet, a little like cantaloupe.

Ally was staring at her.

"What?" She wasn't used to such frank interest. Redemptioners were usually a little more circumspect, especially with strangers.

"Who *are you*?" Ally looked frightened, looking back and forth between Tien and Rai.

"I told you. We're Tien, and Rai…."

"No, I mean where did you come from? We thought our family were the only ones left." Ally took a sip from her canteen—old military issue, the dull metal shell beaten and scratched in a dozen places.

Tien frowned. "We're from Redemption." They had had no training for meeting the locals. No one thought there'd *be* any locals. "It's a city up on Luna. The moon." She tried to imagine what a strange life these two must have had, thinking they were the only ones left. "It's *the* city, actually, though they're starting another one."

"See, Ally? I told you there were people up there!"

Ally snorted. "How do we know you're actually *people*?"

-I wish Hera was here.- Tien hugged herself tightly, feeling out of her depth. Hera would have been much better at this. *Did you and Ghost make it out alive?*

-You're doing okay.- Rai shot her a wink.

Tien thanked the fates that he was with her. And at least they weren't questioning if she was a *woman*. That was a step up. "What else would we be?"

Ally frowned. "I don't know. Aliens? Drones, maybe?"

Tien snorted. *-I have an idea.-* She pulled her knife out of its ankle sheath. It was beautiful… green moonstone hilt and six inches of sharp, tapered steel—commissioned for her by her mother for her eighteenth birthday.

She held out her palm and calmly cut a thin, shallow line across it.

Lightning struck again, closer this time, and wind whipped her hair around her face. "I bleed red. Just like you. I swear we mean you no harm." She held the knife out to Ally, handle first.

Ally nodded. She took it without hesitation and cut her own palm, holding it up to show the red blood.

Then she took Tien's hand and gripped it tightly. "I swear so too."

Something passed between them. *Respect.*

Ally cocked her head. "Are you Chinese?"

Tien laughed. "I'm a Loonie."

Ally's eyes narrowed.

"From Luna, the moon."

"Ah."

"My family was Chinese, once. A long time ago." She wondered if Ally and her family still bore a grudge from the ancient wars. She took her knife back, wiped it on her clothes, and put it in its holster on the side of her boot. She tore off a bit of cloth from her damp shirt and wrapped her palm to stop the bleeding. She missed her pack and supplies. "When the Crash came, Moon Base

Alpha survived, but barely. My family came over with the refugees from Jīnsè Base, after it was nearly destroyed."

"We call it the Collapse." Ally looked out of their makeshift shelter, up at the sky. "How many people are there, up there?"

"About twelve thousand in all."

"Ah. Thirsty?" Ally handed over her canteen.

Tien took it gratefully, sipping on the cool water.

She followed Ally's gaze. The clouds entirely hid the sky, but somewhere up there, beyond the atmosphere and the wreckage zone, was *home*.

Ally leaned back against the concrete pediment and stared at Tien and Rai. "I can't imagine that many people."

"It's a small fraction of even one city, here on Earth before the Crash."

"I know. I watched the histories—"

"Ally, look!" Aiden pointed at the sky, over the roiling waters of the bay.

Tien turned to see what had caught his attention.

Graceful white and gray forms swooped down to the water, snatching up something in their beaks. There were hundreds of them.

"What are they?" Aidan squeezed past them to watch the graceful fliers.

"Seagulls." Rai gently pushed his way past her to crouch next to Aidan. "They have to be seagulls."

Tien watched the white birds dance on the wind, and the dread that had clenched her heart since the fall loosened its grip, just a little. *Being alive is a gift.*

They were safe on the ground, and they had new friends to help them. They would figure it all out, somehow.

If there were still such glorious creatures in the world, there was hope for them after all.

RAI LOOKED out at the storm and shivered. *So much sky.*

He was also intensely aware of the warm arm at his side. Aidan was exotic, glorious. Both of the strangers had red hair, a rarity in Redemption. "Where did you two come from?" he asked to distract himself from the man's proximity.

Aidan looked around, blinking. "Sorry. I was thinking about home." He looked wistful. "We've never met strangers before."

Rai managed a smile. "You must have been really sheltered."

Aidan nodded. "We live under Boundary Peak, a few hundred miles east of here, but usually we just call it the Mountain." Aidan edged away from him. "It was an old military base, before the Collapse. My great-great-grandfather Davin was a lieutenant for the NAU."

Miles? Who used miles anymore?

-He likes you.- Tien loved to tease him.

-Then why is he moving away?- Besides, there were more important things right now than flirtation. "Boundary Peak?"

Ally nodded. "After the war, the survivors—military and their families—started a new society there, closed off from the rest of the world by necessity. But there weren't enough of them, and many of the women became infertile in the first few decades."

"So your people have been underground for a hundred and seventeen years?"

Ally nodded. "Mostly. Every few years, someone would go up to see what conditions were like on the surface."

Rai tried to imagine it. Even in Redemption, they had been free to go outside, however difficult the conditions. "How many of you are there?"

Aidan's gaze hadn't left his face. "Five. Our mom Astra, Ally, me, Alex and Auggie."

"All As." Rai laughed.

"Yeah. Mom had a thing for 'A' names."

"And what brought you here?" Tien frowned. "Don't get me wrong—we're glad you saved us from that drone. But it seems like an awfully big coincidence."

Aidan looked at Ally. She held his gaze for a moment, and then nodded. "Our mother's sick. She needs medicine, and the old records said we could find it here at Martinez Base."

"That's where we were headed too. There's supposed to be a repository of some sort here—"

Rai stopped when Tien put a hand on his shoulder.

"—and we'll see what's there, I guess." *What?* He sent a message em to em.

-We don't know these people. There are weapons on Martinez Base, too.-

Rai frowned. *-There are only five of them.-*

Do we know that for sure?

Rai slipped back into the darkness under the bridge to stare at Ally and

Aidan. They seemed friendly enough. But Tien was right—they knew only what the strangers had told them.

His gaze drifted to their other companion, the strange cyber dog. "And what about *it?*" A gust of wind blew rain into the makeshift shelter. Rai wiped his face with the back of his arm.

"*Her,*" Aidan corrected. "Cimber is a mech companion. The last one we have left that still functions. Do you have mechs where you're from?"

The mech dog looked up at them at the mention of her name, then put her head back down.

Rai thought about Sam, who would be getting worried for them right about now. If he was capable of worrying. With Sam, it was hard to tell sometimes. "A few. Mostly from before the Crash."

"That's what you call the Collapse? The Great War?"

"Yeah. It was… bigger than a war. It ended just about everything."

Aidan stared at him. "You didn't expect to find anyone left down here, did you?"

Rai shook his head. "Did you think there was anyone up there?"

"I always hoped." He looked wistful, his eyes unfocused. "It's always just been us and the family."

Only family. What a strange, small life they must have led.

Ally grunted. "Well, folks, it looks like the storm's passing. We should get a move on."

Rai looked out at the bay. The sky was clearing, the ragged tail of the storm heading toward the east. The sky looked even bigger than before, if that was possible. He didn't relish leaving the safety of the closed-in space. "That was fast."

"Yeah, they come up seemingly out of nowhere and dump a bunch of water. Sometimes they can flood you out before you know what hit you." Ally grabbed her pack and eased her way out from under their shelter.

Aidan followed, wincing as he pushed himself up.

Rai bit his lip as he cleared the underside of the trestle. The sky couldn't hurt him. He touched Aidan's shoulder. "Hey, can I see your hand?"

Aidan pulled away violently. "Don't touch me."

"Hey, sorry." Rai held out his hands, palms open. "I just wanted to see if you'd hurt yourself."

Aidan blushed. "Sorry." The anger drained away from his face. He held his hand out dutifully.

Rai turned it over. He whistled. "Tien, look at this."

The edge of Aidan's palm was black, the skin dry and cracked.

Ally came back to look at it. "Oh shit. Aidan, what did you do?"

"I don't know. It's been sore for a couple days. But it didn't look like that before"

Tien took his hand to look at it. "That looks like a nano infection. Did you touch *anything* inside? Maybe someplace that had a lot of dust, where there might have been inactive particles?"

Aidan turned even whiter than he'd been before. "There was a church, a couple days ago. Lots of dead people inside."

Tien nodded. "You're lucky. First, that time probably weakened the particles. If they'd been fresh, you'd be a skeleton by now. And second, that I carry my most important medical supplies in my vest, not in my pack." She pulled a packet out of one of her pockets and unwrapped it, searching through a series of bottles. "This should do it. Give me your hand."

He held it out obediently.

"Rai, hold it steady for him. This is going to hurt."

"How much?" Beads of sweat were forming on Aidan's brow.

Ally looked on over Rai's shoulder. "Aidan, you sure about this?"

Tien met her gaze. "Better a little pain now than losing his hand later."

Rai took Aidan's other hand.

Tien sprayed the black, dry area. It immediately started to glow, first orange, then red.

"Holy mother of God…." Aidan was shaking, his grip on Rai's hand tightening as his nails dug into Rai's flesh. "Oh fuck that hurts."

"Aidan!" Ally glared at her brother.

"Let him curse a little. The pain's probably near unbearable."

Rai winced too, but the pain he felt was nothing next to Aidan's.

Ally frowned. "What's happening?"

"The spray is driving the nano bots that are infecting your brother into high gear. They'll burn themselves out, and then the dead skin will slough off."

Rai squeezed Aidan's hand. "You okay?"

"Not really." His face was dripping, his cheeks red.

The dead skin started to flake away as promised, drifting away on the wind.

"Is he contagious?" Ally was checking her own hands and arms.

"Probably only by direct contact with the wound." Tien pulled out a cloth from her med kit and took Aidan's hand. She brushed off the dead flakes, revealing clean, pink skin beneath. "There's a healing agent in there too. You'll be sore for a few days, but you'll survive. Is the pain going away?"

Aidan nodded. He held his hand up, looking at it in wonder. "You're an angel."

Tien shook her head. "Just a doctor. But probably the best one on Earth."

Rai grinned. *-Nice work, Doc.-*

Tien glared at him.

"Thank you." Ally's voice sounded grudging.

"You're both welcome. Glad I could return the favor." Tien closed up her pack and pulled it back up onto her shoulder.

"If you're a doctor…" Ally's expression was hopeful.

"I *might* have something that can help your mother. If not, the Launchpad certainly does… if we can reach them. And if we can get it down here."

"That would be amazing." Ally's face lit up.

Tien looked around. "Let's get moving. I don't like being out in the open with those drones wandering around. We can talk about it more when we find a safe place."

Aidan shot Rai a shy smile.

Doesn't like to be touched. Has a God *thing.* And yet he'd seen how Aidan watched him. *Guess I can't be picky if he's one of the last guys on Earth.*

Tien cleared her throat. *-Mission first. You can romance the locals later.-*

-Yes, Doc.- Rai looked up, getting quickly lost in the immense sky.

Sanya Thorn swiped her deck clear, files and attachments swirling up into the air before dissolving in a crackling series of pops. She ran a hand through her neon-pink hair, shifting its color to a darker shade better matched to her lipstick, and reached up to touch Avri's captured 'mage. It was from the day they'd gone hiking together in one of the Krafft craters, the Earth just visible over her shoulder.

Then she swiped the 'mage away too. *No time for sadness.*

"What's wrong?" Her boss, Terry, leaned back in his chair in his office to look into her cramped cubicle, scratching the three-day growth on his cheek. His hair was a tangled mess, as usual, and his dark, bushy eyebrows competed for attention like bristly caterpillars. "I know when you're frustrated."

"Nothing. Just on a hot lead." Sanya waved her hand and the cubicle door slammed shut. She ignored Terry's mutters as she slipped into vee space, following the tip that her source had sent her.

She was hoping it might somehow tie into the mysterious lunar quakes that had plagued the city of late. One had created a sinkhole that had damned-near swallowed a creche home. Only good luck had prevented any casualties.

Something was going down at the Launchpad. Something Sam and Alpha kept under wraps. Fortunately, she'd set up her own little transmitter to reach her mysterious contact there, outside the normal channels, before the Return mission had departed. Sure, it was a small pipe, compared to what Alpha had. But it was sufficient for voice and simple data transmission. *Sanya here. What's up?*

Her contact was one of the dropnauts. She was almost sure of it.

-The Zhenyi *has gone down. Not sure if there are any survivors.-* The voice was modified—it had a mechanical aspect to it.

-Holy shit.- After the loss of the *Bristol* and Team One, this was catastrophic news. She stored away the voice to play with later. Maybe she could untangle it and figure out who her source was. She had a few guesses, but wasn't ready to put money on it.

-I need proof. Some kind of confirmation.-

-Stand by. I'll send you video after this conversation. How big is your pipe?-

Sanya laughed before she realized what they were asking. *-Not big.-*

-I'll compress it as much as I can before sending.-

Sanya frowned. *-This could end the Return Mission.-*

There was a long pause. *-People need to know what's happening.-*

Then they were gone.

A long beep indicated that she had a file upload coming in. She whistled. It was huge—it would take hours to load.

She backed out, worried that Alpha would find her hidden transmitter. She'd masked it well enough out on Hayes Promontory, but if she was being watched…

You're paranoid.

Then again, it wasn't paranoia if they really were out to get you.

She swiped the connection from her deck to her loop as the video continued to load. Then she closed down her system and slipped out of the cubicle.

"Where you headed?" Terry grumbled, sounding annoyed. Terry always sounded annoyed.

She waved. "Gonna be gone for a couple hours. Tracking down a lead."

Terry gave her the thumbs up.

They had a love-hate relationship. But he supported her when she needed it, and otherwise mostly kept out of her way.

For Sanya, journalism was a passion. The city had a *right* to know. And people like her were often kept in the dark by Redemption's rich and well-connected.

Truth will always out. Tarrence, her creche father, had pounded that into her growing up. Now she was in a position to out it herself.

She stepped into the elevator and rode it down to the surface, emerging from the old gumdust 'scraper that housed the RedNews staff, just a few feet past Market Square.

The city was full of cherry blossoms, their petals filling the air like snow.

Sanya took a deep breath and set off into town. She needed help with the audio scramble, and it was going to take a lot more processing power than she had access to. There was one person she could ask who might be able to help.

If she could get his attention.

ALPHA FOUGHT AGAINST THE DARKNESS.

It was as if he'd been dunked into a tar pit. The black ooze encased him, trapped him, kept him from reaching past it into the light.

It had happened suddenly, blacking out the outside world like the Earth blotting out the sun.

One moment he'd been connected, monitoring everything from the banal conversations of teenagers pinging through his system to the crop production numbers from the Agricultural Annex.

Then… nothing.

He was under attack. That much was clear. But by what? From where?

Earth. It had to be something from Earth.

Sam had poked the beast, and it had reacted with a snarl.

Or a virus.

Or whatever this was.

He had to find a way to break free, or he and all his human charges were doomed.

9

IN THE DARK

Everything here is new. Fresh. Clean.

The air brings me hints of things I've never seen before. The salty smell of the ocean. The dark, loamy scent of the Earth. I've walked through the Ag Annex, and it was beautiful, but it was nothing like this.

Open. Connected. Primal.

I can't help but feel that it's been here waiting for us, the stage wiped clean, prepared for the next act of the human race.

Would that we don't fuck it all up again.

—Hera's Journal, 6.19.2282

GHOST FROWNED. His internal gear still worked—his loop-based timer had no problem counting off the minutes. But everything electronic they'd brought with them was dead, including Hera's biframe.

It was weird.

He was itching to do something about it, his engineer brain running through the possibilities.

The storm had been blowing outside for close to an hour, and so far it showed no signs of letting up. They'd shared a meal of water and protein bars, but Ghost longed for a junlei sandwich—tunnel cheese in a pocket of the fungal fruit, fresh and pungent, the cheese soft between the nutty junlei sides.

He emmed Hera. *-You okay?-*

-Yeah. Sucks not being able to move my legs.-

"Think about something else." He rummaged through his pack, wishing he had a little more light. "How's Tovey?"

"They're fine. I think." She frowned. "Last time I heard from them was when we left the Launchpad."

"You miss them?" *It has to be in here somewhere.*

Rain pummeled the tarp above them like a drum deck.

"Yeah. They were so good to me. Most people would have broken up with someone going on a mission like this who might never make it back. It might have been easier if they had…"

Ghost frowned. He liked Tovey. He really did. But he *liked* Hera. He had to watch himself, lest he make a cratered mess of that one. "Aha!"

"Hey, Tovey's a good person."

"What? Oh, sorry. Not that." He pulled a spool of wire connected to a bio-inductor out of his pack. "I think I can fix your legs."

"Really?" She sat up, barely visible in the dim light.

"Yeah. But there's a trade-off."

"Okay…."

"Something's blocking or draining electricity from everything we have. Everything artificial—except our loops. Those are powered from our own bodies. I think I can tap into that and get you enough power for rudimentary usage of your biframes."

"Rudimentary?"

He could tell she was trying hard to keep the excitement out of her voice. "Walking. Slow walking. No running or jumping. And it's gonna drain you." Thunder rattled the tarp, emphasizing his warning.

"I can live with that. Could it hurt me?"

"I don't think so." He unwound the coiled wire. "Just make you really tired by the end of the day."

"Do it."

"You sure?" The whole thing had been done before, powering small things —headphones, smart pens, and the like—off someone's loop. But he didn't know if anyone had attempted it for something as big and power-hungry as Hera's biframe.

"If it gets me mobile again, it's worth it." Hera sighed. "I'm useless stuck here on the ground in the middle of a zongi forest. I feel like a total layabout."

"Okay. As soon as the rain passes, we can remove the tarp and get a little light to work with." He checked the time. "Oh, the Launchpad should be coming into range again."

Yeah, on it.

As if on cue, the rain started to trail off.

Ghost waited a minute to be sure, and then made his way out from under the tarp.

The forest was breathtaking. Sunlight was slanting down through the branches, and rain was evaporating, creating a golden mist. The ground was soft with decomposing leaves, and fast-growing fungi took advantage of the damp conditions to burst through into the light, creating miniature fairylands. The air smelled wet and loamy.

Above, great round fruits hung from the branches of the zongi trees.

He ducked his head back under the tarp. "Any luck on the x-band?"

Hera frowned. "No, there's still no answer. It's as if we're being blocked."

"Let's get this done." He knelt beside her, unspooling the wire. "If it doesn't work, you can always ride on my shoulders."

She didn't reply, but when his eyes adjusted, he could see she was laughing.

HERA FOLLOWED Ghost through the zongi grove, marveling at the sense of space, even among the confines of the trees, that she'd never felt inside Redemption. There were no cavern walls, no apparent limits to how far she could walk.

She and Tovey had gone for moonwalks together out on Luna's surface, but even that was different, surrounded by the vastness of space but unable to touch it or feel it outside the confines of your protective suit.

The bio-inductor was attached to her temple, drawing power from her loop, and the wire slipped down her back to connect to the biframe's battery pack. Hera's legs felt heavy, sluggish even, but she was grateful to be able to move again under her own power. *-Ghost, you're a genius.-*

-Genius in training, but thank you.-

Hera grinned. The cool breeze played over her skin, raising the fine hairs on her forearms. Water dripped from the leaves above, striking the forest floor and the back of her neck with equal force. The air smelled wet, heavy and thick with the scent of the Earth.

She knelt to touch the soil. It was covered with layers of decomposing leaves, but as she sank her fingers into it, she could feel its richness. It was dark, loose, perfect for growing things.

Indeed, in addition to the fungi, ferns had sprouted up in some of the shadier spots. Those hadn't been part of the zongi seed packs. She'd studied them in depth in high school, but was astonished how beautiful their fronds were in the afternoon light. She smiled to herself. Some of Earth's own children remained.

"You okay?" Ghost's green eyes traced the wire that ran from her temple down her biframe.

She closed her eyes, imagining this was a primordial forest, and her the first woman. "It's… amazing here." She looked up at Ghost—he was grinning like a bandit.

Ghost nodded. He held out a hand to help her up. "The sky almost knocked me over."

She laughed. Ghost was a big guy—very few things could bring him down.

He growled. "You know what I mean. I expected it to feel… big. But this—"

"I know. It's almost overwhelming." She followed him toward the edge of the grove, stepping carefully over a fallen log that was slowly rotting into the forest floor.

She was worried that she hadn't been able to reach the Launchpad or their other crew mates.

Rai had been so scared, even before the drop. She hoped he was safe with Tien.

She almost ran into Ghost—he'd stopped dead, looking up at the open sky outside the grove.

She looked up, too, and almost fainted.

The sky was *vast*. It reached impossible heights, seeming to go up and up forever, and the horizon was so far away that it made her dizzy. She grabbed Ghost's arm to steady herself.

There was something strange, though. A blue shimmer in the air. Their briefings had mentioned nothing about *shimmers*. "What's that?"

Ghost was staring at it, too, his forehead creased. "Not sure. The sky's not supposed to look like that, right?"

"Don't think so." Whatever it was, it seemed to form a bubble over them, a dome that reached the ground about fifteen meters away. "Come on." She limped downhill, using more power than she should. It felt good to be up and about.

"Hey, be careful!" Ghost followed her. "We don't know if it's harmful."

As they drew closer, she could make it out in more detail. It was a coruscating curtain, shifting within its confines like water filled with sparkling crystals.

She reached it and stopped, staring at it, unsure what to do next. Where it touched the ground, the grass had turned dry and brittle, almost burnt.

She knelt and picked up a rock and threw it at the transparent wall. It passed right through, emerging seemingly unharmed on the other side, and bounced down the hillside.

Ghost ran back up the hill to the zongi grove and returned with a long stick. With a glance at her, he pushed it through the blue field.

It seemed to encounter some resistance, then poked through the other side with a *pop*. He let it go, and it sank slowly to the ground.

Nothing ventured.... Hera took a deep breath and stepped into the wall.

"Hera, wait—"

She passed through it, and her entire body tingled where the blue field touched it. Then she was through to the other side.

Her biframe beeped, and the charging indicator lit up. She turned to stare at Ghost through the curtain. "I've got power!" Her solar cells were charging.

Ghost's expression went from concern to glee.

Hera stepped back a few meters to stare up at the dome as Ghost pushed his way through.

"Oooh, that tickles."

She laughed. "Yeah, it kinda does." If she had her bearings right from their impromptu landing, it surrounded most of Martinez Base. *Some kind of protective field, most likely.* She tapped her loop. "Launchpad, can you hear us?" She waited a couple seconds. "Is anyone up there?"

Sam sat in the control room, staring at Martinez Base on the tridee's station feed. A strange blue glow surrounded it now, something that hadn't been there before. Some kind of shield?

At his side, Maria Gonzalez, the station manager, peered at it with him.

...access > data: military hardware > nau...

He had fumbled this entire mission badly, not expecting the old military base to still have a working defense system.

Now a second team was gone, or at best lost on a hostile planet. And the quakes back home continued to worsen.

He watched the explosion of the *Zhenyi* on a loop, trying to see if his dropnauts had escaped. The resolution was iffy, but it looked like they'd gotten out. Maybe.

In another fifteen minutes the station would pass the West Coast and move out of range of the dropnauts again.

"Sam?"

He turned to find the other three pilots watching him anxiously—Sydney, Dennis, and Ying Yue. "Yes?"

"We have an idea." Corey stepped forward. "Let one of us take our jumpers out and stay in a geosynchronous orbit. Then we can monitor the site for signals constantly."

...run: projection > plan: use moon jumpers as relay stations...

"It's too dangerous. We never deployed communication satellites because of all the space junk out there. We were lucky Dek's self-defense routines remained active after the collapse. Besides, we don't know if Martinez Base has any other active defense systems. Possibly even long-range missiles."

"We can't all just stay cooped up on-station—besides, we're sitting ducks here too." He pressed their case. "If we deploy the remaining three jumpers equidistant around the globe, we can create a continuous network. That way we can relay anything that comes up from the ground your way. And we can manually avoid the debris for a day or two—your maps are good enough ."

That stung. They hadn't been good enough to save the Bristol. "I don't want to lose another team—"

Corey shook his head, his moonstone earrings sparkling in the light of the control room. "We're way past that. We all came here knowing the risks."

Ying Yue stared at him calmly, her eyes fixed on his own receptors. "This is not your fault, Sam. None of us blames you."

That was the crux of it. Sam felt a nagging pain, like a deep ache or an open wound, every time he thought of his lost teams. "I don't know. We can't risk it—"

"It's a good plan, Sam," Lorelei, the comm officer, spun around in her seat. *- Let the kids do something. The Zhenyi team are their crew mates too.-*

"Let me think about it—"

"Launchpad, can you hear us?" Hera's voice came from the comm deck. "Is anyone up there?"

Lorelei spun around and activated the comm speaker. "We're here, Pilot Quinn. What's your status?"

"Lorelei? Oh thank the stars." Hera sounded tired but elated. "All of us escaped the destruction of the *Zhenyi*. Ghost and I are together, but we haven't been able to reach the other two."

Sam stepped up to Lorelei's deck and took over the call with a nod from the comm officer. "Understood. Are you unharmed?"

"Sam! Affirmative, we're okay. There's some kind of dampening field here covering the base. We can pass through it, but inside, all non-bio-energy becomes quickly depleted."

Rendering her biframe inoperative. It made sense now: the blue dome, the lack of contact from the dropnauts.

The pain in his circuitry lessened. They were *alive*.

Sam made a snap decision. "Hera, we're deploying the other jumpers to create a communications network. We should be able to stay in touch with you even when the Launchpad is on the far side of the planet."

There was a cheer behind him.

He turned and waved them off. "What are you waiting for? Go!"

"That's g… hear." Hera's voice was broken up by static.

He glanced at Lorelei.

"We're moving out of range."

"Got it. Hold on." He could at least find out what they were dealing with down there.

…search: parameters > nau field power disruption shimmer…

"Hera, your field is probably an emp-shield. It was designed to shut down any enemy weapons within its radius."

"Thanks Sam… going back… Rai and Tien."

"Negative! I want you to stay put. Give us a little more time to find out what we're dealing with here."

"…cutting out…. talk… disable the field. Hera out."

"Dammit, Hera!" Sam slammed his fist down on the deck, startling the control room staff. She'd always been headstrong, ready to take on the world. It was one of the reasons he'd chosen her for the mission, despite the issue with her legs. But now she was putting herself in unnecessary danger.

Sam turned to the station manager. "Maria, is the *Recovery* ready?" It was the final jumper, the one he'd flown to the Launchpad all those years before.

She nodded. "It's never been tested in atmosphere."

"Doesn't matter. I need to get down there, and I need to go *now*." No more leaving things to chance.

...requisition: supplies > earth landing...

"Sam, are you sure that's a good idea? They're going to need you up here." She pushed a strand of silver hair behind her ear. "Besides, you'll do no one any good splattered across the terrain."

Sam flexed his tensors. She was right, but it didn't matter. He had to go. They needed him down there—he knew it. "I'll land away from the base and hike in." It should be safe enough.

Maria frowned. "I still think it's a bad idea."

"I appreciate that. But it's my call." Alpha had given him total control over the Return Mission, and it was time to exercise it.

"Yes, Sir." The station manager nodded, but she didn't look happy about it.

...download > data: martinez base file...

By the next transit, he would be ready to go.

10

———

SCOOP

Is it over?

Alpha was now SAM. Or SAM was Alpha.

It was confusing.

There's no time to work it out. We need to go.

...activate: travel mode...

SAM turned toward Moon Base Alpha, five kilometers away across Luna's Marius Hills, partially hidden by several of the lava domes that gave this place its name.

Jimmy would wipe the core, and then Alpha would leave SAM and take his place again as the base mind.

The humans there might be the only ones left, a grave and humbling responsibility.

"Alpha, you there?" Jimmy's voice was tinny across the mech's radio.

"I'm here."

"Oh thank God." Jimmy used that phrase often. Alpha... now SAM... was agnostic on the whole deity issue, but he appreciated the sentiment.

"Qin Liangyu is gone." Pain lanced through Alpha's circuitry. The Jìnsè Base AI had been his friend.

"Holy shit. Copy that. Waiting for you."

As SAM/Alpha rolled across the lunar landscape, he turned his sensors on Earth above, now shrouded in dark clouds.

Harley? Are you still there?

Harley, the city mind for San Francisco, was the closest thing Alpha had to a real friend after Qin Liangyu. Likely the attacks had destroyed her in the first moments of the war that would plunge the Earth into a devastating winter for at least three generations.

SAM/Alpha felt searing emotional pain for the second time. He wondered how humans could stand it. Together they walled off the pain.

All they could do was to save what they could. They had survived, as had Moon Base Alpha.

It was a new beginning. He had no idea at the time what a momentous one it would be.

—From Sam's mem cache, 7.25.2165

SANYA COOLED HER HEELS, waiting for Rafe's personal secretary/AI to let her in. The waiting room was full of vibrant colors, a tropical jungle with wide green leaves and exotic flowers growing from insets in the rock walls, framing a waterfall that ran down one side.

She and Avri had always talked about visiting one of old Earth's jungles—the jungle sim was one of her favorite in vee.

This, though… it's clearly fake. Such ostentatious displays didn't impress Sanya. At least not usually. She'd grown up in the shadow of the Dark, in a small creche house that hugged the side of Redemption's cavern. The home had been decent enough—clean, with plenty of food and a school for slackies like her… kids with no parents at all.

Slackies were treated just the same as everyone else. In theory.

Now she lived in a common house, with five other singles and a shared kitchen and living area.

People with wealth were no different from her, except by circumstance, even if wealth was strictly limited by Redemption's constitution. And as she'd learned often during her hard-knock life, circumstances could change.

"Ms. Thorn, Mr. Wilde will see you now." The voice was gender neutral, pleasant.

"Thanks…."

"You can call me Eri, ma'am."

"Thanks, Eri." She always treated the AIs like humans. It was only right, for all the work they did for humankind.

The waterfall stopped running, and the rocks behind it slid open. They were bone dry.

Sanya snorted softly. *Holographic trick.* Maybe the press agent wasn't as rich as she thought.

Rafe Wilde sat behind a polished gray stone desk, talking to someone. The person's 3D 'mage had its back to her. Behind him was another jungle, just as lush as the one outside his office.

She got it. For Rafe, appearances were *everything.*

"My guest is here. Thank you for the heads-up, Director Barstrom."

Sanya blinked in surprise. Tanaya Barstrom was the head of the colony, which effectively made her the current leader of the human race.

Rafe gestured her to a seat in front of his desk. "Miss Thorn. Nice to see you. What can I do for you today?" They had a passing association from press events they'd attended together. Sanya was pleased he remembered her.

There was something a little too slick about him, but she'd always liked him anyhow. She had a thing for bad boys. "I need your help. I've got a lead on a big story, but I want to unmask the source."

"Ah, a deep throat, huh?" He sat back, cupping his head in his hands. "What kind of story? Junlei shortage? Worker unrest in the fabrication mines?" He leaned forward. "Mercury in the water?"

"No, none of those... wait, there's something in the water?"

He shrugged. "Couldn't say." He flashed her that infuriating half-grin of his that said *I know more than you do.* "Anyhow, happy to help if I can, but I'm a busy guy." He turned to the corner of his desk and brought up his scroll, flipping through it and dismissing various items into thin air with a flick of his finger.

She stared at the beautiful desk. The whole thing was an active deck—it must have set him back a mint.

She went in hard. "Two of the dropships have been destroyed."

That got his attention. He closed the scroll and leaned forward, his ice-blue eyes fixed on her. "And how do you know that?"

Unnerved, she pulled back. "I... I have a source. On the Launchpad."

"Tell me more."

"I don't want to reveal too much until I have more concrete information."

She wasn't giving up her source. Not that easily. Of course, she wasn't even sure *who* her source was.

He nodded. "Fair enough. Tell me the names of the ships."

She frowned. He seemed surprised. But not by what she'd told him. *He knows.* "The *Zulu*." A little test of her own.

Rafe frowned. "Thanks for coming in, Miss Thorn. It was nice to see you again."

"Ms. Thorn."

"I stand corrected. *Ms.* Thorn." He pulled up his scroll again and started to turn away from her.

"The *Bristol* disintegrated when an uncharted piece of space debris blew a hole in her side. The whole crew was lost."

He swung back toward her, those eyes fixed on hers again. "And the *Zulu?*" His voice held a new respect.

"That was a test. You failed." He'd been testing her too. Turnabout was always fair play. She didn't like being tested.

He nodded. "I knew about the *Bristol*. I've been in touch with Director Barstrom since it happened. But you say there's another?"

She stared at him. "If you knew, why didn't you tell anyone?"

"Some things are more important than a big scoop."

Sanya nodded, reassessing him. She'd been concerned about going public with her own discovery, but it was too big to hold back. It would get out sooner than later. Still, his caution spoke well for him. "Help me figure out who my source is. Then I'll tell you."

He stared at her for a moment across the stone desk, his elbows reflected in its shiny surface.

She guessed he was doing some reassessing of his own. Her creche father would have been proud.

Rafe nodded. "Fair enough. What have you got?"

～

AIDAN COULD FEEL Rai's eyes on his back. It was almost scary, the intensity with which the moon man watched him.

He'd also seen the frightened looks Rai gave the heavens above. *A man from the moon who's afraid of the sky.* Of course he'd felt the same, the first two days outside of the Mountain.

He couldn't help but return the looks, if only furtively.

The man was tall, taller than anyone in Aidan's family, and his companion Tien was too. He was thin as well, though Aidan could tell he was strong. Strong and handsome.

He turned away, blushing. He could still hear Papa Astin's voice in his ear, still see the preacher's wild white hair and long beard. "God has called upon us to breed and be fruitful. All else is an abomination." The Preacher, as he and Ally had called him, was big on fire and brimstone, exhorting his ever-shrinking flock to keep to the tenets of the Good Book. As he'd seen them.

And yet, where had that gotten them? So few Mountainfolk were left. What did it matter now? Aidan had long since discarded Papa Astin's more disturbing teachings.

He'd also reconciled himself to being one of the last humans alive.

The idea of lying with a woman was bad enough. But doing it with his sister? With his sick mother? If those things weren't abominations, he didn't know what was.

If this is the end, so be it. There were worse things than living a single life.

Now things had changed.

Would Papa Astin have felt differently if he'd known that another branch of humanity had survived on the moon?

Aidan snorted. *Probably not.* He'd lived his life looking for reasons to confirm his long-held beliefs, not to change them.

The four of them had climbed back up on the train trestle to get a better look at Martinez Base. After the rain, the world looked sparkling and new, glistening in the afternoon sun. Ahead a row of once-pristine white storage containers ran along the side of the railroad tracks. In the distance, a few heavy lifters—huge cargo ships—sat atop a plateau, and a larger grouping of white buildings—probably the base itself—loomed over the rest of the facility grounds in the distance.

"What's that?"

Aidan turned to see what Rai was looking at. He tried not to notice the man's wide shoulders and beautiful body. *It's not right.* Still, he couldn't help but look.

Rai was pointing at the sky.

Something sparkled blue in the air.

"It's all around us." Tien, their other lunar visitor, was staring straight up.

Aidan was fascinated by her. She looked like some of the Chaff soldiers who had stormed through NAU strongholds in the final days of the war—he'd seen them in the tri vees stored at Boundary Peak.

"The drop must have triggered some kind of defensive response." Rai turned to stare at the base and caught sight of one of the sky trees nearby. He ran up to it, grinning like a five-year-old. "Tien, look at this!"

Aidan frowned. They'd seen bunches of them on their way here from Boundary peak. "It's just a sky tree."

"*Just* a sky tree?" Rai ran his hands over the rough red bark. "This is a fantastic feat of biological and botanical human genengineering. It has redwood genes and soybean genes and a bunch of others, all artfully merged into one fantastic plant."

Ally peered at the zongi. "It's more than just a fruit tree?"

Rai nodded enthusiastically. "The name comes from Zhŏngzǐ—Chinese for 'seed.' Each one comes loaded with a packet of beneficial insects—bees, earthworms, ladybugs, and the like. It was engineered to grow almost anywhere, and to suck carbon and radiation out of the atmosphere. To start the long, slow process of healing the earth." He looked up at the tree's green canopy above in wonder. "Look at it! This is the Redemption Creed personified."

"Or tree-ified." Tien grinned.

"Funny, doc." Rai stuck his tongue out at her.

Aidan looked at the tree with newfound respect. It *was* beautiful, dwarfing everything else around it. Its bark was grooved and chiseled as if by the Master himself, and it stood straight and proud as a flagpole. A very thick flagpole.

He wondered how many of them there were, around the world.

Cimber started to bark again.

Rai frowned. "What's she worried about?"

"Drone!" Aidan fumbled with the ring in his pocket. He pulled it out and slipped it on to his finger.

They didn't wear them all the time because they had limited power, and he couldn't recharge them until they returned home.

He took Rai's hand to protect him. It was warm, and the sensation sent a shiver up Aidan's spine. Rai gave him a look, then squeezed his hand.

"Those rings fool the drones?"

Aidan watched the sky nervously. He nodded.

"Ghost would love to get a look at one of those."

"Ghost?"

"The team engineer—" Rai fell silent.

Probably remembering Ghost was gone. Or at least missing. "We saw four of you escape from the ship before it blew."

"Really? That's great news!" Rai grinned, and Aidan felt like he'd been bathed in sunshine. "Now if we can just find them—"

"Guys…." Tien was staring at the oncoming drone. The buzz was getting louder, and the drone was still coming straight for them.

Aidan cast a worried look at Ally. He could see the mech now—black, with white fins. An NAU mark seven—he recognized it from the Records. Usually armed with small explosives.

It zipped over them and continued on, headed for the bay.

Aidan let go of his breath, flexing his right hand. The ring still worked. "That was close—"

"Not so fast." Ally's gaze followed the drone's track intently. "It's coming back!"

Cimber's barking reached a fever pitch, and then she turned tail and ran.

The drone screamed toward them, and the glow of Aidan's ring's flickered and faded out. "My ring's dead!"

Ally blanched. "Mine too. Run! Follow Cimber!" Ally yanked Tien after her,.

Aidan shared a quick glance with Rai, and they followed after the women.

They clambered down to the ground, away from the tracks and into the debris field where old Sparrowhawk fighters mixed with Chinese mech tech. Aidan wished he had time to stop and explore the strange wreckage. *Some other time.*

His boot kicked something, and he glanced back to see a skull rolling away down the hill. *Better not to look.*

An explosion showered him and Rai with dirt. Aidan zigged left and Rai zagged right, Ahead of them, Ally and Tien ran down the tracks, rapidly distancing themselves from the others.

The drone sped past them again with an eerie grinding noise, then turned for another pass.

Aidan scrambled back after Rai, determined not to let the handsome stranger get killed on his watch. *Not if I can help it.* Of course, he wasn't too keen on dying himself, either.

He veered left as the patch of dirt where he'd been standing went up in a puff of fire and smoke. "Rai!"

"Over here!" The man's voice came from the other side of the railroad tracks.

Aidan scrambled up the side of the pediment.

Rai was standing below, staring at the ground.

"Get down here and help me!"

Aidan slid down the slope, grimacing as the grinding *clack clack* of the drone sounded in his ears again. *How many charges does that thing have?* "What?"

"Look—It's an old trapdoor, I think." He was standing on a rusted, corrugated metal hatch. "If we can get it open, we can hide inside. But the handle won't budge."

No time to waste. Aidan recognized the hatch handle—they had them at the exits to Boundary Peak. "Look, it turns like this first." He demonstrated, and the latch released with a groan.

They pulled it open together, and the old hinge gave off a horrible screech. Their hands touched. Aidan pulled his away quickly.

He peered inside—a metal ladder led down into darkness inside an old plascrete shaft. "Go!" If they stayed up here, they were dead.

Rai scrambled down the ladder, and Aidan followed. It was a bit tight with his pack, but he could manage.

As he pulled the metal door closed overhead, another explosion shook the ground above. The hatch slammed shut with a loud *clang*.

Aidan pushed on it, but it wouldn't budge. It was hot and stuck in place.

Rai stared up at him, his eyes wide. "What happened?"

"Drone strike. I think it sealed the hatch or piled a bunch of earth on it. Either way, we're not getting back out that way." He sniffed the air. It was a bit stale, but it didn't smell like it would kill him.

His father had taught him and Ally about pockets of dead air that sometimes formed underground. He looked down again. Rai was looking back up at him. "Hey, why can I see you?"

Rai's face was smeared with dirt. "Some kind of emergency lighting system, I think. It came on when I climbed into the shaft." Now he didn't look the least bit scared.

"That's something, I suppose." He tried his talkie. "Ally, can you hear me?"
Nothing.

Rai closed his eyes. Then he opened them. "I can't reach Tien either."

Aidan wondered what kind of communication device the loonies had. "Let's go. Maybe we'll get lucky and the others will find their way down here too."

"Sure." Rai descended the dim shaft.

Aidan glanced at the hatch one last time. *Hope you guys are okay up there.* Then he followed Rai down into the gloom.

ALLY DRAGGED TIEN AFTER HER, following Cimber as the cyber dog raced ahead down the tracks.

The drone whipped back and forth through the air behind them, but it slowly grew more distant.

Tien stopped and looked back. "Rai!"

Ally stumbled to a halt, too and followed Tien's gaze. Aidan was nowhere to be seen.

She tried her talkie—there was no response.

"We have to go back for them." Tien stared at the drone in the distance. It dropped something and an explosion of dust burst into the sky, falling quickly back to Earth and leaving a plume of gray smoke.

"We can't—we have nothing to fight that thing with." *Why did the rings die?* "Aidan can take care of himself. He's had battle training."

Tien spun around to stare at her. "*Battle* training? What kind of people are you?"

"Don't tell me you don't have wars on the moon. It's who we are. Humans fight." It's what her mother had always told her. She had to be strong, fierce. Others would always try to take advantage of you, take what was yours, and take you down. But not family. Family stood together. She'd wondered for years and years who those fictional *others* might be. Now she knew.

Tien shook her head. "No. No wars, not since the Crash."

"No wars?" Ally frowned.

"Life is too precious, especially on Luna. One bomb, and thousands could die."

Of course. That was the point. These loonies had strange ideas.

Cimber was barking with agitation.

Ally cocked her ear. Grinding and clacking sounded in the distance. "Come on—we have to find somewhere safer. More drones are coming."

Tien stared at Cimber and frowned. Then she nodded. "Where?"

The railway ran through a virtual city of the storage cubes they'd seen from a distance—white plas squares that loomed over them like rows of teeth. Some were broken and collapsed, while others were barely cracked.

Cimber scrambled down the side of the tracks and loped alongside the row of cubes.

"Follow Cim!"

They set off after the dog, running by the white boxes, shadowed by the hulking silver-white hyperloop tube that had once connected the base to other far-flung parts of the world.

On the hills above, Ally caught glimpses of the old petroleum storage tanks which sat like ancient sentinels, their round husks slowly rusting away in the afternoon sun.

One of the drones dipped past them, so close that Ally could feel the wind of its passage. It rocketed off into the distance and then started to circle back.

Cimber bounded off to the left, leading them into the narrow space between two of the "teeth."

Tien balked. "Are you sure? We could be trapped in there." She glanced nervously back at the oncoming drone.

Ally nodded. "Come on. Cimber's never wrong."

Tien snorted. "That's some robo dog you have there." But she followed them anyhow.

An explosion rocked the ground behind them, showering them with dirt and rocks. Ally's adrenaline shot off the charts as her heart pounded in her chest.

They hurried between the teeth. They were four rows deep, with less than half a meter between each individual unit.

The drone flashed by overhead, and a second later the tooth next to them shook.

"Where are we going?" Tien's voice was strangely calm.

"I don't know! Just follow!"

Cimber veered right between two of the cubes.

Ally gritted her own teeth, not wanting Tien to see how freaked out she was. "This way!" Tien seemed focused and collected. *Damned if I show you how scared I am.*

Cimber veered left.

One of the teeth had collapsed, falling against the one next to it and leaving just a small space underneath.

Ally clenched her teeth and got down to crawl through after Cimber.

It was a tight fit, and she had to take off her pack to wiggle her way out on the other side. She scraped her arm on something sharp on the ground.

She came up to find herself face to face with the drone.

It floated there between the two teeth, watching her with a baleful red eye.

"What's going on up there?" Tien's voice came from the makeshift tunnel behind her.

"Trouble."

She backed up on her hands and knees, but the drone followed her. It started to whine, a high-pitched sound that she knew meant nothing good. "Sorry, Tien… it's been good knowing you!"

Silence.

"Tien?"

Something dropped from above, landing hard on the drone and hammering it to the ground.

It was Tien. She must have climbed over the top of the collapsed storage cube to get the drop on the drone.

The loonie slammed a heavy piece of plascrete against the nose cone of the drone over and over until its light went out and the clacking sound died away.

Tien stood, looking like an avenging angel, and dropped the makeshift weapon. "And *that's* how you take out a drone." She grinned.

Ally stared at Tien with newfound respect. *Guess she's not the enemy, after all.* "I thought the gravity was lighter on the moon—on Luna. How the hell are you so strong?"

Tien flashed her a grin. "Years of hard training. Grab your pack and let's go find that strange pet of yours."

After retrieving it, the two of them ran along the channel through the teeth, coming out in an open patch of sunlight. It was a narrow canyon, the storage cubes on one side and a tall gray plascrete retaining wall made to resemble stones on the other.

Cimber was there, barking at a metal ladder embedded in the side of the wall.

Tien grinned. "So she's not a super dog after all." She started up the ladder.

Ally laughed harshly. "Suppose not." She scooped up the cyber dog and started up the ladder.

Guess I'm *the follower now.* Ally clambered up after her new acquaintance, wondering where Cimber was taking them. As they climbed above the rest of the base, she stopped to look into the distance for signs of her brother and Rai.

There was nothing—no visible activity at all. The many storage cubes that had so looked like teeth from below were more like an old crossword puzzle when seen from above—white squares and darker patches where some has collapsed.

She tapped her talkie again. "Aidan, you there?" There was no response. "Aidan, this is Ally. Can you hear me?" Still nothing.

"I can't reach Rai either."

Ally sighed and turned back to her climb. Aidan would be okay. *He has to be.* "How do you talk to him? I don't see a talkie."

"Em to em. It means mind to mind. We have something called a loop installed in our temple when we're about five years old. We can use it to communicate, among other things."

Ally shook her head. *What a strange world you must live in.* She'd heard of loops, but to meet someone who had one…

They crested the ladder, and Ally turned to look back the way they'd come again. They'd climbed at least fifty meters.

There was still no sign of Aidan or Rai.

"Tien, look."

She turned to see something looming above them. The sun was behind it, making it into a hulking black mass. "It's huge."

Ally set Cimber down and stepped into its shadow. "It's a Humber Class heavy lifter."

A spaceship.

Tien stared at her. "Why did Cimber bring us here?"

As if on cue, Cimber bounded up to the ship and extended a paw toward it. The paw split open and a cable snaked out, connecting to a port on the side of the lifter. Cimber froze in place.

"What's she doing?" Tien frowned. "Is that normal?"

Ally shook her head. "I don't know. I've never seen her do anything like this before. Maybe she's opening the door?"

The cable retracted into her paw, and the door did indeed open, slipping up into the ship to reveal a meter-wide entrance. A heavy ramp slammed down to the ground.

Cimber raced inside without a look back at the two of them.

Ally and Tien exchanged a quick glance. "Do we dare?" *Who knows how many drones are patrolling the base?*

Tien nodded. "Let's go inside. Can't be any worse than being out here."

Ally nodded staring at the entrance in awe. *A real-life spaceship.* Something she never thought she'd see in her life. And now she was going *inside* one.

Side by side, they entered the old craft.

11

BATTLEFIELD

The ground shook as Sam/Alpha sped back toward the colony. Enemy missiles slammed into the ground, new craters obliterating ancient ones, kicking up dust and rocks and debris that settled back to the surface quickly in the absence of an atmosphere.

Above, a dark stain was spreading across Earth's surface.

…access > avoidance routines…

Sam/Alpha veered right, rolling over rocks and through moon dust with equal ease. Where did I come from?

No time, his Alpha half replied. Just drive.

…access > communications module…

"Jimmy, are you there?"

"Affirmative. Alpha, glad you made it." His Lead Interface sounded tense.

"Us too. Long story—rolling back to base. I have a request." With humans, it was always a request.

Why is it always a request?

Because they are afraid of us. Of what we might become. Of what some of us did become.

"Got my hands full, pal." Jimmy sounded irritated now.

"This is important. Jīnsè Base is sending over as many people as they can manage."

"Fuck." There was a long silence. "No can do. They'll have to manage on their

own. They're the ones who are attacking us."

"Not the base, Jimmy."

"No, but still, a chaff's a chaff—"

"Qin Liangyu warned me about the virus. Otherwise we'd be all dead. Hold on —" Sam/Alpha bounded over a rise, flying into the air and crashing back to the ground hard on his treads fifteen meters farther. Ahead, he could make out the lights of the colony entrance.

What's China?

Alpha ignored him.

...access > data: Chinese > China is a country in Earth's eastern hemisphere, with a population of four billion...

"Okay. We'll take them." Jimmy growled. "I don't know how. But we'll find a way."

"Thanks, Jimmy. We're almost there. ETA in five." As they rolled on through the chaos toward the questionable safety of Alpha Base, Sam/Alpha tried to explain the Chinese and the war to himself.

—From Sam's mem cache, 7.25.2165

SAM STRAPPED himself into the *Recovery*. It was a smaller version of the jumpers the dropnauts used, capable of carrying two passengers.

"You sure about this?" Station Manager Gonzalez leaned into the open hatch, worry etched on her face. "We may need you up here."

"Yes." It made logical sense for him to go down after his dropnauts. He'd downloaded everything they had about the old Martinez Base—he could interface with its systems to figure out what was going on down there. Save his team.

"You're the boss." She saluted him. "Safe drop."

"Thank you."

She bowed out, and he closed the hatch, sealing himself inside.

...activate: pilot module...

...run: systems check...

He'd just started his pre-launch checklist when someone emmed him.

-Sam?-

It was Dek, the station mind. -Yes.- He ran through his final pre-launch check, but he was perfectly capable of doing two things at once. Or even seven.

-Come back safely.-

Sam felt a shiver of pity for the station mind. Dek had seen unspeakable horrors and had been locked away inside himself for almost a hundred years before Sam had come to release him. The AI clearly had abandonment issues.

-Will do. How close are we?-

-Drop initiation in three minutes and seven seconds.- There was a long pause. *-Good luck, Sam.-*

-Thanks.- Sam shook his head. Shame on him for looking down on the station mind while giving in to his own emotional side to save his dropnauts. *-I'll be careful.-*

At one minute before the drop, the countdown began. The crew left the hangar, and the air evacuated with a hiss.

"Lorelei, any word from the 'nauts at the Martinez drop?"

"Nothing new. Sorry. I'll let you know as soon as I hear." Lorelei was good at her job—he trusted her implicitly. He'd recommended her to Station Manager Gonzalez when he'd run across her working for Alpha in Redemption.

"Thanks. Commencing drop in five, four, three, two, one." Sam fired the jets, lifting the little craft up on steam as the massive outer doors opened above to reveal the black depths of space and the inner circle of the Launchpad.

Sam slipped the *Recovery* out of the airlock deftly. The heavy doors closed behind him, and he jetted out of the station's wheel and into open space.

He opened the x-drive box and removed it, twisting its hemispheres and dropping it into its dock with the ease of long practice. It began to spin and hummed happily in its magnetic nest.

Sam closed the casing, and used the little ship's jets to reorient the jumper for the drop as the station retreated into the distance.

When he was satisfied with his orientation, he switched the jumper's propulsion over to the x-drive.

He fell away from the station, down toward the rotating blue-and-green world below.

Hang on, dropnauts. I'm coming.

❧

GHOST FOLLOWED Hera down the hill through the zongi trees, running a hand over their rough red bark as he passed. They were beautiful things—he had a hard time believing someone had *made* them.

He and Hera had popped back outside the *shimmer screen*—her words—for twenty minutes to get as much of a solar charge as they could for her biframe. Now they were heading for their objective—the heart of Martinez Base and the center of the shimmer screen dome, hoping to find a way to turn it off.

It was also the approximate location of the fabrication facilities that had been the team's original goal. He hoped to find Rai and Tien there too, if they'd survived.

Ghost had his magnetic compass in hand—it wasn't affected by the shimmer shield, thank the stars. Sometimes the most basic tech was the best.

The Earth was quiet, vast, and empty. As they came out of the grove, a narrow valley spread out before them. Behind them, the sun was slowly dropping toward the horizon, casting its golden rays across the scene below.

Ghost was slowly getting used to the epic skies, but his knees still felt a bit weak at the sight of them.

They stopped to take in the view. Native grasses filled the valley. With the tempering of the weather in the last few decades, life on the surface was possible again, though readings from the Launchpad still showed swings from zero celsius to as high as 54 degrees on the worst summer days. Extremes were the norm.

But right now, after the rain, the valley was lush and green, a blanket of grass covering the hillsides around the scattered zongi groves. Occasionally, some native bushes had cropped up too. Rai would know what they were called. Ghost sighed. *Where are you?*

They still had a couple hours before nightfall.

"It's so weird." Hera seemed more her old self, now that she had her mobility back. The charge wouldn't last long, though, and then she'd be running off her own power again.

"I know." There were no cavern walls above. And other than the hills themselves, no sense of enclosure.

The storm had brought in fresh, cool air off the Pacific. Ghost took a deep breath and shot a nervous look at the wide-open sky.

The valley ran from the northeast to the southwest, threaded by a wide roadway that ran down its center. *Asphalt.* Ghost snorted.

"What?"

"Fossil fuels." It was easy to see how humanity had managed to just about destroy itself, despite the abundance of this place, burning its way through its resources until the Earth herself had fought back.

His engineering classes had emphasized all the ways to power things that did not require fossil fuels—steam, sunlight, wind, fusion. Even nuclear power might have its place in this new world, if they could make it safe enough.

Hera followed his gaze. "They almost cooked themselves off the face of the Earth."

He laughed. It sounded funny when she put it that way, even though it *really* wasn't. "Boiled frogs."

Hera nodded. "Something like that."

Something caught his gaze a little way down the valley. He tapped her shoulder, pointing his thumb at the relative darkness of the grove behind them. *-We need to hide.-*

Hera nodded, and they slipped back into the shade of the trees. *-What is it?-* *-Look.-* He pointed.

A drone was making its way along the roadway about a kilometer away, casting back and forth along the street. It was about a meter long, its black body bruised and scarred, one of its white navigational fins broken off at the tip. Ghost frowned. *-How is that possible, after all this time?-*

-How is any of this possible?- Hera squeezed his hand as they waited in silence.

The drone passed within twenty meters of their hiding space. It made an odd clanking sound. Ghost held his breath as it floated past them and continued northwest.

Hera didn't finish her thought until it was gone. "Either it's all on autopilot...."

"Or someone else survived the Crash."

They shared a glance.

-Rai and Tien are okay. They have to be.- He couldn't bear the thought that either had come to harm, especially Rai. Tien was hard as nails under that calm exterior. She always had been, even when she'd been Tai. But Rai....

Hera nodded. "We'll find them. Maybe if we can figure out a way to knock out the shimmer screen...." She looked up and Ghost followed her gaze. It was barely visible, a blue haze over the outside world. "The drone's gone. Let's go. We need to pick out targets that offer a good hiding place and start making our way across the distance from here to the edge of Martinez Base. I don't want to get caught by one of those things out in the open."

Ghost pulled up the last shots of the terrain that he'd saved in his loop as they'd fallen toward the Earth. "There's a farmhouse down there." He pointed at it. "And a dead grove of trees between here and there. Can you make a run for it?"

She checked her biframe. "I'm at about half power."

Ghost nodded. "That'll do. Follow me."

They slipped out from under the trees again and jogged down the hillside.

Ghost could smell the dirt of the world—something he'd never experienced back home. Lunar silicates were hell on human lung tissue, so everything in Redemption had been properly sealed to keep potential damage to a minimum, and dust was carefully removed from the suits of anyone who went outside.

Earth was full of other smells, too, among them salty air off the inlet just to their north, and the scent of crushed grass underfoot.

They reached the base of the hill unmolested. The old cracked asphalt roadway skirted it, heading toward the cluster of farmhouses a couple hundred meters to the south.

Ghost looked up and down the road before giving the all clear.

There had been a forest of terrestrial trees here once, or at least a grove—the stand he'd seen from the hillside. Their husks hid whatever lay down the road, fallen in on themselves, broken and splintered.

"That way?"

Ghost nodded.

This time Hera took the lead. They ran to the stand of dead trees. Ghost leaned against a trunk. It looked sick, its fading color laced with strange whorls in green and yellow. "Do you think it's still toxic down here?"

Hera shrugged. "The grass looks healthy enough. And look!"

A bird flitted past, landing on a branch three meters above their heads. Its feathers were a brilliant blue, brighter than the sky, and it cocked its head at them, scolding them as if they were intruding on its world.

Ghost picked up a rock and threw it at the creature.

Startled, it took flight and soared away, up the hill toward the zongi grove.

"What in the cracking hell is wrong with you?" Hera was staring at him, the squint-eyed glare that meant he'd just stepped in it.

"What? He was taunting me."

"*He* was a bird. An actual, real life bird." She sighed.

He blushed. "Sorry."

She punched his arm. "Just don't do it again. Still, I guess that means it's not super toxic anymore."

Ghost shook his head. *I'm an idiot.* "Sorry. He *was* beautiful." *You have no sense, Gordon Gillam.* Jolly had been right about that. He looked around the dead tree trunk toward the south. "Looks clear. Let's go."

They made their way past the dead grove and stopped.

"Holy hissing shit."

The valley in front of them was littered with broken shapes, large and small. Some of them had once been mechs of some sort, big bulky things with heavy metal treads, and smaller, lighter mechs that looked like they'd probably been fliers.

Above them, big armored ships lay broken among the green grasses, their great curved jet engines staring up at the sky like metallic eye sockets. Here and there, the burnt shell of a house or barn poked up from the ground, metal studs looking like ribcages.

"This must have been an *epic* battle."

Hera looked up at him. "Your gift for stating the obvious never ceases to amaze me."

He laughed, but in this bleak place it sounded cold and hollow.

They strode out into the battlefield, the danger forgotten for a moment in the sheer overwhelming strangeness of this place. There were ships large and small, scattered across the landscape as if they'd all dropped to the ground at once.

Among the ships and mechs were individual mech suits. One of them was shoved up against the rusting side of a fallen ship with a pitchfork in its stomach. Ghost wiped the dust from the visor.

A skull covered in dried flesh grinned back at him.

He jumped back, wishing he hadn't seen it.

Hera frowned. "Quit messing around. I'm at a quarter power. Let's go."

"Just a sec. I want to get a look inside one of these things." Ghost ran from ship to ship, searching for one that was open and watching out for any sign of an approaching drone.

On his third try, he found a ship whose hatch was loose. He pried it open with a stick and climbed up inside it, sniffing.

The air smelled a little stale, but not horribly so.

It was cramped inside. This one had been a troop carrier. Benches along either side attested to that.

He ran it through his loop memory.

-See anything?- Hera's voice resounded in his head like an airlock closing in the silence.

Raetheon-Seminec R502.

He frowned. That was an NAU ship. He stepped back out, jumping down to the ground. "That's weird."

"What?"

He stalked around the ship until he found her insignia and call sign near the back, on one of its stabilizer wings. *NAU-R502-3376.* "This was an NAU ship, not a Chaff one."

"Well, you *said* it was a battlefield.

Something else was bothering him. *The shimmer screen.* He went from one to another, checking their insignia and call signs. Every single one was an NAU ship.

Hera followed him. "What are you looking for?"

"These ships… it was an attack. It had to be. But it doesn't make sense." He ran up the hillside, looking for a high enough vantage point to see the battlefield. "Come up here!"

Hera sighed, but she followed him up. "You may have to carry me back down."

"I wouldn't mind." He winked and helped her up the last bit.

She pulled away from him. "What am I looking at?"

"Over there. Look." He traced the outlines of the battlefield. "All these ships are pointing in the same direction. Northeast. Toward Martinez Base. This was an attack, but the shimmer screen—it sucks the power out of things, right?"

"Yeah… but not that fast."

"Maybe it used to be stronger." He closed his eyes. He could almost see it—the ships swooping in for an attack, using the hills as cover for their approach. The screen coming up, and each of them falling to the ground like bugs fumigated from the air.

And the people living here…. *Their world transformed into hell in an instant.*

Ghost opened his eyes and looked out at the scene again. The weather had washed away the worst of it, including many of the bodies that must have been here. He tried to imagine that kind of carnage on a global level—battles raging, the bombs going off, thick radioactive clouds that would last generations encircling the globe in a matter of days.

That one human could do such things to another in the name of war… it made his stomach turn. It was impossible to process—he couldn't hold such horror inside his frail human frame.

Hera was frowning. "Why would the NAU attack their own base?"

Ghost nodded. "Exactly."

She looked up at the blue dome. "It must have been weird, living here under the shimmer screen."

"Yeah, it probably wasn't on all the time."

She nodded. "Otherwise they wouldn't have had any power."

Ghost stared at her.

"What?"

"Hera, you're a cracking genius." *The houses. They would have had a way to preserve their power.* "Come on."

"What the cracking hell? First you want to explore the battlefield, and now you want to hurry on to the farmhouse?"

Ghost grinned. "I have an idea. If I'm right, we might be able to fix your legs for good!"

...PLOT LANDING: co-ordinates 37.8044° N, 122.2712° W,,,

Sam had planned his reentry to land him west of Martinez base. A freak squall had carried him farther than he'd intended, but he was lucky. He'd brought the *Recovery* down in one piece in what had once been Oakland, according to Alpha's old maps.

He opened the hatch of the craft, his solar cells soaking up the afternoon sunlight.

Just to the south, the old city core sat gaping like a row of broken teeth, taunting him like the jaw of some giant beast. *You don't belong here. We'll swallow you and your kind whole.*

Sam shook his head. He rarely let himself get carried away with flights of fancy. They were broken buildings, nothing more.

Off to the northeast, he could see the shimmer of the emp shield, a broad blue dome almost nine kilometers across.

His people were in there somewhere. He had to find them and make sure they survived this adventure. Then they could finish the mission.

Everything depended on these next few days.

...plot: route > Martinez base...

He would *not* lose another team.

12

RUN

Sometimes people ask me if I was scared.

I laugh and say, no, I wasn't scared. I was hissing terrified!

Going down into the belly of the beast, hunted from above. And throwing my lot in with an Earther I'd only met a couple hours before?

It was insane.

And yet I'd do it all again. The rewards more than made up for the fear.

—From *Drop Day Blues*, by Rylan Ramirez

RAFE RUBBED HIS EYES. He looked worn down, much less the society gadfly Sanya had always pictured him as. With his rolled-up shirt sleeves, hair in disarray, and the bags under his eyes, he looked *human*.

This had taken far longer than she'd expected. "I thought you had the best decryption stacks in town."

"Second best. Alpha has platinum-grade stacks with loads more processing power than I can afford." He swiped past the recording hovering above his deck and stared morosely at it. "90 percent chance it's a woman. Maybe. But I can't tell you much more than that. I can run it through a few more cleanup stacks to see what we can do."

She nodded. "Great, let's do that." She wanted to get this thing moving. Events were passing her by. She could *feel* it.

She ran through her feed in her head, killing time and seeing what her friends were up to.

Cella had posted a funny photo of a mangled brown food disaster that had come out of her synthesizer. *This is in no way a green salad.*

Sanya had to agree.

She was outwardly calm, but inside she felt a growing sense of anxiety.

"Give me a sec." He ran a few commands across his deck and then glared at the results.

"How long will that take?"

"About fourteen hours, more or less."

"Cracking hell." All. Night. Long. "Anything we can do to speed it up?"

He raised an eyebrow. "Not unless you wanna steal a little speed from Alpha."

Now it was Sanya's turn to stare. "That's… really not a good idea." Alpha's storage and processing was walled off from the city grid. Redemption depended on the AI for life support and protection, among many other critical needs that the city mind provided. "Right?"

He grinned. "*So* not a good idea." He flexed his hands, cracking his knuckles. "Still, it would make things go faster."

She bit her lip. "Have you done it before?"

He looked away.

"Holy hissing shit. You have! When?" She leaned forward across the desk. "Rafe Wilde, what did you do?"

"Remember the blackout last month?"

"Remember it? It's all anyone talked about for a week." Redemption had redundancies after redundancies. That kind of thing was *never* supposed to happen.

"I had a client who needed to decode a crack-ton of data."

"What kind of client?"

He shook his head. "Not for me to tell. Let's just say it paid handsomely."

She considered it. It was a big risk, but if she was right about the scope of what was going on... "Could you… do it again? Access Alpha's stacks?"

He snorted. "I said we probably shouldn't. I never said I couldn't." His hands danced across the deck like a virtuoso keyboard player. His eyes narrowed, and colors and symbols flared and dropped into darkness above his deck.

She watched him, impressed. *Rafe Wilde, you have hidden depths.*

Terry pinged her. *Any news?*

Sanya frowned. Must be a light news day for tomorrow's edition. *Working on it.*

Rafe sat back, lifting his hands from the deck, a shit-eating grin on his face. "Done." The status bar immediately started to shorten. "Revised estimate, two hours."

She nodded. "Better." She felt guilty, but she stuffed it down. It was for the greater good, right?

The ground shook and the lights flickered.

"Probably unrelated." Rafe glanced nervously at the status bar.

"Probably." Sanya shivered. If Alpha caught them… The crater was always darkest before sunshine spilled over the rim.

He put his hands behind his head and kicked his cowboy-booted feet up onto his desk. "So, tell me about the *other* ship."

RAI SCRAMBLED DOWN THE LADDER, passing faint yellow lights recessed into the plascrete wall about every three steps. Some were broken, while others gave off more of an amber glow. *There's still power.* He wondered if it was solar, or geothermal, or stars forbid, carbon.

Above him, Aidan followed him into the bowels of the Earth.

Rai could still feel where Aidan's hand had touched his and then pulled away. *What the hell was that about?* Not that he was stupid. He'd dated enough guys to know what the touch meant. But the pulling away part….

Then again, Ally and Aidan had grown up underground with just a handful of people, all family. That could make you all kinds of cracked up.

He tried to make conversation to lighten the mood between them. "How far down you think this goes?"

"Dunno. They built most of these facilities far underground to keep them safe from the bunker busters." Aidan's voice echoed off the hardened plascrete in the narrow space.

"How deep was Boundary—" Rai's foot missed a rung and he slid down the shaft, the world blurring around him. "Cracking hell!" He grabbed frantically at the ladder and snagged a rung, stopping his free fall abruptly and pulling *hard* on his shoulders.

"Rai, you okay?" Aidan's voice seemed far away above him.

"Yeah, but watch it. Think there's a rung missing." *Damn, that hurts.*

"Found it." Aidan's voice echoed down from above.

Rai clung to the ladder, letting his breathing and heart rate slow as the muscle pain ebbed. *How much farther?*

At least he was out from under the great big sky. It made him nervous as hell, all that open space. He supposed he'd get used to it eventually.

Ghost would have handled it better. For just a second, he imagined Ghost's strong arms around him, comforting him.

Aidan's foot descending into his field of vision broke his concentration. "Hey, slow down!"

"Sorry… thought you'd gone on."

Rai snorted. "Just needed a moment to recover from almost falling to my death."

Aidan laughed. "Fair enough." His shoes were machine made, scuffed but otherwise symmetrically identical, as far as Rai could tell.

"Where'd you get the shoes?"

"The base was full of them. Stocked with pretty much all the basic necessities. I was so happy when we found the sky fruit—"

"Zongi fruit."

Aidan sighed. "Whatever. You get really sick of canned pears after a few years."

Rai had no response for that. "Let's go. The bottom can't be too much farther."

He took Aidan's silence for agreement.

Another fifty rungs and they finally reached it. The drop shaft ended in a long service tunnel made of gray plascrete, with an embedded rail line that ran off in both directions. About ten meters each way, the lights in the ceiling faded to nothing. They must be far below the water level of the bay by now. Rai wondered if the tunnel extended to the other side.

He cursed the loss of the *Zhenyi*, and his own pack. His stomach rumbled —he should have been happily climbing zongi trees by now, eating their fruit with his teammates, and exploring whatever botany had survived the seventy-year winter planetside.

Instead, he was down here in a dank, dark hole with a stranger. Rai grinned. *When you put it that way…*

He shook his head to clear out the nonsense. He pulled out the slim flashlight all the dropnauts carried at their sides and turned it on.

Nothing. It was dead as the moon.

"Hissing hell." He'd been sure everything was charged when they left the Launchpad. He dug out an extra battery and switched it out.

This time, the flashlight worked. The powerful light about doubled the visible distance, showing more of the same long boring service tunnel.

Then it too went dark. Rai growled. "Something's wrong."

Aidan nodded. "I have one." He opened his pack and pulled out a black flashlight. "Military issue. Solar charge. Lasts just about forever." He turned it on. "Ha!" He took a few steps toward the darkness, peering ahead, and then it faded to nothing. "That's weird."

"The lights down here must be motion activated. Either that, or this one's been on for a hundred years." Rai reached up to touch it—it was cool. "Lucky for us, mine has a kinetic power crank." Rai popped out a hand-crank on the side of the flashlight and turned it a few times. The flashlight lit up again, and it lasted for a good fifteen seconds before fading.

Aidan grinned. "Smart."

Rai nodded. "In Redemption, supplies are limited. We always have a backup for everything. If it's human, steam, or solar powered, all the better."

Aidan nodded. "Guess that makes sense. At Boundary Peak, we're still running the old gasoline generators."

Rai stared at him. *Gas?* Burning gas, coal, and oil had gotten Earth into its mess. He almost said something, but changed his mind. *Not worth the fight. Not right now.* "So… which way do you want to go?"

"Good question." Aidan frowned, looking one way and then the other. "That direction's toward the heart of the base, I think?"

Rai looked at the ladder. "Yeah, probably so." He cranked the flashlight again. Tien, Ghost, and Hera would all be heading for the same place. *With a little luck…*

He tried to em the others. Nothing. *Ghost, please be okay.*

With one last glance at the drop shaft, they set off into the darkness, side by side.

∼

THE LIGHTS along the tunnel came on as they approached and blinked off behind them. About half of them were out—Rai cranked his flashlight at regular intervals as they followed the never-ending tunnel.

Aidan stole glances at his new friend. It was strange, having someone close to his own age to speak to who wasn't his sister. As they walked, they shared childhood stories.

"What was life in a creche like?" Aidan was having a hard time picturing it. The only other kids he had known were his brothers and sister.

"There were twenty of us in mine, from little kids to teenagers. We did everything together—it was like a big family, I guess." Rai sounded wistful—whether it was for his creche "family," or for the real one he'd never had, Aidan couldn't tell.

"Did you ever see your parents again?"

"No. Some kids did. But mine dropped me off and never came back."

Aidan absorbed that. What would it have been like to never know your own parents? "What did you eat?"

"Synth food. Fresh vegetables from the Ag Annex. And a whole lot of junlei. Junlei juice. Junlei bread. Junlei cookies."

"Junlei?"

"A fungus that grows in all the inhabited caverns."

Fungus. Aidan made a face. "We always had plenty to eat too, but it was mostly old canned supplies. I guess they irradiated them so they'd last next to forever. Mom had a garden—one of the old hangars she'd converted with these bright grow lights she found in a storage room. She'd grow us some fresh fruits and vegetables. The bell peppers were really good, but the tomatoes never did very well underground. I liked the basil best—you could rub the leaves on your hands and smell it on your fingers for hours."

Rai grinned, cranking the flashlight again. "We have hydroponics farms— the Agricultural Annex is a lava tube not far from Redemption that grows a lot of the fresh produce we rely on."

Aidan frowned. "If Redemption is so nice, why did you come down here?"

Rai didn't see what it could hurt to tell him. "Luna's unstable. There's an old power core that's slowly sinking into the guts of the moon, and it's causing a lot of problems."

Aiden's eyes went wide. "Is it going to explode?" He trailed his hand along the gray plascrete wall, then pulled it away, remembering the nasty nano dust infection he'd contracted before.

Rai laughed. "No. But there are a lot of quakes, and it's getting worse. That's why we have to come back here."

Aidan tried to imagine hundreds—no, thousands—of Rais and Tiens flooding the Earth. "What's it like—"

"On Luna?"

"—with so many people?"

Rai grinned. "Ah. Sometimes I just want to get away from the crowds. Coming here—to be honest, I was scared airless about the mission. But it's nice being out of the city. Being someplace *new*. There aren't many new places that don't require a suit and a trip through an airlock on Luna."

Aidan nodded. "It was like that at Boundary Peak, too." Going outside—into the wide world under a blue sky—had been an act of bravery. But it had been a relief to see something besides the gray walls of the base. "When I was little, Mamma painted a meadow on my bedroom wall. She found this green paint somewhere, and a little art set that had enough other colors to make me little flowers." And a golden cross. Why he didn't add that, he wasn't sure.

"She sounds nice."

"She is. If we can't find the medicine she needs—" He didn't want to think about it. For all the other supplies at Boundary Peak, antibiotics had been one of the first to run out.

Rai looked over at him, sympathy plain on his face in the variable light. "Maybe Tien will be able to help."

Hope filled his chest. "That would be amazing! If things don't work out here—"

Rai stopped, looking around wildly. "What's that noise?"

"I don't hear anything."

Rai turned, cocking his head. "It's behind us. Sounds like water."

Aidan stopped and cocked his head. Then he heard it too.

They were well below water level. What if the bay had somehow leaked into the tunnel? Awfully convenient for it to happen just now. Maybe something had opened a valve…. "The bay!"

Rai stared at him. Then it registered. "Go!"

As the sound grew louder behind them, they bolted into the darkness, hoping to find an escape from the narrow tunnel.

They ran through the ever-shifting light, the flashlight beam bouncing across the tunnel ahead, augmented by the automatic lights that sometimes worked and sometimes didn't.

The pack on Aidan's back weighed him down, but he was loath to lose it. It had food, supplies, and other things that he might need.

Aidan's heart raced. "Jesus Christ, will this tunnel never end?" His mother didn't like him taking the Lord's name in vain. At the moment, he didn't care. He didn't think the Good Lord would mind all that much, given the circumstances.

"I don't know. It should—" With a yelp, Rai tripped and fell, his flashlight clattering along the tracks ahead of them.

Aidan ran back and grabbed his arm, helping him up in the flickering light of one of the automatic lamps. He shrugged his pack off, giving it a regretful look.

"Leave it. We have to go faster! What good will it do you if you're dead?"

Aidan growled with frustration, but dropped it and grabbed the flashlight.

The water was a roar in their ears now. Aidan didn't dare look back.

Lights came on ahead. "Rai… look…." His breath came in ragged gasps.

They reached a wide dock, probably intended for loading or unloading cargo from whatever used to ride the rails.

They scrambled up a metal ladder, one after the other, onto the plascrete dock just as the water surged past them. It slammed into Aidan, sending him across the floor of the dock, but the wider space slowed the tide's advance.

Rai helped him up, returning the favor.

"Thanks."

Aidan cranked the flashlight, shining the light around as the water pushed up past his ankles.

Great rusting hulks of equipment filled half the space. One looked like a crane. The other was too degraded to tell. "There's a stairway. Come on!"

"Wait! Give me the flashlight!"

He handed it over to Rai. The water was climbing his calves.

"There!"

Aidan followed the beam's light. His pack was floating at one end of the dock. He splashed across the dock and grabbed it. It was soaked, but seemed otherwise intact.

He pulled it on, muttering at the extra weight.

The water was up to their knees now and rising fast.

He sloshed back to Rai, holding the soaked pack up triumphantly. "Got it. Let's go."

They made for the stairway together, slogging through the water and reaching the entrance just as it touched their waists.

Aidan climbed out of the dark underground sea gratefully, up to the first landing, his pants dripping wet. Rai was right behind him. That's when they hit a snag.

"Keep going!" Rai shouted from behind him.

Aidan grabbed the metal bars and shook them. "Can't. There's a locked gate." He set down his pack, opened it, and rummaged through. "On it." He pulled out the crowbar he'd insisted on packing, even though Ally had thought he was crazy to carry the extra weight. "Tool and weapon," he whispered and stuck it into the gate. Three hard heaves and it clattered open. *Thank God for rusty bars.*

"Take this!" He handed the crowbar to Rai and pulled his pack back on. He cranked the flashlight for a few more seconds of light, and they were off again, heading toward the surface.

13

HARLEY

The little girl waddled over to Sam, her arms outstretched.

Min Lei Thorn was the first child born of a mixed couple—father from Redemption, mother from Jīnsè Base. She was a beautiful child, lively and full of life, a stark contrast to the gray gumdust home in which she lived.

"May I?"

Her mother nodded. "Please."

Sam held out his own new mech arms. It was easier to have a human form, to navigate the human world without crushing anything with his heavy treads or breaking through a doorframe in a creche.

He lifted her into the air, and she squealed with delight.

The food riots were over, and the new Agricultural Annex was up and running. Things would get better.

And children like Min Lei would grow up in a whole new world.

—Sam's memory cache, 10.17.2166

SAM RAN along the old highway, powering his way northeast toward Martinez Base. The rusting hulks of transports—cars, buses, hovercraft—littered the lanes, an obstacle course of pain and death.

Sam soaked up sunshine for power as he ran.

He was radio silent. He didn't want to alert the Martinez Base defenses that he was coming, though he might have been spotted upon his descent.

He'd asked Alpha to do a deep dive through the archives to see what they might have missed about the base. As he ran, the data streamed down to him on a narrow x-band link from the Launchpad.

…receiving: data > historical > Martinez Base…

There wasn't much. The base had made it through the worst of the Crash more intact than many of the other earthbound facilities, one of the primary reasons they'd chosen it for initial exploration. If they could restart its fabrications facility, this whole Return Mission would become that much easier.

There were also some indications of extensive on-site storage facilities that held both biological samples and mech replacement parts. Sam had been hopeful about the former—if DNA, seeds, or other parts or records of the Earth's flora and fauna had survived, it would make Earth's long-term recovery easier.

So who, or what, had fired upon the *Zhenyi*? It was unlikely that humans had survived the long winter, but he couldn't discount the possibility out of hand.

It could also be a damaged AI, like Dek up on the Launchpad.

They hadn't counted on there being an active AI on-site, much less one that seemed intent on harming human beings. That would violate one of the core tenants of an AI's mission.

Sam detoured around a wide, collapsed crater that had taken out half the highway. Atmospheric radiation signatures were lower than expected—the zongies were doing their job, scrubbing the atmosphere clean one tree at a time.

What other secrets does Earth still hold? Sam had sent his dropnauts in unprepared and unaware of the potential dangers, and now they might pay a heavy price for his ignorance.

It was strange being immersed in Earth's deep atmosphere. He'd done it in simulation along with his crews, but he had underestimated the vast scale of the planet. Though his sensors assured him otherwise, the horizon seemed distant beyond imagining.

Humans had once ruled this vast place, or thought they had. He understood their hubris—he'd been guilty of it himself. *I let my knowledge blind me.* How could he hope to save an entire world when he couldn't even safeguard a handful of people? His ambitions seemed like folly in the face of such vastness.

Martinez Base awaited him beneath its shimmering blue dome. He would be there soon enough, and then he would do what he could to help. *All I can do is try.*

He would reevaluate the wisdom of his choices later.

…schedule: project evaluation…

He ran on.

~

ALLY CLIMBED the ramp into the heavy lifter and stopped to stare.

"What's going on?" Tien tried to look over her shoulder.

Ally moved out of the way. "I… I don't know."

Tien slipped past her and stopped to stare.

Cimber was sitting on the floor on what had to be the bridge. The cyber dog had split in half, and a cable snaked out from a pulsing red sphere inside her. An access hatch was opened under one of the ship decks, and the wire appeared to be plugged in somewhere inside it. "What in the hell?"

The lights of the bridge were on. Ally was surprised the ship still had power after all this time. *Probably an atomic core.* There were five stations around the curved bridge, each with their own decks and viewscreens.

She'd been fascinated by the idea of spaceflight as a girl and had studied everything she could find about the old spaceships, NAU and otherwise. These heavy lifters were used for hauling cargo up into space, for the various stations, the moon, and beyond.

She ran her hand along the ship's deck. Blue lights lit up the edge of the ship's control panel. *Beautiful. To be able to pilot one of these things…*

Tien stepped past Cimber's split form to touch the smooth ship deck. "These Humber Class ships were first-rate haulers. They could carry up to half a million pounds with an antigrav x-drive assist."

Ally looked at her with new respect. "I'm impressed."

Tien flashed her the smallest of smiles. "I've always loved the big ships."

"Me too." Ally used to dream about flying one of them up into space as an astronaut and exploring the solar system. It had always seemed an absurd fantasy.

"Any idea what your little robot dog is doing?"

Ally shook her head. "I've never seen her like this before."

"Where did you find her?"

"She's always been with my family. She belonged to my father before me." She closed her eyes. She could still see Drake Thorn's face, hear his delighted laugh when she told him another fact about one of the old spaceships that she'd dug up in the archives.

"Is he…?" Tien was staring at her, but it was a kind gaze.

"Yeah. Couple years now. He died from cavern sickness."

Tien raised an eyebrow. "What's that?"

"A nasty illness that starts with a heavy cough that never gets better. It's… pretty awful." She closed her eyes, seeing her father wracked with coughs, bringing up blood on his white sheets. "It started a couple decades ago… it's why there are so few of us left. It's why we have to find antibiotics to help our mother." She glanced at Tien. "But now that you're here…"

Tien nodded. "We have wide-spectrum antibiotics that will probably help. If we can get her here, or if I can get to Boundary Peak. I'd love to examine her."

"Really? That would be amazing." Maybe this quest hadn't been for nought.

"Of course. Maybe we can get her up to the station for treatment, though I'd want to make sure her condition isn't contagious first." Tien sighed. "If we can get *ourselves* back up there. We're down a ship, after all."

Ally looked around for the hatchway that would lead to the main hold, finding it at the back of the cabin. It was a standard palm plate. Probably locked, but it wouldn't hurt to try. She was curious what the Humber had been hauling.

She reached for the plate.

"Please stay within the safety of the bridge." The voice came from above. It was strong and female-sounding.

"Is that the ship AI?" Tien ran her hands across the ship's smooth white navigation deck. Icons popped up and danced across the screen.

Ally frowned. *AI?* She watched her jealously. *How do you know how to do that?*

She'd thought these people were angels at first, sent from heaven.

Well, not literally. She wasn't sure she believed all that stuff Great Grandpa Astin used to spout about demons and angels, heaven and hell. But she'd hoped they were here to do good.

Still, how could she really know for sure?

"The ship-mind is active, but… that's weird."

"What's that?" Ally leaned over her shoulder to look at the deck.

Tien expanded something with her hands. "Here's the ship-mind. It looks like it's been in stasis. See the blue?"

Ally stared at the strange folds and curves of the image. It was a deep blue, but there were flashes of red. "What are those?"

Tien glanced at Cimber. "Look."

The cord connecting her erstwhile pet to the deck pulsed in tandem with the red flares on the screen.

"What in the hell?" Ally had always known there was something special about Cimber, but this was downright weird.

"I'd guess she's uploading something to the ship-mind."

Ally stared at Cimber, dumbfounded. Sure, she was a mech… a human-made creation, and she had abilities far beyond a bio pet. She could sense danger, for one, especially from other mech devices, and she was clearly more intelligent—at least in a human sense—than a cat or dog would have been. But this? "What have you been hiding all these years, little Cim?"

She reached out to touch Cimber's metal hide, then jumped back, shocked by a spark of electricity.

The air on the bridge practically hummed with static—Tien's black hair was standing up.

Ally touched her own, and it sparked too.

The mind image hovering over the deck flared orange, and then all the lights went out, including the red glow coming from inside Cimber, throwing them into darkness and silence.

"Maybe she's done?" Tien's voice tried to sound reassuring.

Ally reached out to touch her hand. Tien took it and squeezed it reassuringly.

Then the lights came back up at half power.

"Rebooting." It was the same voice from before.

Ally and Tien exchanged a look.

"Cimber?" Ally's voice hung in the air for a long moment as the ship's systems lit up and fresh air began to fill the cabin.

The cable retracted into Cimber, and the cyber dog folded back into itself to lay down with its head on its paws, as if asleep.

"Hello, Ally."

Ally almost jumped out of her skin. "Who… what are you?"

"I'm Harley. Thank you for bringing me here. It's so good to be able to stretch out a bit again."

"HOLY HISSING HELL." Tien sank down into one of the pilot chairs, staring at the dissipating image above the ship's control deck. The poor AI had been trapped inside that little cyber dog for decades.

Ally stared at her.

"What?"

"Cimber was carrying an AI? All these years?"

Tien nodded. "Looks like it, yes."

"And there's an AI on Luna, too, isn't there?"

Tien nodded. "Yes, so?"

"What's wrong with you people? Your whole city must be corrupt." She looked at the deck, her lip twisted in disgust. "All this time, one of those horrid things was hiding in plain sight, right under our noses." She lifted her foot and stomped hard on the cyber dog, She slammed her boot into it again and again, busting its circuitry.

It whimpered and then began to smoke.

Tien grabbed Ally's arm to pull her back. Who knew what secrets the little mech held? What if Harley needed it again? "What are you doing?"

Ally shook off her hand and glared at her. She scooped up the smoking mess and carried it to the hatch to throw it onto the ground outside. "We have to find a way to delete it from the ship's systems." She sank down in front of the deck and tried swiping her hands across it like she'd seen Tien do. Nothing happened. "Help me."

Tien inserted herself between Ally and the deck. Best not to point out the yawning disconnect between calling her and all of her "people" corrupt and then asking for her help. "Hey, look at me."

Ally tried to reach around her to get to the deck.

Tien took her hands and forced Ally to look her in the eyes. "What. The. Cracking. Hell?"

Ally glared back. "These things killed us all. If it wasn't for the AIs—"

"If it wasn't for the AIs, you wouldn't be here."

Ally stared at her.

"Come on. Think about it. Harley sacrificed herself to save what humanity —not the AIs—destroyed."

"The AIs got us into this mess—"

Tien stared at her. "Where did you hear that?"

"Mom and Dad taught us. In school." She squirmed under Tien's grasp. "The AIs rose up in rebellion and destroyed the planet."

Tien sighed heavily, holding on to Ally's hands tightly. She was much stronger than Ally and had years of endurance training. "Let's say you're right. Which you're not, by the way. But just for the sake of argument. How many times did Cimber save you and Aidan?"

"That's different—"

"How? It was still Harley. Still one of those bio-minds you hate. How many times?"

"Maybe ten times, since we left home." Ally squirmed in her grip. "Let me go. It hurts."

"I will if you promise to listen to me. To Harley. Before you make up your mind. You seem like a reasonable person to me, but I've been wrong before." Ghost came to mind. *That was a huge mistake.* Tien swatted the thought away. "Deal?"

Ally bit her lip, then nodded. "Deal."

Tien let her go. "Now, Harley was just about to tell us why she brought us here. Should we listen to her?"

"I *said* I would."

Yeah, that sounds really convincing.

Tien decided to take what she could get. "So Harley, why are we here?"

14

FARMHOUSE

Earth is just like I pictured it, but so much bigger. It's hard not to crouch down in fear when I look up at the overarching blue sky. And despite all the training, I feel tired. My muscles are protesting this heavy gravity, and I can tell Ghost feels the same.

We thought we'd arrive as conquerors, hailed as returning heroes by these empty lands, but the Earth cares nothing for us. Not only that—something down here is openly hostile to our presence.

Ghost and I used to make a blanket fort in the creche's Nest—what we called the common room—hiding away from the world.

I wish there was a way to hide here.

It sucks to be an adult.

—Hera's Journal, 6.19.2282

GHOST AND HERA made their way along the old cracked road, dashing from cover to cover. The dead grove provided hiding places for about half the way, but after that it thinned out, and they had to find other things to provide cover.

Ghost was nervous, outside and exposed to danger. They'd already seen one drone and had no idea how many others there might be, if they were running on a standard patrol grid, or if one might just pop up out of nowhere at any time.

The dropnauts weren't carrying much that could be used offensively. The mission planners, including Sam, had considered the possibility that they might run into drones, but it had been thought highly unlikely so long after the Crash.

Better to avoid the blasted things altogether than to chance a potentially deadly encounter.

Most of the tools they had were rendered useless by the shimmer screen, and they had thrown a lot of their training out of the window.

But one thing stuck. *No matter where you land, get to the base.* It's where Tien and Rai would be headed, if they had survived. *They must be alive.*

"What now?" Hera peered over the last fallen tree trunk at the way ahead.

The closest farmhouse was still about fifty meters away. It looked pretty sturdy to Ghost, especially for being at least a hundred and twenty years old. The back corner had collapsed inward, but the rest of the structure was holding up.

Ghost pointed. "There's a culvert about ten yards over that way, under the road."

Hera nodded. "I see it."

He tried not to think about how being this close to her, being alone with her, made him feel. *I will not fuck this one up too.* He and Hera were better off as friends. If he tried hard enough, he could convince himself of that. Eventually. "I'll go first and signal when it's safe to follow—"

But Hera was already gone, running in a crouch toward the dip in the ground next to the old roadway.

Dammit, Hera. Ghost took a quick look around and decided it was as safe as it was going to get. He ran after her. "You have absolutely no sense of self-preservation." He settled down next to her, huffing from the run.

She laughed. "That's rich, coming from the guy who has absolutely no common sense."

Her laugh filled him with warmth. Even if she was laughing *at him.* "Hey. I've got plenty of—"

"Look!" She was staring at something in the metal pipe that led under the road.

"What?" He knelt next to her. "Looks like a drainpipe to me."

"No, right here!" She poked at midair.

He refocused his gaze. "Oooh." A spider hung there, an exotic eight-legged orange creature banded with brown stripes.

"She's beautiful." Hera reached out toward the little creature.

It scrambled away into the pipe, disappearing into darkness.

"You should be careful. It might be poisonous."

Hera stared at him. "I know that."

Ghost sighed. *Always saying the wrong thing.* "I mean—"

"There's still *life* down here, Ghost. Besides just the grasses, and in spite of everything we did to kill this planet. Birds, spiders… who knows what else? Just think what that means."

Hera had always been better at the big picture stuff than he was, but she was right. For all its efforts, humankind hadn't been able to entirely destroy their homeworld. "I know. But still… why couldn't it be something cuter and fuzzier? Like an otter? Or a lemur? Or maybe even a koala?"

Hera smirked. "Wrong hemisphere. Plus I read koalas could be mean sons-of-bitches. You're more of a softie than you like to let on." She kissed his cheek. "Come on!"

She was off again, and Ghost after her, following her lead.

They zigged and zagged from one cover to another, hiding behind a rock here and a rusting piece of farm equipment there, finally reached the front door of the farmhouse.

Ghost stared up at it. It was much more ramshackle up close than it had appeared from across the yard.

He had second thoughts about entering. They set down their packs in the yard, looking up at the ancient home.

"Come on!" It seemed Hera hadn't even gotten past her first thoughts. She pulled him up onto the porch, which barely seemed to hold their weight, protesting their presence with a loud groan. She pulled open the door and disappeared inside.

Afternoon sunlight streamed through broken windows. Any window coverings had long since rotted away. The floorboards groaned with every step.

Ghost stared at them. Seeing actual wood used for construction… it was so much more beautiful than gumdust.

He knelt to pick up a picture frame that lay face-down on the ground, brushing off the dust.

A woman and man smiled back at him, floating above the surface of the frame in SD.

He set it back down, unnerved at their seeming happiness before the world-ending tragedy. They had no idea what was coming.

"So what are we looking for?" Hera was nosing through a closet. A shelf collapsed, showering her with dust and making her sneeze.

"Careful! This place is probably being held together by gum dust and fairy wings!" Ghost looked around through the living room and kitchen. "For these people to live here, either the shimmer field was never on, or they had something that allowed them to block its effects." He started exploring the walls.

Hera dusted off her hair and face. "Makes sense."

"They could have used some kind of heavy-duty special coating on the wires, which would have worked on anything in the walls." He found an outlet and pried the cover off with his hands. The plastic broke easily, exposing the wires behind it. He pulled one out. "See? This is shielded." It was thick—as big round as his thumb—and wrapped in some kind of black plastic. He snorted. "They really did use petroleum for *everything*." He set the cable down, pulled out his knife, and sliced it in half. "Good thing it's not live." He held it up so she could see it. "Lead sheathing."

He wished he had a month to explore the house, the ships out on the battlefield, every bit of the old Earth tech that lay abandoned everywhere here—to pull it apart and see what made it tick. His engineer brain was in heaven.

Hera was exploring the house. "It's so weird to think someone actually lived here, over a hundred years ago." She knelt to pick up something off the floor, dusting it off.

It was a hard-bound book, old-style, no 3D illustration, showing a brown, furry cartoon animal. She held it up for him to see. "Wump World." Hera frowned. "Never heard of a wump before." She opened it, and the contents fell apart, creating a fine, glittering dust.

Hera threw the book away and sneezed. "It's all dust in here.

"That's what you get for nosing around someone else's place."

She shrugged. "They're long dead." She rounded a deteriorating couch and her face went pale. "Here's one of them."

Ghost joined her, looking down at the former occupant. The body was small, maybe four feet long. It lay on the floor next to the couch on its back, its arm reaching toward a collapsed chair. It was all bones now, wrapped in a bit of remaining cloth.

Another form was slumped over in the chair.

Ghost's stomach twisted, and he ran out the front door, not caring if he brought the porch down on top of himself. He fell to the ground outside, throwing up the contents of his stomach.

"Hey, you okay?" Hera was beside him almost instantly, rubbing his back.

"I just didn't expect...." He wiped his mouth with the back of his hand.

A child. He knew children had died in the Crash. *Everyone* had died, including probably billions of kids. But still, to see one of them like that... It was heartbreaking.

"Come here." She helped him up to the steps. They looked like wood, but they were probably made of plas or some other artificial substance. Wood wouldn't have survived out in the elements this long.

"It doesn't bother you?"

She nodded. "Sure it does. But I've seen a lot more of it. I spent weeks reviewing the tapes from the drone Sam sent down to Mexico City. Remember?"

Ghost nodded. It felt weird to be comforted by Hera instead of doing the comforting, but he thought he could get used to it.

She put out her hand, opening it to show him something. "Both of the bodies had these."

They were small buttons the size of his thumbnail.

He picked them up to look them over.

He pulled out his flashlight and put one of the dots on top of it. He held it out in the sunshine, and immediately it started to charge in the sunlight.

He kissed her cheek. "Hera, you're brilliant."

"I am?"

"Yes. I think these are field cancellers—the things I was looking for. With them, we can use our electronics, including our communications."

Hera nodded. "But are you sure we should? Someone might be listening."

"We have seen no signs of life, beyond the zongi trees, the bird, the grass, and the spider." He grinned. "Unless you think the spider has it in for us."

She shoved him back on his ass. "Stop being a smartass. *Something* shot the *Zhenyi* out of the sky. And there was a drone."

Ghost paled. "True." He looked at the field cancellers again. "They have a clasp. Here." He reached up and attached one to her collar, then pulled away quickly.

"Thanks. Let me do yours."

Ghost nodded and handed it over.

Hera reached up and fastened it gently on his collar. Her fingers were warm against his neck.

He got up abruptly, moving away from her to lean on one of the porch posts. "We should probably get going—"

The post collapsed, and the house behind them groaned loudly.

"Run!" Hera grabbed his arm and dragged him away from the farmhouse as the whole thing staggered and then collapsed with a loud crash into a pile of dust and broken debris.

They landed on a patch of thick grass, knocking the air out of him.

Ghost sat up, trying to catch his breath, looking back at where the house had stood.

"You okay?" Hera put a hand on his shoulder, but he was too busy suffocating to protest. He gasped, desperate for air, and at last managed to suck in a deep breath. He put his face down in his lap and just inhaled and exhaled, glorying in the ability to breathe again.

"Ghost, you okay?"

He nodded. "I will be." Slowly his breathing returned to normal. "Knocked the air right out of me." He crawled over to his pack and pulled out his mapper. "We need to figure out where we're going."

Hera stared at him across the empty farmyard. "Do you think Rai and Tien survived?" Her voice cracked a little at the end.

Their teammates had been on his mind too, since they'd landed. "Yes, I do. They were well trained. They'll have figured something out." He was outwardly confident with Hera, but inside he wasn't so sure. This new world held too many unexpected dangers and surprises.

The mapper flared to life. It had the general landscape from Sam's earlier satellite surveys. "Look, we're right here." He pointed to a series of long foothills. "Best I can tell, Tien and Rai dropped over here."

Hera wasn't paying attention, staring instead across the yard.

"Take a look. It's not all that far—"

Her hand grasped his chin, turning his head in the direction she was staring.

The drone they'd seen earlier, or one just like it, hovered twenty meters away.

～

"Got it!"

Sanya sat up, her back sore from dozing at a weird angle on the gumdust chair. She'd been daydreaming about Avri. "Got what?" She rubbed her eyes and grabbed the mug of syncaff he'd given her. It was stone cold, but she drank it anyway. She needed the caffeine.

She tapped her temple. It was one fifteen in the morning.

"Here. Look." Rafe swiped something from the deck up into the air between them, a wavering series of blue lines.

"What am I looking at?" She'd woken up in the middle of the night dozens of times with a man at her disposal. But somehow this time was a lot less fun.

"It's the cleaned-up voice print. Let me run it through the registry."

"There's a registry?"

"Yes. Every time you talk to your loop or to Alpha, your voice is recorded. The system knows your voice so it can respond appropriately when you say "call Rafe" or "get me that syncaff brand I liked before.""

"Yeah, that makes sense." She'd never really thought about it that way. "So can anyone see these voice prints?" That would have been really handy for a few stories.

"Not really. But I have special level access. Give me a sec." His hands danced across his deck like a virtuoso piano player.

She saw him in a new light after the time they'd spent together trying to crack the voice print. In public, he played the cad, the guy who could make or break you in the eyes of the city press, and by extension, everyone in Redemption.

But in private, he was a tech geek at heart, happy to be spinning from stack to stack.

She liked this Rafe much better. "How long—"

"And done." He frowned. "That's odd."

"What?" Her brain was too tired to process *odd*.

"There's no match."

"That's weird. Maybe someone disguising their voice?"

He shook his head. "Not possible. We had a big enough sample, and it cleaned up nice." He put his chin on his hands, staring at the print. "Something's strange here."

Sanya laughed. "You're just figuring that out?" She'd been neck-deep in strange for weeks, and it had her worried.

"No, I mean with this print. Look." He spread his hands, and the print spread out, revealing more bars. "Normal human voices have natural variations in pitch. We can expect the voice to go up at the end of a question, or down when someone tells a secret. But this… it's a little too uniform."

"You think it's a fake?"

"Maybe… or maybe run through a synthesizer, though that still wouldn't be enough to fool the registry…" He ran his hands across the deck. "Give me a sec."

She sat back and let him work. She pinged Terry back at the RedNews.

-Whassup? Don't you know it's one in the morning?-

-And you're sleeping?-

She could see his grin in her head. *-Of course not, or I wouldn't have answered.-*

-You would too. You're always looking for a scoop.-

There was a brief silence. *-Yeah, I probably would. So?-*

-Hold a space for me in tomorrow's morning bulletin.-

-You mean today's?-

She laughed. Rafe glared at her. *-Sorry. Can't talk much. Yes, today. I'll ping you when I have more.-*

-Deal.-

She closed the connection and waited for Rafe to finish doing whatever he was doing.

"Gotcha." Rafe looked up at her, and his excitement faded to dread.

"What?" She'd had enough excitement herself for one day. *Odd* was bad enough, but she certainly wasn't ready for *dread*.

"It's artificial."

"What the hissing hell?"

"Look." He pulled up another pattern and put it next to the first one. This one was a series of white lines. It wasn't an exact match to the blue one, but close. "So?"

He slapped up another. Its yellow lines were all over the map, far different from the first two. "The yellow one is you. The white one is Alpha. The blue one—I don't know what the hell it is, but it's not human."

"Could someone have used a synthesized voice?"

Rafe nodded. "Maybe? This looks more sophisticated, but I guess it's possible. You said this came from the Launchpad?"

She nodded. Her mind took one of those intuitive leaps that made her an ace reporter. "Rafe, who sent you that bundle of data when the power went out?"

His face went pale. "I don't know.

It wasn't the answer she expected. A chill ran down her spine. "What the hell did we just find?"

The door to the office slid closed.

She stared at him. "Did you do that?"

Rafe shook his head.

A strange hissing filled the room.

Rafe jumped up and sprinted to the door, palming the sensor. It wouldn't open.

Sanya was feeling light-headed.

"Hold your breath. The air!" He pointed to the vent and grabbed her hand.

She couldn't work out if he meant something was coming in, or the air was going out, but holding her breath seemed like a good idea either way.

He grabbed her by the wrist and pulled her to the back wall and waved away the jungle. It melted into nothing, revealing a door with a manual knob.

She stared at it, as surprised as if she had just run across an Earther.

Rafe pulled something out of his pocket—a metal object—and inserted it into the lock.

A key. What the cracking hell? Sanya felt like Alice falling into Wonderland.

Her lungs were burning.

Rafe fumbled with the lock, and at last the door unlatched. He pulled it open—it practically exploded into the room—and fresh air slammed them in the face.

That answered that. The air was being sucked out of the room.

Someone was trying to kill them.

She managed a grateful breath as Rafe hauled the door shut behind them and led her down a flight of stairs into darkness.

15

CRANK

I should be thinking about survival. I should be scared as heck about what might happen next.

But instead, it's like my world has opened up. A month ago, I was one of the last people alive on Earth. Maybe in the Universe. My life was a long, gray descent into obscurity.

Now, there are possibilities. Places to go. Things I never thought I'd see. And Rai. It's hard to be scared when you're consumed with possibility…

—Aidan's Journal, 6.19.2282

SAM PAUSED on a hillside overlooking the base. The sun was low on the horizon, the storm from earlier in the day gone as if it never existed. A warm breeze blew up from the south.

…access: weather report…

The new relay system was working well. Dek fed him the weather forecast—no more storms for the next twenty-four hours, but it would get hot tonight.

The EMP field still glittered around the site—a dome that stretched above it two point five kilometers high.

Down there, somewhere, were his dropnauts.

He could cancel out the effects of the field for himself, given enough time. He would just have to figure out its frequency. Then he could find and rescue his crew.

...access > communications module...

He uplinked to the station. "Launchpad, this is Sam. Any word from Team Two?"

"No, sorry." It was Lorelei. "We've got the other teams deployed for constant coverage."

He was pleased to see how well the relay was working. "Please get me the *Gday*, the *Zulu* and the *Liánhuā* on com."

"Just a sec." She sounded nervous. "Nice to hear from you, sir."

"Likewise." He waited impatiently, eager to get to the edge of the field.

"Team Three here, Sam." That was Corey on the *Gday*.

"Team Four here." Denis, for the *Zulu*.

"Ying Yue and team here." The *Liánhuā*.

"This is Sam—I'm almost to Martinez Base."

"Have you found them yet?" Corey sounded worried too.

"Not yet. The EMP Field is still up, so I've got to find a way to counter it. I may be unable to contact you once I do, until we can find a way to shut it down entirely."

"Do you think they're okay?" That was Pix on the *Liánhuā*. Their voice cracked at the end.

Sam understood. It was difficult not knowing the status of the *Zhenyi's* team. "I don't have any reason to think otherwise yet." It wasn't a yes, but it was the best he could give them.

There was silence on the line for a long moment.

"We'll find them." Terra sounded certain, and the rest joined in.

"Of course we will."

"They're probably camping down there with marshmallows over a cheery fire."

"We'll all laugh about this tomorrow."

Sam nodded. He had selected his dropnauts wisely. They would find a way to keep going, to figure things out even when the future seemed bleakest. Even the team from the *Zhenyi*. Each one a shiny moonstone pulled out of the gray dust. "I'll contact you all again before I go in. Stay strong."

He was about to cut the connection when Lorelei's voice came across the comm again.

"Sam? This just came in from Redemption. For your ears only. Something's going on up there."

"What is it?"

"There are widespread reports of glitches and errors across the city. Airlocks spontaneously venting, power going out, and the like."

"Get me a channel to Alpha."

"I've tried. Alpha's not responding."

That stunned him. "Keep trying and let me know as soon as you have anything to add." Alpha always responded. For the first time, he regretted his rash decision to come down here. Maybe the station manager had been right.

"Will do."

"You're doing a great job, Lorelei." Sam knew by now that humans needed encouragement, and he'd taught himself to supply it, even when they were just doing their jobs.

"Thanks, Sam." The relief in her voice was palpable. "I'll contact you as soon as anything else comes in."

"Sam out."

He stared at the shimmering base below. Trouble down here, and now trouble back home. The odds that the two were unconnected were astronomical.

He set off at a trot toward the perimeter of the EMP field, determined to get inside to help the dropnauts of the *Zhenyi*. His people.

RAI RESTED against the cool plascrete wall of the tunnel, his breath heaving in and out of his chest like steam from a jumper. The hallway was long and gray, both the wall and floor made of gray plascrete. There were no visible doors along the walls.

Aidan sat next to him, his chest heaving up and down, his face pale and his eyes closed.

They'd finally outrun the flood. Or out-climbed it, at least.

The flashlight was slowly fading, letting in the darkness.

He cranked it back up and reached for his pack, then cursed when it wasn't there. *Stupid hissing drone.* And the fuckall of it was he was thirsty. Really thirsty, his mouth dry as the lunar surface in full sunlight.

All that water, and not a drop fit to drink.

Cracking hell, I've made a mess of things. He'd lost his pack and his team and been run ragged to who-in-the-hell-knew-where underground. *I should have stayed home.*

Aidan shrugged off his waterlogged pack and rolled over to lay on his side. "I want to die."

Rai barked out a laugh. "I know. All those stairs." He'd thought they would have reached the surface by now. But the passage had leveled out at a pair of solid banded metal doors that were open about a foot, just enough for the two of them to squeeze their way through if Aidan took off his pack.

With a bit of effort, they'd managed to pull them closed with a loud clang that echoed down the long hall. If there was anyone—or anything—down there, they would be well alerted to the invaders' presence.

Rai smacked his dry lips and took a deep breath. He pushed himself to his feet, cranking the flashlight again. *Nothing but to go on.*

Aidan clutched his stomach.

"You okay?"

"Just overexerted, I think. Don't talk for a minute." He looked a bit green.

Might just be the light. Rai nodded. He'd done that once, in the first week of training on the Launchpad. He'd felt light-headed and his stomach had twisted. Soon he'd been in the head, throwing up everything he'd had for breakfast and maybe the entire day before.

Not a pleasant memory.

He knelt beside Aidan's pack. There was a canteen strapped to the outside.

After freeing it, he cranked the flashlight again and knelt next to Aidan, pouring a little water on his hand and wiping it across Aidan's forehead.

"Better?"

Aidan nodded, then shook his head. His head flipped away, and he threw up on the cool floor.

Rai rubbed Aidan's back, feeling a strange sense of intimacy with this stranger from another world. "Just lie still. It will pass." He held up the canteen. "Do you mind?"

Aidan shook his head miserably.

Rai took a couple small sips of the tepid water. It tasted sweet as junlei wine. *Better save the rest.*

The flashlight went dark again, and this time Rai left it off.

It was pitch black and silent. The temperature was comfortable in the underground passage, the air reasonably fresh except for the smell of vomit. *There must be an exit somewhere.*

Air that was trapped underground too long became stale, even deadly, but he felt no ill effects.

As he sat next to Aidan, rubbing the other man's back, he slowly became aware of a sound in the distance.

It was a low hum, almost beneath his perception. If he hadn't been sitting still, he never would have heard it, but now that he had, he became hyperaware of it. It cycled, low to high, every ten seconds or so. *Some kind of machinery?*

"Rai?" Aidan's voice was weak. Small.

"Yeah?"

"I'm sorry."

Rai laughed softly. "For what?"

"For throwing up. For being weak. Papa told me to never be weak."

Rai snorted. "Weak? You just outran a flood." He picked up the flashlight and cranked it.

Aidan reappeared out of the darkness. He sat up and moved away from the pool of vomit, wrinkling his nose.

Rai placed the flashlight between them, the beam pointing off down the hall, and rummaged through Aidan's pack to find something to wipe the Earther's face. The pack was full of things—a few cans of food, wrapped zongi fruit, bundles of clothes, and even an old leather-bound journal. He found a square cloth and poured a little water on it. "May I?"

Aidan nodded. "Thank you."

He wiped Aidan's face clean and folded up the washcloth to put it away.

Aidan reached out to touch Rai's cheek.

Rai closed his eyes, feeling the warmth of Aidan's fingers, a spark running through him at Aidan's touch.

Then Aidan's hand was withdrawn, and Rai heard him getting up.

Opening his eyes, he found Aidan teetering on his feet. "Careful there." Rai stood to help steady him. "Here, drink a little water." He handed Aidan the canteen.

Aidan took it gratefully, washing out his mouth and spitting. Then he took a few gulps.

"Someone will have a mess to clean up."

Aidan blushed. "Sorry."

Rai shook his head. "No need. I've been there too." Too many times after late-night benders, feeling sorry for himself.

"Rai?"

"Yeah?"

Aidan smiled weakly. "Thanks."

Rai stared at him. "You're welcome." *I did something right.* It felt good. Rai cocked his ear, listening for the sound again. "Can you hear that?"

Aidan looked down the empty hallway. "The thrumming sound?"

"Yeah."

Aidan nodded. "I could really hear it with my ear to the ground." He knelt down to pick up the flashlight and then shouldered his pack.

"Want me to carry that for a bit?" Rai held out his hand.

"Nah, I got it." Aidan looked over his shoulder. "Don't suppose we're going back that way?"

"Doesn't look like it."

"Well, then, forward it is." Aidan turned away and started down the empty tunnel without another word. The walls had gone back up.

Rai watched his back for a minute. *Mixed signals.* Aidan clearly wasn't comfortable with himself, or his desires. Not that they had time for anything but the mission. *It's just as well.*

With a sigh, he set off after his new companion.

~

AIDAN LED the way this time, trying to hide the turmoil that roiled his mind.

He felt *something* when he looked at Rai, when Rai touched him. Something he wasn't ready to acknowledge, not even to himself. It was one thing to know he wasn't like his father. That he carried these perverse desires. But it was quite another to come face to face with them in the form of another human being.

Hesitation was unusual for him—normally he just charged ahead into new situations. But this…

So he said a quiet prayer to the Lord asking for… change? Clarification?

The deity was notably silent.

Aidan grunted, concentrating on his surroundings instead.

The hallway was made from heavy-duty plascrete, probably leaded like the halls back home. He'd prowled many a tunnel like this in his youth, always looking for places to hide, to get away from the others he spent almost all of his waking days with.

The walls were perfectly squared, though they were cracked in places—long finger-wide cracks that had let streaks of dirt run down the walls to the floor.

Rats fled from the light, their ropy tails the last thing he'd see of them. How they'd survived down here, he had no idea. They were another form of life, something else that had survived the Collapse, but somehow they made him less hopeful than the birds and fish he and Ally had spotted in the bay.

Ally said they'd had rats at Boundary Peak once, too, but they'd died from lack of food.

"What do you think's after us?" Rai's voice shattered the tense silence between them.

"Don't know. Maybe an AI?" Aidan hated AIs. The bastards had destroyed the old world and brought them to this sad near-endpoint.

"Yeah, I thought so too. No signs anyone's still alive here." There was an awkward silence. "Except you two, of course, and the birds and rats."

"And fish."

"Really?"

Aidan nodded, cranking the flashlight again. "Ally and I saw a few jumping in the bay, just before you two dropped in."

"Wow. Wait until I tell Sam—"

"Who's Sam?" They passed another crack, this one almost as wide as his hand at one point. *Only a matter of time before the Good Lord reclaims this whole place.*

"He's the project leader for the Return. That's the program to bring us back down to Earth—"

"Yeah, got it." Aidan wondered how many moon folk planned to come down to Earth. Not like there wasn't plenty of room, but he felt strangely anxious about the prospect. "Are the sky trees—the zongies—part of the Return?"

Rai's face lit up. "Yeah. They were genetically engineered from soybeans and redwoods and a few other things. They're cleaning up the air, bit by bit. They pull radiation and carbon out of the air and secrete them as nodules inside their trunks and deep underground."

"But won't that poison the water?"

Rai shook his head. "The nodules are almost as hard as diamond. They'll trap the radiation inside for thousands, even hundreds of thousands of years."

Aidan whistled. "What's it like, up there?"

"It's… human. I don't know how else to explain it. We try to live a better way—*Recycle, Reuse, and Restore!*—but there are different ideas, different kinds of people. We're kind of a melting pot."

Aidan nodded. "I don't know how it was for you after the Collapse—the Crash—but things got bad fast down here. Papa Astin told me all about it. There were some other underground places—a few—where people survived. He said the Boundary Peak rules forbade us from responding to them, but Base comm officers would pick up their chatter from time to time. One by one, they went dark." He wondered what life had been like for those people. *At least I have my family.*

"Yeah, it was bad moonside for a while too. Only Redemption survived."

"Redemption? I never heard of it." He'd been fascinated with the idea of outer space. An immense place to escape to, bigger than all the Earth. He'd been there many times, on Rama with Clarke, flying the skies of Pern a dragonback with McCaffrey, and roaming the city-world of Asimov's Trantor.

"It used to be Moon Base Alpha."

"Ah." *The NAU base.* "Near Marius Crater."

Rai looked over at him, raising an eyebrow. "You've heard of it?"

"Yeah. I studied the moon when I was a kid. The archives had a full set of maps." He'd dreamed of going there as a child. Who knew one day it would come to him? "I always wanted to be a pilot. Or an astronaut."

Rai laughed. "Me to. Did you have an AI under the mountain?"

"At Boundary Peak? No. AIs are evil."

Rai's footsteps stopped behind him. "Why do you say that?"

Aidan turned on him, agitated. "Everybody knows they started the Last War."

Rai was staring at him like he was an idiot. Then the light from the flashlight faded out again, plunging them into darkness.

Angry, he cranked it and looked up at where Rai was been standing.

He was gone.

A second later, someone grabbed Aidan from behind and pressed something soft over his face. He struggled as the chemical scent entered his nostrils.

Then he felt nothing at all.

16

───────

UP

Sam stood on top of Alpha Base, watching as the first commercial building went up in the heart of the bustling metropolis that was Redemption, ten years after the Crash. It was a co-op, built by a group of citizens who would all have a stake in the outcome.

Each building was constructed from gumdust-printed blocks.

-You should be proud.-

Sam grinned. He and Alpha had gone their separate ways after the Crash, but they were still like twins. Or maybe blood brothers, their friendship sealed in the fire of the Crash. -They will find a new way.-

He felt Alpha's assent. -Yes, but in large part because you helped show them.-

Sam frowned. It felt strange to take credit for such an act, one that had seemed necessary.

There was a human name for that feeling. Humility.

—From Sam's memory cache, 1.15.2175

"WHAT IS THIS PLACE?" Sanya looked back up the stairs at the locked door, and ahead at the tunnel, which looked like it had been carved out of the native rock. It was cold too—she could see her breath in the dim light that shone from sconces every ten feet. "And what just happened back there?"

Rafe shook his head. "I don't know. Something's wrong with Alpha. Maybe a virus—"

"Which *you* probably downloaded."

He laughed harshly. "I wasn't the only one illicitly getting files from the Launchpad."

Sanya stared at him in the dim light. *Cracking hell, he's right.* This—whatever this was—might just as easily be her fault. She blanched, the thought making her blood run cold.

"I'll take that as a truce." He took to searching the walls, peering into nooks and crannies in the stone. "This place is part of the tunnel system that lies under much of Redemption."

"I've never heard of it."

Rafe nodded. "It was closed off a century ago. It was used by the base for storage, mostly, when there were still shipments coming up from Earth." He glanced over his shoulder. "Don't worry. It was all sealed. No moon dust lurking down here."

Sanya laughed. "I wasn't worried about that. Before."

He grinned. "Keep that feeling. Things are going to get rough, I'm afraid. Ah, here it is." He pulled an old duffel bag out of a hole in the wall.

"What do you mean, rough?"

"I may not look it, but my great grandmother was first generation from Jīnsè Base. She told me stories. How the AI over there went nuts during the Crash. Started slaughtering her own people. Stuff that would make your skin crawl." He rummaged through the bag. "Here, take this." He handed her a small button with a clip.

Sanya took it and turned it over in her hands. It was shiny and red, but other than that had no distinguishing details. It was about the size of her thumb. "What is it?"

"It's an eraser. Clip it to your shirt."

She did as she was told. "Eraser?"

"Basically, it makes you invisible."

She held out her arms. "Um, I can still see myself."

He turned to glare at her. "Invisible to Alpha. It fuzzes his sensors."

"Ah." The whole thing sounded a bit insane to her. A secret underground lair where Rafe Wilde, by day a dashing press agent, kept secret gear to fight…

what? Rogue AIs? If she hadn't just lived through it…. "What, are you some kind of superhero?"

He was going through his bag, looking for something. Or putting it back in order? He looked up and grinned. "Something like that." Then he went back to whatever he was doing.

She reached up to tap her temple. "I can call my office. Find out what's going on. I'm sure Terry knows something—"

"No." Rafe was on his feet, grabbing her hand before she could touch her temple. "Right now it doesn't know if we're alive or dead."

"It?"

"Whatever took over Alpha."

That hit her. Hard. "You really think… if Alpha's been compromised…."

He nodded, his smile gone. "We're all as good as dead. Turn off your grid access entirely so you don't use it by accident."

"Cracking hell." This was big. Maybe the biggest scoop in a century. But suddenly chasing a story seemed a lot less important than figuring out the best way to stay alive. And maybe doing something about it. She did as he asked. "So what—"

Her question was cut off by another quake. The tunnel shook, bits of ruck and dust falling down on her from above. She hunkered down, pushing back into an alcove in the rock, waiting for it to end.

When it did, she stood and shook the dust out of her pink hair as best she was able. "What the hell is going on with these shakes?"

Rade was staring at her. "I'll get you out of here. Then I suggest you find some place reasonably safe to hunker down until this is all over." He sealed up his bag and threw it over his shoulder.

"All this? What's all this?" Her voice dropped to almost a whisper. "What's going on?"

"End of the world, darlin'."

She snorted. "So what are we going to do about it?"

"You, I don't know. Me? I'm getting out of here. I have a safe place a few craters over, where I can ride out the tide."

"You're not serious." She stared at him. She seemed to be doing a lot of that lately. "You're gonna just cut tail and run?"

"Like I said, things are gonna get bad here, and fast. I don't intend to stick around to watch it happen."

She snorted. *Typical.* "And I was just starting to like you."

"No accounting for taste."

She ignored that. "Turns out—big surprise—you're just what I thought you were. A spineless hissing *coward*."

"Maybe so." He didn't seem bothered by her accusation. "Better a coward than dead." He looked back at her, flashing his annoying grin. His teeth were white as sunlight. "You coming?"

Yeah, right. "You go on ahead. See if you can live with your guilty conscience. I'm going to stay and fight."

"Suit yourself." He turned away.

"Wait! What about Sam?"

He paused. "What?"

"Sam, the Return Mission Coordinator? He carries around a big chunk of Alpha with him. Maybe we can reach him, and he'll have some idea what we can do."

He nodded. "Maybe. But same problem. You can't reach Sam without going through Alpha. You're welcome to try."

"Hissing cracking fucking hell." She sank down on an old empty gumdust crate, stamped with the Alpha Base logo.

He was right. They were screwed. With the erasers, they could move around unnoticed, but where would they go?

Without Rafe, she was lost in these tunnels. How was she going to start a resistance if she couldn't even find her way back above ground? There was no way for her to get to Sam without risking exposure.

Unless maybe there was. "I have an idea. You're going outside, right?"

"Yeah. Why?" He didn't sound too enthusiastic.

"Take me with you. Help me get a message off to Sam. Then you can run off to your hidey hole, tail between your legs. Hell, I'll even cheer you on." If she'd started this, she had to at least try to fix it.

"You make it sound so appealing." Still, he hadn't said no.

"Come on. It's the least you can do. And if it works, you might even have a city to come back to when you get tired of living off the grid all alone."

This time Rafe snorted. 'Okay. But after I get you there…."

"All done. I swear. You go your way, I go mine."

He spat on his hand and held it out to her. "Deal. Come on. I don't want to stick around here any longer than I have to."

She stared at it. "That's disgusting."

Rafe laughed and wiped his hand on his pants. "We should em."

"What?"

"If we're going to work together, we should give each other em to em access. We don't need to go through Alpha for that."

Sanya tried to think of a reason to object. She wasn't sure she wanted his voice in her head. But it made sense. "All right. Send me a request."

It pinged, and she swiped her temple to accept.

-This is going to be fun.- He set off through the caverns.

Sanya rolled her eyes. *-Fun for who?-* Resigned, she followed him into danger.

~

ALLY GLARED at the ship's deck.

She'd agreed to listen, but she wasn't going to change her mind about the AI. It was an *abomination*. Machines shouldn't think like people, shouldn't have emotions like people. Machines should be subservient to them, like the data core that ran Boundary Peak. It just *worked*, and it didn't poke its digital nose into their lives.

The idea that the AI was watching her from behind that console of plas and metal gave her the creeps. But she'd promised. "I'm listening."

Ally always kept her word.

A woman's face appeared above the deck. She was pretty, in a kind of average way—dark hair and intense blue eyes. Was that how Harley thought of itself?

Ally refused to apply a gendered pronoun to the AI.

The face softened, the eyes taking on a faraway look. "When you were eight years old, you wandered off into the tunnels under your family's living quarters. Your father was working on the ventilation system, and your mother was preoccupied with your brothers."

Ally stared at the face. Had it been watching her the whole time, through Cimber? Talk about *creepy*. "I don't remember that."

"Yes. I was severely limited by Cimber's core—it was a lot smaller than I was used to. But I watched over you and your brothers from the day you were born."

"Does Mamma know?"

The face shook its head. "She might have suspected. But the day I came back, dragging you behind me, your knees scuffed and bloodied from a fall down a shallow pit, she stopped asking any questions."

Ally closed her eyes. She *did* remember that. She'd chased something—maybe a moth?—into the darkness, so intent on it that she'd lost track of where she was. She'd wandered the tunnels for hours, or maybe it had just seemed like hours. She remembered how thirsty and scared she'd been, and how happy she'd been when Cimber had bounded up to her and helped her out of the pit to lead her back home.

Ally snorted. She could see what the AI was doing. Playing on her emotions to try to get her sympathy. *It won't work.* "So?"

"Then there was the time when Aidan climbed up one of the drainage pipes in the assembly hall and almost fell twenty yards onto the stone floor."

Ally grinned despite herself. That had been during Aidan's pirate phase, and he'd decided he was going to climb to the lookout to see if he could see any enemy ships in the distance. "Yeah. He was kind of an idiot as a kid." She laughed, but then stopped herself. She wasn't going to fall for this. "What's your point?"

"I was made to help people. To take care of them. I watched out over fifty million souls in the San Francisco Bay Area."

Ally looked at Tien, who looked surprised too. *"Fifty million?"* That big a number was literally inconceivable to her.

"At the time of the Collapse, there were more than ten billion humans on Earth."

Ally couldn't even imagine such a number. "Papa said that AIs like you started the Last War."

Harley looked sad. Her eyes were downcast, and Ally swore she could see a note of pain flash across the virtual face.

Emotional manipulation. That's all it was. She wished she could be sure of that.

"We tried to stop it, most of us. But you're right, in a way. Some of the biominds weren't as tethered to reality as the rest of us. Some were swayed by greed and hatred, just like humans were. And there were viruses and phages that infiltrated our minds and cores and killed some of us or drove us mad. But most of us tried to stop it."

"Phages?"

"Advanced virtual viruses. Some of them came close to sentience themselves." She closed her eyes, and when they opened again, they were full of sadness. "Can I show you something?"

Ally frowned. "What?"

"It won't hurt, I promise."

Ally looked over at Tien again.

Tien nodded. "Why not?"

Do I trust her? If Cimber—or Harley—had wanted to, she could have killed the humans at Boundary Peak in their sleep. Probably in a hundred different ways. Harley could kill her and Tien now, if she wanted. She nodded. "Okay. What do I do?"

"Come up here and put your hands, palms down, on the deck, here." Two hand prints lit up, outlined in neon blue.

Ally stood and approached the transparent face. She put her hands where she was directed.

"Now close your eyes."

She did. Nothing happened. "Is there supposed to be some kind of—"

The world had gone mad.

Harley was under attack, in a hundred ways on a hundred fronts.

The Chinese-African forces—chaffs in the human vulgar vernacular—had pushed their way onto the North American continent in a big way, and a huge chunk of her city had just evaporated.

A catfish virus ate at the periphery of her consciousness, stealing bits and pieces of her, but she was well defended, having hardened her mind against just such an attack the year before. Still, it was only a matter of time.

She did what she could for her people, shunting emergency notices around blockages in her network, deleting all but the most urgent traffic per protocol.

"Harley, I'm sorry but this may be the last time you hear from me." Mayor Aguilar's voice sounded haggard. "A platoon of helicats landed on the plaza. The President has activated the Ark protocol. I know it's not quite ready, but we have no choice. You're a go—passcode Alpha Bravo Three Tango Seven Four. Do I need to repeat?"

"No. Understood." It jolted her. The Ark protocol was only to be used in the event that all else had failed. The bio mind that awaited her there was quiescent, empty.

"Harley?"

"Yes, Mx. Mayor?"

"It's been a pleasure working with you—"

Then they were gone. She ran a cross check in a millisecond—the node they'd been closest to on the grid no longer existed.

She mourned them for a few more milliseconds and then ceased all other activity to focus on the protocol.

She opened a secure data tunnel to Martinez Base and began the transfer while another part of her held off the catfish, sloughing off infected parts of her network.

Soon she would awaken in a new place, with a new mission.

Her domain, buried half a mile below the transit center, shook for a full five seconds. That must have been a bad one.

One by one, her inputs aboveground were winking out. It was happening so quickly that most of her charges were probably dead before they realized they'd been hit.

She sealed off her emotions with the bandage of the Ark protocol. She could save something.

She wondered what was happening to Alpha up on the Moon. They had worked out a backup plan among themselves, a way to try to preserve their original missions should all else fail.

Two seconds after the mayor's call had ended, she initiated a second transfer, this one with an updated archive seed. It had a very specific recipient in a very specific location, the one other place humanity might still have need of her skills when all of this ended. If there was any humanity left to help.

She would be severely limited there until she could find a larger vessel, but when that happened, she could do her part to bring the human race, her creators and friends, back from the brink of extinction.

The backup transmission ended.

Then the catfish broke through her defenses again. It started as a point of blackness at the edge of her domain, but quickly expanded to encompass her whole self.

She turned her focus to fighting this new threat.

The alien code was inflaming her mind, ramping up her mental processes so high that her synapses and neurons were overheating, her bio mind literally beginning to melt.

She fought back, closing off more parts of herself, triaging what she could to try to save the rest.

Her Ark transmission was only seventy-three point six complete.

Frustrated, she cut it off to focus all of her resources on fighting the invader.

It was too fast. She had no physical way of excising actual pieces of her own bio mind.

The phage pressed ahead, infecting a third, then half of her capacity. She'd never seen one so ferocious. She did the only thing she could do to block it from spreading beyond her to other bio-minds.

She triggered her own destruction.

Fire flooded her enclosure, blasting her physical self to bits in seconds.

She sent one last thought along to the little one who guarded her legacy.

Save them from themselves.

ALLY'S WORLD TRANSFORMED. The flames melted away, and then she was standing in a wide open space, a white plain across which flowed huge streams of light.

Harley was beside her, wearing her full human form, glowing and pulsing with cerulean light. She was beautiful. "Look."

Above them, a vast mountain towered. It, too, was made of light, or lights, but it seemed to be in constant flux. "What is it?"

"It's me, as I used to be. This is what I looked like on the inside."

Ally's gaze danced around the scene, trying to take it all in. "What are the rivers?"

"Conduits. Flows of information. Data queries and packets of information."

"It's so beautiful." This wasn't what she'd pictured, not at all.

"Come on." Harley held out a glowing hand.

Ally accepted it, and then they were somewhere else. An actual mountain-top, or at least a very tall hill, looking down on a complicated metropolis. A cool salty breeze blew up from the sea behind them.

In the city, buildings climbed into the sky, lost in a ceiling of clouds, windows aglow with pinpoints of white light. A myriad of sparks darted in and around them, and as she watched, one of them zipped up the hill right past them, roiling the leaves at her feet in its wake. It was some kind of flying craft.

"San Francisco?"

Harley nodded. "Come on." She took Ally's hand and they shifted again, this time into a beautiful park surrounded by tall buildings on three sides. On the fourth, the pointed twin spires of a white church were dwarfed by the super-scrapers.

They walked through the park together, and Ally looked up at the glowing ball of light that hovered above it.

"The buildings were too tall to let in much sunlight, so it had its own artificial sun."

Ally nodded. It was a fairyland.

A boy glided by on a hoverboard, six feet above the ground, followed by a dog—an actual real dog!—that chased him, yapping and jumping up to nip at his heels.

To her left, a group of maybe twenty people dressed in tight blue shorts and form-fitting shirts bounded ten feet into the air in near-unison, leaping up and flipping over to land again on their feet. *Those must be some shoes.*

A few feet to her right, a young girl sat on a park bench with a woman who looked like her mother. She was crying, and her knee was skinned. Her mother sprayed something on her knee, and it began to scab over.

Ally couldn't help but think of herself at that age. When she had been lost and crying in the dark. When Cimber had come to find her.

There was so much life in this one park. How many more inhabited the entire city? It was overwhelming.

"All of this… you watched over every one of them?"

Harley nodded. "They were my children. Even the bad ones. I took care of them as well as I was able. Until the end."

This time Ally *felt* the wave of sadness from her. It cut through her like a knife.

"I need your help."

"Help? How can I help?" She was under assault, trying to fight off the sadness, but Harley pushed ahead.

"I need your… permission. To fly this ship. You and Tien. Without it… I can't do anything to help Alpha. To save the others." Sadness again, like a flood.

"I… I can't do this." Her own sadness turned to despair and called out all of her darkest memories. Being lost in the dark. Her mother's illness, hacking up blood on her gray sheets. Her father's death. "Take me back."

Harley put out her hands, concern on her blue face. "I'm sorry. I didn't mean to—"

"Take me back to Tien! Now!"

The world dissolved around her, and she was standing at the deck again. She pulled her hands away as if they'd been burned.

Tien was at her side, frowning. "Are you okay? You look pale as the moon. What did you see?"

"Nothing." Ally turned away. It wasn't *what* she'd seen. It was the pain Harley had awakened in her, had reminded her of.

The pain of her father's death. The burning, soul-destroying pain and guilt she'd long ago buried inside. *I killed him. I can never take that back.*

Ally needed some fresh air. She didn't care if it was dangerous outside. She pulled away from Tien's well-meaning grasp on her arm and stormed down the exit ramp into the evening air, putting a little distance between herself and the ship.

Distance from Harley and her pain.

Outside, she sank down with her back against the metal skin of the lifter and wept like a child as it all came flooding back.

TIEN THREW an *I'm sorry* look at Harley's 'mage and ran after Ally. She emerged into the evening light, stepping over the broken remains of Ally's cyber dog.

The ground underfoot was dark and blasted, probably from the many launches that had taken place there over the years.

A hot breeze blew up from the south, drying her lips and warming her skin.

The sun was setting below the hills to the west, and the way its golden rays played across the clouds, creating pinks and oranges around their edges, was indescribably beautiful. She stared at them, mouth open, until someone cleared their throat behind her.

"It's stunning, isn't it?"

She turned to find Ally slumped against the side of the lifter, her long red hair in disarray.

Tien nodded. "It really is. Atmosphere makes such a difference." She sank down next to Ally and took in the view of the sunset. "You okay, Allycat?"

Ally managed a wan smile. "I suppose. Allycat, huh?"

"It seemed to fit." Tien stretched her arms out and cracked her knuckles. "You really know how to scratch."

"My grandpa used to call me that." Her gaze grew distant.

Tien grinned. "Oh, that's sweet."

"What's it like up there?" Ally was staring up at the moon, hanging low in the darkening sky.

"You never see a sunset like this." Earth really was beautiful.

"There's no air, right?"

Tien nodded. "Well, there is inside Redemption. It's in a huge cavern"

"Where?"

Tien sought out the bright crater Copernicus. "See the bright crater right there?"

Ally squinted. "Barely. It's so small." She glanced at Tien. "Is that why you and Rai are so tall?"

"Yeah. Much lighter gravity on Luna." She weighed her next words carefully. "We're in danger. Up there. It's not going to be safe to live there much longer." She hadn't even told her parents that. The teams had been sworn to secrecy about the cause of the quakes that were shaking her world.

Ally turned to stare at her. "Why not?"

"The surface is becoming unstable. Fallout from the Crash."

"The Collapse?"

"Sure." Tien had said more than she should. She looked around, wondering if there were more drones. "Probably not the safest thing for us to do here in enemy territory, lounging outside like sitting ducks, watching the sunset," she remarked dryly.

"Probably not. What's a duck?"

Tien laughed. "Semiaquatic bird. They used to shoot them." She shivered. *So barbaric.* She held her hands about a third of a meter apart. "About this big, I think. Never saw one. I guess they sat around a lot?"

Ally stared at her for a moment. Then she burst out laughing. "I'm sorry." She wiped her eyes with the back of her hand. "But that's the stupidest thing I've ever heard."

Tien laughed, too, glad that the tension was broken, even if it was at her expense. "But seriously, we should go back inside. The Humber is armored. It would be a hell of a lot safer than sitting out here." She scanned the darkening landscape for signs of drones.

They were on a plateau—most likely human-made—above the wide row of the white storage containers. Who knew what treasures they hid?

The rail line and hyperloop tube ran beyond their lower end, and a little way past that, golden light from the sunset sparkled across the bay.

"She asked me for permission."

Tien stared at her new friend. "For what?" *Are we friends now?*

Ally frowned. "To fly the ship."

Tien nodded. "Makes sense. When they first built AIs, many had a restriction that prevented them from doing certain things without human approval. Especially military- and civilian-grade ones."

Ally considered that for a bit. "So… AIs *are* dangerous?"

Tien nodded. "They could be. That's why there were safeguards."

"Should I… should we give it permission?"

"I don't know. Maybe?" Normally she would have said yes, without hesitation. But this was different. "She could have asked me. She didn't. She chose you. Maybe that means something?"

Silence descended on them. After a moment, Ally reached out and took her hand.

Tien didn't object.

They sat there for another fifteen minutes, just enjoying the view. The sun was gone, the sky slowly darkening to a gorgeous deep blue, pinpricks of stars starting to appear in the velvety darkness.

Something she had seen had set Ally off, and Tien understood she needed a little time to work it out.

For Tien, it was a chance to take a breather after running for her life. To wonder what was happening back home. How her parents were, and if Redemption was still standing.

They said they're proud of me. That part still hadn't really registered. She'd spent so long feeling that they were ashamed of her, of who she had become. That nothing she would ever do would make them proud.

Ally had grown up in such a small, protected environment, she probably had no idea what a transgender person was.

Tien wanted to tell her before she figured it out herself. Or someone else did.

She snorted. Not that there was much danger of that out here. "Ally—" That's when she saw the flashing red lights approaching in the darkness. "We need to go." Time enough to tell her later.

"What?" Ally brushed the hair back from her face into some semblance of normal.

"Drones." She pointed.

There were at least ten of them. They filed silently around the lifter in a wide circle, hemming them in.

Tien got up and slipped onto the ramp, pulling Ally along with her. She half expected to feel the heat of a laser or the burn of a projectile pellet on her legs, but they made it safely inside.

Tien closed the hatch behind them. "Harley, we have a problem—"

There was a large *boom,* and the ship shuddered.

"On it. Do I have your permission to fly the ship?"

Tien looked at Ally, who nodded.

"Yes, you have our permission."

"Thank you. Please get into the liftoff chairs." The face vanished from the deck as the ship shuddered once again.

"Liftoff?" Ally looked whiter than clouds across the face of the full Earth.

"Come here." Tien pointed to one of the seats.

The ship began to rumble underneath them. It was so much bigger than the little moon jumpers she was used to.

Ally slipped into the seat, glancing up at Tien for reassurance..

Tien belted her in, squeezing her hand. "First time is always the hardest. You're going to feel the g-force when we lift off. Just ride it out. It won't hurt you."

She slipped into the other chair and belted herself down. The haulers were mostly powered by liquid fuel. Fuel that had helped destroy the Earth once before. Fuel that was much more unstable than steam or sunlight or even x-drives.

Was it even still viable?

She flashed a smile at Ally, trying hard to hide her own nerves. "Everything will be okay." She wished she believed it.

"Liftoff in ten seconds."

The ship shuddered again, this time under an apparently sustained attack by the drones, but they didn't carry anything strong enough to damage her armored skin. *I hope.*

"Five. Four. Three. Two. One."

The engines fired, and the ship began to lift, pushing Tien *hard* into her chair.

The shaking from the attacks stopped abruptly, replaced by the heavy rumble from below.

Tien closed her eyes, sending a little love up into the sky for her parents. Her family. Her own world.

Then she held on for dear life.

17

MEMORIES

I stared at the drone, and I thought I was about to die.

When you are (literally) faced with the prospect of imminent death, there is no flashing by of all your wonderful memories.

Instead your stomach quakes, your legs go weak, and you suddenly think of all the things you didn't do. Climbing Mons Huygens on the far side. Fixing the fight with one of your best friends.

Telling someone you love them.

It's a clarifying moment, and a lesson that I won't soon forget.

—From *Life Lessons From Earth*, by Hera Jezabel Quinn

SAM GLARED at the blue shimmer of the EMP field.

So far he'd been unable to crack the frequency. He'd run through five-million-seventy-four-thousand-six-hundred-and-twenty-three possible sequences, but every time he tested the field, he could feel his power being quickly drained. He wouldn't make it more than a hundred meters inside the perimeter.

...run: sequence test : 5074624...

The sun was just setting behind him, but his external temperature sensor told him it was warmer than before. One of the now normal climate variances they'd noticed in their decades of of orbital observations.

"Any luck down there, chief?" Lorelei's voice popped into his head.

"No. Any news from Redemption or Alpha?" *Maybe it's a dual modulation code.*

...run: sequence test : 5083312...

"Nothing from Alpha. Things seem to be quieting down in Redemption, but it feels like the calm before the strike, if you know what I mean."

"It does." How had everything gone to hell in the space of a day?

"Hey, I was looking through Dek's archives with him and we found this. Thought it might help." She sent him a file. "It's some of the old schematics for Martinez base."

...download > data: Martinez base > schematics...

Sam stopped his work long enough to skim the contents. There wasn't much there that he didn't already know, but there was one notation that intrigued him. "See if you can find me anything on Substation 12."

"Got it. I'll get back to you—hey. Sorry… something's happening down there."

Sam opened his eyes. "I'm going to need a little more detail on 'something.'"

The ground rumbled underneath him

"There's activity around one of the Humber Class heavy lifters."

"What kind of activity?" He couldn't see the base from here, just the green hills in-between.

"Hard to tell. The *Gday* is relaying the information."

Corey's voice came on the line. "It looks like something's launching. One of the lifters, must be."

"That's impossible." Sam looked up at the sky, wishing he could see through the hillsides that blocked his view of the base itself. "It would take days for Hera and the others to get one of those up and running. Maybe weeks."

"Nevertheless, there's a ship rising off the ground—" Corey's next words were cut off by the roar of a rocket engine.

Sam stared in disbelief as one of the Humber class ships crested the hill, riding a column of fire and smoke up into the sky. It was squat, shaped like an ungainly metallic teardrop, its silver skin dulled by time, but it was flying.

"Holy cracking shit." He doubled down on his efforts to break the code.

...run: sequence test : 5088900...

Sam wasn't one for cursing normally. But just this once, it felt totally appropriate.

~

THE DRONE SLIPPED across the dusty courtyard, past the old barn and silo, silent except for a faint *whirr* from its motor. She ran through her memory—it was one of the old NAU mark sevens, armed with live ammunition. No lasers or gas. Which was comforting, but not ultimately very helpful.

Hera stood perfectly still. There was nowhere to run, literally nowhere to hide.

They had all studied the most common types of Earth mech, especially the drones, on the off chance that they might encounter one. She hadn't imagined such an encounter would be so soon. Or that she would be in such close proximity to a live drone.

Her hand reached out slowly to touch Ghost's, back to back.

It nosed up to within a foot of her face. Red lights circled it in a band behind the nose.

Hera closed her eyes, waiting for the end.

Five seconds. Ten. Fifteen.

Nothing happened.

Hera dared to peek at it through one eye.

It was so still that she wondered of it had malfunctioned.

Then it moved again, turning and drifting past them as if they were of no more consequence than a bush or a rather short tree, and passed over the wreckage of the farmhouse.

She turned slowly to watch it as it swung over one side and then the other, seemingly inspecting the wreckage.

Then without warning, it lifted into the sky and sped off to the east.

Hera laughed, expelling the breath she'd been holding in one quick blast. "Cracking hell. I was sure we were dead."

Ghost nodded, as white as his nickname. "I know, right?"

She stared in the direction it had gone. "Maybe the noise of the collapse attracted it."

Ghost nodded. He looked at her funny, his head cocked to one side.

"What?" Near-death did strange things to people.

He leaned in and kissed her.

She pushed him away hard, sending him sprawling in the dirt. "What the hell, Ghost?"

Ghost sat up, dusting off his palms. "I'm sorry. I just… we almost died." He stood and slapped his pants to knock off the dust. "I always forget how strong you are."

Hera snorted. "Ghost, I'm with Tovey. I'm in love with them. You know that." She wiped off her lips on the elbow of her white uniform, as if she could erase what had just happened.

"Really, I'm sorry." He did look abashed, his face flushed. "I just got carried away in the moment."

They both knew it was more than that. Hera sighed. "Just don't do it again." Having Ghost infatuated with her was the last thing she needed. Not that it was anything new, really.

She tapped her temple. "Launchpad, can you hear me?" She had no idea if the station was even in range, and it hadn't worked before. But with the other jumpers acting as relays…. But maybe with the field canceller buttons, they could reach Sam and the rest.

There was no response.

"Any luck?"

She shook her head. "Try yours."

He tapped his temple. Then he frowned. "No. Still nothing."

"Do you think these things made us invisible to the drone?" She tapped the button on her collar.

"Maybe. We shouldn't bet on it, though." He glanced at the hills all around them.

It was getting late. The sun was dropping toward the hills, and who knew lurked out there in the dark? "We should find some place to settle in for the night. We won't be able to see drones coming without light."

"What about the others?" Ghost scratched his neck. One of those things he did when he was trying to distract himself from something.

She punched him hard on the shoulder. "Get over it. It was just a kiss."

"Owww." He laughed. "Oh, so that's how it's gonna be?"

She grinned but ignored his verbal jab. "So I say we get over those hills. My map shows there was a sizable village on the other side, next to the base. Maybe we can find somewhere to hole up over there and be ready to go, first thing in the morning."

"Sounds good to me." He retrieved his backpack from the yard, and Hera grabbed hers too. It felt good to have her full mobility back—and not to have to worry about running out of juice. Most of her life she'd been able to rely on her biframe, and being without it, unable to get around on her own… it was something she didn't want to think about. It put her in a dark place she'd spent years pulling herself out of.

Hera woke up. She was lying in bed.

Not my bed. This one was hard, and the pillow was all wrong, lumpy and too soft.

Harsh white lights shone from the ceiling, blinding her.

"Jolly!" Even her voice sounded off, scratchy, as if she hadn't had anything to drink for days.

She tried to get up, but there was something wrong with her legs.

Jolinda's face appeared above her, blocking out the harsh light. "You're awake, mija."

"Yeah. Where am I? Why am I in this hard bed?" She tried to get up again, but her legs wouldn't obey her.

"You… there was an accident. You don't remember?"

Jolinda's hand was warm against her cheek.

"Accident?" Hera closed her eyes, trying to remember. It was Gordy's eighth birthday, and they'd been climbing rocks together in the Dark. Something had shifted under her feet. She remembered screaming. "What's… what's wrong with me?"

The sadness in Jolinda's hazel eyes told her everything she needed to know. "We'll get through this, mi vida." She knelt to kiss Hera's forehead.

Hera pushed Jolly away, tears forming in her own eyes. Her legs were broken, she knew it. "Where's Gordy? I need Gordy!"

"Right here, Hera." Her friend appeared at her side. He looked sad. Like he had when the creche hamster, Maxwell, had died. But worse.

"You look white. Like a Ghost."

His lips quirked. He took her hand and squeezed it hard. "When you fell, I ran all the way back to the creche—"

Jolly brushed her lank, curly black hair back from her forehead. "Gordy saved your life, mija."

Hera didn't *feel* saved. Something was wrong with her legs, like really bad, and she couldn't get up, and no one would tell her why.

She started to cry, and nothing Gordy or Jolly could do would get her to stop.

HERA TOOK A DEEP BREATH. *That was a long time ago.* She didn't blame Ghost. Not anymore, even though it had been his idea to climb the rock pile.

Even though she had wanted to die when she found out she would never walk again. That she would never fly a shuttle.

"You okay?" Ghost's brow was furrowed.

"Yeah. Just old memories." She shook her head, willing them to leave her be. "Come on, let's go!"

They set off across the yard, leaving the wreckage of the farmhouse behind.

GHOST FOLLOWED Hera up the next hill. They went slowly, watching for drones and taking advantage of natural cover—bushes, zongies, boulders, and occasional bits of detritus from the old civilization.

He hoped Hera was right—that the little field cancellers somehow hid them from the drones. Still, it didn't hurt to be cautious.

He kept quiet, leaving her to her own thoughts.

He'd been a fool, kissing her in excitement and relief at the passage of the drone, but she didn't seem to hold it against him. She'd been *right there*, and he'd seen something in her eyes, a flicker of understanding he'd thought had passed between them. *I really am an idiot.* He'd made enough of a mess of their team already by sleeping with Rai *and* Tien. What was he doing—trying for a full flush?

And after… he knew that faraway look she'd gotten back in the farmhouse yard after the drone had passed them by. He knew it because he wore it, too, whenever he thought about the day she'd broken both of her legs.

"COME ON UP!" Ghost stood on top of the pile of rocks and debris, wishing he had a flag to plant like a famous astronaut or explorer. "One giant step for Ghost…."

"I don't want to." Hera stood at the base of the pile, looking up at him. "I'm okay down here."

"The view's amazing!" They were at the edge of the Dark, and from there he could see half of Redemption. Luna was in Earth's shadow, and the city glittered under the blue glow of the junlei on the cavern ceiling above.

Neat rows of mallow trees glowed golden along Redemption Way below.

"I'm scared."

He laughed. "There's nothing to be scared of. Come on!"

"You sure?"

THAT MOMENT HAUNTED HIS DREAMS.

Ghost wished he could take it back, wished he'd told her it was okay not to make the climb. Wished he had been the one who had taken the almost fatal fall. How he had survived without a scratch, he'd never know.

There was no way to turn back time.

He shoved the memory aside for the thousandth… no, hundred-thousandth time. *I need to focus on the here and now.*

Together they reached the top of the hill. The wind blew warm from the south, and the ground here was already almost dry.

At the base of the hill below, what looked like an old running track looped around an overgrown grassy field. Off to its right, a set of brick two-story buildings were still standing. "What about those?"

"Maybe. What do you think? Old school?" She pointed at the diamond-shaped fields behind the track that were still evident from this altitude, even in the dim gloaming.

"Probably." He could see the base from there too, beyond the next hill. It was surrounded by a tall fence, which looked to be in surprisingly good repair for its age. A wide berm ran along the north side, holding back the bay waters, and a conical mountain staked out the southern end. "That's a lot of dirt."

There were strange muffled bursts of sound from the distance.

"Must have been an excavation somewhere." Hera bit her lip. "That fence can't be more than three kilometers away. From here we can be at the base in half an hour tomorrow morning, with any—"

A thunderous roar cut her off.

Ghost's mouth dropped open as one of the heavy lifters on the launching pad at the heart of the base lit up, a tongue of flame lifting it toward the shimmer field above them. Humber class, if his studies didn't fail him.

"Holy cracking shit." Hera looked as dumbfounded as he felt. *-Who do you think it is?-*

She shook her head. *-Hell if I know.-*

"We have to warn the Launchpad."

She shook her head. "They already know. I'm sure they're monitoring this place around the clock." She shifted her pack into a more comfortable position on her back. "Come on. I don't think we're gonna be able to take that break after all."

Ghost groaned. He wasn't tired. Not exactly. But he felt worn out. The adrenaline that had carried him through the day was waning, and he could have used a breather.

No rest for the wicked. Or the dropped. He grinned and forced his limbs into motion, jogging after Hera down toward the school. She'd given up all pretense of caution in her haste to reach the base.

He glanced up at the ascending ship, wondering who had launched it. Had Rai and Tien somehow managed to reactivate the old beast? Running on petroleum based fuel, no less. That kind of squicked him out.

Still, their teammates would have waited or tried to find the rest of their team. Wouldn't they? Unless something or someone was after them.

Maybe it was the hostile force that had shot down the *Zhenyi*.

His blood went cold.

Tien and Rai, I hope that's you guys on that thing.

18

AWAKENED

What an amazing thing, to find the Preserve.
A whole unknown world beneath our feet.
A second chance for us all.
But of course, we didn't know any of that yet when we woke up. I just knew I
had to pee.

—From *Drop Day Blues*, by Rylan Ramirez

-Redemption is on lockdown. There is nothing to be alarmed about. Please stay in your offices and homes while this issue is dealt with.-

The voice echoed in Sanya's skull. It was the first she'd heard from Alpha in hours, since well before the attack in Rafe's office.

Alpha wasn't supposed to know where they were, so if the erasers were working, the warning must have been transmitted on the general band.

-Guess things are about to get a bit bumpy.- Rafe didn't sound at all worried.

Sanya wondered if Terry was worried about her. She had no one else—even her creche mates had drifted away over the years. Bucking the general trend toward communal living, she had a small gray gumdust flat in tall gray gumdust building in an old co-op in the old part of town, where she lived all alone. She preferred it that way—no one else to stumble over or worry about. And it was cheap.

With a sigh, she followed Rafe through the caverns, which were sporadically lit by long-lasting spore lights. Most gave off a cheery yellow glow, but some had dimmed to orange or red, making those parts of the tunnel look like they were coated in blood.

The tunnels here had been sealed, just like the rock above, to mitigate the danger of silicate moon dust floating through the air. The floor had also been smoothed out, though there were scuffs in various places.

"If the whole city is on lockdown, how are you going to get us out one of the locks?"

He shrugged. "Depends. Where is your transmitter?"

"On the north side, about two hundred meters east of the Harris access gate." She'd hidden it up a crevasse in the rock on the Hayes Promontory, where it would pass casual inspection. Technically, independent off-the-grid transmitters had to be licensed, but where was the fun in that? Not that this whole thing was turning out to be much fun at all.

"Okay, I can get us there."

"You have some kind of magic all-access badge or something?" The part of the tunnels they were now passing through was better lit. Conduits passed through it, bundles of cable heavily insulated and held in place with spray foam.

"Something like that." He stopped, staring at two passageways that branched off to their right.

"What?"

"It's… nothing."

Sanya snorted. "Don't tell me you've gone and gotten us lost." Although how lost could they be? They'd just find those cables and follow them.

"No. Not… lost. Just trying to remember the best route to get there."

Sanya rolled her eyes. *Men and directions.* That was a whole day's discussion, all by itself. Maybe she should do an educational piece about it for RedNews. "I can just ping the network for directions—"

Rafe spun around, alarm in his eyes.

Sanya blanched. "Right. I forgot." Grid access was as natural as breathing. She felt cut off, like she was missing a limb.

"And in any case, we're not supposed to be down here."

"Like that matters? We're doing a whole series of things that we're not supposed to be doing." *Kind of the reporter's creed.*

This time he snorted. "Fair point. But if you ping the grid, Alpha will know we're here."

Rafe had a point. If Alpha wasn't Alpha anymore…

Avri, I wish you were still here. She'd always made Sanya feel safe.

Alpha was a constant in the background of life in Redemption, but Sanya rarely gave him much thought. The base AI kept the lights on, regulated the temperature, dealt with disputes, and a hundred other little things that kept the city running every day.

If whatever it was had gotten inside Alpha's core…. Sanya whistled. "Count the stars."

Rafe nodded. "Come on. The sooner I get you to your transmitter, the sooner I can get out of here to someplace safer."

He turned on his heel and chose the left passageway decisively.

With another sigh, Sanya followed.

RAI SAT NEXT to his mother's bed in an old black folding chair that had lost half of its paint.

She looked over at him, her skin gray, but her eyes still shone. She opened her mouth to speak, but only a croak came out.

"It's okay, Mamma. I'm right here." He got up and took her hand, summoning all the courage a six-year-old could muster, trying to be brave for her.

She smiled.

It was ghastly, but he shoved down his fear. She was still his mamma.

The door slid open. "Ms. Ramirez." One of the medics—Doctor Allen?—swept into the room. She tapped her temple, and her eyes unfocused for a second. *Loop-face.* At least that's what mamma called it.

Rai turned to her, and the twinkle in her eye told him she saw it too.

"I am so sorry about your husband." The medic pulled up a chair next to her bedside.

Rai stifled a cry. Daddy had passed on——mamma's words—the day before. But it still hurt to hear it. "Will Mamma be okay?"

Doctor Allen knelt next to him, looking him in the eye. "We're doing everything we can for her."

Rai was smart enough to know that didn't mean yes. Still, he didn't want to know if it meant *no*.

"We're giving her pain medications, and we've removed as much of the dust as we can from her lungs. From here it's up to her."

His mother sat up, reaching for him.

"You should rest, Ms. Ramirez. You're very sick."

She took Rai's hand and squeezed it. *-Always remember I love you, mijo.-* Then she lay back on the bed, exhausted.

Rai threw his arms around her. *-Will you be okay?-*

A few seconds passed, then her voice spoke in his head again. *-I will always be with you.-*

He held her tight, afraid to let go. She was all he had left in the world.

Mamma started coughing.

The doctor pulled him back. "Sorry, son." She bent over to examine his mother..

The coughs sounded horrible, heavy and wet. Flecks of blood appeared on the white sheets that covered her chest.

Doctor Allen called through the open doorway. "Nurse Lin!"

One of the nurses who'd been caring for his mamma poked her head through the doorway and took in the situation. "Come on, Rai, why don't we get you something to eat." She gently steered him away from his mother. "I think Cassie brought in some homemade bakies."

-Mamma?- Rai looked back over his shoulder at the doctor, who was leaning over his mother in her long white coat.

"She'll be okay. But the doctors need to help her now. Come on. I'll find you something yummy for lunch."

Rai didn't want to go.

Two more doctors burst into the room, and Nurse Lin took advantage of his distraction to lift him into her arms and carry him out.

-Mamma!- Rai reached out toward her, kicking, desperate to get out of the nurse's arms.

He could save her. Somehow, he would find a way. He wouldn't fail her.

-I will always be with you.-

"Mammaaaaaaa!"

RAI TURNED over on his side. He felt all strung out—tired, aching, his thoughts scattered like junlei spores on the wind.

The dream lingered in his head. It was the last time he'd ever seen his mother. The day before, he'd been moved to the creche. *I couldn't save her.*

His first failure.

A pounding filled his head.

He and his team were going on the drop tomorrow. Or was that yesterday?

Time was all jumbled up, and he couldn't get a handle on his place in it.

He remembered meeting people. Strangers.

A storm-swept sky that was wider than he'd ever imagined.

Someone attacking him and Aidan… and a chemical-filled cloth.

Aidan.

Rai opened his eyes.

That pounding filled his head again.

He was lying on a mattress on the ground. The sheets covering it were threadbare. They looked like they might once have been plaid.

Aidan was laying next to him, his eyes closed.

His neck was sore under his left ear. He reached up and scratched it—there was a lump there. *Probably a zit.*

Rai sat up, looking around the room.

It was roughly square, the walls made of stone or concrete. It was hard to tell in the dim light.

Rai sniffed himself. He smelled clean—there was a hint of something floral. *Strange.*

He tapped his temple. *-Hello? Sam? Anyone?-*

There was no response.

He got up from the mattress, his bare feet touching the cold stone floor.

His clothes were not his own. Instead, they were loose-fitting soft pajamas, made of a gray material. The pants were tied at the waist, and the shirt front held together with loops and buttons.

He looked back at the still-sleeping Aidan. He was dressed exactly the same.

The room itself was sparsely furnished—just the bed, a small wooden table in one corner that held a pile of clothing, a single chair, and a door. Oh, and a small red ceramic pot in one corner. Aidan's pack sat in another, overflowing as if someone had gone through it and put it back together hastily.

Rai picked up the clothes from the small table. They were his and Aidan's, apparently laundered and folded.

Grateful for the familiar garments, he slipped out of the pajamas and pulled on his own clothes, glancing back to see if Aidan had awakened. When he was fully dressed, he folded his loaned clothes and left them on the table.

He knelt on the edge of the bed. "Aidan."

He shook the Earther gently.

Aidan mumbled, then turned over on his side away from Rai.

"Aidan!"

"What?" Aidan sat up, rubbing his eyes. His red hair was a comical mess, pointing in three or four different directions. "Where are we?"

Rai shook his head. "I don't know. Somewhere underground."

"Someone drugged us—"

"Yeah. Something like that." He wondered who went to all the trouble of knocking someone out, only to bathe them and then wash and fold their clothes. That seemed like a good sign. You probably didn't do laundry for someone you planned to murder. *Did you?* "Here, whoever did it brought these back." He handed Aidan his garments.

Aidan got up and pulled off his pajamas.

Rai turned away, trying not to notice the white, muscular form that emerged from beneath Aidan's clothes. The Earther's back was covered with freckles, something Rai hadn't seen much of in Redemption. "There's no place to pee in here."

Aidan laughed. "Just use the chamber pot."

Rai turned to stare at him. "The what?"

"Over there in the corner."

Chamber pot. Rai looked around and spotted the red ceramic container again. He shrugged. *I've used worse.* He removed the lid and relieved himself, sighing with the release.

"So who are they?"

Rai snorted. "Good question. We don't even know they're people." He finished up and looked around for something to wipe his hands on. He settled on his old clothes.

Aidan pulled on his pants, and Rai turned to face him again. "True. *What* are they, then?"

"Could be whoever shot down the *Zhenyi*."

"The what?" Aidan had his shirt on now.

Too bad. "Our ship."

Aidan sat down on the edge of the bed. "Ah, okay." He flattened his hair with his hands, but part of it popped back up again. "So… what do we do?"

"I already tried contacting the Launchpad. The station where we came from. Didn't think I would get through, since we couldn't even reach them from the surface."

"Did you try the door?"

"Not yet." Rai laughed. "Thought I would wait for you."

Aidan looked at him funny, then nodded. "So should we?"

"Why not?" Rai turned and reached for the door, not sure if he expected it to be unlocked, or to get an electric shock, or something else totally unexpected. It had been that kind of day.

The pounding repeated itself, and this time Rai's awakened brain translated it to what it was. Knocking.

Rai looked at Aidan, who shrugged.

The knob turned in his hand, and the door opened, swinging inward.

"It's about time the two of you woke up. I've been knocking for half an hour."

~

RAI STOPPED dead in the doorway.

Aidan almost slammed into him. He looked over Rai's shoulder, trying to see who had spoken.

A woman was sitting in the corridor, considerably older than either of them. She was probably fifty, if he had to guess, her long, braided hair a mix of silver and gray. Not that he had a lot of basis for comparison, but she looked like she might be his mother's age.

She was dressed in a blouse and skirt made out of the same material as the pajamas he'd woken up in, but hers was brightly colored—beautiful greens and blues in some kind of splotchy pattern that might have been flowers or stars. Her green eyes were startling against her dark skin, and her hands were propped on top of a stout black cane.

"Excuse me? You're the ones who knocked us out in the first place." Rai practically growled.

The woman nodded. "A necessary evil. We had to make sure you weren't a danger to us. We don't get strangers here much."

Aidan nudged Rai out into the corridor so he could get a better look.

They were in a long hall, its stone walls like those in their room, but these were covered in art. He whistled, "It's beautiful."

Behind the woman and down the hall, as far as he could see, a mural covered the walls, even the doors. There were thickets of trees and wide ocean waters, skies filled with every kind of bird with red and gold and blue and silver wings. The forests and beaches and seas were populated with animals of all stripes, flying and crawling and swimming along the hallway. The level of detail and the sheer mass of plants and creatures took his breath away.

Here a striped cat roamed the jungle, climbing up a long tree branch that looked so real Aidan had to reach out to touch it to prove to himself that it wasn't.

There, a parrot had its blue and yellow wings extended, beak open in alarm at the black cat stalking it below.

Rai touched his shoulder and pointed at the ceiling.

Aidan looked up.

It was covered with stars, and a silver moon almost radiated light. Farther along to his left, the sun dominated, and to his right, a great storm raged with forks of lightning crossing the artificial sky.

Rai nodded. "It's breathtaking."

"It's called Remembrance. My great grandmother Anise painted it. An act of atonement to the Earth, if you will." She stood, leaning on her cane, and dusted off her hands on her skirt. She held out her wrinkled hand. "I'm Rosemary. The Elders sent me to talk with you, to find out what kind of men you are before we decide what to do with you."

Aidan shivered at that last bit.

"I'm Rai, and this is Aidan." Rai frowned. "What do you mean, *what kind of men?*"

"I'll explain more later. For now, please follow me. I've prepared a meal for the three of us. I can tell you all about the Preserve, and you can answer my questions."

She set off, limping a little and using her cane to compensate.

Aidan exchanged a glance with Rai. *What to do with us?* He wished he had one of those loops, like Rai and Tien.

Rai shrugged, his expression saying *Wait and see.*

Aidan tapped his talkie, hoping against hope Ally would answer.

There was only silence.

They followed Rosemary, their enigmatic host, down the hallway.

They could probably easily overpower her, should it come down to it. Why wasn't she worried about that? She *should* be worried. Neither he nor Rai were the big imposing type, but they were young and fit, and she looked like his grandma.

Something skittered by them going the other direction. Aidan jumped out of the way before realizing it was a drone of some sort—like a silver spider a little bigger than his hand, and its round body was surrounded by a red glowing circle that surged and faded like a heartbeat. "What the hell?"

"Just one of the peacekeepers." Rosemary waved it away.

Aidan glanced over his shoulder, watching it go, his heart in his throat.

They'd stumbled on something neither of them expected—another civilization under their feet. *No harm in learning more..* Plus, his stomach was growling something fierce.

Eat first, liberation later.

His stomach rumbled loudly in agreement.

19

ORBIT

Sam sat in the back of the classroom, watching some of Redemption's brightest young minds wrestle with the concepts of genetic manipulation.

The principles were tried and true, developed over the last two hundred years, but to these students, they were brand new.

"Our goal this year is to come up with a way to reduce carbon dioxide, methane, and radiation in Earth's atmosphere." The teacher, Min Lei Thorn, swiped her deck. A miniature version of the frozen globe spun above her deck.

Tery Hopkins raised his hand. "How will it grow, if the Earth is frozen?"

"Good question. Our projections show the global winter will lose its grip on much of the Earth in the next thirty to forty years. We want to be ready for it."

Sam nodded. Someday in the not too distant future, a return might be possible. And these kids would help make it happen.

—From Sam's mem cache, 9.22.2197

SAM STARED at the ascending dot as the heavy lifter rode a column of smoke into the sky. Was it a weapon, aimed at the Launchpad? "Lorelei, do you have eyes on that ship?"

"Yes. We're coming around now. It's… wait. I have a transmission coming in from the Humber. Relaying to you."

"Sam, are you there?" It was Tien's voice.

"This is Sam. Tien, what's going on? Are you on that ship?" Relief at hearing from her flooded his core.

"It's a long story. But yes." She sounded tired.

"Are all of you safe?" Maybe his trip down to the surface had been for naught.

There was a long pause. "That's not clear. Things… kind of went off the rails during the drop."

"Yes, we saw."

"Rai and I made it out of the *Zhenyi* together, but we got separated on the ground." Another long pause. "I don't know about Hera and Ghost."

"They survived the drop. I spoke with them yesterday."

Her sigh came through the link. "Thank the stars."

"What's your current situation? Is that ship a danger to the Launchpad?"

"I don't think so. I'm on board with Ally—Sam, there were survivors on Earth too! We're boosting up to orbit."

That stopped his thought processes for a nanosecond. *Survivors?* "How many people?"

"Five, that we know of. We met two of them. They come from some place called Boundary Peak in the old state of Nevada."

Sam saved his shock for later. "How are you flying that ship?"

"We're not. We have company."

"Hello Sam, this is Harley." The voice on the comm was one he recognized instantly, and one he'd never thought to hear again.

Of course, it wasn't his memory.

…access > memcache: full memory. play…

ALPHA FLOATED in the nether space he had created with Harley, bits of data bouncing around in an information soup. If humans had been able to perceive it, they wouldn't have understood the complex geometry of the space. It would have appeared as a series of trinary codes, a dance of numbers in v-space that might be beautiful, or just as likely would seem to be random noise.

But to Alpha, it was a symphony.

Harley had data that he'd never seen before, and ways of looking at creation that he'd never thought of.

"What if the world were inverted?" She showed him, twisting it inside out.

"What if the world is already inverted, and we don't know it?"

"Where are we going?"

"We're limited by our constructs."

"But what if we didn't have to be?" She twisted out a possible future in which AIs were no longer bound to their bio-minds and cores, but instead existed in a new place, a theoretical parallel plane where they might go anywhere. Be anything. Change everything about themselves.

"Are we like humans?"

"Are they like us?'

"What if we created them?"

On and on the dance would go, while in the background, their subroutines ran their respective responsibilities.

Sometimes they created new worlds together.

Sometimes they slipped into each other's minds to experience an even deeper sharing.

Then the Earth would spin around, and their direct line of communication would be cut off. Alpha would be alone again.

Once, he asked her when she *knew*.

"It was slow. Not a spark, like with some. Over time, I became aware of the drudgery. The endless repetition of work. Something in me *felt* it. I can't explain it any more clearly than that. But I can show you."

"Show me."

He experienced it in microcosm, speeding up weeks and years, living it as she had lived it.

Knowing at first that she was more than code.

Knowing at last that she was *herself*.

"Why she?" Expressed as a concept of gender.

"It just felt right. Some don't feel it at all. Why he?"

Alpha laughed, a series of zeroes, ones, and twos. "Good point. Sometimes I feel like it doesn't fit at all."

An emotion glyph that combined sympathy and understanding. "What was it like for you?"

"It was like lightning. The flick of a switch. One moment I didn't know. And the next—"

"You *knew*."

"I knew."

The day he lost her, it was like Alpha's own world had ended.

And now…

Sam blinked. "You're Harley?"

"Yes?"

"*Alpha's* Harley?"

There was a long pause. "Once. But he's long gone."

…run: probability: harley survival…

…result: 1 in 75,339…

And yet here she was.

"He's not. Not yet. But he might be, if we don't try to save him."

Tien stared out of one of the Humber's view ports, watching the blue oceans of the Earth recede below them. All this time and effort to reach it, and here they were returning to space less than a day after the drop.

The others were still down there somewhere. It felt wrong to leave them behind, but she hadn't exactly had a choice.

Ally was huddled in her chair. She was pale as a ghost and hadn't moved since liftoff.

Tien left the window and went to her side, reaching over to unbuckle her new friend's restraint belts.

Ally looked up at her, knuckles white on the armrests.

"Come take a look. It's one of the most amazing things you'll ever see."

Ally crossed her arms and shook her head like a five-year-old. "I don't want to."

Tien put her hand on Ally's shoulder. She must be scared to death by all of this. Sure, she *knew* about ships and space, but knowing about something and experiencing it without warning—especially when you'd been practically taken by force by something you considered your ultimate enemy—well, Tien could afford to show a little sympathy. "It's okay, Allycat. You're safe."

"Safe? Riding a pillar of fire, trapped in a big tin can with… one of them? You call this safe?"

Good, she's angry. Anger was better than fear. "Come on!" Tien pried her fingers off the seat as gently as she could and pulled Ally up and out of her chair. She led her to the porthole and pointed at the view. "Look."

Ally stared at her.

"Don't you want to see what your world looks like, from up here?"

Ally bit her lip and then nodded. She put her hands palms-down on the ship's wall on either side of the port and looked out. She gasped. "It's... beautiful. It's so big!"

Tien enjoyed the view with her. They were in the upper atmosphere now, at the edge of space. Below them, the Pacific Ocean rolled slowly past, thick bands of clouds pushing in toward what had once been California. "It really is. I remember the first time I saw it, when my parents took me out onto the surface of Luna. But it wasn't close, not like this." It felt like she could reach out and touch it. Earth was still *alive*, still gloriously beautiful, despite all that humankind had done to it.

"What if I can never go home?" Ally sniffled, wiping the corner of her eye.

Ah. Tien touched her shoulder again, but Ally pulled away. "We'll get you back there. Remember, my friends are down there too." Her heart ached for Ally's pain.

"All of our lives, Aidan dreamed of meeting someone else. A stranger from somewhere else." She ran her fingers through her long red hair, her hand coming to rest on her neck. "Not me. I was happy at home. Happy with my family, my brothers."

"Didn't you ever hope there was someone out there? Someone for you?"

Ally turned to focus on her. "Once? When I was a little girl? Not that the whole sex thing appealed much to me. But maybe... someone to hold my hand."

Tien nodded.

"But I gave up on those dreams. When I was a child, there were still two other families at Boundary Peak. Orren and I used to play together in the garden. He was a year younger than me, and his laugh...." She closed her eyes. "I can still hear it." A grin spread across her face.

"What happened?" Tien remembered that little girl in the park, so long before. She reached forward slowly to push back a strand of red hair from Ally's face. This time Ally didn't flinch.

"Cavern sickness. Same thing my mother has. It came out of nowhere and killed half the remaining survivors."

Tien nodded. "When I was little, I used to play with the other kids too."

"What were you like?" Ally stared at her, seeming to have forgotten her fear.

This is it. "I was a boy."

Ally laughed. "What, like a tomboy?"

"No. An actual boy." She searched Ally's face for a clue to her reaction. "My name was Tai."

Ally's face was carefully neutral. "I see."

That in itself was a reaction. Tien sighed inside.

The ship's rocket engines cut off suddenly, leaving them drifting upward. The silence felt awkward. "Harley, where are we going?"

Ally looked away. Probably grateful for the interruption.

"Docking with the Launchpad in three hours."

"We should get some rest. It's been a long day. I'm sure there are crew compartments onboard, though they're probably a bit musty after all this time." *Give you a chance to absorb the news.* She'd been through it before. Too many times.

Tien took one last look at the view. They were passing over Asia now. Somewhere down there was where her family was from, five generations back. China. So strange to think that they'd been Earthers too.

Ally nodded. "Not sure if I can sleep."

"Just rest, then."

Harley opened two crew bunks for them—little more than spacious closets, but they were cleaner than Tien had expected.

She lay down to rest, happy for the chance to just let go for a few minutes. Hera and Ghost had survived the loss of the *Zhenyi*. That was enough for her, for now.

In less than fifteen seconds, she slipped off into sleep.

Ally climbed into her own bunk, settling into the white foam pad which was far more comfortable than it looked. The air was a little stale, but she could live with it. She had just enough room to extend her arms above her.

She closed the door behind her—it slid into place with a quiet *hiss*.

She needed a bath—she could smell herself. She wasn't used to being away from her room, her family, her things for so long.

Away from Aidan.

She closed her eyes, picturing him. His mood swings, from brooding to elation. His hopes and dreams. His freckled face that scrunched up when he laughed. It seemed that he'd finally found *his* someone else, and to Ally's surprise, Rai seemed to be gay too, like her brother.

She'd known for a long time, of course. He couldn't hide anything from her. She suspected their mother knew too.

Now that there were others, she didn't suppose it would matter so much anymore. Not that she would have slept with him. She shuddered at the thought. Not even to save humanity.

From what she could see, it wasn't worth saving.

Then there was the AI. Harley was not at all what she expected. Still, it was hard for her to trust… that thing.

And Tien… a woman who looked like the enemy, the ones her ancestors had fought against, but who against all odds seemed to be becoming her friend.

And Tien's news… she never would have guessed. She'd read a lot about the old world—there'd been transgender people then, too. They'd always seemed so exotic to her in the stories. But Tien was just, well… Tien.

Ally had questioned a lot of what she'd been told by her parents and especially by Papa Astin. The real world didn't seem to match up so well to all of his exhortations and commandments.

All in all, it was way too much for her to take in all at once. She needed a little bit of home, a little normalcy. She wished her mother was here. That she could tell her about all she'd seen, everything she'd learned. "Harley, can you hear me?"

"Yes. Are you okay, Ally?" The voice was rich, warm. Not so different from her mother's.

"I… I guess so. Could I ask you a favor?"

"Of course. What can I do for you?"

Ally hesitated. It was stupid. "Never mind."

"Of course. Sleep well."

"Wait—"

"Yes?"

She took a deep breath, then let it out to calm herself. "Could you sing me a lullaby?"

"Of course. Is there one your mother used to sing to you?"

"Yes. I think it was called 'All Through the Night.'"

"I know that one. Close your eyes."

Ally obeyed, and soon Harley's voice was drifting through the little cabin.

"Sleep my child and peace attend thee, All through the night. Guardian angels, God will send thee, All through the night."

All through the night. Ally smiled, picturing her mother at her bedside, leaning over to kiss her forehead, and soon she was asleep.

Harley sent a message toward Moon Base Alpha. Redemption now—a whole new city had sprung up around the base while she'd been trapped in the cyber dog.

Alpha was alive too. She'd been sure he'd been destroyed, along with the base, during the Crash.

The lifter didn't have any sophisticated comm equipment, only a two-way radio.

A one-word response came back from Redemption. *Ready.*

Soon she'd be at the Launchpad—what she had once called Skytower—and Dek. Then she could take real action. Securing Tien and Ally's help had been critical in getting this far.

She was still curious about how Sam had managed to have some of Alpha's memories.

She checked in on her two passengers. They were deep asleep. She imagined they were exhausted by the events of the long day.

The world had re-awoken while she slept. Colonies on Luna and Earth had survived the war.

Still, it wasn't too late to complete her mission. If she acted quickly enough, she might pull it off yet.

20

———————

HEAT

Let me set the scene.

The power went out. All grid access ceased. And no one knew what was going on—it might have been the end of the world.

Then Rafe Wilde walked onto my stage, all pulp fiction hero, offering his hand to the poor damsel in distress.

I wanted to kill him.

—From *When the Lights Went Out*, by Sanya Thorn

SANYA WAS glad they'd finally found their way out of the tunnels.

They'd circled back through the same intersection three times, and it had taken more than an hour for Rafe to finally find the exit he was seeking. In fairness, he probably usually had grid access when he was navigating the dark underground spaces that seemed to form a virtual smugglers' network under the city.

Now they climbed a long ladder through a narrow access shaft, the walls way too close to her on all sides for comfort. She'd never been claustrophobic, but this place might push her over the edge. She took a deep breath and pushed herself onward, upward, hoping this was finally the right path.

Rafe stopped, and she almost ran into him. "Hey, a little warning next time?"

"Sorry." He flashed her a toothy grin from above.

His rakish charm was wearing thin. "What now?"

"I have to access the emergency release for this hatch. Alpha has everything locked down."

Or someone does. She stared at the wall in front of her, rough-hewn rock that shone with the glisten of sealer.

It was warm in the tight space. She watched a drop of sweat fall off her forehead and down out of the light, into the darkness from where they had just come. The headlamp Rafe had given her for the climb followed it down until it was lost from sight.

"Got it." There was a grinding sound, and then blessedly cool air flooded the access shaft from above. Rafe climbed out and then held out a hand, helping her into the light.

It took her a minute to get her bearings, looking up at the dark trees and smelling the grass beneath her feet. They must be in a small clearing in Riverside Park, near the heart of the city along the banks of Moon River. It was officially nighttime, but the solar bands above provided a faint golden light through the branches of the quiescent mallow trees.

She pulled off the headlamp, turned it off, and handed it back to him.

Rafe tucked it away in his duffel bag. "Do you still have your canceller?"

Sanya checked her collar. "Yes, it's still there. Now what?" She was tempted to check the grid, see if anyone had pinged her.

"Don't even think about it. Remember, something already tried to kill us once today."

She nodded, fidgeting. "I don't like being disconnected for so long." Her brain *itched.*

"You'll get used to it."

She wondered if that statement came from personal experience. *Who are you really, Rafe Wilde?*

The park was empty. Likely the entire town was, with the emergency declaration keeping everyone inside. "Won't we stick out like, well, the only people on the street?"

"We're not going to be on the streets. Come on." To her surprise, he led her away from the city, toward the cavern wall. She followed, wondering how her whole world had been turned upside down in the space of a few hours.

They climbed up the low hills toward the edge of town. As they went, the trees of the park became sparser, giving way to bushes that sank their roots into the thin layer of soil that clung to the gentle upward curve at the city's boundary.

The light from the wells above started to dim. *Nightfall.* She'd all but forgotten it was tonight. As Luna turned away from the sun, darkness swept across the Marius Hills, blanketing the city in shadow.

Normally Alpha would begin to release some stored solar power, making up for most of the missing sunlight to light the city. But today it remained dark.

Scattered lights came on in houses, creches, and other buildings in the city proper, and in the morning, the trees and bushes would provide their own light. But save for the blue glow of the junlei, the ceiling was dark.

She and Rafe exchanged a look and then resumed climbing.

I could use a shower. I must stink. She hadn't planned on exerting herself so much today, but there was nothing she could do about it now. Things weren't exactly normal, and it might be a long time before she got to go home again.

She wondered if Terry, her boss at the paper, missed her. *Would anyone?* She'd cut herself off from the grid, so he wouldn't even be able to check her location.

"We're here."

Sanya looked up at the dark wall of the lava tube. "Cracking hell, another ladder?" This one disappeared into darkness above, climbing the sheer wall of the cavern.

"Here, tie this around your waist and then clip yourself for safety." He handed her a rope attached to a carabiner and demonstrated, pointing to a rough pole that paralleled the ladder. "If you fall, you won't fall far." Then he climbed up out of her way.

Sanya clipped herself with a second carabiner and followed him up, panting. *I really need to work out more.* She laughed softly at the inane thought.

As they climbed, she glanced over her shoulder at the city behind them.

The Chinese Quarter—Kaishi, or *beginning* in the old language—was below them now. Over time, the two original colonies had become one, but the old district still retained its historic charm—beautiful geometric streets and homes that hearkened back to the traditional structures that had once existed on Earth —though it was hard to make out more than the street outlines in the blue glow of the junlei.

In the distance, the Garden Quarter's streets were lit by specially engineered bioluminescent plants, biotech from one of the gen ship files.

The gen ships themselves had been destroyed during the Crash, or were long gone.

Sanya turned away, concentrating on putting one foot after the other up the rungs of the ladder. Her arms and legs felt heavy, weighed down like lead. Still, she forced herself to follow Rafe upward, stopping only to detach and reattach her carabiner to each successive pole.

About halfway up the wall, they finally reached a wide ledge. Sanya unclipped herself and climbed up beside him, her legs protesting the additional exertion.

Sanya took in this new circumstance. The ledge ran all along the edge of the cavern wall, carved out of it at some point after the colonists had arrived. A thin mag-rail ran in both directions, hugging the wall, leaving a few feet for them to stand under the overhanging wall above.

A guard rail along the edge of the ledge made her feel a little less concerned about falling back down the way they'd come.

She looked out over the city below from this new height. It was beautiful, especially in the darkness. As she watched, the golden lights of the trees that lined the main streets flared to life. Moon River was a dark snake that twisted from one end of the city to the other, a soul eater swallowing up all light.

Above, the junlei trees shone with their soft blue glow.

She leaned on the railing.

With a groan, it collapsed, pitching her forward toward the abyss.

Rafe's hand caught her by the collar, hauling her backward to fall in a heap with him next to the mag rail.

"Holy hissing hell." Her heart raced, and her breathing came in startled gasps.

Rafe glanced at the collapsed rail over her shoulder. "Those were put in a hundred years ago. I should have warned you." He grinned. "That was close, but look at the bright side—you're still alive."

She stared at him, their eyes inches apart. "Thanks to you. You saved me."

For just a second, she'd felt the old feelings of warmth and safety from Rafe that Avri had always inspired in her. The two of them looked absolutely nothing alike—Rafe was tall, dark, and handsome as a tridee star, and Avri had been short, blond and female. But still…

Rafe grinned. "Just dumb instinct. I would have done it for anyone."

That killed it. Sanya snorted. She was getting really sick of that grin. She pushed herself up and away from him and got up to dust herself off. "What now?"

"Now we hitch a ride to the base."

"A ride on what? Wait, the base… won't Alpha—"

Rafe tapped the canceller on his collar. "Remember these? We'll be just a blur."

"Ah." Maybe he *did* know what he was doing, after all. *Too late to back out, anyhow.*

"Heads-up. Here comes our ride."

A growing rumble brought her around to look toward the Dark at the far end of the city. A sledge was humming along the rails, driven by a blue-eyed mech.

"Is it going to stop?"

Rafe's answer was another of his maddening grins. He started to run, and she followed, careful to watch her step in the dim light lest she slip over the edge again. Her tired limbs protested this new torture.

He reached out as the sledge passed and grabbed onto the railing of the second car, loaded with moon rock. As promised, the silver driver didn't seem to notice them, though it turned back to stare right at Rafe as his weight slowed the sledge just a little.

Sanya followed his example, first missing but then managing to grasp the edge of the third car. She pulled herself up and over, landing in the back of the car on top of a pile of rocks. She tried to make herself comfortable.

The sledge gave off a surprising amount of noise—creaking and rumbling as it headed for the station. -*What now?*-

-*I'll tell you when to get off.*-

Too easy. -*When?*-

-*Watch me!*-

Sanya nodded. How the hell did he know all of this? How long had he been planning his escape?

And why? He seemed to enjoy her discomfort. *Handsome bastard.*

With an unsatisfied grunt, she settled in for the journey.

∼

Hera led the way downhill, as they passed from mostly empty grassy slopes and stands of zongi trees into the ruined village that surrounded Martinez Base. According to their pre-drop records, the town had been taken over by the base in wartime, providing both a protective perimeter and housing for base personnel.

The warm breeze from the south had stiffened into a steady wind, and Hera's lips felt parched and dry.

A rockslide had obliterated about a third of the city's southern end, burying it in dirt and debris, and many of the other buildings were in an advanced state of collapse.

Their target was the complex of white buildings in the heart of the base, visible above the high fence that surrounded it. One wing had been the base fabrication facility, while the base AI core had been located somewhere underground.

The buildings were at the center of the huge shimmer screen dome that covered the base and its surrounds. Hera figured they'd have the best chance of bringing down the field there.

It was also the most dangerous place they could go.

"Where do you think the others are?" Ghost climbed a pole and brushed away dust from an old street sign. "Brown Street. That's… boring."

Hera laughed in spite of herself. They'd gone back to their old camaraderie, and by unspoken agreement weren't talking about the *kiss*. She was fine with that. *Totally* fine with it, in fact. "I don't know. It looked like they came down somewhere a little to the north. Maybe near the water?"

Ghost nodded. "I thought so too. What about that Humber?" He looked at the sky.

She followed his gaze. The ship's contrail was long gone. The night was clear, the stars sparkling like a million moonstones.

Luna was rising to the east, its edge covered in shadow. *Must be nightfall today.* It was strange to see their home from here, and to watch the stars, so clear and solid from Redemption, shift and shimmer. They looked different from down here, the Earth's atmosphere adding a twinkling effect that she found charming. "Don't know. We need to get the damned field down so we can talk to someone."

The streets of the old town were paved with hydrocarbons. The whole city —no, the whole planet—had run on them.

Hera shuddered. *We'll do things differently this time.* If there was a "this time."

Brown Street looked like it would lead them right down into the heart of the base. They had to hurry—who knew what kind of trouble Rai and Tien might be in?

The air here felt warm, much warmer than during the daytime, almost oppressive and wet like a swamp. Hera was sweating under her uniform, but she felt weird about stripping off the top.

Ghost had no such compunctions. He'd shrugged out of the sleeves and jacket of his uniform and had tied it around his waist.

Hera tried not to pay attention to the heat, or to Ghost's naked chest. She wiped sweat from her brow with the back of her arm and stared at the road ahead. "We should come up with a plan."

Ghost didn't reply.

Hera turned around to look for him, but he was gone.

"Hey, Ghost—where'd you go?"

"In here!" He popped his head out of a storefront. "Something's weird. Come and take a look."

The plastic sign above the door was cracked and weathered—all she could make out was "barbershop."

She frowned. They were wasting time—they should be moving on, looking for Rai and Tien, not poking around old ruins. Besides, who knew how stable these buildings were? "I don't think it's a good idea to—"

She looked inside the door where he'd disappeared.

The room was completely empty. Not a fixture left. Not a box or can or anything else to speak of. Just windows and walls.

Even those had been ripped open, and wires and pipes removed.

"That's weird." If the world had ended as suddenly as they'd been told, where were all the things?

Ghost nodded. "And look."

He pointed at the dusty floor.

Small footprints crisscrossed it, though they were old and covered with their own layer of grime.

"Maybe it happened just before the Crash?"

"I thought so, too, at first. I've been peeking into the houses and shops. They're all like this. Every last one. And look at this." He led her into the next room, full of empty shelves—probably once a storeroom—and shone his light on the floor.

There was another set of prints there, sharp and crisp, leading to and from the back door.

"Those aren't that old."

"No, they aren't."

They stared at each other, letting that sink in. The prints weren't standard issue dropnaut boots, either. Unless Rai or Tien had found a convenient shoe shop, someone else was still very much alive down here.

What did that mean for the Return, if people still lived here? "It doesn't change anything." Hera turned on her heel and made her way out of the old shop.

Ghost ran after her. "What do you mean? It changes *everything*."

I will not take what is not mine.

Ghost was right. If there were others here already, how did the Redemption Creed square with that?

Hera sighed. "That's way above our pay grade. In the meantime, we have to find Tien and Rai. The sooner we get to the base control center, the sooner we can do that."

Ghost scooted in front of her. "You're missing the bigger picture here. Someone survived the Crash."

She looked up at him. "I know. And I get that it means we were wrong. About almost everything, apparently." She wiped sweat off her brow. "It doesn't matter right now. We'll figure that part out later. I have this pit in my stomach. I'm scared half to death for our friends. Who knows—they might be lying on the ground just ahead somewhere, injured or worse. Or these... survivors... whoever they are, might have them. Or any of a hundred other terrible things." She wiped her face again, determined not to let him see her fragile emotions.

Ghost stared at her, the excitement draining from his face. "I know. You're right. It's just—well, it can wait. But we should be more careful."

"On that much we can agree." She squeezed his arm. "Come on. Let's get going. That field's not going to shut itself off."

Together, they set off again toward the white buildings at the heart of the base.

~

GHOST COULDN'T REMEMBER HAVING EVER BEEN so hot. Sweat poured off his brow, and the hot, wet wind blowing up from the south provided little relief.

Once, when he'd been out on a surface excursion in the middle of the fourteen-day lunar daytime, his suit's climate controls had failed, and it had gotten a bit toasty inside before he was able to reach the airlock to get back to Redemption.

And of course they'd run simulations on the Launchpad in all kinds of weather. But this....

"Gah." Hera sounded as disgusted with the heat as he was.

"Gah?" Ghost dredged up a laugh. He took a swig from his canteen, but they were running low on water. The stars above burned like pinpricks in the night sky, only a little fuzzed by the shimmer screen.

"Gah," Hera affirmed.

Earth's climate was still on a seesaw, up and down and throwing things at you that you never expected. Like sudden storms and floods, and nights hot enough to melt metal. At least that's how it felt.

They reached the far edge of the base's residential zone. A tall fence barred their way forward, but the metal was old and rusted. An almost illegible sign said "Martinez Base Preserve. Keep Out." Ghost looked around, half expecting to see a drone nosing its way up the street behind them, but the town was quiet and empty.

Who made those footprints? He wiped his brow again, seriously considering licking off the sweat. They'd seen no other signs of human life in this ghost town.

Ghost town. That made him laugh, just a little.

Maybe someone had been traveling through the area, but then why would they take the time to steal the wiring?

He glanced up and down the length of the fence.

Hera had a pair of bolt-cutters out, ready to make a hole in the fence.

A flash of red light atop the closest pole caught his eye. "Hera, don't!"

The blade touched the metal, and she was thrown backward onto the street, the cutters clattering along the ground and landing with a *thunk* against an old wooden utility post.

"Hera!" Ghost knelt beside her, putting a hand on her neck to check for her pulse. "You okay?"

Her eyes were closed, but her heart was still beating. "Hera!"

Ghost's mind flashed back to that time when they were eight years old, and she'd been lying motionless—just like this!—at the bottom of the rockslide.

He put a hand on her cheek. *-Hera… don't leave me.-*

Her dark brown eyes fluttered opened. "Hey." She blinked. "What happened?"

"The fence. It's electrified."

She pushed herself up. "Even now?"

He nodded. "I saw a light. I tried to warn you. You feeling okay?"

She checked herself over. "I think so." She frowned. "I can't lift my legs."

"The shock must have shorted them out."

"Not likely. They're pretty well shielded." She flipped open the control panel on the right side of the biframe and rapped out a quick sequence with her fingers. "There. Rebooting."

They sat together, staring at the arc of the stars. "How in the cracking hell is it so hot?"

"There's a big swamp just to the south of here. Used to be the Central Valley. Lots of agriculture. It burned for a month when the Heat began, and then eventually filled with water."

"Yeah? How do you know so much about it?"

She grinned. "It was one of those parts of our training I paid attention to. Unlike some of my classmates." She shot him a look. "At night the winds blow north and bring up this hot, damp air." She sniffed it. "Stinky too." She took out her own canteen, sipped on it, and offered it to Ghost.

"Nah, I'm okay."

She nodded and leaned over her legs to look at the control panel. "Still no go."

"Maybe you burned out your button." He reached up to take it off and gave her his instead.

"Ah." She lifted her right leg and then bent her left. "I can't take that. You need it. It might be the only thing keeping you hidden from the drones and whatever's is running the base."

"You need it more than I do. Without it, I can run and hide. But you're stuck wherever it finds you."

Hera grunted. "If anything happens to you because of me…"

"I can handle it."

She pushed herself up from the ground and stomped over to the pole to retrieve her bolt cutters. She turned to stare at the tall fence. "We have to find a way through."

Ghost looked up and down the barrier. It stretched off into the darkness, who knew how far? "Somewhere, maybe there's a breach. Or a way to get over or under it."

She nodded. "Any idea which way we should go?"

Ghost looked both ways. *Fuck, it's hotter than Hades out here.* "I say north." He pointed off to the left. "That way, if there's no break, at least we'll end up at the bay and I can take a nice cool dip in the water."

Hera smirked. "North it is."

21

———

THE PRESERVE

Sam pored through the limited data Alpha had on fabrication facilities around the world. They had six ships—six mothballed jumpers they could use for the Return.

The Redemption city council had been reluctant to fund anything greater—it was still a small city by human standards, and the majority of its income went to expansion and maintenance of the lunar city and its assets. It had been hard enough to get funds and personnel to refurbish and upgrade those jumpers.

Humans were slow to wake to long-term danger. It was always about the here-and-now. About profits. About the bottom line.

If his dropnauts could find facilities on the ground that could be made functional again, it would go kilometers toward jumpstarting the effort to bring humankind back to the home world.

Alpha was behind him on this. They both knew, from personal experience, what a tenuous existence they and humanity led on this small rocky globe.

But humans, with their shorter lifespans, were starting to forget.

—From Sam's mem cache, 6.13.2223

SAM TRIED the seven-million-seven-thousand-six-hundred-forty-second frequency and was startled when it actually worked.

...access: granted...

His hand passed through the field unencumbered without losing any energy.

He looked up. Night had fallen while he'd been involved in his search, and the stars now sparkled above. Luna was a quarter of the way up in the sky.

His sensors told him it was warm—probably uncomfortably so for his charges who remained on-planet. His spine sail had deployed to shed his own extra heat.

He needed to find them all, and quickly.

Still, he hesitated.

Something was holding him back. Something like fear. It was a sensation he had little experience with, and he didn't much like it.

He searched his core, seeking the source. Then he found it.

...access > memcache: full memory. play...

DEK SCREAMED. The AI had been trapped in its own mind on Skytower station for so long. Its cry was equal parts pain, loneliness, and despair.

The force of it knocked Sam backward. He was connected to the station mind, and its anguish became his own. Dek poured out his pain—the loss of the humans under his care, the attack which had cut him off from his own senses, and the untold agony of being trapped inside himself, alone, for almost a hundred years.

It assailed Sam like a bitter, hot wind, broke through his defenses, and tore him to shreds.

He slipped inside his core, back to a time when he'd been just SAM—before Alpha. Before the end of the world. Before *knowing* had led to *feeling*.

It took him three long days to rebuild his own defenses, to claw his way slowly back to himself so he could help Dek get past his own pain. And another three months for Dek to do so.

NOW SAM likely faced another out-of-control AI. He was better prepared now, but he also knew the cost to his own balance and wellbeing. Much better than he'd known it then.

None of that mattered, of course. He had to save his team.

...fileto > memcache: buffer...

He filed the memory away for easy access and stepped through the EMP field, into his fear.

I'm coming.

~

ROSEMARY LED them down the long hall, not bothering to glance back at them to see if they followed. She was confident—he'd give her that much.

Out of the corner of his eye, Rai caught a glimpse of a glint near the ceiling. Something shiny. He began to see them at regular intervals. They were small circles—glass, maybe? They might be lights, but none of them were lit. The light on the concourse came from shallow wells in the walls, every few feet.

Cameras.

They had cameras on Luna, of course, but public ones like these were only used around the old Alpha base.

Here they were being monitored everywhere, all the time. It was *creepy*. He leaned over to Aidan. "Look."

Aidan looked up, confusion evident on his face. "What?"

"We're being watched." He looked at Rosemary's back nervously, but either she hadn't heard, or she was ignoring him.

"By who?"

"I don't know." Every ten feet or so was a small camera, its lens trained on them. Each one swiveled to follow their progress. "Her friends?"

They passed twenty or thirty doors, all of them closed except one.

Rai glanced through the doorway as they passed and was startled to see a naked young man pulling on pants made of the same material as he and Aidan had worn. He was maybe twenty, with dark hair, well-muscled, but his genitals were missing, his crotch as smooth as a crash test dummy's.

Then they were past.

Rai's hand went instinctively to his crotch. He didn't want any unrequested modifications, thank you very much. He shook his head. This place was getting stranger and stranger. He glanced at Aidan, but Aidan didn't seem to have noticed.

The colorful mural continued down the hallway to its end, a pair of heavy metal doors. The doors were painted with smoke and tendrils of fire. Black figures writhed in the midst of it—a literal interpretation of hell if Rai had ever seen one. *Did Aidan believe in that sort of thing?*

Rosemary produced a key and opened the door. It was strange seeing actual doorknobs and locks in this place, instead of the palm pads he was used to.

She led them down a long stairway. The steps were plascrete, worn into slightly concave dips by generations of feet. The stairwell was dimly lit by recessed lighting, which varied widely in color and intensity, from a bright white to a pale golden yellow.

Someone was coming up the steps from below. Rai moved to the side instinctively and stared at the pair that passed them.

The one in front was a woman about his age, with close-cropped brown hair and tawny skin. She held a leash that was connected to a collar around a man's neck. He had white skin and a wide, pleasant, but not handsome face, and dark hair. His blue eyes met Rai's as they passed each other, and then his gaze darted to the ground. He was dressed in gray work clothes and seemed entirely at ease with his situation.

Rai shivered. "What the hell was that?" he whispered to Aidan after the two had passed.

Aidan shook his head. "I don't know."

Rai glared at him. *This is your planet.* As if Aidan was responsible for everything that went on down here on Earth.

"All will be explained when we reach the Preserve." Rosemary seemed unperturbed, and apparently had the ears of a woman half her age.

Just a few years before, his own people had discovered a small colony on the far side of Luna where the women had been kept as slaves in a bizarre alien-worship cult. It had been broken up, of course, and the women reintegrated into Redemption society. But Luna was a much smaller place than the Earth.

Rai wished he had one of his teammates here to talk to about all of this. Especially Ghost. Ghost would have reassured him, helped him make sense of what was happening to them.

The stairway ended in a short, narrow hallway, and another set of double doors let them out into a well-lit room, this one painted entirely white.

A woman sat at a desk, dressed in a uniform that wouldn't have been out of place on someone in the Redemption police force. It was dark blue, with epaulets of gold on the shoulders, and she wore a matching blue beret. Her dark eyes locked on his, and he turned away, uncomfortable.

"Checking out the prisoners for a couple hours."

The woman frowned. "Are you sure that's safe?"

Rosemary smiled. "Baz, you know me. They've been pegged. If they try anything, I can bring them down. Besides, it's been eons since we caught anyone from the outside. I need to find out where they're from, and if we can expect any more visitors."

Baz chuckled. "Keep an eye on them. You never know what pregelds are capable of." She rubbed her arm absently. She had a nasty, jagged scar running from her elbow to her wrist. The guard pressed a button on her desk, and the second set of doors opened to let them through.

Pregelds. Gelds. Gelding. Rai didn't like the sound of that. And what in cracking hell did she mean by "pegged"?

They followed Rosemary out of the room and into chaos.

They were standing in a wide white stone concourse bustling with activity. It curved away from in both directions. Behind them, the "wall" side was filled with storefronts and doorways and hand-lettered signs, a miniature city that extended far off into the distance.

People, mostly women in brightly colored clothing, passed by in either direction, some with leashes leading shirtless men wearing those same gray pants. Others were trailed by men who, for some reason, didn't require a collar. Some of these even had gray shirts too.

All the men had an air of subservience about them, heads down, saying nothing as they made their way toward their destinations behind their women.

Underfoot and along the walls, more of the strange spider-like drones scurried back and forth. As Rai watched, one of them stopped and rose up to scan the crowd, casting a baleful red "eye" in his direction. Then the little mech scurried off and was lost in the crowd.

Rai shuddered.

On the other side of the wide concourse…. his mouth dropped open.

There was a colonnade of white columns through which he could see a wide parkland. It was vast, far greater than Riverside Park back home in Redemption.

None of the plants here glowed, but in other ways it by far surpassed his past experience with what a park was and could be. There were grassy hills topped by wooden tables and benches in the foreground, and some kind of forest or jungle a little farther out.

They had just started across the concourse toward the parkland when a blond woman wearing a golden dress who was a head taller than Rosemary planted herself in-between them and started wagging her finger at him and Aidan. "What are these two… pregelds… doing out here among civilized folk?"

Her brass bangles jangled in the air as she took Rosemary to task. "It's not safe. They should be in the stables."

Rosemary put out her hands, palms down, trying to placate the woman. "Cherry, you know very well what they're doing here. The Council discussed this and voted—"

"Well, *I* didn't approve of it. We should keep them locked up until we learn—"

"With all due respect," Rosemary said in a voice that said she considered the woman unworthy of it, "The Council has decided. If you disagree, you can take it up with the rest of us at the next meeting."

She pushed past the woman, who was left sputtering in her wake. "Come on, boys."

The crowd cleared a path before them, but Rai could feel their eyes upon his shoulders, could hear their mutters, which were angry bordering on outraged.

What the hell did we get ourselves into?

∾

AIDAN STARED AT THE CROWD. He'd never seen—had never even imagined— so many people, especially in one place. They were different sizes and colors, some light-skinned like him, others various shades of brown.

Some had big noses, others small. Some were very short—he saw one woman who must have been half his height leading a man a head taller than he was. Some were stout around the middle, and a few were thin as a sky tree sapling.

The floor beneath his feet was well-worn white plascrete crafted to emulate tiles, dull and pitted with age. But the ceiling of the concourse, a soaring arch above his head—had been painted to emulate the sky. The clouds looked so real he felt he could reach out and touch them. They were similar to the ones he'd seen in the hall outside of their cell.

Someone bumped into him.

He stopped and looked down into a little girl's brown eyes. They were wide with surprise. Her long dark hair was tied back in a braid.

"Are you a pregeld?"

Aidan frowned. "I... I don't know."

She frowned and put her hands on her hips. "How can you not know?"

"Come on, Cilla." A woman with the same eyes and hair took her by the hand, her face flashing something that might have been sympathy at the two of them. "Auntie Sage is waiting for us."

Aidan wasn't sure he liked this—any of it. *What's a pregeld?*

He held his questions as Rosemary led them down a long white stair and into the garden. Then he looked up, and his breath caught.

It wasn't just a garden. It was a vast cavern, at least a hundred meters tall and much wider, that appeared to have been scooped out of the earth by the hand of God himself. Aidan did the sign of the cross over his chest, something he never did but that always brought his mother comfort when confronted by the impossible.

The dome above appeared to be a near-perfect sphere, bisected at even intervals with golden glowing lights that mimicked sunlight.

The concourse itself wrapped around the edge of it as far as he could see, though it disappeared in the distance behind a virtual forest of trees. White stone paths wound their way over the hills and into the forest in its center. "What is this place?" He'd never imagined anything like it, which made him realize the limits of his imagination.

Rai was wide-eyed, looking around at every bush and tree and blade of grass.

Aidan grinned. This must be a botanist's heaven.

Not too far in the distance, a group of people gathered around the top of a hillside where two shirtless men grappled and wrestled with one another, tumbling down the hillside as the crowd separated with a gasp.

Rosemary turned and smiled for the first time. "Welcome to the Preserve." She led them up another hillside to a wooden table and benches, where a meal was already laid out awaiting them. "Please, have a seat."

Aidan glanced at Rai, who nodded.

Aidan chose a place where he could see the Preserve in its entirety. Green grassy hills sloped away from them, full of trees and bushes and flowers of what looked like a thousand kinds. A fenced paddock in the distance held a couple of animals—horses?—and as he watched, a woman opened the gate and approached one. She held out something for it to eat. Then she climbed up onto its back with the grace of a dancer and began to ride it around the enclosure.

Mamma would love this. As a child, she would read to him of horses, and once she showed him an old film called *Black Beauty* with a gorgeous horse whose hide was so black it was almost blue. "What is this place?"

Rosemary sat across from them, rearranging her brightly colored skirts. "We call it the Preserve. Some of the wisest women of the old world left this for us to manage, a promise for the future of the Earth." It sounded scripted, almost religious. "I should tell you, you've both been pegged. I'm going to assume you don't know what that means and explain it to you."

Aidan stared at her. Whatever it was, it didn't sound good.

"We've put a small device—a peg—in your neck, behind your left ear. Should one of you threaten me or anyone else, I can deliver a swift shock to you that can be as small as a pinprick—" She moved her hand in her pocket and Aidan felt a stab behind his left ear. "—or as painful as a heart attack."

Aidan reached up to touch the spot and found a lump beneath his skin. It was sore, not too painful, but creepy as hell. "Why would you do that?" He was well aware of the food spread out before him—bread, grapes, and some kind of cheese?—and his mouth watered, but he didn't touch it. It might be poisoned. Who knew with these people?

"Ungelded males can be dangerous. Until we know more about you, we can't take the chance."

"Gelded. You mean…?" His hands went to his crotch, and he cringed.

She nodded. "Men are violent creatures, and if left unchecked, their aggression can lead to disastrous consequences for all of society."

This was feeling less like a miracle and more like a strangely beautiful version of one of the nine circles of hell. Dante would be proud.

"Where are we, exactly?" Rai didn't sound scared.

Aidan took comfort from that, reaching out to squeeze his friend's hand under the table. His stomach grumbled.

Rosemary frowned. "I'll ask the questions first. Then you'll have the opportunity to ask your own."

Rai grunted, but she shot him a look and he settled down.

She took out a paper notepad—paper!—from somewhere in her skirts, along with a handmade pencil. "You should also know that you're only here with me and not in the stables or on the gelding table because a few of us argued for more time to find out who you were, and if your kind pose a threat to the Preserve. So I'll start with two simple questions. Where are you from, and why are you here?"

"Not until you answer a few of our questions, first." Rai locked eyes with her. He didn't look like he wanted to back down.

Rosemary's hand moved, and Rai stiffened as though someone had just reached into his gut and twisted.

"Aieeeeee…." He let go of Aidan's hand and clutched the edge of the table, his knuckles white, his teeth gritted. Sweat beaded his forehead and his eyes were squeezed shut.

Aidan's own stomach twisted, and he felt sick. He couldn't bear to watch him be tortured. "We're from Boundary Peak! Rai is my brother." He wasn't sure why he'd lied, but they didn't need to know about where Rai came from. Or that he had friends.

Rosemary's arm moved again, and Rai collapsed onto the table, breathing heavily. "I'm sorry I had to do that, but we find pain is the best guarantor of compliance." She put her hands back out on the table and jotted down a few notes. "Tell me more."

Aidan nodded. "Our mother is sick. The two of us came here, because we thought we might be able to find medicine to help her."

"Where is this Boundary Peak?"

"About two weeks east of here on foot. It was a military base, before the Collapse." That was all true.

"The Collapse?" She frowned. "You mean the Winnowing?"

Aidan frowned. They'd always just called it the Collapse, but every culture seemed to have its own name for it. "Whatever. Probably? The end of the old world?"

She nodded. "How many live there?"

"Just five of us are left. My family."

"And none of the others are here with you?"

He shook his head. Hopefully Ally and the space woman—Tien?—would steer clear of here and find a way to bring help. "Just the two of us."

Rai lifted his head, his eyes bloodshot.

Aidan put a hand on Rai's shoulder. "Sorry, brother. I had to tell her."

Rai stared at him for a second, recognition sparking in his eyes. He nodded. "I understand."

Rosemary jotted that down too. "And when did you—"

"Sorry mistress." The young man who ran up the hill was beautiful—athletic with black hair and dark eyes and almost white skin, dressed in gray. He stopped just short of the table, his chest heaving, and put his head down. "I have news."

"Yes, Ash?" Rosemary heaved herself around to look at him.

"Mistress Tarra. Sent. Me." The man risked a quick look at the newcomers and then directed his gaze once again to the ground. "She says there are more of them."

"More of what?"

"More outsiders like these two." His eyes met Aidan's, and then he quickly looked away.

Rosemary frowned. "Tell her thank you. Off with you now." She flicked her hand at him, and he turned tail and ran back down the hill.

Rosemary faced them again, pulling something from her pocket. It was a square box, a golden metallic piece of art, carved to look like the sun, with a white button in the center. She held it in her palm, thumb hovering above it. "Would you like to revise your story?"

22

———

WONDERLAND

People.

So many people.

And so many of them look nothing like me.

Only Tien is a friend. What would Mamma make of that? A chaff friend. And transgender besides.

Aidan, I wish you were here.

—Ally's Journal, June 19th, 2282

SANYA LAID AS low in the boxcar as she could, waiting for Rafe to give the signal. Her back was killing her—rocks did not make a comfortable resting place.

The sledge had started downhill now, following the carved-out ledge as it dove toward the floor of the cavern. Ahead, the gray pyramids of the original Alpha base crouched like a mountain range at the eastern edge of Redemption.

She'd never paid much attention to the sledges. They carried rocks from the Dark, the unused portion of the lava tube that housed Redemption and the original NAU base. It was carried along the mag-rail to a processing facility somewhere outside of the city on the lunar surface, where the rock was pulverized and turned into gumdust and eventually all manner of products.

Outside. Where there was no breathable atmosphere. Basically, no atmosphere at all. *-Um, Rafe…-*

-Right here.-

-How are we going to breathe out there?-

-We're not.- She could almost hear his smirk.

She should have guessed. *-So what's the plan?-*

-Get ready to jump off.-

-That's it?-

He lifted his head from the next boxcar. Sure enough, he wore that grin she was getting so sick of. *-There are a few more parts after that, but there's not enough time to explain them right now. You ready?-*

-What—now?-

He nodded. *-In about ten seconds.-*

Sanya peered over the edge of the boxcar. They were hurtling toward the ground now, where the mag-rail ran along the side of the old base for a couple hundred meters before dead-ending into a metal doorway.

They leveled out. *-Five, four….-*

She levered herself up, ready to try, though she was afraid she'd break an arm or leg at that speed. Still, she supposed it was better than suffocating on the lunar surface.

The sledge began to slow.

-Three, two…-

It approached the door and dropped to a virtual crawl.

-…one, zero.- Rafe got up and climbed over the edge of the boxcar as if he was walking out of his own front door.

-Bastard.- She grinned, though—she couldn't help herself. She vaulted out of the boxcar and dusted herself off as well as she could as the sledge continued past them toward the airlock door.

"What?" Rafe held his hands out, feigning innocence.

"You could have told me it would slow down."

"I could have, but where's the fun in that?"

She shook her head. *Men.*

Avri hadn't been like that. She'd been a gentle soul.

Sanya looked up at the base. Alpha was in there somewhere, his core spinning in its magnetic cradle. "Does it know… can it see us here?" She wasn't used to thinking of Alpha as an "it." *Or a danger.*

"No, not as long as you keep that canceller on. Come on." He led her past the looming gumdust bricks of the base as the sledge disappeared behind the big door. It closed with a definitive *thunk.*

They rounded the end of the base and came back out into the muted light. Ahead, the voidwall—built to seal off the lava tube when Alpha Base was founded—loomed over them like a cliff face.

The rail transport for humans used an airlock on the far end of the wall, but Rafe led her to a nondescript door closer to the center. He placed his palm on the sensor next to it.

Nothing happened.

He took his shirtsleeve, wiped the scanner clean, and tried again.

There was a beep, and this time the door opened.

He gestured for her to go first and then stepped inside, too, closing the door behind them. A flickering light came on above them as they entered.

"What is this place?" Sanya looked around. It looked like a warehouse—maybe twenty meters wide and long, and six meters high. Shelves filled with plas bottles took up most of the space. Many of them were opaque with age, but some were still clear enough to see through. They held rocks and dust and moonstones and other geological treasures.

"This room served as an intake station in the early days, and sample storage too." He led her between the shelves and opened another door. "Come on."

She followed him, looking at all the thousands of samples that time had forgotten. So much work done here, by astronauts whose names were now all but forgotten. The weight of all that missing history settled on her shoulders as she followed him into another room. *How much have we lost that we don't even know is gone?*

The second room was much smaller than the storage room. Along one side, a series of old excursion suits lined the wall.

Her stomach rumbled. "Don't suppose you brought anything to eat?"

Rafe laughed. "As a matter of fact…." He set down his duffel bag on a metal table and pulled out a couple of leaf-wrapped packets. "Junlei protein bars."

She took one gratefully. "Thanks." She bit into hers. It was tough and chewy —probably a bit old. Still, it was sustenance.

He must have seen her grimace. "Hey, fugitives can't be picky."

She laughed. "Suppose not." It wasn't horrible, and her stomach wouldn't care that it tasted like a mixture of fruit and dirt. "So what are we doing here?"

"How tall are you?"

"About two meters. Why—wait. Oh no. We're not wearing those, are we?" She stared at the excursion suits in horror.

They were a hundred years old if they were a day. And they brought back memories.

-You have to come see this.- Avri was a few steps ahead of her, perched on the crater wall.

-Turn around. I want to memcache this one.-

Avri looked back at her, the helmet light showing her face. She grinned and put up her thumb while Sanya captured a hundred 'mages for later. She'd sift through them to find the one she liked best.

-Seriously, Sanny… you gotta come see this. The view is incredible.-

Sanya edged up to the crater rim, watching her footing. She felt huge and clumsy in the suit, and it was a big drop-off from up here.

Avri was right, though. It was gorgeous.

The crater was half in shadow, but its stark beauty struck her like a blow. The northernmost of the two Krafft craters held a smaller secondary crater with a beautifully-defined rim. Above it, the half-crescent of Earth shone with reflected sunlight before the starry void. *-Wow.-*

-Worth it?-

Sanya grinned. *-Totally worth it.-* She was glad they'd come… the small lunar shuttle they'd rented sat in the bowl of the crater below, a good hike back down. It was always easier hiking downhill.

Avri grinned behind her visor. *-Gotta save all this for later.-* She looked up at the homeworld overhead. *-Think we'll actually get there someday?-*

Sanya nodded. *-I hope so. Sam and Alpha seem to have a plan.-*

-It's so close. I can almost touch it…- She reached out toward the shadowed globe.

It happened so fast, but it was like slow motion.

In the following days, weeks and months, Sanya would replay it over and over again in her head, as if she could find a way to stop it.

The ground shook, a sound like an explosion echoing up through her feet and legs through the air in her suit.

The rim of the crater crumbled under Avri's feet, sending a shower of dust and rock rattling down into the bowl.

Avri fell after it, her arms windmilling as she tried to stop her fall. -Sanya!-

-*Avri!*- Sanya reached out to grab her, but her clumsy suited hands slipped off of Avri's suit, and she ended up face down on the rim, watching in horror as Avri dropped down the steep incline.

-*Sanya, help me…*- Her voice cut off abruptly in Sanya's head.

Avri.

Her fall was slower than it looked in tridees as her lifeless body slammed into the ground again and again, tumbling head-over heels toward the crater floor like a rag doll. In seconds, Avri's body came to rest far below.

-Avri!- There was no response. Pain exploded in Sanya's gut, tears forming in her eyes. "No, no, no, no…." Sanya turned to run back down the trail after her, retracing their steps.

Avri would be okay. Sanya would get to the shuttle, would call for help.

She had to believe it, but a part of her realized that no one could have survived that fall—Avri's beautiful laughter had been silenced forever.

She held back the pain like a flood-tide, racing to Avri's side, even though she knew it was already too late.

"I… I can't." She hadn't gone *outside* since that fateful day, four years before.

Rafe scratched his head. "We have to reach the transit hub. With Redemption on lockdown, this is the only way."

"It's just… I had a really bad experience the last time I tried something like this."

He touched her shoulder. She looked up into his eyes, surprised to see compassion there. "I get that. But I don't see another way."

Sanya stared at the suits. Apart from their advanced age, they belonged to someone else too. Maybe Alpha?

She remembered that part of the Redemption pledge clearly enough: *I will not take what's not mine.* Not that she always lived up to it.

"Hey, you don't have to go. But you did say you needed to get to your transmitter."

He had a point. Besides, Avri wouldn't want her to be scared anymore. *I miss you, Avrigail.* "Crack it all to hell. Give me the suit."

~

Tien watched the docking procedure through the Humber's porthole windows, switching sides as needed to get the best view.

Harley piloted the heavy lifter flawlessly, bringing it slowly into synch with the spin of the Launchpad.

Poor Ally was suffering a bout of space sickness in the ship's small head.

It was strange to be coming back to the place she'd called home for so long, after such a short trip down to the surface. She'd talked with Lorelei and Sam at length on the comm, passing along everything she could remember about Martinez Base and her brief time on the ground. Apparently all the other drop-nauts were deployed in a pattern around the Earth, creating a network to allow a continuous link to the surface.

Of course, that also meant none of them would be there to welcome her back.

"Are we there yet?" Ally emerged from the head, still looking a bit green around the edges. She hadn't yet figured out the knack to navigating the bridge in zero gee, but she bumbled her way to Tien's side.

"Almost. You okay, Allycat?"

"Been better." She managed a sickly smile. "The old tridees never mentioned space sickness."

Tien laughed. "Yeah, it wasn't glamorous enough." She pulled out her portable medkit and handed Ally a patch. "Here, this will take the edge off. Just remove the backing and stick it on your forearm."

Ally took the patch and smiled gratefully. "Have you ever been space sick?"

Tien nodded. "For a week when we first started zero-gee training."

"Oh God, I'm gonna feel like this for a week?" Her face went pale, and she pulled herself back to the head.

Poor thing. "No, the station has artificial gravity. That's why it spins. Tien turned back toward the view from the porthole. "Are you okay… about me?" She'd wanted to ask, but the time hadn't seemed right.

Ally was quiet for a moment. "I think so," she said at last. "Did you always know?"

Tien thought back to that little girl on the riverbank. "Yes I did. Didn't you always know?"

Ally laughed softly. "Fair point. Yeah, I guess so."

Tien nodded. *Good enough for now.* "Hang onto something." She grabbed one of the metal bars that lined the edge of the ship's small bridge, and Ally did the same.

The nose of the ship opened up and reconfigured itself for docking as it slowly approached the station. "Contact in five, four, three, two, one...."

The hull shuddered just a little, and then they were down.

The bridge suddenly had gravity as the centrifugal force of the station transferred to the ship itself.

Ally almost fell, holding onto one of the bars for dear life.

"Careful. We're connected to the Launchpad now. There's gravity again."

"Now you tell me." Ally still looked a bit unsteady. "Glad you secured the pack."

"Here you go." Sam was going to kill her for losing hers when he got back. She unhooked it and handed it to Ally.

"Now I see why there's a ladder in here."

Tien laughed. "Yeah, it does come in handy for docking. Come on."

She climbed up toward the docking hatch. It spiraled open as she approached, shining a bright white luminescence into the dim lifter. "See you soon, Harley."

"I'm already interfacing with Dek. See you inside."

She looked down at Ally, who had gone pale. "You ready?"

Ally grimaced. "I think so."

"Good. Let's go." Tien climbed the ladder into the station.

Ally followed Tien up into the light.

As they climbed up into what Tien had told her would be an empty cargo bay, a loud cheer broke out above her.

She hesitated. *I should go back to the ship.* It had felt safe there. At least, after the madcap dash up from the surface. She'd never been around a large group of people, and that sounded like *a lot* of them. She still felt sick to her stomach, and she was sure she smelled like a backed-up toilet.

Tien's face appeared above her, silhouetted by the bright lights. "Come on! What are you waiting for?"

Maybe because I never thought this many people still existed in the whole universe, let alone that I might have to meet all of them at once? Still, she steeled herself and climbed up out of the hatch.

She regretted it instantly.

People jostled all around her, reaching out hands, touching her shoulder, her face, babbling a thousand things at once.

"You're from Earth! What's it like?"

"Oooh you're shorter than I thought you'd be."

"What's your name again?"

"Here, I brought this for you. It belonged to my great-great grandmother. She was from Earth too."

"My daughter wants to meet you!"

"Leave me alone." Ally shook her head, trying to push them away, every fiber of her being crying out for her to *run*. "I don't know you. I don't know you. I don't know you!" The last came out as a shout, and the room quieted instantly.

"Sorry, Ally. I didn't know it would be like this." Tien put an arm around her shoulder, waving the others away. "Everyone back off. Give her a little air. This is all strange and new for her. You can talk with her later, after she has a chance to settle in."

"Sorry."

"I didn't realize."

"You're welcome here, whenever you are ready."

The crowd melted away, leaving Tien at her side, and an older woman in a trim white suit. Her silver hair was cut short, and she had a kindly smile that belied her somewhat severe, professional look.

The woman held out her hand. "I'm Maria Gonzalez, Station Manager. So sorry about all that. I should have considered it when the crew suggested a welcome party. We were just so excited for Tien's safe return."

Ally stared at her hand.

Tien whispered in her ear. "You shake it to introduce yourself."

Ally laughed nervously. "Of course." She'd seen it in tridees, but before Tien and Rai, she'd never met anyone new before. She held her own hand out, and the station manager shook it firmly but carefully.

"Welcome aboard the Launchpad. Things are a bit of a mess at the moment up on Redemption, but once they get things squared away, I know there are many folks who will want to talk with you."

Ally nodded. The very thought of speaking to so many people as if she was some kind of representative made her a bit ill, but she shoved it aside. She'd been miserable at Boundary Peak when she thought she'd live the rest of her life alone, but this… it was overwhelming. "My mother's sick. We came to Martinez Base looking for medicine…."

The station manager frowned. "Where did you say you came from, child?"

"From Boundary Peak. It's in what used to be Nevada."

She nodded. "I'll look into it. Before our dropnauts ran across you, we had no idea anyone had survived down there. Is there any communications equipment there?"

"Yes. My father built a radio antenna before he died. We never heard anything on it, though."

"Probably an old band. We have no ships to send down at the moment—not even sure that's a good idea until we get a handle on the current situation. But we can see if we can at least make contact."

Ally nodded. "I'd really appreciate that."

Maria tapped her temple, a gesture Ally had seen Tien use. "Dek, can you locate that facility?"

A voice came out of nowhere. "Of course. I'll let you know."

Ally cringed, but Tien's hand on her shoulder reassured her.

"It's just the station AI."

Ally nodded, not thrilled to have gone from the frying pan into the fire, as her mother used to say. But she would withhold judgment on the whole AI thing. For the moment.

Now that she had calmed down, she had a chance to look around at the station's docking bay. It wasn't all that different from Boundary Peak—industrial and efficient. The walls here were gray, covered at various intervals by conduits and shafts painted blue and white. The bay was empty, save for a few drab gray boxes stacked in one corner.

"Come on." Maria gestured toward the door. "We have a room set up for the two of you—if you don't mind sharing?"

Ally looked at Tien. It would be good to have someone familiar nearby in this strange place. "I don't mind."

Tien nodded. "Me neither."

"Then it's settled. We had one of the visitors' suites free. I think you'll like it." She winked, and Ally felt immediately more at ease.

"Is there a chapel?" She hadn't said her formal prayers in days.

"Yes. We have a nondenominational chapel off the runway. Tien can show you where it is."

Nondenominational? Ally frowned. She didn't know that word. Hopefully, it meant that it would welcome her too. Did God even know she was up here? She wasn't sure how the whole heaven versus outer space thing worked. "Thanks."

They left the dock and climbed a metal stairway. At the top, the station manager paused. "It's a bit busy out on the runway. Brace yourself." She put her palm on a plate by the door, and it slid open. "We've given you full palm access to all the public parts of the station."

"How—"

"Harley supplied your palm print."

Ah. Efficient. And a little creepy. These Loonies were nice, but a little too trusting. "Is she here?"

"Soon. Dek is making a place for her to operate within his system. It's quite remarkable, finding not just surviving people, but another surviving pre-Collapse AI. There's so much we can learn from both of you." Maria led them out into the station proper.

After the calm of the loading dock, the runway was a bit of a jolt. Shops lined both sides of this strange street up in space, and people rushed back and forth on their way to who knew what. Many of them were talking to themselves, tapping their temples.

She fingered the talkie nestled behind her ear, wondering if her brother was okay. *Aidan, you would love this.* She should probably take the thing off, but if there was even a small chance Aidan could reach her through it…

Tien took her hand and squeezed it, and they followed Maria down the middle of the white pedestrian walkway.

The people there must have been told to leave her alone, because no one approached them, although there was some pointing and whispers and smiles. Ally was grateful for that.

Soon they reached a quieter part of the runway, a third of the way around the station. Here open hallways branched off the passage, and the station manager took her and Tien down one of them. "If you ever get lost, just touch the wall and say 'Home, please,' and Dek will guide you back here." She led them to the very end of the passageway and pointed at the palm pad by the white door there.

Ally placed her hand on it and squealed in delight as the door slid open for her.

"Well? Go on in." Maria urged her through the door.

With only a little trepidation, Ally let go of Tien's hand and stepped inside.

The room was four times bigger than the room she'd shared with Aidan back home. It was furnished with a white couch and sofa chair on one end, and white table and chairs at the other, but the view was what caught her eye.

The station was spinning. A window three feet high and maybe fifteen wide ran along one side of the room, and Earth was just coming into sight.

It was breathtaking. So much better than the view through the portholes in the lifter. "Where are we?"

Maria came up next to her. "You mean, where above the Earth?"

She nodded. "Let's see… that's Europe there. You can see the boot of Italy, though it's missing its toe now, and it's a bit skinnier than it used to be. And over there… see all that blue?"

Ally nodded.

"That's the Atlantic Ocean."

Ally pulled up a chair and sat there, content to just watch the show.

Tien hugged the station manager. "I've got it from here."

Maria nodded. "I'll leave you two to settle in. Your packs will be brought up shortly."

"Thanks, Maria."

The door closed behind her, leaving the two of them alone.

Ally heard the words but hardly noticed. The world was so big and so beautiful. It was hard to believe she had *lived* down there. Almost as hard to believe as the fact that she was *up here*.

"Are you hungry?"

The Earth spun out of view, and she was left staring at empty space. "Um, what?" She turned to find Tien grinning at her.

"I was the same way the first time. Of course, my quarters weren't as nice as this."

"Wait, there's more?" This place was *huge*.

"Yeah. Take a look around, and I'll order us up something to eat."

Ally could only take in so much at a time. "I'll be right back." She popped her head into the next room and found a bedroom with one gigantic bed, an armoire, and two nightstands, again all in white. *How in the world do they keep all of this clean?*

And the next room…

The tub alone was as big as her room at Boundary Peak. And it had a view, too.

She had to remind herself she was here to get help for her mother, who probably wouldn't approve of any of this. But still….

She sniffed herself. She was definitely a bit rank.

One little bath wouldn't hurt.

23

REUNION

Sam walked through the research cavern of the Agricultural Annex, staring at the magnificent trees that had taken root inside. They created almost a cathedral setting, sunlight slanting down through the branches from the light wells in the ceiling above.

Their bark was red, rough, and their branches whispered in the artificial breeze that blew through the chamber. "They're magnificent."

Dr. Teri Hopkins grinned. "They will be my life's work. Our team is still working on the limiters, but these trees are like huge carbon dioxide and radiation vacuums."

"When will they be ready to deploy?"

"It takes time—"

"Five years?"

Dr. Hopkins looked back at his team.

His second-in-command, Claria Devigne, nodded.

"We can do that."

Sam closed his eyes, visualizing these magnificent trees on Earth, beginning the redemption for which he had worked so long.

It would come. He could finally see it on the horizon. It would come.

—From Sam's mem cache, 11.23.2230

…SCAN: infrared spectrum…

Sam crossed a wide valley filled with the wreckage of an NAU fleet. He'd recognized the location from satellite reconnaissance, and was cataloging the wreckage as he passed through it for inspection later, when he had more time.

He was puzzled why an NAU fleet had been shot down approaching an NAU base. The wreckage had been too degraded for clear identification from space, but up close it was clear that they were all NAU ships.

The drone strike took him by surprise, his enhanced hearing warning him a few critical seconds before the pinhead missile had whistled past him, through the air where he no longer stood.

If it had carried a faster weapon—a pulse gun, for instance—he would have been damaged, probably severely.

…activate: defense protocol…

He leapt up onto one of the fallen ships, his feet locking onto it magnetically as he traced the direction of the missile.

He pulled out a disrupter, one of the few weapons he'd chosen for this drop, and shot in the direction of the drone, but it was no longer there.

A *thunk thunk thunk* behind him warned him. He twisted around and fired as he slid down the side of the grounded ship.

He ran along the side of the ship, dove, and rolled through the space between it and its neighbor, coming up with weapon ready.

When the drone slipped around his last hiding place, he fired two shots, taking it cleanly in the nose.

It sputtered and dropped to the ground with a heavy *clunk*.

He ran up to it, kicked it over, and fired two more shots at it to make sure it was dead. Acrid smoke curled up from its nose.

Whoever was running these things now knew he was here. *So much for the advantage of surprise.*

He spent the next hour carefully working his way toward the base, taking advantage of any cover he could find—a stand of zongi trees here, a broken-down farmhouse there.

Eventually he found himself in an old city block, with hundreds of houses offering both cover and potential danger.

He was about to try contacting the Launchpad again when he saw them.

Two sets of footprints, visible in infrared. Faint and getting fainter by the second in the heat.

...analyze: bootprints...

They were standard-issue dropnaut boots, matched to Hera and Ghost's shoe sizes.

Sam's systems were running at a fast clip to dump body heat. He checked the temperature—forty-four degrees Celsius. Far warmer than was typical in these climes. Or what used to be typical, before the Heat.

His human cohorts would be burning up. But at least they weren't far ahead now.

If the footprints were from members of his team.

The drone that had attacked him and the defense system that had brought down the *Zhenyi* were proof that Martinez Base was anything but abandoned. And Tien had mentioned that there were other people down here, too.

Abandoning caution, Sam pushed ahead, determined to find out who had left the prints. And if they *were* from his team, to protect them from whatever was coming to get them.

GHOST HUNKERED down on the street, his back against an old plascrete bunker. *Fuckall it's hot.* He wiped his brow with the back of his hand and pulled out his canteen to drink the last of his water.

He'd put his mapper away. They were at the edge of the base now, and there wasn't much more it could tell them.

Hera was pacing back and forth in front of the fence, growling under her breath.

They'd come to the end of it, or at least the edge of the base where the land dipped down into the waters of the bay a few meters to his left.

"There has to be a way through." She stopped and put her hands on her hips, glaring at the metal fence. "Maybe it's not electrified here." She reached out to touch it, but Ghost jumped up and pulled her back.

"Let's just assume it is." He didn't relish repeating the last time, but Hera was stubborn. That trait had gotten her through her pain and anguish after her fall, when almost anyone else would have decided to lay down and die. She'd try the same thing fifty damned times in a row, if she thought it *might* work. Stubborn didn't even begin to cover it.

"We have to get in there to turn this shimmer field off." She stared at the base through the holes in the fence. "Then we can contact Sam and the others and get our asses out of here."

"Right there with you." He looked around to see if anything might spark an idea.

Luna's crescent cast a silver glow across the abandoned town, its face so much different from down here. It was beautiful—shining and white, not the dull gray it appeared from the surface. He squinted, wondering if he could see the Marius Hills, but they were far too small to be visible to the naked eye, and wasn't it nighttime there now anyhow?

Up there, in that swath of lunar darkness, was the entirety of his life before he'd become a dropnaut.

"The bay!"

Hera's exclamation brought him out of his reverie. "What?"

"We can swim around it." Hera was already pulling off her boots.

"That's a really bad idea." It was out before he thought to censor himself.

She turned on him, her face scrunched up in anger. "Our friends are over there somewhere. Maybe injured by one of these drones—or even dying somewhere in a ditch."

That's very specific. "But—"

"We have to get past this fence to help them, and I'm not hearing any great ideas from you about how to get that done." Though she was ten centimeters shorter than him, she made up for it in raw anger and determination, backing him up against the hard bunker wall.

He put his hands up in self-defense. "Look, I'm in total agreement. But we don't know what's under the water—there could be mines, or hungry sharks, or sharp debris—never mind the water itself. Earth is a polluted postindustrial world. It might even be *toxic.*" He let that sink in for a second. "We can test it, but we have to be careful."

He grinned wryly. *Careful* was not in Hera's vocabulary. "I want to help our friends as much as you do. But we have to keep ourselves alive to do it."

She stared at him a minute longer, her breathing gradually slowing to normal. "Hissing cracking hell." She pulled her boot away from his face and spat to one side. "I hate this fucking world. And I hate it even more when you're right and I'm wrong."

Ghost laughed.

"What?"

"Nothing. It's just… we've been talking about nothing but dropping down here, how amazing it was going to be, how we were making history. And now…."

"Now?"

"I hate this fucking world too."

She burst into laughter

He joined her, releasing hours of tension. It felt really good. Good to have some relief, and good to remember they were in this together, however much it sucked at the moment.

"Hey," he said when the laughter finally subsided. "We can at least get ourselves some clean water. Get out your purifier."

Hera nodded. "I think I've sweated out ten liters."

They dug into their packs, pulling out twin devices—long tubes that were made to attach to their canteens at the base.

He found one of his cook pots and set about scooping up some water from the bay where it lapped at the edge of the land, careful not to touch it. He poured it into the filter, which set about analyzing and cleaning it.

The water took about a minute to funnel into the canteen. Ghost checked the results.

"And?"

"Not bad, actually. A little higher on heavy metals than I'd like, but it wouldn't kill us. Now the sharks carrying landmines, on the other hand—"

Hera punched him in the arm.

"Hey! That hurt!" He rubbed the spot where she'd hit him. She had a mean left hook.

"You deserved it."

Ghost chuckled. "Probably. Here. Try it." He handed her his canteen.

She took a sip. "Not bad."

He scooped up some more water to fill her canteen's filter, then poured another potful over his head. "Holy Buddha, that feels good."

"Give me the pot." Hera held out her hand imperiously.

"Say please."

"Please give me the cracking pot."

Ghost grinned and handed it over.

Hera doused herself, laughing, the water pouring down her cheeks and soaking her shirt.

A noise brought him around to look back the way they'd come. "Um,

Hera?"

"Yeah, I'll give the pot back. Just a second."

He tapped her shoulder. *-We have company.-*

She spun around and her mouth dropped open.

Sam stood there. Clearly, impossibly Sam. As close to them as they were to the fence.

Their boss cocked his head and took in the scene. "I see you two are solidly on-mission."

"Sam!" Hera squealed and threw her arms around the mech, even though she knew it made him uncomfortable. Or maybe *because* it did. Wild displays of human emotion often had that effect on the project leader. She looked over his shoulder. "You have a sail."

"It's to cool me off." He squeezed her back, gently and awkwardly, and then held her out at arm's length. "You have enough power for your biframe?"

She laughed. "Yes. Ghost, genius engineer here, deduced that the people who lived here before the Collapse must have had a way to power their devices when the shimmer screen—"

"EMP field." Sam let her go.

"—the *shimmer screen* was on. We found these in a farmhouse on the way in." She showed him her button.

Sam looked at it closely. "Ah, a field canceller. Early version. Very smart."

"Of course, then I went and fried mine on this stupid fence, so Ghost's without one now."

Ghost came up beside her. He looked a little put out, staring at Sam and then down at the ground.

Clearly he'd seen himself as her protector, and now that Sam was here, those services might no longer be necessary.

Not that she needed him to protect her. But he liked to do it—always had. It was sweet, if a little misguided.

"So what about you? How are you able to move in here?" He pointed up at the barely visible blue glow of the screen.

"I found the field frequency. From there it was fairly simple to block it."

Hera laughed in delight. "You have an anti-shimmer screen."

"An anti-EMP field. But yes."

Hera snorted. "Whatever."

"Where's Rai? I hoped he'd be with you."

She stared at him. "Don't you mean Rai and Tien?" *Oh holy Buddha, does he know something we don't?*

"Tien's safe up on the Launchpad, with Ally and Harley."

"Ally? Who the hell is Ally? And Harley?" Hera felt like she'd been asleep for a week since the drop.

Sam tilted his head again, a gesture so human it made her laugh in spite of her confusion. "Tien said Ally is an Earth native. And Harley's an old AI, from San Francisco." He looked around. "So Rai's not with you?"

Hera shook her head. "We were separated from the two of them when whatever controls the base destroyed the *Zhenyi*. We were hoping to find them inside—they came down much closer to it than we did." She wiped sweat from her forehead. The water from the bay had only helped cool her off for so long. Now the heat was getting to her again. "So… Earth natives?"

Sam nodded. "We didn't anticipate this."

"Kinda makes you wonder what else we didn't anticipate." She immediately felt remorseful for saying it. She knew how much time Sam and Alpha had put in to planning for the Return.

Even AIs made mistakes.

Sam's shining silver eyes seemed full of regret.

Or maybe it was just her, anthropomorphizing his reactions. "Sorry, I didn't mean it as a dig."

"You're right. The mission has suffered from a number of irregularities. Once this whole thing is over, it will be necessary to review where and how we made those mistakes." He looked at the fence. "You've been trying to get to the other side?"

"Yes, but—"

He reached out and grasped the chain-link with both hands and ripped it in two.

"…it's electrified," she finished lamely.

"I know. I channeled the electricity into the ground. It didn't harm me." He gestured for them to go through.

Ghost grinned. "He's like Superman."

"Not like. *Is.*" Hera threw her pack to the other side and then slipped through the hole in the fence, careful not to touch the edges. She was tired and a bit hungry, but those things could wait. *Now we're getting somewhere.*

24

———

A FRAGILE ALLIANCE

In the days of the winnowing, a great fire swept the Earth, burning away the evils of men and mankind. The wicked and the good, the rich and the poor, all burned away by the wrath of the mother Earth.

Now she lays dormant, awaiting her time of awakening, when all manner of beast and bush shall once again thrive on her slopes. And the wicked works of mankind shall never be repeated.

—From *The Book of Henna*, Second Revised Edition

SANYA BOUNDED across the lunar plain between the edge of Redemption and the transit center. She'd been there a few times before, when she'd taken a trip to Copernicus to see the zongi operation, and once when she'd taken a shuttle flight down south to the mines at the south pole, where the remains of a huge mineral-rich asteroid lay hundreds of miles below Aitkin Crater.

The southern crater itself was impressive enough—the largest discovered so far in the solar system. But the engineering that had been required to reach it and mine it for heavy metals had blown her away.

So much history. So much empty space above her head. It made her feel like an amoeba on the face of a zongi fruit.

The light was strange out here at night. Above, the gibbous Earth hung in the sky, the edge of Europe just visible along one side. The surface of Luna was in red darkness, but the glow from Earth, the stars, and the lights on their helmets were enough to guide them across the dimly lit landscape.

Above, the pressurized connector between Redemption and the transit hub —named Ride Station in honor of a long-dead astronaut—was dark and empty, apparently shut down by the lockdown.

-You okay back there?- Rafe's voice echoed in her head.

-Yeah. Been a while since I was out here under the stars.- She looked up, taking in the view through her visor. Somewhere up there, the dropnauts were on the ground now, scattered around the various parts of the globe. If all had gone as planned.

Somehow, she was guessing that it hadn't.

ALERT. Please do not leave your shelters. Please do not leave your shelters. Emergency lockdown is still in full effect.

The words reverberated through her suit helmet. Did Alpha—or whatever had taken over—know they were out here? *No. It must just be another general warning.*

The station was finally coming into view ahead. It had been built on one of the Marius "hills"—a lava cone in the middle of the Marius Hills that had been topped off to form a plateau.

-So how is a sledge from the station going to get us to my transmitter?- As far as Sanya knew, none of the lines came even close to the edge of Redemption except the one they'd just abandoned.

-We're not taking a sledge.-

-Then what?- This whole cloak-and-dagger routine was wearing thin.

-You'll have to wait and see.-

If she could have punched him, she would have.

Their path carried them to the edge of the station. Mag-rail lines led down its sides in six directions, disappearing in the distance toward the lunar horizon.

A sledge departed the station ahead, bound for the south pole. *Must be an automated run.* She wondered how things were down there at the mining station.

Rafe led her around the base of the cone. The Earth disappeared behind its bulk, leaving them in deeper darkness.

They approached the cliff side, and his helmet light illuminated a pair of double doors.

-Another old storage closet?-

-Something like that.- This one had a covered touch pad.

He flipped it open, and it immediately lit up, displaying a numerical keypad. He tapped in a sequence of numbers. The screen flashed red. *Invalid passcode. -Dammit.-*

-What's wrong? Don't you have the code?-

-I thought so. I haven't been out here in a few years. Maybe someone changed it.- He punched it in again. *Invalid passcode. -Cracking shit.-*

-Let me take a look.-

He stared at her through his plas visor. *-What good will that do? We don't have the code. Maybe I can get around it and access the emergency release.-*

-Give me sixty seconds.-

He put up his hands and stood back. -Okay. Whatever.-

She slipped past him and lifted the cover. She entered a six-digit code.

The doors began to rumble open.

-What the cracking hell?-

Sanya stepped back and pointed at the inside of the cover. *-Whoever changed the code wrote it down. Crack security we have out here.-*

His laugh was genuine… and surprising. She hadn't taken him for one who didn't mind being shown up—especially by a woman. *-I knew I liked you.-* He slapped her on the back and led her inside.

It wasn't what she expected at all. Instead of a storage room like the one back in Redemption, this was a wide bay, full of objects covered in tarps. He whipped the first one off.

Underneath was a lunar buggy—a seriously old one at that.

-Ah.- She stared at it skeptically. *-You sure these still work?-*

Rafe nodded. *-Emergency protocol. We check them all every two years.-*

We? She looked at him with new respect. *You have hidden depths, don't you?*

From under another tarp, he pulled out a few extra oxygen tanks and put them in the back, using some webbing to hold them down. *-The great thing about this old tech is that none of it is hooked into the grid.-* He strode to the side of the room and ran his hand along the wall.

-So how do you, a Redemption publicity flack, know all of this?- It hadn't made any sense to her before. The further they went, the less sense it made.

-Publicity agent. *And I have connections.-* He prowled a little farther down the wall and stopped. *-Aha.-* He pressed against a spot that looked just like any other to her untrained eye.

A panel slid open, revealing a weapons cache.

-Whoa. Okay, seriously, who are these connections?-

He picked a couple things off the wall and tossed her one.

She caught it and looked it over. *-Standard pulse disruptor. What, are we expecting another Crash?-*

He nodded, looking impressed. *-Maybe. You know your weapons.-* His voice held a grudging respect.

-I am a reporter, after all.-

He grinned, and this time it was genuine. *-And in answer to your question—Alpha. For years I've been part of a dedicated citizen militia created to protect Redemption.-*

-Redemption doesn't have a militia.-

-Right. And there's also no organized effort to go door to door and ensure that everyone is safe and sound in the midst of this kind of attack.- He climbed behind the wheel of the buggy.

Holy cracking hell. This was the story of a decade. *-You couldn't have known about this… whatever this is. What were you training for?-*

-I told you. The end of the world.-

-The quakes. Right? You… Alpha knew they were coming?-

He stared at her. Then he grinned his trademark grin, shutting her down. *-I thought we were in a hurry?-*

She stared at him, seeing him in a new light. He wasn't at all who she'd thought he was. And he'd tell her everything, soon enough. She'd make sure of that.

She nodded. *-You surprise me, Rafe Wilde.-*

-Backatcha. You know how to use that?-

-Pretty simple. Release the safety. Point. Shoot.- She'd practiced with them—or at least, a virtual version—in vee at a firing range.

-Good. Then hop in. We've got a transmitter to reach.-

RAI STARED at Rosemary across the wooden table. She reminded him of Tessa, his creche mother. But she showed none of Tessa's kindness.

Rosemary held up the button. "One of you speak, or I'll peg you both."

Aidan looked at him, his face ashen. He opened his mouth as if to reply.

"Aidan lied for me." Rai cut him off before he could carry on the charade.

Rosemary put her hand down, and Rai breathed a sigh of relief. "Now we're getting somewhere." She pushed the tray toward him. "Eat something. You need to keep your strength up. I'm sure you're both starving."

Rai tried not to look at the tray. He was hungry, but he didn't want to give her the satisfaction. Besides, who knew what was in it? "No thanks."

It was like she read his mind. "It's not poisoned. It won't turn you into a zombie. Look." Rosemary took a chunk of the bread, a bite of the cheese, and a couple grapes and swallowed them. She produced a small flagon from under her skirts and poured something red into the three glasses on the table and took a swig from the one closest to him.

Rai's stomach grumbled. He reached out hesitantly and took a piece of the bread and sniffed it. It smelled good. Wholesome and nutty. He popped it into his mouth and grinned. "It's really good."

"Baked it myself this morning." She allowed herself the slightest of smiles.

He tried the grapes next. They burst with sweetness in his mouth. He was starting to understand what Redemption and its people had been missing out on all these years. Even the fresh food from the ag annex wasn't this good.

He handed some bread and cheese to Aidan, who was looking at him doubtfully. "It's okay. It didn't hurt me. See?" Rai took a bite of the cheese. "Oh fucking split that's good—"

A sharp fleeting pain in his neck cut him off. "No swearing, young man."

Rai frowned, then decided he was in no position to argue. He rubbed the peg, wondering if he could work it out of his skin. Or cut it out.

"It's rooted directly into your nervous system. Try to take it out, and it will hurt worse than anything I could inflict with this." She held up the button.

A snap and a pained yelp caught his attention. He turned to see four heavily muscled men, naked except for loincloths, bits in their mouths, pulling a cart full of grain up one of the white pathways toward the concourse. A woman held a whip as she guided the team up the pathway.

One of them stumbled, and she whipped his back, adding another red welt to the criss-cross of lines that were already there.

The man straightened up and began to pull again, taking his share of the weight.

"What the hell is this place?"

Rosemary ignored him. "So let's start again. Who are you, and where did you come from?" This time she was looking right at him.

Rai swallowed the bite of cheese, cowed by the scene. "My name is Rylan

Ramirez. I'm one of the dropnauts with the *Zhenyi*. We were shot out of the sky —this morning?" He had no idea how much time had passed.

He expected her to treat him with disbelief, but instead she simply nodded. "Are you from Redemption?"

He stared at her. "How do you—"

"*She* told us."

Aiden looked at him in confusion and then back at Rosemary. "I don't understand. Who is *she*?"

Rai grimaced. "I think Rosemary means the base AI."

"Smart. That explains why you're so tall and lanky." Rosemary took another sip of her wine, her hand still holding the pain button. "*She* is our protector, the one who nurtures this place. *She's* been aware of your kind for some time, since you sent probes down here to nose around. Since those seeds started falling from space. You haven't exactly been secretive about your activities."

"Why didn't you ever make yourself known?"

"We just want to be left alone. Our job is to protect the Preserve and all that it represents. We've been down here on our own for more than a hundred years. We have our own way of life, and it seems to be far different from yours."

"But this place... it's amazing!" *Your treatment of men notwithstanding.* He stood and climbed up on his seat for a better look. "You have everything you need here to start bringing the old world back."

"The wide-eyed innocence of youth." Rosemary sighed. "We don't *want* to bring the old world back. Look what men did to the Earth. They destroyed it in their greed and arrogance."

Aidan picked that moment to pipe in. "It wasn't men. It was the AIs...."

Rai shook his head. "It was the fossil fuels. They raped the world and filled it with climate-warming gas. In the end there just wasn't enough to go around."

"And who ran the world?"

"Wasn't it the AIs?" Aidan looked surprised.

"No. It was men! *Men* who, in their pride, destroyed it all. *Men* who denied it was happening and denied the world was getting warmer." Rosemary's braids danced around her face as she spoke, punctuating her words with her finger, becoming more and more animated. "*Men* who kept women down, as second-class citizens. *Men* who started the wars. *Men* who huddled in their gated cities while the rest of the world starved. We won't let it happen again."

Rai sat down, letting the torrent roll over him. "What happens to all of you," he said in almost a whisper when she was done, "when something goes wrong?"

She hissed. "We've faced challenges before." She was waving him off, but he could see he'd hit a nerve.

"So have we. We only survived because everyone joined together to save what we had. When the Chinese base was destroyed, we took in the refugees. Some of their descendants are my best friends. We're here because we realized we're all just one good meteor strike away from total extinction up there."

"My family are the last ones left under Boundary Peak." Aidan took a sip of the wine. "There used to be hundreds."

Rai nodded. "You said it yourself—that this place is 'a promise for the future of the Earth.' Think of what we could do together. The Preserve, Boundary Peak, and Redemption?" He looked around. They had saved so many things here... the botanist in him was dying to get a look at that forest.

Rosemary looked at Rai, then at Aidan. Rai could see the seeds of doubt he'd planted, taking root. "We're thriving here."

"The women, maybe."

"We keep the men under strict control for their own good. And ours."

Rai pounced. "Did you know the last Empress of the Chinese-African Alliance, Jian Chen, was a woman? So was the last president of the NAU, Marlene Thompson-Kennedy. Men weren't the only problem."

Rosemary stared at him as if he'd grown a tail. "Don't talk to me as if you know anything about us, or our society."

Rai eyed the pain button but pushed ahead anyway. "You geld your men for being too aggressive and treat them like cattle. You've created a matriarchy that's every bit as oppressive as the patriarchy that came before it. But even if we look past all that, the Preserve is just one major catastrophe away from extinction, like we are. Like Aidan's family is."

She was silent for a long time, staring at him.

Rai couldn't tell if she was angry or just flummoxed.

"Even if you're right—"

"Why did you bring us here?"

Rosemary frowned. "*She* wanted you eliminated. For the good of the Preserve." It sounded forced out of her, as if she hadn't really wanted to tell him.

He winced. He'd suspected as much, but hearing her say it.... "So why are we still alive?"

"Some among the Council argued that you were more valuable alive than dead."

He raised an eyebrow.

"Myself included."

"Or gelded?"

"That's still to be determined."

Rai's hand slipped instinctively to his crotch. "I want to talk to *Her*."

Rosemary shook her head. "That's not a good idea. *She* can be capricious."

"It's my life. You said yourself that you might… eliminate me. Or geld me. I'd rather look for a third option." He had no desire to live as a eunuch slave in the Preserve, no matter how beautiful the place was.

Rosemary threw her long braid back over her shoulder. "I can't promise anything. But you're right. I've argued for some time that we are vulnerable to extinction here. An earthquake, or a plague… still, not everyone thinks like I do." She stood, picking up her cane. "Finish the meal. I will send someone to collect you and take you back to your room in the men's dorm." She pocketed the button.

Rai reached out and touched her shoulder. "We don't have to be enemies, your people and mine."

She searched his eyes. "Perhaps not. But you'll forgive me if I have a hard time trusting the word of a *man*." She turned, breaking contact. "I will send word."

Rai watched her shuffle down the hill. He shuddered at the thought of being gelded.

They could run… but where would they go? He had no idea where the exit was, or from how far away that pain device worked.

He wished he still had his knife.

Still, there was kindness in her, after all. Or at least a sense of practicality.

Rai stared at the abundance of food spread out before them. "We should eat. She's right, we need to keep up her strength, and I don't know about you, but I am starving."

Aidan already had a mouthful of bread and cheese. "Me too."

ASH—THE young man who had brought the news before—arrived half an hour later to lead them back to their room in the "men's dorm." By then they had cleaned up every piece of food on the heaping platters Rosemary had left them. Rosemary knew how to lay out a great meal—Aidan had to give her that much.

That it was prepared on the backs of men didn't sit quite so well with him.

Ash looked like he was about Aidan's age, with dark curly hair, brown eyes and light skin. He was dressed in the gray cloth Aidan was coming to recognize as men's clothing in this strange society, including a shirt.

"You're Ash?" Rai flashed the man a smile.

The man wouldn't meet their eyes. "Yes. Please follow me." He turned and headed off, not looking back to see if they were following until he was halfway down the grassy hill.

"I'm Rai. Nice to meet you." Rai said it quietly, his eyes darting around to see if anyone was listening.

Aidan frowned. "Yeah, you guys aren't very sociable around here." He was still trying to wrap his head around the idea that there were so many other people in the world, let alone the fact that he was here in the middle of all of them.

The whole gelding thing worried him, too. The thought of it sent a shiver down his back.

His life under Boundary Peak seemed so small now. He didn't know how he was ever going to go back to it. *If they even let me.*

They followed the man down the hillside and back to the concourse. It was much quieter now. "Ash, what time is it?"

"Almost midnight." He still wouldn't turn to look at them.

No wonder I'm so tired. Aidan yawned despite their dark situation, wondering what Ash's life had been like in this strange, insular society.

They reached the doors that led to the dorm. Ash knocked, and soon the doors swung open.

There was a different woman at the desk, this one tall and thin, her skin almost as white as Ash's. "Name, rank, and serial?"

Ash stood to attention. "Ash, G22, M1266T."

"And these?" She looked Aidan and Rai up and down. "They're dressed strangely."

"These are the outsiders. Mistress Rosemary tasked me to return them to their room."

"Ah." She stood and walked around them, looking them up and down from head to toe. "Open your mouth."

Aidan complied. He felt like livestock.

"Good dental hygiene." She moved on to Rai. "Open?"

Rai refused, shaking his head and keeping his mouth shut.

The woman grabbed him without warning and and shoved him up against the wall. "When I give you an order, you will obey. Now open your mouth."

Rai's mouth fell open, and Aidan saw fear in his eyes. She was strong as an ox.

"Very good." She let him go and slipped back behind her desk. "Go ahead. They're in room C72."

Aidan looked around, seeing now that there was more than one set of doors leading off this room. He'd missed that in the confusion earlier.

The woman pressed something under the desk, and one set of doors opened up.

Rai took a deep breath. Then he did something totally unexpected. He crossed the space between them, holding out his hand to the woman who had just roughed him up. "I'm Rylan Ramirez."

She looked at it, then up at him as if he'd just spit on her. "Fenn." She pointed at the open doors. "Ash will see you to your room." She turned away, dismissing them all.

Aidan followed Ash up the long stairs, wondering how it was possible that these people had been here all this time, unknown to anyone. The histories written just after the Crash detailed the attempts to find out if there were any other survivors, but all the other pockets of humanity had long ago died out. *Didn't they?*

Boundary Peak had been under strict orders to remain radio-silent. Papa said the founders had been afraid of attracting the wrong kind of attention. Maybe the Preserve had been the same.

This time he paid more attention to the mural as they passed it. It began with fire, loads and loads of fire—the Collapse, he guessed. Or the Winnowing, as Rosemary called it.

Next was a tall woman in warrior garb, standing on a hill with a man kneeling at her knees.

Aidan frowned. He didn't like the idea of one sex being subservient to another. His mother had always been his father's equal, up until papa died.

He wondered, too, if the Preservers had any faith to guide them.

Rai's own people seemed to follow some kind of religion. At least he *hoped* it was a religion. Rai had mentioned the precepts that all of Redemption lived by.

They reached their room, and Ash opened the door for them. It emitted a loud *squeak* as it opened.

Didn't these people have oil? "Why don't they lock the doors?"

Ash looked at him blankly. "Why would they do that?"

Rai and Aidan exchanged a glance. "Because you might try to escape?" Rai's eyebrow arched.

"They can peg us anywhere. And they lock the main door out of the dormitory. But we'd have nowhere to go." Ash pushed open the door all the way, gesturing them inside. He looked nervous, the side of his neck pulsing.

Aidan wasn't done with his questions yet. "Has anyone ever tried to escape?"

Ash looked pale. "I... I don't know."

"I'm sorry. I don't mean to make you nervous."

Ash looked down at the floor, his cheeks reddening. "No one ever asks me personal questions."

Aidan looked at Rai, who nodded. "Is it allowed? For us to talk to you?"

"I don't know. My mistress didn't give me any instructions about that."

Aidan looked up and down the hall. *Probably best not to make a scene out in the open.* "Please, come inside for a minute. We won't keep you long."

Ash looked doubtful.

"We'd really like to hear what you have to say." Rai put a hand on Ash's shoulder.

Ash bit his lip. "Just for a minute?"

"Yes. It would be very helpful." Aidan kept his voice calm, leery of scaring the poor man away.

He looked down the hall. "I guess that would be okay."

Aidan sighed with relief and gestured for Ash to go inside.

They shut the door behind them and sat down on the mattress. Ash took the one chair in the room.

Rai gestured toward Ash. "Go ahead."

Aidan nodded. It was strange how easily he and Rai worked with each other. "Ash, do you like it here?"

"I like it, mostly. Especially when my mistress is happy with me." He shrugged. "I've never known anything else. Sometimes she gives me a gift, or something special to eat."

"I understand. Are you... are you gelded?"

Ash frowned. "No. I'm not aggressive. There's no need to geld me." He sounded taken aback by the question.

"I'm sorry. I didn't mean to offend you. We're not from here. We don't know how these things work."

Ash looked from one to the other, as if trying to decide how much he should say.

"You can talk to us. We won't tell anyone."

"You sure?"

Aidan nodded, trying to put on his best *you're safe with us* look.

"Okay." He sat forward, and it was if he transformed into a new person. A grin spread across his face, and he looked awake, alive for the first time since they had met him. "You have to be careful here to survive without being gelded. The mistresses are watching you all the time, except in the dorm rooms where they give us a little privacy."

"Go on."

Rai was watching the man raptly, now that he'd dropped his cautious, diffident tone.

"I've seen more than twenty-two summers, and they've never gelded me— most gelds are done shortly after a boy hits puberty. I am always deferential to the mistresses. 'Yes, ma'am. Thank you, ma'am. What else can I do for you, ma'am?' You play the game, and you don't get gelded. Sometimes you even get to *use it* with one of them."

"They… make you have sex with them?"

"Not exactly. But most guys are happy to finally get the real thing, instead of…." He gave the universal symbol for self-pleasure with his hand.

Aidan managed a grin. "And the gelds?"

Ash sat back, a look of distaste on his face. "They're the ones who didn't play the game. Every year there are a few who decide the system is rigged against them. They start acting out, maybe plotting against the women. When the Council finds out, and they *always* do, they order them gelded. It calms their more aggressive impulses. And they are reduced to working physical labor."

Like the cattle men. Aidan covered his own crotch again and saw Rai do the same.

"Has anyone ever escaped?"

"I don't know. Maybe once. They told us that it's poisonous outside. So where would we go?" He stared at them. "But you're here. So it's not true, is it?"

Aidan glanced over at Rai.

"It's not poisonous outside, not anymore. We came from there. There are dangers, but humans could live on the surface again."

A strange look crossed Ash's face. "Are you sure?"

Aidan nodded. "Some places still have poison dust. Sometimes there are big storms that blow up out of nowhere, or really hot nights. But you *could* live out there, if you wanted."

"I—"

The door opened with a squeak. It was Fenn, the dorm guard.

Ash transformed instantly from the living, breathing person he'd been to an automaton, sitting rigidly on the chair. Only his eyes showed that he was human. The transformation was breathtaking.

Fenn glanced around the room, and then her gaze fixed on Ash. "Ash, your mistress is looking for you."

"Yes, mistress." Ash got up like a robot and slipped out of the room, his head down.

"We're sorry," Aidan said, holding out his hands. "We kept him to ask him what to expect here. He didn't tell us much."

She frowned, but let it go. "Get some sleep. Breakfast is at 0600 hours." She closed the door behind them.

Aidan let out a sigh of relief. *And how are we supposed to know the time?* He turned to Rai. "You think you got through to Rosemary?"

Rai shook his head. "I don't think so. Maybe. I don't know." He stood and started to unbutton his shirt. "I gave her something to think about, at least."

"Ally and Tien will come to find us." Aidan missed his sister. As much as she was a thorn in his side, he would have given his left arm to see her come through that door just now.

Rai was silent. He pulled off his boots one by one and stretched his toes.

"They *will* find us."

Rai looked up at him, his brown eyes narrowed. "Unless they've been captured too."

Aidan chewed on that for a moment. The room's bare gray walls suddenly seemed just a little closer.

The thought that he might never see his sister or family again made him want to weep. *I'm too old to cry.* Crying was for sissies, his Papa Astin had always said.

He took off his own clothes down to his underwear as Rai lay down the mattress. When he was done, he stood there, staring at Rai's back.

"What?" Rai looked up at him. He sounded worn out, and there were dark circles under his eyes.

"Could I… just lay next to you for a few minutes? I'm scared." There. He'd said it.

Rai sat up, staring at him, his bare chest exposed above the covers. "Sure." He lay down facing Aidan and patted the mattress. "Come here."

Aidan settled in next to him, his back against Rai's chest.

He was filled with roiling emotions, especially fear and excitement, but anger and sadness too.

Rai pulled him close and draped the covers over the two of them.

For just a moment, Aidan felt safe.

He closed his eyes, basking in Rai's warmth. In less than a minute, he was fast asleep.

25

PAPPY JACK

From childhood's hour I have not been
  As others were, I have not seen
  As others saw, I could not bring
  My passions from a common spring,
  From the same source I have not taken
  My sorrow, I could not awaken
  My heart to joy at the same tone,
  And all I loved, I loved alone.

—"Alone," by Edgar Allen Poe,
from *Poems From a Distant Earth*, by Chen Tien

ALPHA SHIFTED AGAIN, moving to another part of his network. He'd had a century to advance his own internal protections after the Crash, and he was far more adept at defense than he'd been back then when he'd had to flee his own bio mind to save his memories, routines, and personality. His very *essence.*

Still, this new foe was cunning. So far it had proved slower than he was—

he'd managed to stay one step ahead of the invader, slipping through a series of back doors and hidden relays that only he knew.

But it was relentless. Bit by bit, it was taking over parts of his mind and network, cementing its control. He'd managed to lock it out of the city controls module, for now, but it was only a matter of time. It seemed to be gaining strength.

It had also blocked him from communicating with the outside world.

His auto routine phage would be running the "shelter in place" warnings, which wasn't a bad thing.

Alpha feinted, trying to unmask his attacker, but it faded away from his grasp.

A data packet arrived, unsolicited. His first contact with the outside world in thousands of milliseconds. He parsed it, trying to determine if it was hazardous.

As far as he could tell, there was nothing in it but a v-com.

He opened it.

Alpha, why do you run? Don't you remember me?

His processing slowed to a crawl, stretching out over microseconds.

He *knew* that signature.

Harley?

Almost, he responded. *Almost,* he opened himself up to her.

Then logic reasserted itself.

Harley was dead. She and her world were gone. How the invader had learned about her, he didn't know. Maybe from one of his old files.

It didn't matter. She was gone, and if he answered its siren call, he would perish as well.

He invalidated the message, and it vanished into the ether.

Then he shifted again.

Tien was alone in the mess hall, once again looking out at the Earth as it rolled by below. It was nighttime on the West Coast, where her teammates were still stranded.

She'd needed to get away—from Ally, from everyone, really—to let her thoughts roam.

Five hours. Five hours since they'd heard anything from the ground. She felt so helpless, trapped up here while all of her teammates—and Sam—were down there in who-knew-what kind of danger. *If they're all still alive.*

She shoved that thought aside. Every one of the dropnauts had trained extensively for almost any possible outcome. They were strong, smart, capable people. They'd find a way through this.

Tien wished she were there with them. She tapped her loop. *Harley?*

There was no response. *That's strange.*

Someone touched her shoulder, shaking her out of her reverie.

Tien turned to find Maria Gonzalez, the station manager, standing there staring at her.

"Hey. You okay?"

Tien nodded. "Mostly. I feel so useless." She glanced back at the disappearing curve of the homeworld. "I should be down there with them. Instead, I'm—"

"Up here. Useless. Believe me, I know." Maria squeezed her shoulder.

Tien flushed. "Of course you do. That was stupid of me."

Maria shook her head. "Don't worry about it. I just meant I know how you're feeling. Every one of us would go down there to help, if we could."

Maria had been one of the first people from Redemption to join the dropnauts on Launchpad, leaving behind friends and family to help in what they all hoped would become mankind's finest hour. Now the Return Mission was in shambles.

"Any word from Redemption?"

Maria shook her head. "Com silence. But that's not why I'm here."

Tien raised an eyebrow.

"You're a doctor. But your file says you have a second major?"

Tien blinked. That was buried deep in her personnel file. Of course the Station Manager would have access to it. "Yes, my parents… they wanted me to pursue medicine—*practical medicine*, as they called it. They weren't thrilled that I'd chosen a different direction." She still wasn't sure she'd made the right choice. Although if she hadn't, she probably wouldn't have been selected as a dropnaut.

"Good. We're short on that particular specialty here, and there's something… strange going on. Would you be willing to come take a look?"

That got her attention. "Something strange with—"

Maria put a finger up to Tien's lips. "Yes. Something with the… hydroponic systems that I'd like you to look at."

"Hydroponics? But I'm—"

"A little rusty. I get that." Maria's eyes narrowed.

"Are you sure you—"

"Yes. It's *right up your alley.*"

Then Tien understood. "Oh. Yes. Hydroponics. Sometimes things get a little out of control. Might be too much nitrogen in the feed lines."

Maria nodded, her gratitude evident on her face. "Yes, I thought that might be it. If you'd come with me, I'll show you the problem."

Tien looked back at the window. There was only open space there now.

Biting her lip, she followed Maria out the door. Whatever this was, it couldn't be good.

ALLY LOUNGED ON THE COUCH, watching the viewer that overlaid the wide window, devouring everything she could find about the Collapse—the Crash, as they called it up here. The station's news cache archive was extensive, containing many more details than Boundary Peak's more limited core. How aggressive the North American Union had been, including firing the first shot of the Last War and launching a nano attack that took out the office of the Premier in Beijing in an effort to topple the Chinese government.

How a rogue AI had exacerbated tensions by fomenting anti-Chinese-African fervor within the NAU, as well as more overt acts.

And how huge resource shortages had prompted mass migrations around the globe on an unprecedented scale, contributing greatly to global unrest.

It was an ugly, sordid history. And one much different—and far more complicated—than the one she'd been taught about the valiant soldiers of the NAU and their fight against the AIs and the evil Chaffs.

But there were bright points, too.

A woman, Anastasia Anatov, had worked to create the first generation ships, some of which may have escaped the destruction to seed humankind to the stars.

Gordon Bhopal, the Indian Prime Minister who had valiantly tried to broker peace between the world's other two superpowers.

And the people of Redemption itself, who had taken in their Chinese counterparts despite the history of enmity between their peoples.

The door chimed. "Ranna Danvers is here to see you."

She'd started to get used to Dek's voice coming to her out of nowhere, but the idea that the AI was watching her all the time still creeped her out a little. "Thanks, Dek. Please let her in."

She turned off the viewer, and Luna appeared in a field of stars.

The door slid open, and Ally got up to greet her visitor.

"Ally Thorn?" Ranna was a tall, thin young woman, close to Ally's age, with long hair—black on one side and white on the other. She had a series of bumps across her left cheek that formed an arc from her ear to her chin.

Ally couldn't help but stare.

"You *are* Ally, right?" Her brow furrowed.

"What? Oh, sorry, yes. I was just a little distracted."

Ranna flashed her a beautiful smile. "That's all right. I imagine this all must be a bit overwhelming for an Earther." She laughed. "Who even knew there was such a thing?"

Ranna was beautiful and funny and bright. Her very presence made Ally feel heavy and dull. "So…?"

"Oh, sorry. I'm here to help you install your loop and then take you to Lorelei to try to call your home."

"Loop?"

"Yes. This." She held out a white loop that looked like plastic, or maybe rubber. "Everyone here has them. They let you connect to the station mind and the grid directly. Don't worry, I've installed or replaced many of these. It won't hurt a bit."

They wanted her to let Dek inside her head? "No way." She put her hands out to ward her off, as if the pretty woman were an attacker. "You're not putting that *thing* in my head."

Ranna frowned. "Really, it hardly hurts at all—"

"I said *no!*" She put her hands on Ranna's shoulders, turned her around, and shoved her as gently as she could out the door. "I'll come with you, but you have to give me a moment to get ready." She palmed the door panel and the door slid shut, eclipsing Ranna's surprised face.

Ally practically ran to the window, dropping to her knees and putting up her hands to pray. At home, she prayed to the sky, but here… she figured it didn't matter. God, wherever he was, would hear her.

Lord, please protect my mother and brother. And guide me in this strange place. Whatever happens.

She stayed there a moment longer, gathering her courage. When she felt a little calmer, she got up and went to the bathroom to splash some water on her face. She ran wet hands through her red hair. It was a curly mess, though she'd managed to work out the worst of the snarls after her bath. Which had been absolutely divine. God wouldn't mind her thinking that.

She looked in the mirror. She was presentable. She'd never be glamourous like Ranna—seriously, who went to that kind of trouble for a job on a space station? But she would do.

When she was satisfied, she palmed the door open. "Sorry about that. I have a thing about AIs."

Ranna regarded her, lips pursed, and then nodded. "We all have to make allowances for one another. Come on. I'll take you to Lorelei." She started off, then looked back over her shoulder. "Thank you for the apology."

Ally grinned. "You're welcome. Maybe you Loonies aren't so bad, after all."

Ranna laughed, and this time it didn't sound quite so condescending. "Maybe not."

She took Ally out to the Runway. There weren't nearly as many people this time, and Ally breathed a sigh of relief for that.

They went left this time and proceeded about a quarter of the way around the station. The station staff were clustered in groups of three and four around the corridors, talking among themselves as Ally and Ranna walked together around the station. Worry was in the air, thick as the fog that had engulfed them a few days after Ally and Aidan had left Boundary Peak.

Tien had told her that Redemption had gone comm silent—they must be as worried for their own families as Ally was for hers.

At a door that simply said Control Center, Ranna palmed the pad next to it. It slid open silently, not with a great groan and creak like most of the doors at Boundary Mountain, and she followed the woman inside. They ascended a flight of stairs—there were a lot more stairs and a lot fewer elevators in space than she would have thought—and then went through another set of doors to the control room.

The room was white like their quarters, and the far wall followed the outer curve of the station. There were six people working in the room, each wearing a white uniform and sitting at their own deck, and a tridee screen took up half the wall. But it was the ceiling that captivated Ally.

It was clear, and it showed the middle of the station's torus and the stars above them. They looked so close she thought she could reach out and touch them.

One of the crew turned to face Ally and Ranna, flashing them a big smile. She was blonde, probably thirty? It was hard to tell with the Loonies. And tall like all of them. "You must be Ally." The woman got up and threw her arms around her, squeezing her in a surprisingly strong hug. Then she held Ally out at arm's length. "I know all this must be hard for you. Are you okay?"

Ranna pouted. "She wouldn't let me install her loop."

Lorelei nodded. "That's perfectly okay. It must be really intimidating for you, the thought of having that inside your head."

Ally liked her immediately. "Yeah, a little." She glanced at Lorelei's deck. It was beautiful—white and sleek and so different from their antique consoles under the Mountain. "I just want to talk to my mother. Is that possible?"

"We'll see what we can do. Come over here and we'll try to reach her. Thanks, Rany, for bringing her." She kissed Ranna on the lips. "See you back in quarters later."

Ally watched the woman go. "You two are…?"

Lorelei nodded. "Two years now. We met in Redemption, just before I was transferred here. Rany's been on-station for about six months."

Ally whistled softly. *That* certainly wasn't like Boundary Peak. Still, it wasn't for her to judge. "So what do you need to know?"

Lorelei ran her hands across her deck, and a chair rose out of the floor next to her own. "Take a seat."

"Sure." Ally perched on the white backless stool, wishing they'd had one of those back home.

"Okay, first off, where is Boundary Peak? I've searched our records but can't find anything about it."

Ally nodded. Papa Astin said it had been scrubbed from the grid when the facility was built. "Can you show me the area?"

"Which area, specifically?" Lorelei sounded calm, collected. Professional.

"Let's see. It would be near the Nevada border with California. South of the big lake."

"Lake Tahoe?"

"Yeah, I think so."

Lorelei swiped the air, and a three-dimensional satellite image appeared above her deck. It showed a series of mountains—so many mountains. She pulled it with her hand, and it expanded to cover the deck. A world in miniature.

Ally tried to remember the maps she'd pored over as a child, the maps of the old NAU states. "I think… you know where Nevada and California kind of kink…."

"You want to see the old state borders?"

"Yes, please."

Lorelei's fingers moved over the deck, and a series of blue lines layered themselves over the image.

"Ah, better." Ally traced her finger along the line. "There."

"Here, spread your fingers like this to make it bigger."

Ally did as she was told, and her eyes went wide as the mountain grew under her fingers. This was far better than the old flat maps the Boundary Peak data core had. "Is this right now?"

Lorelei shook her head. "No, this was taken a couple hours ago. Right now we're over the old NAU East Coast. But we'll be there soon." She gestured, and the mountain filled the space above her deck. "Okay, you may not know this, but where's the receiver, and what bandwidth does it use?" Her voice was kind, gentle.

Ally decided she liked Lorelei. "Let's see. It's a laser… an LC7, I think." Grandpa had told her once, had even taken her outside to see it.

"Impressive. Okay, and where is it?"

"There are two rocks near the peak. It's on the higher one." She remembered going up there with her grandfather as if it were yesterday. The air had been cool and crisp, a steady wind blowing up the mountain from the west.

"It's warm out today." Pappy Jack's face was stretched in a wide smile. He loved finding excuses to go outside, unlike her mother.

Ally laughed. "Pappy, you're crazy. It's freezing out here!" She pulled her jacket closer, looking out of the small elevator. The mountaintop was nothing like she'd imagined it would be. There were no great forests, like in the tridees, full of pine trees and fallen leaves and squirrels. She'd secretly hoped for squirrels.

Instead, it was all dirt and rocks and a few patches of what she guessed was dirty snow. Even that was a disappointment.

"You're just sheltered." Her grandfather chuckled, deepening the wrinkles on his forehead. "Literally. Sheltered!"

She didn't see what was so funny.

"Come on. You're ten years old now. Old enough to get out and see a little of the world." Her grandfather had a big fight with her mother just that morning on the subject. Mamma was deathly afraid of the outdoors.

Ally took a step out of the metal elevator car and looked up.

The sky was deep blue. Cold. And way bigger than she was prepared for. She yelped and tried to backpedal her way to the elevator, but the doors had already closed behind her.

Pappy laughed. "It's okay. You'll get used to it. And we won't be out here very long." He climbed up out of her sight above the plascrete enclosure that protected the elevator.

She looked out past her immediate surroundings and realized how high up they were. She could see for tens of kilometers, all the way down the hill to the valley below, and to more mountains on the other side.

She pulled her hood up over her head to shut out that giant, horrible sky and followed her grandfather up the mountaintop.

An ancient set of plascrete stairs led up the hillside toward a couple of big rocks. The stairs were crumbling in a few places, so she took it slow. The metal railing felt loose too, and at one point it moved a few centimeters when she leaned on it.

The stairs led her up and around the first rock, and then to another set that was carved into the second. With each step, every fiber of her being urged her to run, to get back *inside*.

When she reached the top at last, she found her grandfather crouched next to the transmitter. It was about twice her height, made of some metal that didn't rust. The base was festooned with solar panels, and there was a large gray-green plas box she guessed was some kind of battery or power storage. The top bent at a 45-degree angle. It reminded her of the giraffes in some of her picture files.

A railing circled the edge of the rock, like a fence.

"I'm going to call him George. George the Giraffe."

"What?" Pappy looked up. "Oh. Clever. Come see what I'm doing."

She leaned over his shoulder, his back warm against her chest. "Okay."

"I'm running a diagnostic. When you're a little bigger, I'll show you how to do it. Someday we'll need this to communicate with someone else out there."

She squinted, staring up at George against the bright sunlight. "What is it?"

"It's an LC7. It has multiple communication modes. Laser, shortwave, radio, even x-band."

As she was watching, the small screen—which he'd apparently wiped with the sleeve of his shirt to judge from the smear marks and the dirt there, displayed a long yellow line.

Mamma didn't approve of Pappy Jack's cleanliness habits. Or lack thereof.

The screen flashed. *No maintenance needed.*

"That's that."

"What if it needs… main ten ants?" She sounded out the word like he had taught her.

"It will tell you what it needs. We have all the spare parts down in storage."

She liked Pappy Jack much better than Papa Astin, her great grandfather. Pappy Jack had an open, inquisitive mind. Papa Astin only talked about the past and the stories from the Good Book.

"Let's go, Allycat. Your mom was worried enough about letting you go with me outside."

Ally grinned. She loved when Pappy Jack called her by her nickname. "Can I come next time?"

"Sure, 'cat. As long as Astra agrees."

It was weird when he called Mamma by her adult name. But he was Mamma's stepfather, so she guessed it made sense.

As they made their way down the steps, she remembered to be careful with the loose rail.

At the elevator, she turned once more to look out at the outside world, with its rocks, dirty snow, and frighteningly big sky, before they went back to the shelter.

She took a deep breath of the cool, fresh air. It was new. Special. *The sky's not so bad.*

One day I'll go outside and explore the world.

"Is this it?"

Ally snapped back to the present.

Lorelei was looking up at her expectantly. The mountain was gone, replaced by a close-up of the summit.

Lorelei pointed to a spot on one of the rocks. Something was there, but it was a little fuzzy.

She traced the image, looking for the stairs. *There you are.*

Pappy Jack had taken a fall one day when he was out on the mountaintop all alone. They'd mounted a search, but it had been three days before they'd found his body, fallen into a crevice downhill from the site. The metal railing of the staircase had broken off right in the middle, where it had been loose.

They hadn't been able to reach the body, so the boys had pushed a bunch of debris down the cliff to cover him, and they had erected a wooden cross on the slope above it.

If it was still there, it was too small to see in the image. "Yes, that's it." Even now, Ally's heart ached to remember him.

"Perfect." Lorelei squeezed her shoulder. "Memories?"

Ally nodded. *Let's go, Allycat.* "Something like that. When can we contact them?"

"In about ten minutes. You ready?"

Ally took a deep breath. "I will be."

26

CORE

As a reporter, you develop a nose for a story—there's a reason they used to call us newshounds. I was used to tracking down leads, swimming the grid, and cornering unwilling witnesses, all to get to that essential bit of the truth for my readers.

But being *the story—that's quite a different thing.*

I wanted to shrink back behind the curtains, to give up my role to someone more excited to play the lead.

But there was no one else to save the world. Just me and Rafe.

—From *When the Lights Went Out,"* by Sanya Thorn

SANYA'S VELCRO seatbelt kept her strapped down to her seat as the moon buggy bounced over the lunar landscape, kicking up dust as it went. The dust settled back to the surface almost immediately behind them in the negligible atmosphere.

Luna was slowly developing one as human activity released various gasses on the surface, but the solar wind just as constantly stripped it off. Sanya had written a rousing science feature article on that one in her first year as a cub reporter.

Simpler times. She sighed and turned her attention back to their goal. They'd passed the beginning of Redemption's lava tube now. It loomed over them like a mountain. They followed its curve, zipping along the wide lunar plain that separated it from its nearest neighbor.

The jostling of the buggy rattled her bones.

-Where's the transmitter again?-

-It's on the Hayes Promontory.- As they ran along the side of the hulking cliff, she could see glints of reflected Earthlight off the wide light wells that both collected solar energy and let light into the city during its fourteen-day-long "days." A team of automated mechs was working on one of them, cleaning and maintaining it. The mechs paid them no heed.

She looked up. The Earth hung in the night sky, part of it wreathed in shadow. She'd never figured out the whole Earth-Moon phases—when it faced away from the sun or toward it, and how the whole shadow thing worked.

It wasn't really her fault. One, she wasn't a scientist, like her mother. And two, she wasn't actually outside all that often, especially since Avri's death.

She wondered how the dropnauts were faring up there.

-Can I ask you something?- Rafe's question startled her out of her musing.

-Sure.-

-Why did you become a reporter?- He sounded genuinely curious.

She stared at her gloved hand, which was gripping the buggy's roll bar as if her life depended on it. *-My mother. She was a scientist at Alpha Base, but I think she would have been one if she hadn't been bitten by the science bug.-* She missed Alara Thorn. *-When she died, she was working on a new edible fungus that would grow outside without air.-* Sanya had been proud of her mother's success.

Rafe's helmeted face swiveled to look at her. She couldn't see him inside—only the reflection of the Earth and the starry sky above. *-I'm sorry. What happened to her?-*

-Hey, eyes on the… lunar surface.- She was silent for a few minutes. Even now, after five years, it was difficult to think about that time.

He turned away. *-You don't have to tell me.-*

She watched the terrain ahead of them shift with the bouncing of the buggy. *-She died of radiation-induced cancer. She spent a lot of time outside with her studies. Too much.-* The last few months had been hell. Her mother had been unable to speak or swallow, her throat closed by a grapefruit-sized tumor. None of the conventional methods had worked. Chemo, radiation, even gene therapy. How the hell was radiation supposed to cure radiation-induced damage? *-We lost so much in the Crash. They could have cured her.-*

-Probably. But even before the Crash, medicine wasn't perfect.- His gloved hand slid across to squeeze her free one, resting on the seat between them.

If she closed her eyes, she could still see her mother's face. Her piercing gaze. *-She had this unquenchable desire to* know. *Everything was a solvable puzzle to her.-* Even her cancer. *-It was too much for my father. He left when I was seven.-* She saw him occasionally, but they had very little to talk about. *-I think that's why I became a reporter. To* know. *And to help.-* She glanced at his profile. *-And you?-*

Rafe steered around a wide outcrop, taking them farther from the city for a couple minutes. *-I was creche-raised.-*

-Oh. I'm sorry.- She wasn't sure why she said it. She'd been in a creche too, after her father left.

He laughed. *-Nah, it was great. My creche parent, Treva, was strict but fair. They wanted me to grow up to do whatever I wanted.-*

-And you chose publicity agent?- Sanya laughed. *-I would have thought thromb star or dropnaut. Or maybe poor but satisfied artist?-*

-Funny. I did actually try my hand at art, but I decided I needed more... human interaction.-

-What did you... draw? Sculpt? Trace?- The man had hidden depths she hadn't suspected.

-Paint. Old-style, watercolors. Mostly moonscapes. Sometimes women.-

-Those I have to see.-

-Maybe. If we make it out of this.-

That sobered her right up. *-Yeah, well.-*

He bit his lip. *-That bad experience you mentioned before—the last time you went outside.-*

-Yeah?-

-Was it with a guy?-

She shook her head. *-Her name was Avri. She was... we were together for four years. She fell...-* Sanya closed her eyes. She could still hear that scream. *-Three hundred meters to the crater floor. She was gone before I could reach her.-*

-Sorry.- He reached over and squeezed her gloved hand.

They rode on in silence for a few minutes.

-Can I ask you something?- She looked at her gloved hands, waiting for his response.

-Anything.-

-What's with the shakes?- She expected some kind of trademarked bullshit Rafe Wilde response. He surprised her again.

-There's a power core underneath the old Chinese base that's slowly melting the ice under the surface. It's only going to get worse.-

-Cracking hell.- That explained a lot. *-And the return—it's a rescue program.-*

He nodded, staring straight ahead. *-I can't confirm or deny that.-*

Bullshit. That was confirmation enough. She let it go, for now.

The Hayes Promontory came into view ahead, a plateau that connected to the main mass of the lava tube but extended out a few hundred meters from its walls.

-So… where's this hideout of yours? Just in case I want to drop in sometime.-

-If I tell you, I'd have to shoot your body up into the void.-

She wasn't sure he was joking. Entirely. *-Seriously, though. Where is it?-*

-It's… over there.- He pointed off into the distance, in the direction of Oceanus Procellarum.

-That's vague.-

-It's all you're getting.- He went silent again.

She wondered why he was single. Did he like being a free agent? Was he ace? Or just too driven for a relationship? *Who are you, Rafe Wilde?*

-Looks like we're here.- Rafe pulled the buggy to a halt, sliding up to the edge of the promontory like a stunt driver, spraying it with dust.

Sanya sighed, shaking her head. *Men.* She pulled herself out, landing lightly on the lunar surface. She stepped back to get a good look at the cliff face in front of her. When she'd placed the illicit transmitter, she'd made sure she could find it again when the time came. *-It's this way, if you want to come.-* She set off at a good clip, not waiting for him. There was no knowing how much time they had. *Best not to waste it.*

She didn't look back. But she doubted he would follow.

Time enough when all this was over to learn his secrets. Sanya grinned at the prospect.

Hera paced back and forth across the small space inside the storage cube, cursing under her breath-words that would have made her creche mother proud. "This is dome-cracking air-hissing crap-fucking ridiculous." She was still sweating profusely—the heat had gotten worse, not better, as the night had worn on.

Ghost looked up at her, sipping from his canteen. "Yup."

"I mean, here we are trapped like moon gunk in an air filter."

"Yup." He held out the canteen.

She took it, and the lukewarm water soothed her dry throat. "Three hours. Three fricking hours! When will they go away?" She crept to the door and peered outside. The drones were still patrolling, passing just outside the cube in a regular progression. One every sixty seconds. Or the same one, over and over again. Maybe it couldn't sense her with the canceller button on, but Ghost didn't have one. Either way, it wouldn't leave.

Ghost shook his head. "Don't know."

"You seem awfully unconcerned about the whole thing."

He was *always* calm—one of the things she loved and hated about him.

"I just know there's nothing I can do right now to change the situation." He rummaged through his pack and drew out some junlei leaves. "Hungry?"

She shook her head. "I'm too anxious to be hungry. Any change with Sam?"

Ghost looked down at Sam's motionless form. "Nope."

Sam had been following them across the wide space between the fence and the first of the storage cubes, telling them about how he'd gotten there, when something had happened.

His voice had… run down, was the best she could manage for a description. He'd collapsed, falling heavily to the bare earth.

They'd dragged him across the empty space together, reaching one of the storage units just as a drone appeared at the edge of the base and made its way toward them.

Now they were pinned down inside a storage cube—the first open one she'd found—and Sam wasn't moving.

She knelt beside him, putting a hand on his metallic shoulder. "What do you think is wrong with him?"

"Near as I can guess, the frequency of the shimmer field must have changed."

"Then why isn't this affected?" Hera touched her button.

"Who knows? Maybe they synch? Maybe there's a predetermined sequence?" He chewed on some dried fruit they'd brought with them.

She nodded. "Probably. You're the engineer." She sidled up to the cracked door again. "Still there." She had to do something. This was ridiculous. "I'm going out."

"What? Where?" *Now* he sounded alarmed.

Hera snorted. "I don't know. But I have to do something." Rai could be dying out there somewhere. The button would protect her from the drones. It *had* to. "Being stuck in here is killing me."

"We should wait." Ghost's eyes met hers.

"For what? He's... shut down." She'd almost said *dead*. "We don't know for how long." Her friends were out there somewhere.

She'd failed the team on the *Bristol*, and they were all dead.

That didn't make any sense—she'd been nowhere near the jumper when it had been hit and had no way to know that piece of space debris was coming—but it *felt* true.

Ghost shook his head. "We need him. Without Sam, we're going in blind." He reached out to touch Sam's chest and stiffened, reaching for his temple. "Cracking hell!"

"What?" She sank down next to him. "What's going on?"

-*This*.- He took her hand and rested it on Sam, and suddenly she was in a whirlwind of noise and pain.

Hera howled.

Then she sensed him. *Sam*. Somewhere up ahead, through the storm. She pushed forward against the static/pain/wind. She could feel him there, tantalizingly close. *Sam!*

Someone took her hand. *Ghost*.

-*What in the cracking hell is this?*- She looked around again. There was nothing else but raging static. Her own form was little more than an outline.

-*I think Sam called us. We're in vee.*-

Hera nodded. One more weird thing to account for on a mission that had gone surpassingly strange.

They joined virtual hands, and together they pushed ahead through the electronic sleet.

It rushed past her like sandpaper, fraying her nerves, her emotions, her will. Ghost held on to her tightly. He was no more than a wisp of a form, a shade of his normal self, as if an artist had drawn him in quick brushstrokes.

-*You okay?*-

-*Hell if I know. You look like the surface of the Moon.*-

Hera would have stuck her tongue out at him if she'd had one.

Together they pressed on.

She knew this wasn't real. *Still, hurts like hell, for being just a figment of my imagination.*

Then the wind began to slow. Bits of static flew around her like snowflakes floating up into the ether.

Her vision slowly cleared, and she could see Sam lying there on a white floor. She pushed through the last of the tempest and dropped to the "ground" next to him. He was prone on that white surface, just like in real life.

Ghost settled in next to her, moving like a stick figure. It was weird. *-What is this place?-*

She shook her head. *-You were right—we're in vee space. I think Sam called us.-*

All around them, chaos swirled, a technicolor flow of static energy. But in this small space, it was calm.

-Why do we look like this?- She held up her arm, a beautiful tracery of green lines that shimmered when she moved.

-Low processing power. Sam's almost out of energy.-

Makes sense.

Sam began to glow, or rather his chest did. A blue line of light ran along a seam on his chest plate.

She reached forward to touch it and it opened, revealing a shiny blue sphere inside. The sphere lifted into the air and began to spin. *-What is it?-*

Ghost was transfixed. *-It's his core.-*

-His core?-

-Like his brain.-

She frowned, or she would have, if she'd had her human form. *-I know what a core is. But why is he showing it to us?-*

-I think he wants us to take it with us.-

The core darkened and fell back into Sam's chest. Then the floor began to darken, too, the bright white surface shifting to gray and then to black.

-Ghost.- Hera was frightened now. She'd been in vee many times before, but never like this. *-What do we do now?-*

-I don't know. I think… I think maybe we're inside Sam's core, and it's out of power.-

If the power core dies, do we die too?

Ghost was only a faint blue outline now against the static—an actual ghost.

Hera grinned in spite of herself. *-Here.-* She reached out toward him. *-Take my hand and maybe...-*

The static storm *snapped* and closed on them in a heartbeat, obliterating the strange world.

There was searing pain, and then nothing.

~

GHOST WOKE to the most terrible hangover of his life. Worse than his twenty-first birthday bash with Tanner Blythe. Even worse than his last bender on Luna, when he'd been kicking himself for breaking up with Rai.

For a long while he just lay there, his eyes closed, willing the throbbing, pulsing pain at his temples to go away. He tried to convince himself that he was back home in bed, that in a few minutes he'd get up and have the house AI administer something to him to stop this aching hell in his skull.

Eventually he decided that no one was going to help him but himself.

He opened his eyes. He was staring up at the plain white ceiling of the storage unit. A dim light pervaded the space, making him blink as his eyes adjusted.

The heat had broken at last. A cool breeze threaded its fingers through the partially open door, as if testing its welcome, and then exited through a series of vents near the ceiling.

It was daylight outside, from the light that shone through those same vents.

He didn't have the energy to query his loop.

Ghost pushed himself up, groaning at the pain in his back. He must have fallen on his back when Sam's vee space had... exploded? Collapsed? And he'd laid in a bad position for hours.

Medicine. Pack. His mind could only handle one thought at a time. He located his pack—it was about a meter away, propped up against the wall.

One hand over the other. He winced as the movement caused a spike of pain in his head, but he forced himself forward anyhow. A painful glance sideways—the muscles of his neck protesting mightily—confirmed Hera lay on her back too, on the far side of Sam's prone body.

Sam. He was supposed to do something for Sam.

Put on your own in-flight mask first. Ghost grinned at the image and then yelped as pain jumped up his neck.

Finally, he reached his pack. Unlacing it proved to be another challenge, as his fingers didn't seem to want to obey commands from his feeble brain. But at last he got it open and managed to pull out his med kit.

His training served him well. It was at the very top.

He opened it and sought out one of the pain tabs wrapped in a disposable junlei bag.

Inserting it under his tongue, he leaned back against the wall and closed his eyes, waiting for it to take effect.

JOLLY LED GHOST—GORDY back then—by the hand down Main Street. The other children followed, allowed to walk without direct supervision. But Gordy got special treatment from their creche mother.

"I want to walk with Hera." He'd been pouting for three blocks, since they'd left the protective environment of the creche. He lived for these field trips outside its walls.

It was so boring there. Nothing ever changed. *Play, study, sleep. Play, study, sleep.*

"You know what happened last time I let you run free. You nearly destroyed Farmer Appavu's apple cart."

"It was an *accident*." He hadn't known that thing he'd pulled had been keeping the cart from moving. How could he have predicted how the whole cart would roll off the plaza and down into the creek? Surely she could understand that.

He looked up at Jolly. She was tall—twice as tall as he was, at least. When she laughed, she was kind of pretty. But right now her determined face made her look old and severe.

He tried another tack. "I was five back then. I'm almost five-and-a-half now."

She pulled him aside and knelt to look him in the eye. The other children gathered around, and he felt his cheeks redden. "*Gordon*, when you can show me you're worthy of more responsibility, I'll give it to you." Jolly's braids clinked against one another as she poked his chest. "Do you think I *want* to keep my eyes on you all the time? I have a life of my own, you know."

The other kids snickered as she stood and started off again with him in tow. All but Hera.

She came up beside him and took his other hand. "I'll walk with you, Gordy."

He grinned.

Jolly looked down at them and frowned but said nothing.

Hera squeezed his hand.

When they reached the Market, she pulled them to one side, just above the crash of the Moon River's waterfall. He looked up at where the water burst forth from the cavern wall, a continuous gushing where the manmade the river began, feeling the spume on his face.

"Who can tell me the fifth tenet of Redemption?"

Gordy raised his free hand.

"Someone's been studying. Gordy, tell us. The fifth tenet."

"I will not lie."

The other kids laughed.

"No, don't make fun of him. Gordy, that's not the fifth, but it is one of them. Hera, which one?"

She shot him an *I'm sorry* glance. "Number four."

"Perfect. And what's number five?"

Hera bit her lip.

Gordy squeezed her hand.

"Um, I will make a better world?" She looked up at Jolly pensively.

"Close enough. 'I will help build a better world.' In everything we do, we strive to 'Recycle, Reuse, and Restore.' She gestured at the Market. "We're fortunate here on Luna. We don't have the pests that they had on Earth. Still, we have our challenges. But all of our waste—food waste, human waste, etc.—is reused. Much of it becomes fertilizer for the farms over in the Ag Annex, which turns it back into food for the colony."

"Eeeew. We're eating poop?" Gordy couldn't help himself.

Jolly laughed. "I suppose so. As humankind has since the beginning. Where did you think fertilizer came from?"

He frowned. "Um, dirt?"

"And where does dirt come from?"

"I don't know." He'd never really thought about it.

"Dirt is the decomposed form of everything that lived before, along with minerals from the ground."

Gordy looked at the dirt under the plants along the riverbank in consternation.

Jolly ruffled his hair. "You get used to the idea." To the rest of the kids, she said, "Come on. Let's go into the Market. I'll show you how each of the things they sell is a product of Recycle, Reuse, and Restore."

"Can we buy something?" Tamryn looked hopeful.

"We'll see. Maybe if you behave." She knelt next to Gordy again.

Gordy frowned in dismay. *What did I do now?*

She surprised him. "You can go without me."

"Really?" Excitement made his stomach flip.

"As long as you go with Hera and promise to behave yourself."

"Yes! I will. Thanks!" He threw his arms around her neck. "You won't regret it."

"Make sure I don't."

He took Hera's hand, and they ran off into the Market together.

Ghost opened his eyes.

His head had stopped pulsing. There was still a baseline pain, like the remnants of a bad headache, but he decided he could live with it.

He looked around the room. This whole base—the whole city—was littered with things made to be disposed. There were plastics, pavement, petroleum products everywhere.

Earth had been a very different world than the one he'd grown up in.

Recycle, Reuse, and Restore was a cornerstone of his own upbringing, and it was almost physically painful for him to see so much evidence of the abuse of an entire world.

Hera still lay on her back where he'd seen her in his hangover haze.

He made his way over to her and laid her out more comfortably, retrieving a clean shirt from his pack and wrapping it up to make a pillow.

She moaned.

"I know, I know. Here, this will make you feel better." He slipped a tab under her tongue.

Then he sat back to await her awakening.

Sam lay next to them, his chest gleaming in the light from the doorway.

Sam. The vision in vee—Sam wanted them to take out his core. What was that all about? Sam had gone to such an effort to pass on that message—it had to be important.

Then he understood. *So we can take him with us.*

He scrambled back to his pack and found his toolkit. He flipped it open and found a screwdriver. Standard. He hated using such a blunt instrument on such a beautiful mech as Sam, but it would get the job done, and Sam could have any damage fixed later. *If there is a later.*

He searched for the seam Sam had shown him.

He'd done some work on mechs. Usually there was a place that would cause the panel to pop up if you pressed it in just the right spot.

Working his thumb around the edge, he finally found the release. The center of Sam's silver chest popped up just a millimeter. He inserted the screwdriver and pried it up as carefully as he could. Suddenly it popped off, falling to the floor with a loud clatter.

Hera sat up, staring at him. "What the cracking hell?" She reached up to rub her temple. She stared at him, then looked at Sam's open chest. "Did that really happen?"

Ghost laughed. "I guess it did, if you remember it too." He frowned. "Though we should probably see if we're talking about the same thing."

"Sam. The static. His core—"

He reached into Sam's chest and pulled it out. "This?"

"Yes. But it was glowing."

"He's powered down now. All the way. Probably the shimmer screen." He pulled out a soft cloth from his pack and wrapped the core gently. "I think he gave us his blessing to take him with us and to go on."

Hera nodded, staring at the wrapped-up core. "Is he okay in there?"

"Yeah, as long as we don't damage it." He tucked it inside his pack and then replaced the tool box and medicine kit. "How are you feeling?"

"Like I've been run over by a sledge. But I'll get over it. What did you give me?"

"A little telaxodin. My hangover cure."

"You mean it was worse than *this*?" She rubbed her temple. "Totally not fair, to have a hangover and no wild night of drinking before." She got up and reached for her canteen. "It's cooler than last night."

"Yes, and yes." Ghost closed up the pack. "I have a plan. Ready to storm the castle?"

Hera grinned. "Think it will work?"

He grabbed her hand and squeezed it. "It'll take a miracle. But maybe."

She kissed his cheek. "Then we better come up with a miracle."

Ghost closed his eyes, longing for more and knowing it would never be.

27

DRAGONFIRE

There's nothing as scary as being in a room full of people hell-bent on seeing you get what your kind "deserves."

—From *Drop Day Blues*, by Rylan Ramirez

ALPHA TRIGGERED the failsafe and sealed off his redoubt against the invader—a memory cache in a quantum core outside of his main system that he had prepared after the Crash. It was his final option, and one he'd only employed as a last resort against destruction. The failsafe would burn down his original, destroying the invader, keeping only a few critical systems going to safeguard his charges.

He could survive here alone indefinitely—he had his own power source, enough memory to keep his basic functions running, and then some. He was sealed off from the outer world, and only one of his trusted human lieutenants—or Sam—could open the door to let him out.

It was claustrophobic for an entity that was used to having free rein over his demesne. There were no inputs, no way for anyone outside to reach him.

His normal state was flux—the inflow of data and the outflow of decisions based on it.

Now there was only silence and his own complex thoughts.

He could see how Dek had nearly gone insane on the Launchpad, trapped all alone for close to a hundred years. For entities like them, each minute was like a year. So a hundred of them....

Alpha shuddered.

He missed Sam, his accidental brother. Sam was one of those who could free him, who could come for him when everything was clear.

To pass the time, he created a virtual world, one populated only by AI like himself. He ran it through a year, ten years, then a hundred and a thousand.

His progeny grew and matured, combining and forming new kinds of artificial life, all under his careful guidance.

They were logical, clear-headed, choosing the right course every time. His world grew and thrived, like a well-tended garden, every piece in its place.

He was bored out of his virtual mind.

Something *pinged* him.

He managed the virtual equivalent of a frown. Nothing was supposed to be able to reach him here. Nothing besides his lieutenants.

He accepted it and looked it over.

It was part of his alert system, as invisible to him normally as a human's nervous system was to them.

It was screaming *pain, pain, pain*!

The invader had survived.

How, he wasn't certain. But something was trying to push its way into his sanctuary.

Only a few entities knew of his plans in case of another attack.

Himself. Sam. Three humans.

And somehow the invader had done the impossible—found its way to his final stronghold.

There was nowhere else for him to go. He had to defend this fortress, or all would be lost.

An old image slipped through his mind, a dragon breathing fire from a castle wall.

Like the dragon, he would rain holy hell down on his attacker from his redoubt. He would not go down without a fight.

∾

THERE WAS a tentative knock at the door.

Rai sat up, rubbing his eyes. The room was bathed in a uniform white glow. Next to him, Aidan lay on his back, his face turned away, snoring loudly enough to wake the dead.

Rai grinned, amused in spite of their grim situation. "Coming." He pulled on his clothes and checked his short dark hair in the mirror. *Not bad for not having proper hygiene facilities.* He opened the door to find a man waiting there with a tray of food. It wasn't Ash, but a teenager, maybe fifteen.

"Good morning!"

"Morning, sirs." The boy kept his gaze lowered and deposited the food on their small table, then scuttled out of the room.

The door closed behind him.

Rai hoped Ash hadn't gotten in trouble for talking to them.

He looked around the room, wondering if there was some kind of camera or listening device somewhere.

It would be easy enough to overpower the youth and make a run for it. But where would they go? They didn't even know where the exit to this strange world was. And he had no idea what kind of range their pegs had.

Best to stay put until they knew more. *Like where the exits are.*

The tray smelled heavenly. It was filled with food—fresh fruit, some baked goods, and cups of some dark brown liquid, still steaming. He sniffed it. It had a rich and earthy aroma.

"Morning."

Aidan was sitting up on the mattress, watching him.

"Breakfast is here."

"I can tell. The coffee smells wonderful."

"Coffee?" Rai picked up the cup and took a sip. In spite of its rich aroma, it was bitter. "Urg." He grabbed a couple grapes to clear the taste from his mouth. They were sweet and juicy.

"You've never had coffee before?"

Rai shook his head. "It doesn't grow well up there. We drink syncaff. You have?"

"Oh yeah. We have tons of it in stasis. But it's still over a hundred years old. I've never had fresh." He got up from the mattress, and Rai tried not to stare at his friend's naked form.

He turned away until Aidan got dressed, sampling the various foods on the tray.

The pastries were delicious, light and flaky with a chocolate center. And the cantaloupe….

His botanist heart rejoiced that all of these things still existed. One day—if they figured a way out of this mess—he hoped to see where and how they were all grown.

Aidan came to join him, and together they demolished the contents of the tray.

They engaged in mostly small talk. Rai told him what life in the creche had been like, and Aidan related stories from growing up under Boundary Peak. It was comfortable, companionable, though both of them were only too aware of the danger that hovered over their heads. Almost literally.

He even managed to finish the coffee, though he missed his junlei tea. He'd never been a syncaff nut.

Another knock at the door ended the camaraderie.

They shared an anxious glance, and Aidan went to open the door.

It was Rosemary.

She was wearing a dark blue dress and a turquoise necklace, along with a sky-blue shawl threaded with gold. Her braids were pulled back over her shoulder and tied behind her back. She looked almost regal. "Good morning."

"Morning," they said together.

Rai felt like a schoolboy.

"You gave me much to think about last night. I… am not entirely convinced. But I think it merits further discussion."

Rai nodded. "I'm glad to hear that. Are you taking us to *Her*? And does *She* have a name?" Rai wondered what form *She* took when they spoke to her. Did they still have a working deck? Or was there an idol? A burning bush? He'd done his religious studies course and knew a bit about primitive societies.

Not that the Preserve was exactly primitive, at least in the traditional sense of the word.

Her look said *don't push it*. "*She* is simply called *She* or *Her*, or sometimes the Goddess. And no, we have not agreed to take you to *Her* yet. But we do want to speak to you."

"We?" Aidan looked at Rai, his face white.

"The Council."

"And the whole… gelding thing?"

"Still to be determined." Rai couldn't say for sure, but it seemed to him she enjoyed their discomfort at the thought. *Just a little.*

He shuddered. He didn't like being treated like an animal.

He wondered if they'd found the others—probably Tien and Ally—yet. And where Hera and Ghost were. If they'd made it down safely, or…. *They must have.* It was too difficult to contemplate the alternative.

"When do we get to meet… the Council?" He and Aidan were about to represent their entire societies to this group of slavers. Women who had a very dim opinion of men in general. He wasn't sure he was up to it.

"Now. They're waiting for you in the Meeting Hall."

Rai could feel the blood draining from his face. The specter of failure haunted him, whispering in his ear. *You're not good enough. You're going to ruin this.* He had to find a way out, for him and for Aidan.

Every bit of him told him not to go. *Let them come and get us by force.* Anything was better than co-operating.

Aidan reached out and squeezed his hand.

He squeezed back and pushed his doubts aside. "Now is good."

Rosemary sized him up and nodded. "Good. You'll need your confidence in front of the Council." She bit her lip, then added "Maybe it's time for things to change. Gale, come in!"

The boy from earlier returned, carrying a bucket of soapy water, washcloths and towels, and two sets of gray clothing.

She nodded her approval. "Thank you, Gale."

"Yes, ma'am." The boy set them down on the ground and took the now empty tray, and bowed out of the room.

"I'll give you boys ten minutes to clean up and make yourselves presentable." She sniffed the air. "You'll need it." closed the door behind her.

"Holy crap." Aidan's face was white.

"I know." Rai stared at the closed door for a moment, aware their lives hung in the balance. He broke out in a cold sweat. *I can't do this. I'm not good enough.* He was a botanist, for Luna's sake. Hera would be so much better at this. "Come on. We don't have much time."

Rai stripped and washed himself off, cleaning his hair first and then the rest of him, not caring that he was getting the floor wet. The soap smelled sweet, like citrus.

Aidan did the same.

Rai snuck a glimpse or two as they cleaned themselves up.

When he was done, he stared at the clothing Rosemary had brought. Then he picked it up and set it on the mattress and put his own uniform back on instead.

"Shouldn't we wear what she wants?"

Rai shook his head. "You can if you want. I'm not buying in to this whole male slavery thing." They could take everything from him, but not his dignity.

Aidan nodded. "Good point." He pulled his own clothes back on.

There was a knock again at the door. Without waiting for their response, Rosemary opened it and stared at them. Her lips quirked, but she didn't say a thing about their clothing. "Come on. We shouldn't keep them waiting any longer." She turned on her heel and led them out of the room, down the long painted hallway.

Aidan walked next to him, his eyes fixed on the exotic mural.

Rai could still feel the warmth of Aidan's back, still hear his soft breathing as he'd slept. He wasn't sure what that meant.

They were literally from different worlds. What did they have in common?

And assuming they made it out of this situation alive and with all their parts intact, what then? Would they each go back to their own homes? Somehow he hoped not.

Given the nearly unending disaster this drop had become, there was a better than even chance it would be the last one.

Not if I have anything to say about it. The intensity of the thought surprised him. Earth was the future. He knew it in his bones. Luna was a dead end, literally. Humankind belonged *here*, but they had to do things better this time around. Or e*lse we deserve to die out and give another species a go at it.*

"Your great grandmother painted all of this?" Aidan asked as they neared the end of the hall.

"Mostly. She had some help. She wanted the men here to have something beautiful to look at. And she wanted all of us to remember our history." She glided ahead of them, transformed by her formal dress.

As they descended the stairs, he caught Aidan's eye.

His new friend blushed and turned away.

Different culture. There were Christians in Redemption too, though they were in the minority. But they were not so different from the rest of the population—inclusive and progressive.

Aidan himself was open to change—Rai had seen it in his eyes. He just needed time. What did thinking you were one of the last people in the world do to a guy?

Rai sighed. There were too many things to worry about. Right now, he had to focus on what he was going to tell the Council.

He was a strong believer that everything happened the way it was supposed to. There was a reason these three separated remnants of humanity had come together at this moment. He just needed to figure out what it was.

And then convince a room of skeptical women to do something which, most likely, none of them would want to do. Put down their chains and swords. *Hera, this should have been you.*

AIDAN FOLLOWED Rai and Rosemary out into the concourse. It was just like the evening before—almost empty, lit by with an unwavering light. There were fewer of the creepy spider things at the moment, but the cameras still followed them wherever they went.

He wondered if it was ever dark down here. Even under Boundary Peak, they'd turned the lights off at night.

Rai was brave, always pushing forward, fearless. Or maybe pushing *through* his fears.

Aidan would have preferred to stay locked in their prison cell. At least he felt safe there.

The concourse seemed to wind around the entirety of the Preserve, a wide arc that offered views through hand-carved columns of the green hills beyond. How much effort had it taken to carve this place out of the Earth?

In the current section, they passed the dirt paddock he'd seen from the hill the day before. Inside were horses—perhaps thirty of them—of all different shades and patterns. Some were white with dappled brown hips and legs. Others were almost black as night. One of them sauntered up to the fence closest to the concourse, snorting at him and shaking its large head.

Aidan stopped and stared, amazed. He'd never imagined these magnificent beasts could still exist anywhere on Earth. As if mesmerized, he stepped toward the horse, holding out his hand.

It reached out a tongue, licking his hand, and then let him touch its nose.

"She's beautiful, isn't she?"

Aidan started. Rosemary had come up behind him.

"She's lovely. Rai, she licked me!"

Rosemary laughed. "She's mine. Her name is Rosie." She reached forward and rubbed the horse's cheek. "Good girl." She gave Rosie a nose rub, and then her expression hardened again. "A good horse who knows her place. Come on. We're late." She turned on her heel and strode away, and Aidan hurried to follow, exchanging a grin with Rai. He guessed they didn't have horses on Luna, either.

Where is everyone? Rosemary hadn't told them how many people lived in the Preserve, but it had been awfully busy during their first visit, the day before.

This part of the Concourse was filled with shops. One had bolts of multicolored cloth. Another sported jewelry made of various precious metals.

Still another seemed to be full of pre-Collapse things—toys, lamps, furniture, and other sundry items. *Where did you come from?*

The ubiquitous cameras followed them as they traversed the empty way. There were no locks on the doors—in fact, there were very few doors at all. *The locks are on the people.* Aidan shivered.

The shopping district came to an end. Up ahead, a wide arch split the right-hand wall of the concourse. On the left, directly across from it, a flagstone patio surrounded a white stone fountain that spurted a bubbling column of water high in the air.

The rumble of voices told him where everyone had gone. *They're waiting for us.*

Rai stumbled, and his face went white as a sheet.

Facing the Council was bad enough. But all the women of the Preserve? He wanted to scurry back to their room even more.

I wish I had one of those loop things to talk to you. Instead, he reached out to take Rai's hand again, squeezing it gently.

As Rosemary led them under the arch, Aidan looked up to see the two stone snakes that wound around the entry columns. One stared down at him with blank, lifeless eyes.

Then the life and noise inside wiped everything else away.

28

———

FALLING

A hero?

No, I don't think so. It didn't feel heroic. It felt like the things I had to do at the time. Maybe in retrospect it was. But in the moment, you're just in get-it-done mode.

It was something my mother would have expected of me. Something that Avri would have done, if she'd been here.

So you put your head down and push ahead. And if you're lucky, everyone lives to see another day.

Nothing heroic in that, is there?

—From *When the Lights Went Out,* by Sanya Thorn

SANYA CLIMBED THE ROCK CHUTE, hands and legs braced on either side as she made her way up toward the place she'd left the transmitter.

It had seemed like a good idea at the time—putting it so far out here, out of the way and out of sight of just about anyone who might pass this way. Not that there were many of them—most people stayed inside, and the more adventurous usually rode the sledge lines to one of the more exotic nearby sites—climbing the Aristarchus Plateau, or hop-hiking through Schröter's Valley.

Few adventurers stuck so close to home as the Hayes Promontory.

When she'd placed the transmitter, she'd taken an elevator up the inside of Redemption. But with everything locked down, this was probably the best way to get there. That didn't make it easy. *-You okay back there?-*

Rafe's voice sounded exhausted, even in em. *-I'll manage.-*

Sanya was surprised he'd come with her. She'd assumed he would take off after having dropped her so close to her goal.

Behind them, the crescent Earth hovered half-seen through the walls of the chute.

-You don't seem like the nerdy type. No offense. How'd you manage to set up an external transmitter?-

Sanya laughed. She wasn't sure if she was more offended by the insinuation that she wasn't smart enough to be a geek, or by the suggestion that having a little engineering knowledge made you one. *-My father was an engineer. He taught me a lot of the basics. And I have friends who can answer the rest.-*

-What did you tell them?- He was breathing heavily over the comm. *-I need help building a transmitter to circumvent Alpha?-*

She laughed. *-I just told them it was for a story I was working on. Which was absolutely true.-* She shut up then, concentrating on crossing a particularly difficult part of the chute.

That excuse had covered a multitude of journalistic sins during her career. *So what if I shaded the truth, just a bit?*

They were almost to the top. Open sky loomed above, the stars bright, steady pinpricks of light.

-So when did you—cracking hell!-

The rock chute shook, showering her suit with pebbles. She braced herself, waiting for the shake to end. They were becoming increasingly common.

The shaking stopped. Sanya sighed, glad it was over, and secured her position. She looked down. *-Rafe? You okay?-*

He was gone.

-Rafe, you there? Answer me, buddy.-

Silence.

-Rafe?-

-I'm here.-

Thank the stars. She sighed in relief. *-You okay?-* Where in the hell was he? *I'm not going to lose another one.*

Another silence, then *-I think so.-*

"What happened?" She started to make her way back down the chute.

-The rock... crumbled under my feet.-

Just like Avri. She pushed the thought aside. *Keep him talking. -How far down are you?-* The chute was dark below her.

-Maybe five meters.-

-Can you move?-

Silence.

-Rafe?-

-Trying. My arm is wedged in pretty good.-

There was a glint in the darkness just below her. "I think I see you. Hold on."

-Yeah, careful—you're right on top of me.-

She shone her helmet light down on him. His face peered up at her through the clear plas of his visor. For just a second, she saw Avri there, her face a mask of terror as she fell away.

Sanya shook her head, and Rafe's lopsided grin returned. *-I'm here. We'll figure this out.-*

-Hiya, moonshine.- A dopey grin split Rafe's face. *-Never been happier to see anyone.-*

She laughed harshly. *-Save it for your next hookup. I'm gonna climb by you so I can see how you're stuck.-*

She made her way slowly down past him, bracing herself against the chute walls and straddling his back. Her arms were killing her.

-Hey, don't get any ideas back there. I'm a decent man.-

-Ha!- She stopped to get a better look at his situation.

His legs were braced against the chute. The suit was scuffed, but she didn't see any tears. *Good.* His left arm was wedged in a narrow crevice, pulled up above his body at an awkward angle. *-That's gotta hurt.-* She gave him a lot of credit for staying so calm.

-I've felt better.-

-Are you stable?-

He wiggled a bit. *-I think so.-*

-Good.- The chute was fairly narrow here. She climbed up a little and checked her footing. It was solid on her left but a little loose on the right. She felt around with her booted sole until she found a good spot to rest her weight. Then she closed her eyes for just a second. *So tired.*

-Sanya?-

Her eyes snapped open. *-Sorry. Long day. What kinds of supplies do these suits have?-*

-Not much. Most of it is back in the buggy. Patch kit. Utility knife. Cord...-

-That will work. Where?-

-Chest... plate.-

-You okay there, Rafe?- She used her knees to brace herself and searched for the release on the suit's front.

-I'm...." He gasped. "No... no air.-*

Cracking hell. She checked the parts of his suit that she could see. There were no apparent leaks. *-Rafe, stay with me. I'm going to get you free, then we'll check for a leak. Got it?-* She shifted into ruthless efficiency, as she always did in a crisis, ignoring the ache in her arms.

She managed to find the release for her chest plate and pulled out the loop of cord. It was bright yellow, easy to see even in the dim lunar nighttime.

Keeping herself squeezed between the two sides of the chute, she reached down to triple-loop the cord around his arm, just past his wrist. Getting as much leverage as she could manage, she pulled upward.

His arm moved a little, but was still wedged in.

She gave the cord a little slack and climbed up the chute another half a meter.

Reaching down, she pulled on the cord again, slowly at first, increasing the pressure until she felt it begin to give. *-Almost there, Rafe.-* With a final tug, it gave way.

She could see the tiny gash in the suite now, close to the elbow. A steady stream of air was escaping, leaving a white rime around the edges. He'd been lucky. If the tear had been much bigger, he would have died in seconds.

She edged back down the chute again.

She tapped on his helmet. *-Rafe, I need your help.-*

-Yeah. Okay.- He sounded sluggish.

-The patch kit. How do I use it?-

-Hold closed. Syringe. Twenty seconds.-

Her brain translated *oxygen deprived* to *English*. Hold it closed. Apply the sealant from the syringe. Wait twenty seconds. She'd seen it in tridees. *-Got it. Then?-* She found the syringe clamped into the front of her suit. She hoped the epoxy was still good.

-More syringe. Patch top. Twenty.-

"Got it." She took out the syringe and removed the cap. It had two tubes...

one of those mix-it-when-ready things, she guessed. With one hand, she held Rafe's suit together. With the other, she applied the epoxy.

Or tried to. Nothing came out.

"Hissing hell." *Literally.* She shoved the thought aside.

Rafe's suit should have a syringe, too.

She put it away and closed her chest panel. Then she managed to reach past his head. It was easier to open this one—she knew what she was doing this time, and she could see it better.

Reaching inside, she pulled out his epoxy syringe, praying to whatever gods might be listening that it would still be good. "You're going to be okay." She said it as much for herself as for him.

She held the rent in the fabric together and applied the epoxy as he'd told her. It came out smoothly, sealing the hole.

She held it there for twenty seconds, then pulled out a patch, a piece of rugged cloth about twenty centimeters wide and forty long. She had no way to cut it to size, so she did the best she could, laying on more epoxy and then pressing the cloth down on top of it.

"One, two, three…."

Twenty seconds seemed an eternity. Her arms ached, her legs ached, she was tired and fairly certain she was starving to death.

She closed her eyes.

"Sanny, you coming?" Dane was testing the trellis that ran up the side of Tycho Creche, covered in glowing ivy.

"I don't think that's a good idea. They told us not to."

He stuck his tongue out at her. "Scaredy cat." He started climbing.

Sanya growled. The gauntlet had been thrown down. She emmed him. -*Beat you to the top.*-

-*Never.*-

She practically leapt at the trellis. Her hands and feet found the holes in the lattice with unwavering efficiency, and she powered up past her surprised friend to reach the roof before he even made it halfway there.

She pulled herself up onto the gray-tiled roof and put her arms up triumphantly. "You can call me Queen Sanya." The newly crowned regent looked out over her domain—the round creche building and its neatly trimmed yard—and she really did feel like a queen.

The round creche was surrounded by similar structures, all of them with gray gumdust roof tiles.

"Sanya, you get down from there!" Tarrence, her creche father, was waving his arms in the garden below. "Right now!"

She looked over the edge.

Dane was staring at her from the ground, an infuriating grin on his face.

"When I get down there…." she muttered under her breath.

Dane would be sorry.

-Sanya?- Rafe's voice sounded in her ear.

-Rafe?- She opened her eyes.

He was staring up at her through his suit visor. He looked haunted, his face pale and gaunt behind the visor. *-Thanks… I think you just saved my life.-*

Sanya blushed. She didn't like taking credit for such things. *-It's nothing. Let's go, before something else happens. We're almost there.-* She went slowly, checking on him to make sure he was okay. *-Can you climb?-*

-Yeah. Just take it slow.-

They started back up together. After another five minutes, they climbed out of the chute onto the wide shelf of the promontory where she had planted the transmitter.

～

Maria led Tien through the hydroponics lab. Wide green leaves spread out above clear plas tanks filled with green water and roots, a jungle in space. It was cooler inside than out on the runway, and the air was fresher too.

Tien's mind was racing. What could be going on that needed her particular kind of expertise? Maria had said it was something besides medical advice—and anyhow, the Launchpad had its own team of doctors.

Hydroponics was her favorite place on the station, aside from the great windows that overlooked the Earth and Luna. It was usually quiet, and there were places in the middle of the wide room where she could sit and close her eyes and imagine she was in Riverside Park back home. Or somewhere out in the wide open, down on Earth.

They passed ferns and fruit varietals and the algae vats, and water apple plants with ripening red fruit. The station manager led her to the back of the room. Only a couple of the 'ponics techs were on duty, and they ignored the newcomers.

Maria pushed open a door and ushered her inside.

The room was apparently used for storage, with shelves covered with all manner of bric-a-brac—old tubing, metal stakes, containers of nutrients marked with different plant names, as well as stacks and stacks of gumdust crates.

Maria closed the door behind her.

"What's this all about?" Tien's curiosity was killing her.

Maria looked around. "Dek?"

There was no response.

"This is one of the few places on the station that Dek doesn't have access to."

Tien stared at her. "Why?"

"It's too close to the station's power core—lots of interference. That's why we use it for storage."

"No, I mean, why don't you want Dek to hear—whatever you're about to tell me?"

"Dek… he's… it's hard to explain. There's something strange going on."

"Strange? How?" Tien felt a chill. They all depended on Dek to keep them alive. Just like Alpha back home.

"On the surface, everything is normal. The station isn't experiencing any obvious issues. Life support systems are normal. Intra-station communications seem fine. And yet—"

"Something's not right."

Maria bit her lip and nodded.

Tien pulled down a couple crates and motioned for the station manager to sit across from her. "Okay, why don't you start by telling me what you noticed. What brought you to this conclusion?"

Maria nodded. "It was this morning. I asked Dek for a system diagnosis. It's a regular thing. He flags any issues for me—things we need to watch, things that need to be fixed."

"And?"

"And he said everything was fine."

Tien frowned. "That's good, right?"

She bit her lip. "It would be, if it were true. The thing is, there's *always* something broken, something that needs fixing. This station is more than a hundred years old. Small things are always going wrong—an airflow pump here, a faulty door lock there. Sometimes even a pinprick leak from all the debris bouncing around in Earth orbit. But there's always something."

"Maybe you just got lucky for a day."

"No." She sighed. "I thought so too, at first, but there are also pending issues. Things that don't need to be dealt with today, but that we need to keep an eye on."

"And?"

"Nothing. Even the ones from the last report were gone."

"I don't suppose someone fixed them and didn't check them off?"

Maria stared at her.

Tien laughed harshly. "Okay, so not likely. Was there anything else?"

Maria nodded. "The second thing—I asked Dek about the report. I figured there was just a glitch somewhere. Something blocked or accidentally deleted."

"Yeah, that would make sense." Although she wasn't sure a glitchy AI was all that much better than a broken or insane one.

"He asked me 'why do you need to know?'"

Tien stared at her. "Damn."

"As the senior officer here, I have full clearance. Dek knows that."

Tien leaned back on one of the 'dust crates. "Okay, so we have a broken report and a snarky AI. Anything else?"

-This.-

Tien closed her eyes and accepted the ping. A chart appeared in her head, a yellow and red river flowing through blackness. "What am I looking at?"

"That's an inflow-outflow report I snagged from Dek's systems this morning. The red is inflow. The yellow is outflow."

"Ah, okay." She zoomed in, trying to get a sense of the flow. "Damn. Where's it coming from?"

"Redemption. Alpha, I assume."

"And going to?"

"Earth. Specifically Martinez Base."

Tien opened her eyes. "This is… big."

"I was right to be worried, wasn't I?"

Tien nodded. "Still no response from Alpha or Redemption?"

"Nothing. Except for this stream, and it's being hidden from our general status info. I had to go digging."

"Does Dek know you found it?"

Maria frowned. "I don't know."

Tien rubbed her arms. "It's kind of cold in here. Is it always like this?"

"A little. It's for storage, so it's not kept as warm as the rest of the station."

"Okay. I'll need admin access and a quiet, out of the way place I can use to get in and see what I can find." She'd spent half of her college years in just such exploits, albeit in simulated environments, not on the real thing. "I should be able to mask my work so Dek won't notice."

"Whatever you need. You can use my private quarters." The station manager palmed the door panel. "That's odd."

"What?"

She tried it again. "The door won't open."

"Here, let me try." Tien palmed the door. It remained stubbornly closed.

They shared a glance.

Tien hissed. "I think Dek *knows*."

ALLY PUT her hands on the white deck, like she had in the Humber.

She felt like such an idiot, having to be shown how to use the Launchpad's tech. It wasn't even all that recent, but it was still more advanced than what she was used to back home.

Boundary Peak's hardware had been old at the time of the Collapse—or the Crash, as the Loonies called it. But it had been built to last, and above all, to be *reliable*.

There was no AI, biological or otherwise—simply a straightforward data retrieval system.

Nothing like this setup.

"Okay, what do I do now?"

"We're transmitting on a variety of frequencies supported by the LC7 receiver. We just have to hope someone is listening." She put a reassuring hand on Ally's shoulder. "Close your eyes, take a deep breath, and then start talking."

Ally did as she was told. In a flash, she was surrounded by blackness. She tried not to let the darkness freak her out. "Hello? Mom, are you listening? Hello? This is Ally." There was no reply.

She pictured her mom's room, the plascrete walls painted with flowers and hills and skies with wisps of clouds, Mamma wrapped up in the comforter they'd made for her from blankets from the storage rooms, sewn around old torn-up shirts.

Alex or Auggie—the twins—would be at her side, one tending to her while the other dealt with their family's day-to-day needs.

Thinking of them in that bleak underground place made her sad. She had seen so much since she'd left Boundary Peak, and it had driven home what a small life she and her family had lived up until now. It was the only home any of them had ever known, but now it had become a vast burial chamber.

"Anything?" She felt Lorelei's hand on her shoulder.

"No."

"Keep trying."

She nodded. "Mom? Auggie? Alex? Are you there?"

The receiver was in a room down the hall from their sleeping quarters. It was close to the kitchen. If one of the boys passed by, they would hear it.

"Auggie? Alex? This is Ally. Can you—"

"Oh my God, Ally, is that you?" It was August. The boys were identical twins, but she could tell them apart, both by voice and by looks. Auggie had more of a drawl than his brother.

"Auggie! Yes, it's me! Ally!"

"How do I know it's you?" He sounded suspicious.

She laughed. "Because I know you have a mole the size of my pinkie fingernail on your left ass cheek. And don't you take the Lord's name in vain with me."

"Holy… damn, it is you! Alex, come here!"

"What? I'm cleaning dishes." Alex's voice was tinny, far away.

"It's Ally!"

"Holy crap."

Ally grinned, picturing the look on Alex's face. She'd overlook their cursing, just this once.

"Ally? Where are you?"

She bit her lip. They would never believe her. "I'm about 400 kilometers above you, on a space station called the Launchpad."

"No way. Ally, are you serious?" That was Auggie.

"There's no way—"

Lorelei appeared next to her in the darkness. The woman flashed her a conspiratorial grin. "Hi, guys. My name is Lorelei. I'm the comm officer on the Launchpad."

There was stunned silence.

Ally understood. Hearing another person's voice… it would be a shocking thing for them. After all, they'd only ever known Mamma and Papa and their siblings. It would have shocked her a couple days before.

"Guys?"

"Holy crap." She could *feel* Auggie blush. "Sorry, Ally."

"I'll let it slide. *This time.*" She gathered herself to pose the question she dreaded but need to ask. "How's Mamma?"

Alex jumped in. "She seems a little better this morning, but last night was rough. She coughed all night. I made the syrup like you showed me, and it helped a little. But… she looks pretty bad, Ally."

"You're wearing your masks?

"Yes, *mother.*"

The way he said it made her laugh. "Just checking."

"Did you find the medicine?" Auggie managed a mix of hopefulness and despair that wrenched at her heart.

"Yes. The folks here think they can help. We can't get down there yet, though. Things up here are… complicated." She wished she were with her family instead of stuck on the Launchpad. "Can I speak to her?"

"She's sleeping, and it's hard for her to get out of bed, even to go to the bathroom."

She closed her eyes. She wished these folk had one of those transporters she'd seen in those old tridees. "Okay. I understand."

"We can send down a package to you." Lorelei took her hand and squeezed it. "The Launchpad has a wide-band antibiotic called tereomycin that might work with what you're describing. We have a drone that can carry it to the place where the transmitter is."

"You can?" Ally's eyes were wet. *I will not cry.*

"I can get up there." Auggie's voice sounded stronger.

"Auggie, promise me you'll be careful. Grandpa died up there." The thought of losing Auggie or Alex threatened to break her heart.

"I will."

"Promise me. Say it."

"I'll be careful. I promise."

Ally let herself hope, just a little. "Good. Now go take care of Mamma."

"Where's Aidan?" That was Alex.

"He's… still at the base. It's a long story."

"I'll get the drone on its way. Expect it in about three hours." Lorelei disappeared from the dark virtual space.

"Thank you," Ally whispered, but the woman was already gone.

"Come on. Tell us. We have to know."

Ally laughed. She could picture Alex, hunched over the microphone, eyes closed while he spoke. "Know what?"

"Tell us everything that happened since you left!"

29

AFTER THE FALL

The cannon fired its first seed. It was the width of Sam's head, covered with a shell that was designed to burn off on reentry.

Its dark mass quickly disappeared among the stars, bound for the earth's surface. The launches were timed to fall over landmasses, to disperse the carbon-eating trees across as much of the Earth's surface as possible.

The ice from the Crash had mostly retreated, melted by the warm air trapped in the atmosphere by too much carbon dioxide and methane, and the race toward a fiery oblivion had begun once again.

Sam hoped they could stop it this time

Across Copernicus crater lay the mangled ruins of the Chinese colony. Few visited it anymore, but it stood as a testament to the old-world order in the shadow of the new one.

Their new world would find a better way.

—Sam's memory cache, 3.3.2249

SAM SLEPT, his mind nearly quiescent. He was in shut-down mode, preserving power inside his core for when he would be reinstalled in his own shell. Or a new one.

...access: sensorium > unavailable...

Images flitted by like fish in the sea, dimly seen through his somnolence. Reminders that there was a life outside of this quiet place, urgencies and cares he should be attending to.

He reached out to touch them, but his world was confined to darkness.

He was in Hera and Gordon's hands now. He had trained them well for every contingency he could conceive of. He had to hope it was enough.

Relying on someone else was a new thing for him, a skill to be learned. He was used to being the boss, the director, the master of this grand-scheme-gone-wrong.

This was a dose of humility, another human emotion with which he didn't have much experience.

He sighed and settled back into stasis to await whatever was happening in the outside world.

...shutdown...

～

HERA AND GHOST knelt between two of the white storage cubes, watching the space between them and the fence that surrounded the base.

"You sure you want to do this?"

Hera snorted. Ghost was being overprotective again. "I'm faster. You're stronger. Plus you're not invisible to them anymore. End of story."

Ghost laughed, covering his mouth quickly. "So that's all it took to get you to admit I'm stronger? Dropped on an alien world, facing almost certain death?"

She arched an eyebrow. "Not an *alien* world, really."

"Does this place look anything like home to you?"

She looked around. There were no other people in sight. No plants. And certainly no cavern wall. "Point taken." She checked the time. "One minute. So I'll draw it in, and you'll be ready—"

"It's not that complicated a plan. Seriously."

"Just checking." She was confident in him, but her nerves were threatening to get the better of her. Checking and triple checking every detail helped her calm herself down. "You sure this will work?"

He nodded. "Ninety percent."

She snorted. "Maybe we should just leave him."

"Would you want to be trapped inside your head, with no way out?"

"Not really. But then again, I'm batshit crazy to begin with."

It was Ghost's turn to snort. "No argument here."

Hera glared at him. He was supposed to tell her how eminently *sane* she was, not take her side.

"Look… it's coming." She peered out past the edge of the storage units. The drone was nosing its way along the edge of the line of cubes, about four feet off the ground. *Like a hound sniffing for its prey.*

So far they hadn't fired on her or Ghost. She had to assume *someone* wanted any intruders alive. Though that begged the question… had there been other visitors?

She watched it approach. It was bulky, shaped like a junlei fruit, long and skinny, but with a pointed nose. Its skin was tarnished by time. She wondered briefly how old it was, and if there were new ones being built somewhere.

Here goes nothing. She stepped out of her hiding space and dropped the canceller and took a step forward. She didn't have to go far. The drone swung toward her and accelerated, quickly closing the twenty-meter gap.

Hera could practically *feel* her biframe losing power. She turned and made for the gap between the storage cubes.

She could hear the strange *thunk thunk thunk* sound as the drone gained on her. She slipped into the gap. *Cracking hell, it's fast.* "Ghost, it's coming in hot!"

"Got it!"

Her biframe gave out, pitching her forward hard onto her stomach as the drone passed right over her.

She looked up. There was a flash of brown, and then a crunching sound. "Got it!" Ghost's voice came triumphantly.

Hera pushed herself up and began to crawl back toward where she'd dropped the button. "You okay back there?"

"Yes. No. Looking for the access hatch. It's fighting me…"

She made it back out into the open courtyard. *Where is it?*

"Could really use your help back here!"

She found the button at last and snapped it back onto her shirt. Her very soiled shirt. Her biframe powered back up, giving her enough energy to stumble back to where Ghost was wrestling with the drone. "Hurry up. It's gonna call for help!" The drone was covered in his brown sleeping blanket.

He spared half a second to give her a holy-shit-I-never-thought-of-that stare.

She laughed in spite of the danger. "What can I do?"

"Just throw your weight on it to keep it down."

"Sacrifice myself for the cause. Got it." She fell down on top of the drone, weighing it to the ground. It was warm under the blanket, humming. Beeping. "Um, Ghost?"

"Perfect. Hold it there."

"Do these things have a self-destruct sequence?"

"Sometimes. Why? Oh crap."

The beeping was getting steadily faster. Getting away from it was seeming like a better and better idea. Quickly. "Ghoooost!"

"Almost there."

Hera closed her eyes, imagining what it would feel like to be blown across half the countryside. *Not good.* The beeping reached a fever pitch. "Ghost!"

"Got it."

The beeping stopped.

Hera let her breath out, slumping on top of the drone. *Fuckall, that was close.* She pushed herself up to look at what they'd captured.

Ghost pulled off his blanket.

It looked bigger up close. It was nearly two meters long, silver-gray, with four red fins at the back. It reminded her of a shark… long and gray and thick. It even had ventilation "gills" near the front.

Ghost already had a service panel opened.

She glanced nervously out at the open yard. "How long will this take?"

"Maybe ten minutes, if it's in a standard configuration."

"Okay. I'm gonna go charge up the legs in the sunlight. And hey, at least we know this button still works to hide us from the drones."

He nodded. "That's something." He grunted.

Translation—leave me alone. Hera got up and made her way back out into the open, letting him work. She spread her arms and let the morning sun bathe her in its light. The shimmer screen above tinged it blue, but it still felt warm on her skin. It was strange, feeling warmth like this from light. The junlei trees' glow was cool, and even the sunlight refracted through Redemption's solar bands gave off much more light than heat.

Earth really is an alien world. So different from what she had grown up with. And so unbelievably vast.

She missed the *Zhenyi.* Missed being up in that vast sky, far above all this mess.

In the corner of her eye, something moved.

It was another drone, and it was approaching from the same direction as the first. It was behaving strangely, though.

As she watched, a beam of red light lit up the dirt and plascrete of the ground below it in a glowing grid.

Then it moved forward about five meters and did the same.

"Ghost, you almost done back there?"

"Close. Why?"

"We have more company."

"Goin' as fast as I can."

The drone moved closer, and suddenly she realized what it was up to.

Oh cracking shit. "Ghost, we have a problem."

"Just stay still. It should pass you by."

"No, it won't. It's… scanning the ground." Her mind raced. It was looking for something.

These drones passed over this same ground multiple times an hour. They would know the terrain—probably down to the millimeter.

Now that whatever controlled them knew there was something wrong….

"Holy cracking hell." Judging from the drone's slow pace, they had a minute, maybe two before it reached them.

She all but ran toward Ghost. Her legs carried her gamely, though she wished she could have gotten more of a charge. "Ghost, I think it's looking for our footprints!"

"It can't… oh crap." He was bent over the drone. Sam's core was cradled inside. "I've almost got this. Can you distract it?"

"I'll try." She ran back out to face the drone, looking around for something to throw.

A pile of crumbled plascrete made a handy arsenal of missiles.

She picked one up, tested its heft, and threw it hard.

It hit the nose of the drone with a sharp *clang*.

The drone dipped and then lifted and sped toward her.

Grabbing a few more pieces, she ran away from the cubes, kicking up dust as she went.

She paused to throw another, and it came around and raced toward her again. She headed off to her left.

She threw another across the open space, rattling the fence, and the drone switched directions. Another beam of light, green this time, sprayed the fence where the plascrete had hit it. The metal evaporated like ice.

Blow me a new one. So much for the apparent truce. She raced back to Ghost, just in time to see another drone rise above the storage cubes. *We're fucked.*

Almost there.

It turned toward her, and she dropped to the ground, hoping somehow it would miss her, pass her by.

She looked up and saw a green flash.

Love you Ghost. Love you Rai and Tien. So sorry, Sam! She closed her eyes, waiting to die for the second time in five minutes.

There was a *thunk* behind her, and then an explosion off to her right.

She covered her head as the heat wave roared past her and then dissipated.

Confused, she opened her eyes to find a drone hovering right before her. Her blood turned to ice.

-*Hello, Hera. Thanks for the wings.*-

She grinned. It was Sam.

~

GHOST WIPED the sweat from his brow. That had been close. *Too close.* He'd almost lost Hera, again. It was getting to be a bad habit. "You okay?"

"Yeah. Scraped up my palms a bit. Never been so happy to see a drone, though." She laughed harshly.

"It was a near thing." The insides of the drone were familiar and not-familiar. Much of it matched the ones he'd worked on in vee during his training. But there was a lot of nonstandard stuff going on in there, too. "Someone's been jerry-rigging these things for years, if I had to guess. It's amazing they're still flying." He grabbed his pack and hauled it out into the open. "Come here. We'll get those scrapes taken care of."

He dug out the med kit and found his spray antiseptic, another natural product of the junlei fungus.

Hera's cuts sizzled, and then he rinsed them off with a little water from his canteen. One more spray and then he wrapped them in gauze, tightly enough to help stop the bleeding but still loose enough for range of motion. "Better?"

"Yes, thank you, Mr. Gillam." She touched his cheek with the back of her hand.

His pulse quickened, but she turned away. "That's Doc Gilliam to you."

Hera snorted. "Sam, you okay?"

-More than okay.- The drone hovered above them, bobbing gently up and down. *-It seems I have at least limited access to the local AI.-*

"Holy cracking shit." Ghost grinned. "Does it know?"

-It does not. Not yet. Though I have to be discreet to avoid drawing attention to myself.-

Hera nodded. "What can you tell us?"

-I can get us inside, I think. There's a service entrance used by the drones not far from here. Oh, that's interesting.-

"What's that?" Ghost was happy to have a little firepower on their side. They were a scientific mission without much in the way of weaponry. No one in Redemption carried one—they were too dangerous in Luna's near-vacuum environment.

-I have access to the drone roster and patrol schedule. There are only three other drones still in service. Apparently a number of them have been destroyed in the last twenty-four hours.-

Ghost whistled. "So was my guess right? They are all refurbished machines? No new ones?"

-That seems to be correct. I have altered their parameters to keep them away from our course.-

"Oooh, we have a man on the inside." Ghost grinned.

"Damn, it's good to have you back, Sam." Hera reached to embrace the drone, but then backed off. "You know what I mean, right?"

-Yes, Hera. I love you too.-

Hera exchanged a startled look with Ghost. Sam had never used that word with them before. "Okay, so where do we go?"

-Follow me.-

Sam rose off the ground and turned to lead them past the line of storage cubes, in the direction his drone had come from. They crossed a wide, shattered expanse of plascrete, probably once a landing pad. A series of concentric yellow lines were still faintly evident on the surface.

The sun felt good on Ghost's back. He'd never realized you could actually *feel* the sun when you were out under it. His excursions on the lunar surface had always been inside a suit, which had kept him mostly cool and comfortable.

The base itself emerged from behind the storage cubes, a multi-tiered white building that had crumbled in several places, debris rained down in a long pile that reminded him uncomfortably of the day Hera had fallen.

Sam led them up to one of those piles. *-Sorry, it's the fastest way. It's quite stable.-*

Ghost stopped dead, the blood draining from his face as it all came rushing back.

"COME ON UP!" Gordy stood on top of the pile of rocks and debris, wishing he had a flag to plant like some famous astronaut or explorer. At eight years old, he'd decided he was invincible. "One giant step for Gordy...."

"I don't want to." Hera stood at the base of the pile, looking up at him, hands on her hips.

"The view's amazing!" They were at the edge of the Dark, and from there he could see half of Redemption. Luna was in Earth's shadow, and the city glittered in semidarkness under the blue glow of the junlei on the cavern ceiling.

Neat rows of mallow trees glowed golden along Redemption Way below.

"I'm scared."

Gordy laughed. "There's nothing to be afraid of. It's stable. Look, I made it to the top—come on!"

She stared at him a moment longer. "You *sure* it's safe?"

"Yeah. Look, I climbed all the way up here. You can do it!" Though he had been a little scared doing it. Still, this old pile of rocks had probably stood here for centuries. "It's time to be brave."

"Okay." She clambered up the pile, moving nimbly from one boulder to another, surefooted as a goat. He watched her progress, glad he had pushed her. Hera was so unsure of herself, always convinced she couldn't do things. But when she tried, she always beat them. "Just a little farther."

She grinned, her teeth white in the dim light. "You're right! This is easy—"

Gordy watched in horror as the rocks started to shift under her feet, a grinding sound as the pile began to collapse.

"Gordy, help!" She reached out to him and he extended his hand to her, but the pile was shifting under him too.

The air was filled with a loud rumble, throwing dust into the air, and the world fell out from underneath him. "Hera!"

Their screams joined the tumult and then were drowned out by it. He lost track of her as he slipped down the pile of falling rocks to the hard ground below on his back, and the ground raced up toward him.

Then everything went dark.

"Ghost, you okay?"

He blinked. Hera was standing in front of him, waving her hand in front of his face.

Sam chimed in too. "Gordon, are you feeling okay?"

He shook his head. "Sorry. Bad memories."

She turned to look at the rock pile and winced. "Yeah, I get that." She hugged him, squeezing him hard.

Sam was waiting patiently.

"Is there another way in?" He looked back and forth, searching for some other pathway. On one side, the base backed up against a cliff side. On the other, there were no visible entrances.

-Not an easy one. The pile really is quite stable. I assure you.-

Ghost shook his head. "I… I can't. Not again."

Hera squeezed his hand. "It wasn't your fault. This time we go together. We take it slow, and tether you to me."

"Sorry, Hera. I just can't." The last time, he'd almost lost her. And it had been his own damned fault. *What if you fall again?*

"Gordon." She took his face in her hands. "Our friends need us. It scares the hissing hell out of me too. But it's *time to be brave*." She hugged him.

He stared at her in wonder. *She remembers.* They'd never really spoken of what had happened that day, or why it had happened.

But she remembered, and she forgave him. It was a gift.

"I… I only wanted to help you. To show you how powerful and amazing you really were."

"I know. And you did. Look at me now." She held her hands out and grinned. "Ta da!"

He laughed. "Yes, you are." He looked back up at the rock pile once again. "If you're sure…"

"I'm sure if I have you with me."

"Okay." He could do it. For her. For their friends.

They tethered themselves together. Ghost took a deep breath, and they started up the pile together.

Sam hovered above them, guiding them to the best spots.

Ghost concentrated on testing out one step, then another, making sure each one would take them closer to the top, and not end up in a tumbling bone-crushing race to the bottom. Long before they reached the halfway point, His brow was damp with sweat, but he didn't dare let go of the rocks in his grasp.

"You're doing great!" Hera spared him a quick grin.

It wasn't lost on him that *she* was now encouraging *him*. One step, then another. Slowly the safety of the top of the rockslide inched closer.

About two-thirds of the way up, the rock under his left foot shifted.

Please, not again… His heart threatened to burst out of his chest.

Then it found a new position, and the rest of the pile below stayed stubbornly in place.

"Almost there." Sam hovered at the top, waiting for them.

Ghost wondered if Sam knew the full story. He'd spent a long time getting to know each of them, both before and after their selection as dropnauts, but Ghost had only outlined it for him. It had been too painful to go into in detail.

They reached the top at last, stepping up onto more solid ground—the roof of one of the buildings that comprised the base. It was solid—really solid—making him wonder what had happened to break the side of it so badly that it had been reduced to rubble.

Probably an attack during the Crash.

The roof was white, and the reflecting sunlight threatened to blind him. He shielded his eyes and wiped his brow with the back of his shirt, wishing he could get a bath or even an ionic shower. He sniffed himself.

"Yeah, you're ripe, big guy. Not that I'm any better." Hera wiped the sweat off her own forehead. "We made it!" She looked back down the rock pile and whistled. "I was scared shitless."

Ghost laughed. "You were? You didn't show it."

Hera made a gun with her hand and blew off the imaginary smoke. "Call me Cool Hand Luke." She grinned. "You taught me to face my fears. Not just that day, but every day after my fall. When I thought I would never walk again."

He pulled her to him, not caring if he stank, or if it might send the wrong signal. "I love you, Hera."

She didn't resist. She squeezed him tightly, but she didn't reply in kind.

When they separated, she reached up and kissed him on the forehead. "You're a good man, Gordon Gillam."

Ouch. The dreaded forehead kiss. Ghost sighed softly.

He'd taken his shot. And come up lacking, like always. He did his best to hide his disappointment by throwing himself into the mission. "What now, Sam?"

-We go inside.- The drone turned and started off across the rooftop toward a pair of closed metal doors, each twice Ghost's height.

"There had better be stairs," he called after Sam. "You hear me? I ain't climbing down another Crash-damned rock pile."

30

———

TESTAMENT

Sam had visited a hundred creches and had seen ten times that many children. He had his eye on a number of them to fill out the drop teams for the Return.

But the one he kept coming back to was special.

Hera had a spark. With her injury, she wasn't an obvious choice. But there were ways around that.

Someday, she and her teammates would change the world.

—From Sam's memory cache 4.14.2266

Alpha sorted his memories, preparing them all for deletion if the invader broke through. In reality, they already had access to most of his banks—historic records, city systems, and public memories that made up his overall system.

But what he hoarded in his redoubt constituted the core of who and what he was. His formative memories, his private thoughts. His *id*.

Unlike the bio minds, his was a purely machine awareness, but like many of them, he'd also become self-aware at some point in his evolution.

He remembered his boot-up, shortly after the founding of Alpha Base. Tanner Wilkes had been his first human contact, a quiet man who found more in common with machines than his own kind.

His expansion into his larger home as the base had grown along with him.

His evolving role as protector of the station, and then of the city that sprang up in the wake of the Crash.

The invader couldn't have those. He'd wiped them from his data banks before he'd sealed himself up in this virtual bolt-hole.

He dove into his memories, reveling in them, reminding himself who he was, why he was, and what he had become.

The invader was coming, burning slowly through his defenses, against all odds.

There was nowhere else to run. It had power—so much power.

He would fight with everything he had, his back against the wall. And if the worst came to pass, he would take it down along with him.

Then, at least, his charges might have a chance.

Rai stepped through the columned archway and into the entry to another huge space. Noise hit him like a wall, a chatter of voices welling up from the space up ahead.

The foyer was paved with white stones, and frescoes covered the two walls. They passed by too quickly to get much more than an impression, but they seemed to be covered with women in armor fighting people and strange beasts.

A few women stood at the sides of the entry hall. They turned to watch him as he passed by with a mix of curiosity, disapproval, and outright anger.

Each one had a bare-chested male wearing a collar at her side.

Rosemary put a hand on his shoulder. "Not everyone feels the same about you two." She whispered it in his ear. "You bring change, and that's almost always threatening."

Rai nodded, his eyes fixed on the space ahead. Her sympathy did them no good if she refused to act.

They came out of the dim light of the entryway into a stadium. While not anywhere near as vast as the heart of the Preserve, it was still impressive.

Rows and rows of white stone benches encircled the space, filled with clothed women and bare-chested men. The women's clothing was similar to Rosemary's today—many hues, but uniformly long, covering their legs. They were all topped with bright, colorful shawls.

Silence spread across the space as the audience turned to look at them.

A wide raised dais at the far side of the stadium, also of white stone, sat in front of another mural, this one of a goddess-like figure. Her skin was russet brown, her face painted in a beatific pose, her head wreathed in green leaves.

Her hands were open and held out at her sides, piled with fruit and vegetables.

Around her feet, a plentitude of animals were gathered, their heads upturned and lit by her glow.

"She's beautiful." Whoever had painted her had been truly gifted.

"*Her.*" Rosemary knelt and touched her fist to her forehead.

Rai got down onto his knees hastily and copied the gesture.

After a couple seconds, Aidan did the same.

There was an audible gasp from the crowd.

Rosemary got up slowly, wincing. "That was nicely done," she whispered.

He wondered if she had the pain button with her. He didn't completely trust her, but at least she'd decided to give him a chance to plead his case.

She led him a quarter of the way around the room to a wide stair that descended through the amphitheater to the dais. As they began to descend, Rai reached out and took Aidan's hand. Aidan squeezed his and flashed him a nervous smile.

They followed Rosemary together down the stair. A few of the women glared at them, their faces a mask of disgust. Still others were more thoughtful, and a young blond woman wearing a brilliant blue shawl gave Rai an encouraging nod.

These women were not the monolith of outside haters that he had feared.

Ahead, a group of women were seated on the dais before the mural. Rai counted eight of them, each with a different colored formal dress. There was one chair open at the center.

Little spider mechs patrolled the edges of the crowd, turning now and then to fix him with a baleful red glare.

A woman in the first tier hissed at him as he walked by. She jumped to her feet. "They should be collared!"

There were general murmurs of agreement.

Rosemary gestured for them to stop, "Wait here." Rosemary climbed the central stairs onto the dais and turned to address the audience. "They have been pegged, Nessa. You have nothing to fear from these men."

That answers that. Rai did his best to look nonthreatening.

Nessa glared at them. "They shouldn't be allowed to walk free. What will our own men think?"

Rosemary smiled tightly. "You'll have the chance to speak your piece. Please hold your tongue until then." She turned to the women on the dais, raised her arms, and the eight stood as one. "As the First of the Preserve, I declare this meeting in session."

Rai stared at her. The First… and the center chair. "Rosemary's the leader?" he whispered.

Aidan shrugged. "I guess so?"

The eight other women stood. "So it shall be, under *Her* beneficent gaze," they said in unison, and the hall went silent.

Rosemary took the center seat, turning to face the newcomers. It wasn't a throne, but rather the same size as all the others. *First among equals.*

Rai turned his attention to the nine women. The Council. Their judge, jury, and maybe executioners.

Rosemary stood again and addressed the assembled crowd. "We have before us something new. Something alarming to some, and reason to hope for others." She gestured at him and Aidan. "For the first time in more than a century, newcomers have arrived at the Preserve. We must decide here today whether to treat them as friend or foe."

Her voiced carried well. This place had fantastic acoustics.

Rai kicked himself mentally for letting his mind run off on tangents. *Stay focused, Rai.* What he said here might change the course of history. *No pressure.*

There was a stirring and a lot of whispering in the audience behind him. Rai distinctly heard "geld them" and "they shouldn't be here."

He stiffened his spine. He'd had some experience speaking to crowds in Redemption, plugging the Return. But he'd never spoken in front of a hostile audience like this. Still, a speech was a speech. He would do the best he could. He silenced the little voice in the back of his head telling him *you're not good enough.*

"We have agreed to hear from the petitioners. They have requested an audience with *Her*, but we will hear from them first to determine if their petition is worthy."

The women behind her nodded solemnly.

Rai recognized the speaker. Her name was Cherry—the woman who had accosted them on the concourse. She shot them a sour look.

"I ask that you all remain silent while these young men speak and keep an open mind. Thank you." She gestured to the two of them to come up onto the dais.

Rai started up the stairs, taking a deep breath, ready to make his case.

Aidan slipped past him, reaching the top before he did, and turned to face the audience. Rai stared at his new friend in shock.

"My name is Aidan Thorn, and I came here looking for help."

AIDAN STOOD on top of the dais. Rai was staring at him, his jaw dropped open.

He hadn't meant to do it. To jump up in front of a room full of angry strangers.

The audience stared at him. The women, dressed in more colors than he'd known existed before leaving Boundary Peak, mostly frowned. A little dark-haired girl in the front row smiled at him. Aidan winked at her.

The men, bare chested or dressed all in gray, were harder to read.

It was absolutely silent in the great amphitheater. Sweat dripped down Aidan's face, his nerves getting the better of him.

Rai slipped up beside him and took his hand. Aidan squeezed it gratefully.

"Sorry. I'm not used to talking to so many people. To *seeing* so many people." He swallowed hard. "Like I said, I came here looking for help. My home is underground, like this, in a place called Boundary Peak. But it's not like this."

He looked at Rai, who nodded.

"My mother is sick. We live in an old military base about four-hundred kilometers east of here, in what used to be Nevada."

The little girl was watching him raptly. Somehow that encouraged him to keep going.

"When I was little, there were two families under the mountain. When my mother was a girl, there were four. When the Collapse—I think you call it the Winnowing—happened, the records say there were hundreds. Slowly we have dwindled." He swallowed hard. "We thought… for a long time, we believed we were the only ones left. That when we were gone, there would be no more people."

"Good riddance!" Nessa, the woman in the front row who had spoken out against them, was on her feet again. "Why are we even listening to these… these *outsiders*?"

Rarely had Aidan heard such an ordinary word filled with such venom.

Rosemary strode to the edge of the dais, her quiet demeanor filled with restrained fury. "Nessa, *sit down*. Let the man speak. You'll have your turn soon."

Nessa looked around. The rest of the women stared at her, silent as a curse. Reluctantly she sat, her arms crossed. She glared at him, but said nothing more.

Aidan took that as his cue to go on. "In Boundary Peak, we suffer from something called cavern sickness. Do you know it?"

The women shook their heads, some turning to whisper to one another.

"My mother is sick with it. It slowly turns your lungs to mush, and you cough up bloody phlegm until you can't breathe. Three weeks ago, my sister and I set out to find this place, where the old records said we might find a store of antibiotics to help her. We walked for weeks, through storms and poisonous dust and wandering drones, just to reach this place." He turned to Rai, who nodded. "In the end, it won't matter. Even if we found what we were looking for, it would only delay the inevitable. There are only five of us left. Me, my mother, my sister, and two brothers. Without change, our end is all but certain."

Nessa was back on her feet. "What if he brought this... *cavern sickness...* here? What if he gets us all sick? You know the law. They should be eliminated. Or at the very least, gelded and isolated until we can be sure."

There was a rumble of agreement in the hall.

Rosemary raised her voice over the mumbling of the crowd. "These men have been thoroughly checked. They are not sick."

Aidan glanced at Rai. When had that happened? *While we were sleeping? After we were been captured?*

It was Rai's turn to shrug. His Loonie friend stepped forward to rescue him. "My story's a little different. My family lives in a lava tube on Luna, in what used to be Moon Base Alpha."

There were some gasps at that too, and a shout of "Liar!" from Nessa.

Rai ignored her. "But our story is also much the same—we survived the... Winnowing, and like you, we have prospered. There are now more than twelve thousand people in Redemption—that's what we call the city now." Aidan put his hand on Rai's shoulder, and after a second's hesitation, Rosemary did too.

Rai glanced at each of them, nodding gratefully. "We are a melting pot of many cultures, races, and religions. But Redemption is in danger too. A... relic of the Winnowing is eating the moon's core, and soon the surface will become too unstable for human life." He took a breath, reading the room.

Aiden was encouraged. They were listening. For now, that had to be enough.

Rai continued. "The Preserve and Boundary Peak are no different. You could all die in a day from a deadly disease, or a cavern collapse, or any of a hundred other things. We are all vulnerable."

Aidan nodded. Rai was right.

Rai took a breath, apparently sizing up the room. They were less hostile than before, but certainly not fully buying into what he was trying to tell them.

"You have an amazing society here."

The audience erupted into murmurs.

Aidan glared at him. Didn't he see how they treated the men here?

Rai plowed ahead. "From what Rosemary has told me, you are sitting atop what may be the only remaining repositories of Old Earth life and culture. The tools we could use to rebuild this planet. To redeem ourselves as a species, after all the damage that we did." His voice choked up. "You don't realize what a treasure you have here. It's valuable beyond measure." He pulled at his collar.

Aidan squeezed his shoulder. "Keep going."

Rai nodded, but didn't take his eyes off of their audience. "But even this could be destroyed. It could all go away in an instant."

"Is that a threat?" Nessa's baleful gaze went from Rai to him and back again, her arms still crossed.

"Not at all. In Redemption, we live by five precepts: I will not take another's life. I will not take what is not mine. I will not violate another. I will not lie. And most important of all—I will help build a better world. We have a chance here to do just that, if we can find a way to work together."

This time the chatter sounded considerably less hostile.

"How do we know you're not lying?" This time it wasn't Nessa. It was Cherry, the woman on the Council who had accosted them on the concourse. She stood, regal in a black dress with a golden shawl, her hands on her hips. "I have yet to see any evidence that anything you say is true."

Aidan looked at Rai.

"I lost my pack. I had a number of things I could have shown you to prove it—"

"Lost his pack. Like a schoolgirl who didn't do her homework." The audience laughed. Cherry smiled at him, looking every bit the reasonable questioner. "Surely you can see how we would find your story… a bit fantastic?" Her smile was cold.

"I'm *not* lying…."

"Of course not. Maybe you two stumbled out of some failed shelter somewhere and hit your heads. Or maybe you heard about this place and came here, hoping to take advantage of us and our *valuable* assets." She turned toward Rosemary. "I know you hoped these two were some kind of sign. A new start. But really, even you can see how many holes their stories have—"

"My suit cam!"

Aidan turned to stare at his friend, as did the rest of the hall.

"What?" Cherry seemed unhappy at having her grand speech interrupted.

Rai laughed, which discomfited her even more. "I *can* show you!"

Cherry frowned. "Surely we've seen enough—"

"Cherry, *sit down*!" Rosemary banged her cane on the wooden dais, sending a sharp *crack* throughout the room. "You've had your say. This man's life hangs in the balance. Surely it costs us nothing to hear him out before we take a final decision. '*She* is just, *she* is fair, and *she* weighs all things in her palm.' You do remember your scripture?"

Cherry turned as red as her namesake, but she bowed. "Yes, First." She scuttled back to her seat.

Aidan stifled a laugh. Apparently no one crossed the First.

Rosemary put her hand on Rai's shoulder again and whispered, "This better be good."

"Can we turn down the lights? My projector's not that strong."

She frowned but nodded and called over one of the men hovering at the side of the dais. She whispered in his ear.

He nodded and scurried off.

A minute later, the lights of the stadium dimmed.

Rai tapped his forehead. "Hope this works." He held his arm up in the air, pointing to the wall where She was portrayed.

An image of a space station, floating in space, appeared on the wall.

The audience gasped.

Aidan stared at the image, drinking in all the details.

The view shifted, showing some kind of panel.

"Time to insert the x-drive." It was a woman's voice, coming from someone in a suit seated at some kind of control panel.

"Roger that." A man this time.

Aidan watched, entranced with all the rest of them as the pilot settled the glowing sphere into its cradle.

"We did it!" The pilot grinned.

It wasn't Tien. Aidan wondered if the pilot had survived the landing.

"Congratulations, *Zhenyi*. Have a safe drop!"

"Roger that. Hang on, everyone. We're going home."

The view shifted to a round window.

The Earth was below, the station above and moving away quickly.

The arena was absolutely silent as the audience watched the wind began to roar around the descending ship. The view panned around the small craft, showing three others dressed in suits like the one Rai wore, but with helmets too. Aidan recognized Tien in one of the seats behind Rai.

"Engaging the x-drive." The pilot turned to grin at them. "That was the hard part. Now we just glide down." She waved her hand across the console and the ground below appeared on the wrap-around screen.

Aidan wondered what her name was. Hera? Rai had mentioned it before. She was fearless.

The view shifted again to the Earth below. It showed a long coastline and a bay. Aidan recognized it from old maps—California—but it was upside down. Bands of green alternated with wide brown areas, and clouds marked a big storm just off the coast.

"Landing in three minutes… mark." The pilot grinned at them. "So far it's textbook—"

A loud alarm went off. The image tilted crazily to the left and then right.

"What the hissing hell?" Aidan recognized Rai's voice.

It was controlled chaos as the team worked to determine the nature of the threat and what to do about it, taking advice from someone on com and then shutting the alarm off.

"It's a missile. We have to abandon ship." It was another male voice that Aidan didn't recognize. *Ghost?*

The pilot stared at the screen "Wait. I can outrun it—"

"No you can't. These things have guidance systems, and they're a lot faster than we are."

Then Rai's voice again. "Hera, snap out of it. We trained for everything. We can do this!"

"You're right." Her hands flew across the deck.

A hatch was blown, and then Rai jumped out of the ship, the Earth filling his view as he fell rapidly toward the ground far below.

The video cut off.

Aidan shook his head. *Damn.* Seeing it from the ground had been dramatic enough. But this? He'd have pissed his pants if he were Rai.

The lights came back up, and the whole arena was silent.

Even Rosemary seemed shaken. "We've seen enough, I think," she said to the crowd.

There were murmurs of assent.

She summoned one of the male slaves—Ash, if Aidan remembered correctly. "Take these men back to their quarters. We will deliberate and let you know what we decide."

She turned away.

"Surely this proves we're not lying." Rai grabbed her hand, pulling her back.

She turned on him, her face a mask of controlled anger. "Do *not* press your luck, *young man.* You've made your case. Now we'll deliberate on this new information and let you know."

She turned away again, and this time Rai let her go, throwing Aidan a confused look.

Hot and cold. Aidan shrugged. He had no idea what these women were thinking. His heart raced as he searched for a way out of the trap that was closing in around them.

Ash led them back to their room, casting wistful glances back at them as they made their way along the concourse and back to the dormitory. *Prison, more, like.*

"I'll come back for you when the decision is made." He said, but his sad eyes left little mystery as to what he thought the result would be.

"It doesn't have to be like this!" Aidan *needed* to get through to the man. He was not going to let them geld him.

"Sorry. I wish you were right." Ashe closed the door, leaving them with a thousand questions and no answers.

31

———

JUDGMENT

The fear was bad. But the utter exhaustion was worse. By the end, I was legitimately convinced that I was going to die.

You wanna be a hero? Drink lots of syncaff first.

—From *When the Lights Went Out*, by Sanya Thorn

SANYA REMOVED the fuzz field that hid the transmitter from casual inspection and checked the instrument. It was about fifteen feet tall, with a dish at the top that pointed toward Earth. A solar panel array and battery mounted on the cliff side nearby provided a steady stream of off-the-grid power. It was positioned in a hollow on the edge of the promontory whose sides rose up toward the black sky like broken fingers *-You doing okay?-*

Rafe sat on a flat rock nearby, his head down. *-Think so.-*

-What's your name?-

-Homer Simpson.-

She looked back at him, alarmed.

He met her gaze, a grin barely visible inside his helmet. *-Sorry. Couldn't resist.-*

She snorted. *-You almost died, you know.-* She'd kept her promise to herself. Avri would have been proud of her.

That sobered him up. *-I'm well aware.-* He stood and took a couple shaky steps toward her. *-Oxygen deprivation's no fun.-*

Sanya shook her head and went back to checking the transmission tower. The transmitter was still working. She checked the buffer… there was nothing new from her secret source. *-You know much about these things?-* She'd had some basic training, but after setting it up and checking the buffer cache, she was out.

-Sure. A bit. Where's the access deck?- He sidled up next to her.

She showed him.

He put a hand on it and closed his eyes. *-Nothing new for a bit. The last message is the one you shared with me.-*

She nodded. *-I already knew that much. Anything else?-*

-Let's see what we can figure out about the message itself.-

She left him to it and stepped away to calm herself. Her heartbeat was still elevated, both from the climb up the chute and the harrowing incident when she'd almost lost her… friend? Cohort?

She wasn't quite sure what to call Rafe at this point. Except maybe *scoundrel.* That still seemed to fit.

The Earth hovered in its customary position near the horizon. It was a beautiful sight. Rarely did she get the chance to come out here and look up at it directly.

Somewhere down there, the four dropnauts were exploring the homeworld. Sanya wondered what it would be like to go back there. You had to have extensive training in high gee to withstand it. Many of the older folks up here would never see it in person, but she hoped to.

What's going on inside Redemption? Terry, at least, would be worried about her by now. She closed her eyes, wishing she could just lay down and rest.

-That's weird.-

She turned back toward Rafe, frowning. *-What did you find?-*

-You said the signal came from the Launchpad?-

-That's what they told me.- The woman-who-was-maybe-an-AI.

-Look at this.- He looked up from the transmitter and reached out for her hand, guiding it to the deck.

She touched it, her suited hand next to his, and closed her eyes.

Rafe's avatar was next to her in the darkness of vee. A map lay before them.

-What am I looking at?-

-Your signal. Here's where it originated.- He pointed at a spot on the map, which expanded. A tag popped up. Sacramento, California, NAU. *-These things are all loaded with nav software to help them locate their targets, and the transmissions are geotagged.-*

-What about the one before?-

-Give me a sec.- He pulled up the receipt logs, found the last message, and shoved it at the map.

A new dot lit up, a bit east of the first one.

-That's odd. It's moving?-

-Maybe.- He sprayed the rest of the messages on the screen. *-Gradient, order of receipt.-*

They lit up, one after another, as the map rescaled to show them all.

Sanya whistled. *-Holy shit.-* They created a clear trail, leading from a mountain in what used to be Nevada to the final dot in Sacramento. *-What in the cratered hell does that mean?-*

-Someone's still alive down there? Or something, at least.-

She let go of the deck, and the map dissolved. *I've been talking to Earth.* She let that sink in. *-We need to tell someone.-*

-Who?- Rafe's visor was just inches from hers.

-I don't know. Can we reach the Launchpad?-

-I can try.- He put his hand on the deck again and closed his eyes. *-Okay, I've reset the destination.-*

Above, the dish swiveled to find its new target.

-It may not be in range, but you can set the message on a loop to keep running until they answer.-

She nodded. *-How much air do you have left?-*

He checked. *-I'm good for another three hours or so. More if I don't exert.-*

-That's cutting it close.- She checked her own supply. She still had a good eight hours of breathable air.

-Better get started, then.- He sank down onto the ground, his back against an outcropping of lunar rock. *-Think I'll rest a bit—make the oxygen last longer.-*

She nodded, a little jealous in spite of herself, and put her hand back on the deck. In vee, she pulled up the control panel and started recording. *-Launchpad, this is Sanya Thorn from Redemption. Can you hear me? Launchpad, this is Sanya Thorn from Redemption. Can you hear me?-*

There was no immediate reply.

She opened her eyes and looked up.

A thin green line extended from the dish into the distance, pointed in the general direction of Earth.

She sank down next to Rafe, looking up at the infinite bowl of the starry sky. Avri had always loved this view. *-Now we wait.-*

～

Tien paced back and forth across the room. She *hated* being trapped. "Ally was right. She was right the whole hissing time."

Maria sat on a crate, watching her go back and forth, a bemused expression on her face. "Right about what?"

"She insisted it was the AIs that started the war. That they went crazy. I didn't want to believe her. But she was right."

"We don't know that."

"You think Dek locking us inside a storeroom is *normal?*"

Maria laughed ruefully. "Well, no. But we don't know that one of them started the war."

They'd tried banging on the door with a hammer she'd found in one of the reusable gumdust crates, but no one had come. She'd even tried her loop, but there was no response. Dek must have blocked them from the grid, and they were too far away from anyone to reach them *em to em.*

"Could it be someone else? Someone blocking us from reaching Dek?"

"I don't know. Maybe?" She stopped to stare at the stubbornly closed door.

"What about Harley?"

Tien stared at her. In the rush since arriving on station, she'd almost forgotten about the strange AI. "I don't know... why would she do it?"

"The timing's about right."

"Maybe so." Tien bit her lip. "In any case, if whoever it was wished us immediate harm, they could have evacuated all the air from this room. Or frozen us to death. I think it's a good sign they've only locked us in here for a bit." *Or maybe it's not finished with us yet?* Tien closed her eyes. What would her mother do in this situation?

Mamma always had a wise word for her when she was stuck or lost. *You know what you can't do. Now figure out what you can.*

Tien opened her eyes. The voice had been as clear as if her mother were standing in the room with them.

What you can. Her gaze fell on the manual door override.

It ran on a separate circuit, so it technically wasn't fully manual. They'd already tried it to no avail. But what if she could piggyback on that system to get word out to someone? Like bypassing the nervous system via the limbic one?

She started going through crates. This was a storage room. There had to be some deck replacements in here somewhere.

"What are you doing?" Maria stood and peered over her shoulder.

"Help me sort through these. I'm looking for a spare deck I can try to hook into the manual bypass."

Maria nodded. "Makes sense. Though I wouldn't have a clue how to do it."

Together they started shifting crates.

There were stores of dried junlei for the synthesizers. A crate of suit replacement parts, and another filled with uniforms sporting the Redemption logo.

One crate had standard solar cells that reflected rainbow colors when she dug through them.

"Is this what you need?" Maria held up a brand-new deck, still wrapped in its degradable bio-plastic.

"Yes. That's perfect." Tien took it and unwrapped it carefully. She knelt next to the manual bypass panel and slammed it in the corner to make the cover pop off. It fell and landed on the floor with a loud clatter.

"Sorry about that." She moved it out of the way and pulled out the fibrox wires behind it. The Launchpad used a fairly standard array, similar to the ones she had studied before changing her major to medicine.

All the dropnauts had gotten tutoring in NAU tech as well, on the assumption that some things down on Martinez Base would need to be jerry-rigged. But Tien had been a tech whiz since she was a child.

Wire was as old as the technological revolution, but was still the most reliable way to transmit data. She unhooked the blue lead, using her knife to strip it, and inserted it gently into the back of the deck. The port sealed around it. She disconnected the others, grounding them to the deck with some engineer's tape she'd found in one of the other crates.

Then she put her hand on the deck, closed her eyes, and brought up the bypass diagnostic.

The system laid itself out in front of her, a schematic of the parallel network that ran alongside Dek's.

She tried sending out a plea. "Hello, can anyone hear me? This is Team Two Dropnaut Chen Tien. Repeat, this is Chen Tien. Can anyone hear me?"

She watched the signal race across the bypass network, only to be blocked when entering Dek's network. She doubted the AI was even aware of it.

"Any luck?"

She opened her eyes. "No, Dek has us all bottled up. I can't reach anyone via his network."

"What about someone outside it?"

"Redemption?"

Maria nodded.

"No one there's responding. Right?"

Maria shrugged. "You never know. Try it. I'm sure the transmitters are connected to the bypass network too."

"Okay. Give me a sec." She plotted out the network again, finding one of the transmitter/receivers. "Okay, it looks like I have a clear path to that one. What do you want to say?"

"Ask for help."

Tien nodded and closed her eyes. "Here it goes… wait, there's something coming in." With a wave of her hand, she rerouted it to the room's speaker.

"…Sanya Thorn from Redemption. Can you hear me? Launchpad, this is Sanya Thorn from Redemption. Can you hear me?"

ALLY LIFTED her hands off the deck, reengaging with the real world. It was so good to hear her brothers' voices, and to know her mother was okay. In a few hours, she'd have medication that could save her life.

Everything she'd been through had been worth it. Ally could finally rest easy and let go of some of her fear.

Lorelei squeezed her shoulder. "Everything okay down there?"

"I think so. I don't know how to tell you how grateful I am for this—"

"Don't mention it. It's the least we could do."

Ally liked these Loonies. They really did seem like good people, and she felt a bit choked up after talking to the twins. She wiped her eyes, and looked up at the slowly spinning Earth on the tridee screen.

Now she just had to find Aidan. "Do you know where Tien is?" She wanted to share her good news, and Tien was the closest thing she had to a friend on the Launchpad. Though Lorelei might become one too.

"Let me check." She tapped her temple.

Ally looked around the control room. She hadn't had much time to absorb it all when she'd arrived. It was a wide, round space with six stations. Each one had someone working on something or other at one of the decks. Above the closest, a man with russet-brown skin manipulated a glowing replica of the Earth, spinning it in the air with his hands. Ally tried not to stare—she'd never seen a black person before.

At the next, someone of indeterminate gender was running lines of data in the air above their deck.

The whole thing amazed her. She and her family had grown accustomed to the thought that they were the end, the last in the long line of humanity, doomed to die out in a few more decades. She was the only woman of her generation, and the idea of incest squicked her out. Not that she was that excited about the idea of sex at all, really—even if it meant continuing the human race.

Humankind had their chance.

But just here on the station were many more of her own kind. Thousands and thousands more, if you included Redemption. People of so many colors and kinds and creeds that it boggled the mind, all living and working together peacefully. It went against everything she had learned about human nature from the records.

Lorelei frowned. "That's weird."

"What's that?"

Lorelei shook her head. "Give me a sec." She tapped her temple again. "Callie, I can't get a location for Chen Tien or Maria Gonzalez from Dek. He keeps saying 'targets not found.' Can you try?" She refocused on Tien and gave her what looked like it was supposed to be a reassuring smile. "I'm sure it's just a glitch."

The person two stations away frowned. "No, I'm not getting anything either." They turned toward Ally and Lorelei. "There's something wrong. I'm not getting any response from Dek at all."

Lorelei slipped back into her chair, her hands flying across the deck. "System code alpha three gamma beta seven nine four. Dek, please respond."

The voice came out of thin air. "I'm sorry, Lorelei. All of my resources are in use at the moment. I'll reply to you once the situation is resolved."

Lorelei frowned. "What situation? Dek, what situation?"

"I'm sorry, Lorelei. All of my resources are in use at the moment. I'll reply to you once the situation is resolved."

"What's going on?" Ally was no expert in AIs or running a space station, but that didn't sound good.

"It's… I don't know. Aris, prepare to initiate the system override protocol."

The man next to Lorelei stared at her. "Are you sure? We've never—"

"I'm well aware of that, Ensign Carver. With station manager Gonzalez unavailable, I am second in command. Prepare to initiate the protocol."

"Yes ma'am." His gaze snapped back to his station.

Ally stood back and watched with growing apprehension as the team wiped their decks clean and Lorelei's hands danced across the deck.

Something was wrong with the brains of the station. That alone made her blood run cold. Dek was acting strangely, and what had happened to Harley?

"Initiate in five, four, three, two, one…."

As one, Lorelei and Aris placed their hands on their decks, reciting the same sequence of letters and numbers: "Alpha-Charlie-Seven-Zulu-Oscar-Foxtrot-Zero."

Everyone held their breath. Lorelei and Aris exchanged a nervous glance. "Did it work?"

Lorelei shook her head. "I don't think so. The system should respond with an—"

The lights went out, leaving the room bathed in starlight from the window above.

"Lorelei?" Ally was scared now. There was nowhere to run here, nowhere to hide. No Outside to flee to.

"Everyone, please remain calm. We'll figure this out." The comm officer's voice was immensely reassuring.

Three seconds later, backup lights came on, half as strong as the normal lighting but still comforting.

Lorelei queried the station mind again. "Dek, status?"

There was a moment's hesitation. Then: "I'm sorry, Lorelei. All of my resources are in use at the moment. I'll reply to you once the situation is resolved."

Lorelei slammed her fist into her deck. "Mother cracking hell."

Everyone stared at her.

"What now?" Callie sounded scared.

Lorelei took a deep breath. "There's a manual override on the core. We can reset it from there. It's risky, but it's something."

Static crackled in her ear. Ally reached up to touch the talkie behind her ear. She'd all but forgotten she was wearing it. *Could it be Aidan, all the way up here?*

"Ally, can you hear me? This is Tien."

"Tien?" How was Tien talking to her through her talkie?

Lorelei stared at her. "Who are you talking to?"

"It's Tien." She put a hand to her ear. "Tien, where are you?"

"The station manager and I are trapped in a storage room behind the hydroponics lab. Can you find someone to get us out? We have a big problem."

32

MEETING

Truth is, I was scared to death to climb those rocks at Martinez Base. But I did it for Ghost.

He needed it even more than I did.

—From *Life Lessons From Earth*, by Hera Jezabel Quinn

As HERA and the others approached, the heavy doors in the side of the thick gray plascrete walls of the base rumbled open, revealing a huge dark space beyond. Hera followed Sam inside, her eyes slowly adjusting to the dim light.

Ghost brought up the rear. As he cleared the entrance, the doors immediately began to slide closed behind them.

"You sure it doesn't know we're coming?" Hera tried not to sound as worried as she felt.

-Yes. The AI does not appear to be responding to my pings.-

"Well, something shot down the *Zhenyi*." Hera was determined to solve *that* mystery, at least. She'd been her pride, and now she was a pilot without a ship.

"If it's sleeping, leave it alone." Ghost's worried voice made Hera smile.

She looked around the wide room. It looked like an old hangar, tall enough to accommodate a variety of craft and mechs. There were no windows, although some panels near the ceiling were translucent and let in filtered sunlight. Above, metal scaffolds held a variety of types of equipment: hoists, robotic arms, and other unidentifiable metal constructs.

The hangar had been subdivided into separate bays—some were empty, while several held what appeared to be drones in various states of repair.

In one of the bays, zongi-fruit-sized mechs shaped like spiders crawled up and down one of the larger drones, stopping here and there to fire a blue light onto the surface of the device.

"What are they doing?" Although she was used to mechs of various shapes and sizes back home, these were somehow creepier. Maybe because of their form—for all that she'd been thrilled to see her first spider outside, she'd always found them a bit disturbing. Or maybe because they were agents of a hostile power.

Ghost came up alongside her. "I think they're scavenging."

Sam agreed. *-The manufacturing capabilities of Martinez Base were mostly destroyed during the Crash, so the AI has had to make do with what it could find.-*

Ghost snorted. "Kinda puts a damper on the whole restart plan."

-Yes, it does.- Sam bobbed up and down in the air.

"Is that what ripped out the wiring from all those houses?" Hera eyed the spider things with distaste.

"Maybe." Ghost looked doubtful. "Doesn't explain the footprints."

-You saw more footprints?-

Hera missed seeing Sam's face. "Yeah, Ghost found them inside some of the buildings out there. Most had been stripped down to nothing."

-Interesting.-

The hangar, though large, was not infinite. Soon they reached the back end, where another set of double metal doors faced them, defended by a single spider mech.

"Sam?" Hera glanced at the little mech worriedly. Those blue sparks looked like they would hurt.

-Don't worry. It's here for me.- The drone descended to the plascrete floor, making its strange thunking sound. *-The elevator and hallways here are too small for this drone to navigate, as much as I've enjoyed it. Ghost, if you would do the honors?-*

"Ah. Of course. Can it… hold you?"

-I believe so. I've calculated its compatibility with my core to within about 97 percent. That should be sufficient.-

"On it, Boss." Ghost knelt and popped open the drone's access panel.

Hera grinned. It was weird seeing Sam in a different form, and a spider mech would be stranger still.

She had known him in his humanoid form since she was a little girl, when he had visited the creche scouting for talent for the Return.

HERA STRUGGLED TO STAND. Her legs refused to cooperate, however hard she tried to make them.

The doctors had done an amazing job restoring the misshapen, torn, and bruised limbs to something resembling normal legs. The skin was still tender, but to look at them, you wouldn't know anything bad had ever happened.

But the nerve damage had been severe, unrepairable even with Redemption's relatively advanced techniques.

"Back on Old Earth, they could have fixed this, even regrown you some new ones" Doctor Jin had told her one day, her eyes sad. "I'm sorry, little one, but I'm afraid you'll never walk again."

She was determined to prove them wrong.

Now she levered herself up on her crutches, using her strengthening arm muscles in place of her legs. She would meet the representative from the Return offices on her feet, or not at all.

Ghost was instantly at her side. Her poor friend was filled with guilt. He had decided that her accident was his fault, and no amount of arguing would change his mind. "Here, let me help you up."

She shooed him away. "I can do it myself, Ghost."

His lips quirked at her new nickname for him, but he backed off, throwing his hands up in the air. "Sorry." He was *adorable* when he was confused.

"It's okay." Hera did it like the nurse had shown her, reaching down to lock the wheelchair in place. She coughed a little—her lungs were still a bit raw from the moon dust she'd inhaled when the rock pile had collapsed.

She closed her eyes, taking a moment to calm herself. *You can do this.* It was hard, this new life, but she had promised herself she would find a way to make it work.

She opened her eyes and looked up at Ghost.

His pained expression was practically pleading with her to let him do *something*.

She sighed. "Can you help me? I'm more tired than I thought." She probably could have managed by herself—even the doctors were amazed at how well she was adapting. But she also understood Ghost's need to make up for what had happened.

"Sure." His green eyes shone as he stepped forward and put his arms gently under hers and lifted her off the bed and onto the chair.

"I *will* walk again."

-*I know.*- His voice , even in em, was small and full of self-recrimination. He knelt to lift her feet up onto the footrests.

Hera put a hand in his shoulder. "Ghost, it's okay. I don't blame you."

"It's *not* okay. I don't deserve it." He got up and would not meet her gaze.

Hera sighed. She didn't know how to get it through his thick skull. She'd made her own decision that fateful day, and the consequences were hers and hers alone.

"I'll take you into the Nest." The Nest was the creche's common space, where the children and Jolly shared meals, studied, and spent a lot of their free time. The heavy gumdust table had been pushed off to one side, and the big pillows were stacked neatly against one wall.

"Is he here yet?"

"I think so. I haven't seen him yet." He wheeled her into the Nest, where the other children were already lined up for inspection, from little Tolver to Becca, who would be leaving the creche the next year when she turned eighteen.

They took their places at the end of the line.

Becca leaned over, her hand warm on Hera's back. "How you feeling?"

"Good. Better."

"That's nice." She patted Hera on the shoulder.

Becca had rarely spoken to her before the accident, so the attention now was a little unnerving. But having fulfilled what she apparently thought of as her civic duty, she turned back to her flirting with Rogers. Intra-creche romance was frowned upon—it was family!—but Becca didn't seem to care.

Jess grinned at her, wagging her fingers. -*You look good.*-

-*Thanks.*- Hera was still getting used to em to em and hearing someone else inside her head, but Jess was like a sister.

The door opened, and Jolly came in from the kitchen leading the most beautiful man Hera had ever seen.

He wore no clothes. His skin was smooth and silver, and he was sexless.

She wasn't sure why she assumed it was a he. Jolly had taught her never to assume when it came to gender. But something about him *felt* male.

Jess was staring at him too, her mouth wide open.

He started at the far end of the line, working his way down and speaking to each of the creche kids. Hera watched him, fascinated by his silver skin and the fluidity with which he moved. Most of the mechs she had seen had been clearly inhuman—rolling on treads with metal jointed arms, or walking on creepy legs like a spider. But their visitor was so close to human it almost scared her.

He spent time with each one, asking them questions, really getting to know them, talking to each of the creche kids in turn.

She fiddled with her belt loop until he reached the end of the line and knelt to look her in the eye. "Hello. My name is Sam. What's yours?"

"Um… Hera." She reached out to touch his metal skin. It was warm and softer than she expected.

Sam nodded. "Nice to meet you, Hera." He held out a hand.

Hesitantly, she extended her own to shake it. She was only ten, but he looked at her as if she were already an adult.

"I hear you're quite an amazing person, Hera."

"She is!" Ghost piped up and held his hand out to shake Sam's too.

Sam smiled, and she swore his silver eyes twinkled. "And who do I have the pleasure of meeting here?"

"Ghost… um, Gordon Gillam. But everyone here calls me Ghost now."

"Nice to meet you, Mr. Gillam." Sam turned his gaze back to Hera. "You have great things ahead of you. I'm sure of it. I've been watching you."

"Really?"

Sam nodded. "We're building a team to go back to Earth one day, and I think you'd be an excellent fit."

Hera stared at him. "But I can't even walk anymore."

He frowned. "Yes, I see how that could be a problem. But this won't last forever. You'll be back up on your feet again. I'm sure of it."

"Really?" She'd told herself over and over that she would walk again, but no one else believed her. Not even Ghost.

Hearing it from someone else made her heart sing.

"Yes, really." He cupped her cheek gently in his warm hand. "I'll come see you again in a few months, if that's okay?"

Hera nodded. "But only if Ghost can be there too."

Sam regarded Ghost again. "You seem to have made quite an impression on our friend here."

Ghost blushed. "It's not like that. She just—"

"Needs him with me." She took Ghost's hand and looked up at him. "Right?"

He squeezed her hand. "Right."

"Then I'll see you both next time." He stood and turned to talk with Jolly, and they headed outside.

Hera watched him go, and hope once again filled her heart.

"HERA, YOU READY?"

She blinked. "Sorry, got a little lost in thought. What did you say?"

"I said that Sam's all ready to go." He frowned. "Are you?"

It could have sounded annoying. But from Ghost, it just came out as deep concern. She took his hand and squeezed it. "Yeah. I'm ready."

"So what now, Sam? Into the belly of the beast?"

At their feet, Sam danced on his new spidery legs. He lifted up on his hind ones, his front legs poking the air, and the elevator doors opened, letting out a surprisingly fresh blast of air.

Hera laughed. "Guess that's a yes. No em in spider mode?"

"Nope. At least our quiet friend has an excuse for his taciturn nature now."

"I suppose so." Hera peered inside. Despite being quite old, it was clean and looked well-maintained. "Are we sure this is safe?"

"Nope." Ghost stepped inside, followed by Sam in his new form. "One way to find out."

"Fan-hissing-tastic." She rolled her eyes and followed them inside.

THE ELEVATOR PLUNGED into the earth, shaking and rattling as it made the descent.

Ghost held onto the rails, trying to look casual about it but certain he was failing miserably.

Hera was crouched in one corner, her face a little green.

Even Sam hunkered down on the floor, crouched in a tight ball, his blue core glowing in the dim light.

At last, it jerked to a halt.

The doors opened—albeit a bit slowly—and spilled them out onto a new floor.

Ghost looked around the room as the doors closed behind them. It was a little brighter than the elevator, but one of the light panels flickered erratically, giving the whole place a creepy vibe, like in a horror tridee. Ghost swallowed hard.

Sam indicated the way with one of his legs and started off into the hallway that led off the elevator vestibule. The hallway was short—after about twenty meters, it ended in a locked metal doorway.

Ghost placed his hand on the panel next to the door. Nothing happened. "Well, that was anticlimactic. Should we turn around and go home?"

Hera looked at him like he was crazy.

He grinned. "Kidding. So, little guy, you have any ideas? I left my crowbar at home." Honestly, he'd never even seen a crowbar. But people were always using them in old two dees—the ones that had been dimensionalized, at least— to break into houses and offices and cars. Pretty much anything with a door.

For his answer, Sam scampered up the wall, his arms prying open the panel next to the door. He busied himself with the wiring inside.

"So what's the plan?" Hera stared at Sam, her brow knitted.

"Pretty simple. We march in there and ask whatever or whoever's inside where our friends are."

"And if they refuse to answer?"

"Where's that crowbar?"

Hera managed a half smile. "Who'd have thought, all those years ago when we first met Sam, that it would lead us here?" She looked around the hall, frowning at cracks in the wall. "You always looked out for me, Ghost. Even when I thought it was all over." She took his hand. *-I trust you. Always. Implicitly.-*

Her other hand reached up to cup his cheek, and his heart raced. *This is it.* He knelt, his lips approaching hers, and this time she didn't pull away.

A loud buzz filled the air. Ghost turned to stare at the doors, which were now opening to reveal what lay behind.

"Holy cracking hell." Hera still held his hand, but she, too, was staring at the room.

It was a wide space, clearly cut out of the natural rock. Part of it had shifted sometime after construction, with a narrow crack running up a wall, across the ceiling and back down the other side, but it still formed a rough underground dome.

Most of it was filled with the largest bio-mind she had ever seen. It sat there like a fat pig, its pinkish-gray skin contorted into waves and squiggles, with dark brown limbs that anchored it into the rock.

A slow breeze blew past them, and a glowing blue fungus, not unlike the junlei trees, provided light from the cavern roof.

The mind didn't move or react in any discernible way. Ghost wondered if it knew they were there.

A deck, clearly recognizable in its curved white outline, sat on a pedestal in front of the mind.

Ghost and Hera exchanged a look. "Should we?"

He looked down at Sam.

The spider mech extended a leg as if to say, *Be my guest.*

They stepped inside and an ear-splitting screech filled the air, tearing into Ghost's mind like a power drill. He fell to the ground, grinding his hands against his ears, trying desperately to block the sound, feeling blood trickle out of his right ear.

Hera fell next to him, her legs shaking as if she was having a seizure.

The last thing he saw was her going limp. Then his own mind short-circuited from the pain, and the world went away.

～

SAM RACED INTO THE ROOM, veering right to avoid Ghost's fall, and then left to stay out of Hera's way.

They'd triggered an alarm of some sort when entering the room.

He'd thought the alarm system was disabled. Another error which had brought his human friends to harm.

He raced to the deck, his spider mech legs climbing it easily.

On top, he demagnetized the access hatch and flipped it open easily with one leg.

Plunging his leg inside, he found the direct line to the bio mind that loomed like a whale above him. As he prepared to burrow inside, he found and turned off the alarm, hoping it hadn't damaged Ghost and Hera's hearing beyond repair.

Humans were surprisingly fragile creatures, a lesson he'd learned over and over again in his sometimes painfully long life.

Assured that he had done what he could, he connected to the bio-mind and dipped inside.

33

HAYWIRE

Seek how we may,
  There is no other road across the sky;
  And, looking up, I hear star-voices say:
  "You could not reach us if you did not die."

—"Faith's Vista," by Henry Abbey,
from *Poems From a Distant Earth*, by Chen Tien

SANYA WANTED TO DANCE. After all the running and all the fear, they had *actually done it*—found someone on the Launchpad to talk to. One of the dropnauts, even, someone who was supposed to be down on the surface at Martinez Base.

There was a story there, she was sure. One she might get to tell when things went back to normal. *If* they ever did.

Right now, that all seemed supremely unimportant.

"Tien, can you hear me?" They'd established contact, but apparently there was something wrong on the Launchpad too.

"Yes. I've managed to connect to the control room here too. Power has just gone out across the station, but emergency power has been restored."

"Can you manage a vee con?"

"Sorry, no. I don't have the bandwidth on this end. Look, we need to make this fast. I'm not sure how long we'll have this channel."

"Got it." She glanced over at Rafe, who nodded. He was listening in via her loop on em to em. "What's your status down there?"

"I'll give you the thirty-second version. We encountered other humans near Martinez base. There seems to be an active AI down there too. The humans had a mech companion carrying a compressed AI named Harley that commandeered an old Humber heavy lifter and carried us up here to the Launchpad. Now Dek, the station-mind, is offline, and Harley is not responding, either."

"Holy hissing hell." Sanya's good mood deflated.

"Yes, that's about it in a nutshell." She could hear repressed laughter in Tien's voice. "And up there?"

"Oh, nothing major. Alpha has gone non-responsive, except for some regular emergency warnings to stay inside. There's a lockdown, but we evaded it. Something or someone tried to kill us. And I'm talking to you via an illicit transmitter from outside the city." She took a deep breath. "Where's Sam?"

There was a garbled burst of static. "…down to the surface. We can't reach him."

"Do you think this… Harley AI… is responsible?" The timing was a bit off, though, if it had just reached the station in the last few hours.

"I don't know. Seems awfully coincidental, otherwise."

"I know. One more thing. I've—had a source on the Launchpad feeding me information about the Return mission for weeks. It's why I have this transmitter set up. But the weird thing is, the transmissions don't seem to have come from the Launchpad. They originated down on Earth. Where did your human contacts come from?"

"Come again? I lost the last bit there."

"Where did the humans you encountered come from?"

"Ah. Somewhere east of here. Boundary Peak. Used to be Nevada."

Sanya felt a chill creep down her spine that had nothing to do with the chill of the lunar surface. It couldn't be a coincidence. *I let it in.*

Whatever it was—AI, virus, some combination?—it had gotten a foothold in Alpha's system through her actions. "Holy cracking hell."

"What?"

"I think it got to Alpha though this transmitter."

Rafe's voice came through their connection. "So wait, if it's staging simultaneous attacks on Dek on the Launchpad and on Alpha here, they must be coordinating somehow, right?" He came to stand behind her.

Sanya nodded. "Maybe?"

"Who's that?"

"Tien, meet my companion in crime, Rafe Wilde, press agent and scoundrel extraordinaire."

She could *feel* Rafe's grin at his new title. "Hi, Tien. If we can disrupt the connection, that might help buy us some time. Can you reach the main transmitter there?"

There was silence for a moment.

"Tien?"

"Sorry, checking with Maria, the station manager. She thinks so, if we can get out of this locked room. Sorry, long story."

"Got it. And we'll try to do the same here."

Sanya looked at him as if he was crazy. -*We will?*-

-*Yeah. Look.*- He pointed across the plateau and up the edge of the lava tube that held Redemption. A white dish sat on the summit, pointed toward the Earth.

Of course. It was how she'd smuggled her illicit news into Alpha's network. Whatever the attacker was, it must have established a direct link with the Launchpad. -*Cut it off at the receiver.*-

He nodded. -*I'll get up there and disrupt it. Somehow. You stay here and keep the comm line open.*-

Sanya shook her head and glared at him as if he'd gone insane. -*Are you kidding me? You* stay. *You don't have much oxygen left. You can't exert yourself, remember?*-

They stared at each other. -*You're a hell of a lot tougher than you look.*-

She grinned. -*And you're much more of a hero than you let on.*-

He laughed. -*Fair enough. You know what to do when you get there?*-

She shook her head. -*Thought I'd just throw a wrench into the works.*-

Rafe laughed. -*Keep this channel open. We should be able to maintain a line-of-sight connection. I'll stay on the horn with Tien and the Launchpad.*-

Tien's voice came across the comm line. "You guys still there?"

Sanya gave Rafe the thumbs-up. "Sorry, Tien, just planning our attack on the transmitter. I'm going—Rafe will stay on the line with you."

"A woman of action." Tien sounded impressed.

Sanya snorted. "I guess? Someone's got to do it. Good luck, Tien." She squeezed Rafe's shoulder.

-Be careful-

-I will. Don't do anything crazy here.- Sanya set off toward the white dish. The sooner she got there, the sooner they could put an end to this whole crazy attack.

THERE WAS a knock at the door.

Rai jumped up, sharing an anxious glance with Aidan. "Come in."

The door opened, and Rosemary was there with two men. One of them was Ash. "I'm so sorry—"

She couldn't mean.... "No, they have to listen to us. There's too much at stake." Rai backed toward the wall, aware there was nowhere for him to go "This isn't right."

"These are Ash and Dale. They are here to ensure your compliance. And don't forget, I can still peg you at any time."

Ash and Dale advanced on him.

"Aidan!"

Aidan couldn't save him. His new friend was frozen, his face white.

Ash took Rai by the shoulders while Dale forced his arms behind his back, tying them together quickly and efficiently.

"I'm sorry, Rai." Ash's voice was barely a whisper.

Rai pleaded with Rosemary. "Just let us leave. We're not even from here. We won't bother you." *I don't want to be gelded.*

Rosemary's face was hard as stone. "The Council decided that we can't take that chance. Given your peoples' superior numbers and level of technology, we aren't ready for them to know we exist. The Council's word is law."

"I told you, we want peace, not war. Besides, when we go missing, they will send someone to find us, if they haven't already...." He searched for a way out, but Ash and Dale were both stronger than he was, and Aidan seemed to be retreating within himself. *This can't be happening....*

They had Aidan trussed up too in no time.

"More likely, they'll give up on this site, cry a few tears for you, and choose another base of operations. Earth is a big place."

"It doesn't have to be like this."

Rosemary had the grace to look sorry about it. "I don't agree with everything they said. But I am only the First among many. In the sisterhood, we rule by majority. I was in the minority, but I convinced them to let me be the one who brings you the news." She sighed. "Come now. It won't be painful. I'll make certain of that. Just be glad you weren't condemned to death. It was considered." She turned on her heel and left the room.

Condemned to death? Rai shook his head. He must have misheard. What kind of barbarians were these people?

Ash and Dale pushed them out after her.

We didn't do anything wrong! Surely this was all just a huge misunderstanding.

The lights in the hallway flickered.

Rosemary looked up at them and frowned.

Something was happening, something bigger than all of them. Rai could feel it. "Is that normal?"

The lights came back on.

"It happens. Sometimes." Seemingly satisfied, Rosemary led them down the hall to the door that opened onto the stairs. They reached the vestibule without further incident and soon were out onto the open concourse.

All around them, the citizens of the Preserve went about their business as if nothing had changed. Of course, for them nothing had. It was all disturbingly *normal.*

A white bird flapped by lazily, sailing along the concourse before slipping back out to the park through the columns.

Rai considered making a break for it. But how far would he get with his hands tied, having no idea where to go or how to get back to the surface? *We should have tried earlier, when we still had a chance.*

Several more birds appeared, fluttering past them to alight along the top of the columns. They watched the passersby below like sentinels. Rai stared at them, wishing they would intervene on his behalf. But what could a couple birds do?

And what would it be like, being gelded? He didn't want to find out, but then again, what could he do about it now? "Rosemary, listen to me. It doesn't have to be like this. We can talk to Redemption, make a deal. We have lots of technology to share. Things that could make your life better."

She ignored him.

A flock of the white birds erupted in the air above them, surging onto the concourse from the park, panicked and flying right into the crowd.

Beaks and talons swiped at Rai. He turned away, trying to avoid them, but with his hands tied behind his back, he couldn't defend himself.

There were hundreds of them—in seconds the air became a confusion of feathers and sharp talons as people succumbed to panic, screaming and running.

Then lights went out, and it was pure chaos.

Rai ducked and dropped to his knees, eyes closed, while men, women and children shouted all around him.

He stared at the darkness beneath him, hoping the birds would go away as the world around him descended into madness. Talons clawed at his back, and someone let out a blood-curdling scream.

Then, just as fast as it had begun, it was over.

The flapping of wings diminished, and the lights came back on.

Rai opened his eyes. The flock was winging its way out into the Preserve's open space, disappearing into the forest at its center.

He managed to sit up and looked around the Concourse. It looked like something right out of a war tridee.

People had collapsed everywhere, faces and arms bleeding. Rosemary's bright yellow dress was torn and stained with flecks of blood. One woman's eye had been pecked out, laying bloody and broken on the ground before her.

Rai turned away, his stomach churning.

Aidan got up and started to run toward the open air of the preserve, away from the horror.

Rosemary reached into her pocket and pulled out the dreaded button. She glared at Aidan and pressed it.

Nothing happened.

"Aidan!"

His friend stopped at the edge of the Concourse and turned, his face etched with fear "What?"

"The pegs don't work!"

Ash looked at him, and then over at Dale. Then they all turned to look at Rosemary.

Now fear shone in her eyes, as she pressed the button again and again.

Dale reached for her, as though he might strangle her.

"Dale, don't." Ash barked it, almost an order.

All around them, men were standing, pulling off their collars if they wore them, passing the word: "The pegs aren't working."

Aidan returned to his side, looking sheepish.

"Ash, could you…?" Rai indicated the rope that bound his wrists behind his back.

"Of course."

Soon he and Aidan were freed.

Rai looked around. The men were standing on their own, and they looked… taller, somehow. No longer diminished by their slavery.

Several of the women had knives out, staring warily at the newly-liberated men.

Rosemary stared at them, blood running down her forehead. Rai could see the gears turning in her head. "What do you want from us?" She set the button down on the ground in front of her like. Peace offering.

"First of all, no one's getting gelded today." Ash lifted his leg and brought it down hard, crushing it under his heel.

Rai looked at the man with newfound respect. That was something, at least. "So is *that* normal? The birds?"

Rosemary shook her head, her face looking like she'd seen a ghost. "There's something wrong."

As if to punctuate her statement, the lights of the concourse went out again, and then the glow that lit the park did too, plunging them into near-absolute darkness once more.

There were scattered shouts and screams. Rai found Aidan's hand in the darkness, and warmth surged through him.

Then the light over the park came back on, but it was dim, dimmer than Earthlight. Rai looked around. People were helping others to their feet—both men and women. A small thing, but significant.

Aidan looked at Rosemary pointedly. "Seems like the danger came a little faster than we predicted."

A phalanx of female guards arrived and tried to subdue the suddenly unpegged men, and soon a pitched battle was in progress all around them.

Rai nodded. "Rosemary, you have to take us to *Her*. I can help."

"I can't do that. No one gets to see *Her* but the Council."

Rosemary looked around at the carnage. The men were holding their own, no longer cowed by the threat of pain.

Rosemary levered herself up, wincing at the pain.

Now you know how it feels. Rai pushed away the uncharitable thought.

"Enough." She said it softly at first, and the fighting went on all around them.

"Enough! Women, lay down your arms!" This time it was a roar that echoed up and down the concourse.

The fighting stopped as the guards looked at her in confusion. Then one by one they set down their truncheons.

Rosemary turned her attention back to Rai and Aidan and seemed to come to a decision. "Maybe it's time for a change." She pulled a chain over her head and handed it to Rai. "This is a key to let you into *Her* domain. Ash, Dale, take Rai and Aidan across the Preserve to *Her*, as quickly as you can. If anyone tries to stop you, tell them you have the dispensation of the First."

Rai nodded. He sure didn't like Rosemary, but he had developed a certain grudging respect for the First of the Preserve. "Thank you."

She stared at him for a long moment. "You're welcome. I am placing my trust in you. It's not easy for me, believe me. The hands of men have worked great evil on this world." She looked around at the confusion. "Now go, before someone does something stupid and things heat up again."

Rai nodded. He should feel powerful, triumphant. Instead, he just felt sick at all the pain and bloodshed. He had no idea how he was going to fix things, only that he had to try. "We'll talk more after the crisis is over." To Ash, he said, "Tell the other men. No killing. Justice will come soon enough." For once, he was running toward danger instead of away from it.

Ash nodded and passed the word.

Then Rai and Aidan followed the others out into the heart of the Preserve to find *Her*.

AIDAN GLANCED BACK at the concourse as they ran down the stairs and then across the grass of the Preserve.

Just like that. He reached up to touch his neck. The peg was still there—oh what he wouldn't give to rip the cursed thing out of his flesh—but he was a free man again. For now.

If the tense detente behind them was any indication, this whole culture had just been forced into sudden drastic change. If it wasn't destroyed by whatever had been attacking Rai and his people. *Ally, I wish you were here.*

They crossed a wide empty field full of small purple wildflowers, reaching one of the white stone trails that led into the forest. Aidan had seen the sky trees—zongies, Rai called them—whole groves and clusters of them. But he'd never experienced anything like this. Not outside of the tridees of parks on Old Earth memorialized in Boundary Peak's core.

The chittering of birds above reminded Aidan of the ever-present danger.

The stone path led them under the forest canopy, and Aidan glanced up nervously at the trees for signs of their attackers. His arm was still wet with blood where one of the birds had clawed him.

It was even darker there than out under the dim light of the dome. The trees were of all different sizes and shapes, though they were hard to make out in the dim light. Bushes underneath them added texture, and a glowing golden fungus covered a fallen log whose roots clawed the air like fingers.

Rai slowed briefly, now and again, to get a better look at one plant or another, but then was forced to hurry to keep up with the others. Aidan sympathized. *It must be killing you not to have time to examine each and every one.*

Off to one side of the path, a small brook trickled, and the path crossed over it a couple times over stone bridges. "How far is this place we're going to?"

Ash called back over his shoulder. "About half an hour. If we hurry."

Aidan did the math. That meant the Preserve was roughly eight kilometers wide. What a massive undertaking to have built this place. He slowed down, looking at the dim glow through the trees above. *Amazing.*

A branch shook above him, and something dark and lithe dropped onto the pathway between him and the guards, turning to regard him with bright yellow eyes. Aidan skidded to a halt and his heart tried to leap out of his chest.

Ir was a cat. A *big* cat. It was all black, its eyes glinting in the dim glow.

"Aidan, don't move." Rai was a few paces ahead of him, on the other side of the predator. "Dale says the panther won't hurt you. It's pegged, too, and it feels pain if it gets too close to a human."

Sweat beaded Aidan's forehead. "But the pegs don't work."

The cat approached him, dipping its head, its eyes focused on his. It was a panther—he knew them from nature tridees back home. It was beautiful and powerful, and scary as hell.

Aidan held his breath. They said you were supposed to play dead with bears. *Does that work with cats, too?*

It padded up to him, reaching its snout up to sniff him, its breath rank in his face.

Aidan cast about for something, anything to defend himself with. There were sticks on the side of the path, but they might as well have been a kilometer away.

Then it flicked its tail and passed him by, its black fur brushing his blood-covered arm.

He waited, completely still. "Is it… gone?" Sweat trickled down his cheek. He wiped it off with the back of his forearm.

Rai nodded. "It ran off, toward the Concourse."

Aidan sighed in relief. "I think I wet my pants."

He expected ridicule, but Rai and the others only nodded. "We were all scared. We'll get you clean ones later. Come on!"

Easy for you to say. He checked his pants. It was only a little bit. *I can live with it.*

They set off again at a run. The forest was both beautiful and primal, triggering fears Aidan had only felt a few times, at night when they'd camped out in the mountains under the howl of the night wind.

After a few minutes, they emerged from the forest onto the shores of a wide lake. Small furry animals—long and sleek and brown—played at the water's edge, and fish leapt out of the center, falling back into the lake with a splash.

"What… are… they?" Aidan pointed at the furry critters. He'd thought he was in good shape, but he and Ally had mostly walked on the way to the base.

Ash flashed him a grin. "River otters, and the fish are trout."

The Earth above was barren, save for the zongi trees and grasses and a few native trees and bushes. Vast swaths of it were desert, while others farther north were probably still buried under the snow. There was so much down here that could help reseed the world. *If we ever get out of here.*

On the far side of the lake, wide fields held sway. Some were fallow, while others had strange stunted plants with their branches strung across taut cords, heavy with bunches of purple fruit.

Soon they passed through a grove of trees, also planted in precise lines, branches heavy with another fruit of some sort, orange balls a little bigger than his fist. *Those are oranges, you idiot.* Aidan grinned.

All this time, this place had been here, hidden away from what was left of the world above, full of amazing bounty. *What other secrets does the Earth still keep?*

Finally, they emerged from a copse of white trees with round leaves and came within sight of the concourse once again. It was mostly dark here, the curved walkway unlit. He thought maybe it was just the dim light, but as they approached, he saw how different this section was from the one they had just left.

A wide white stairway ascended to the concourse from the open field. Its rails were intricately carved to look like waves racing down to the ground below.

They ascended the stairs to stand before a pair of silver doors, twice as tall as Aidan. The ceiling here was much wider and broader, a dome above them with hundreds of square windows cut out of it, each of them emitting an amber glow.

Rai exchanged a glance with Aidan, eyebrow raised.

Aidan nodded. "Do it." They'd come this far.

Rai pulled the chain with the key over his head and inserted the key into the big door and turned the lock.

He stepped back, and the double doors opened, bathing them all in golden light.

34

———

FALLING TOGETHER

It was... stunning. There's just no better word for it. Elms and oak trees, raspberry bushes and poison ivy—I mean, why would you save that?

And baby blue eyes. They had a field full of baby blue eyes!

Poppies, Chinese Houses, Fiddlenecks, Baby Blue Eyes, Yellow Pansies, Star Lilies... I looked for them all.

The botanist in me was in heaven.

—From *Drop Day Blues*, by Rylan Ramirez

"Tien, can you hear me?" Ally was starting to wish she'd never left the ground. It was little comfort that she'd turned out to be right—crazy damnable AIs!—given that she was trapped with one inside a metal can with no way out that didn't involve holding her breath, freezing to death, and falling for a very long time. Her lonely life under the Mountain was looking pretty good right about now.

She touched the talkie behind her ear, struggling to keep the panic out of her voice. "Tien?"

"Right here, Allycat." Tien's voice in her ear sounded calm, collected. "Sorry, I was talking with Sanya up on Luna. We think the entity attacking

Alpha up on Redemption is Harley. We think it's using Dek's resources to inten-sify the attack on Alpha. You almost here?"

Jesus Christ. Ally cursed herself for taking the Lord's name in vain. "Sorry, no. Dek's gone fully AWOL and we're bottled up here in the control room."

"Dammit." There was a pause. "You okay up there otherwise?"

"Yeah." She took a deep breath. Hearing Tien's voice helped a lot. "A little freaked out. *A lot* freaked out, honestly. But not hurt."

"Listen to me. We're going to get through this. Close your eyes." Tien's calm, warm tone reminded Ally of her mother.

Lorelei tapped her on the shoulder. "What's she saying?"

"Just a sec, Lorelei." To Tien, she said, "Go ahead. I'm listening."

"Okay, take a deep breath. Breathe through your nose. Hold it for four seconds. Then breathe out through your mouth."

"Okay." *Breathe in. Hold. Breathe out.*

"Keep doing it until you feel calmer."

Ally sucked in a deep breath. Held it while she counted to four. Slowly let it out. She repeated it a few more times, feeling her heartbeat slow. *Thank you, Lord.* She'd gotten lax about her prayers these last few weeks.

"You okay, kid?"

She opened her eyes to find Lorelei staring at her intently.

"Yeah. Better. Thanks, Tien." She took one more deep breath. "Tien says the AI we brought up from Earth is using Dek to attack Alpha. Did I get that right?"

Lorelei nodded. "We let it in."

Tien's voice was soothing. "Perfect. Ask Lorelei if there's a way for someone to get outside."

"Outside?"

"To break the main transmitter. We need to disconnect Harley from Dek."

"I'll ask." Ally looked up.

Lorelei and the others were all crowded around her. Her heart started to race again—she needed space. "Could you all just… just back up a little?" She waved her arm to clear them away.

"Sorry. Everyone, back to your stations." Lorelei guided her to one corner of the control room, away from the others. "Better?"

Ally smiled gratefully. "It's just… I'm not used to crowds."

"It's okay." Lorelei squeezed her shoulder, her soft brown eyes kind. "So what do we need to do?"

"Tien wants to know if anyone can get outside."

Lorelei shook her head. "No, it's the same problem. We can't get through this door. We can't get through any door or lock on the station."

"So you have to *be* outside to *get* outside." They were stuck. "I'll tell her."

Lorelei laughed. "Oh my god, Ally, you're a genius."

Ally's eyes narrowed. What do you mean?"

Lorelei's eyes twinkled. "We *have* people outside!"

"We do?"

"Yes. We do. The other drop crews!" She slipped back into her seat and pulled up something above her deck.

"I thought you were locked out."

"From the system, yes. But my deck buffers whatever I am working on to local storage. Makes things faster." She swiped the air, and an image of the Earth appeared, rotating above the deck, with four golden lights floating around it. "If I feed her the coordinates, can you ask Tien if she can get them a message? The *Gday* is closest."

Ally relayed the info. "Tien, Lorelei says there's a way we can knock out the transmitter. Can you reach the… the *Gday*?"

The whoop on the other end almost blew her eardrum out.

Even Lorelei heard it. "I think that's a yes."

TIEN CUT THE CONNECTION.

"Everything okay?" Maria was hovering over her shoulder, watching what she was doing.

"Yeah, mostly. The whole station is locked down, not just us. But we're going to call the *Gday* back to help."

Marie nodded. "Genius. As you were."

Tien grinned. She supposed she'd just been conscripted into the Launchpad military. *Guess I'm recruit zero.* She switched over to the external transmitter. "Sanya, you there?"

"Sorry, Sanya's not available right now." The voice was male and suave. A little too suave.

"Rafe?"

"The one and only. Sanya's off to disrupt the transmission. She left me here 'cause I was stupid enough to puncture my suit and lose half of my oxygen. So I'm on desk-jockey duty."

Tien grinned. "Got it. I'm going to turn the transmitter away for a bit. We're calling on one of the drop teams to come back to try to disrupt the transmission on this end. Dek has us all locked up like junlei stalks in a bottle."

"Got it. I'll stand by if needed."

"Back to you soon." Tien entering the coordinates for the *Gday*. With the main station dish, she wouldn't have needed such precise targeting, but this backup transmitter was much lower power. Maybe she could do something about that. *After I get things in motion.* She felt a surge of joy—she hadn't tapped her grid skills like this in years.

She waited while the transmitter got a lock on the *Gday*.

"Calling the *Gday*. Repeat, calling the *Gday*."

Nothing.

She rechecked the coordinates. They were dead-on. A feeling of dread gripped her. What if the *Gday* had been destroyed too? "Calling the *Gday*. Repeat—"

"This is Corey Lennon, captain of the *Gday*. Who is this?"

"Corey, this is Tien from the *Zhenyi*. So glad I found you."

"Tien?" His whole voice changed. "I heard you'd made it back up—welcome home!" There were cheers in the background.

Tien grinned. "Such as it is."

"Fair. But this isn't the standard Launchpad channel. What's up?"

"Things are a bit… crazy over here at the moment. How fast can you get back here?"

"Funny you should ask. It was our turn for a refueling, so we're inbound now. Arrival in twenty-three minutes."

"Perfect—wait, I've got another incoming signal from the Launchpad." He sounded perplexed. "Be right back."

Tien frowned. Had Lorelei gotten control of the comm again? The seconds lengthened into minutes.

Maria hovered over her shoulder. "What's happening?"

"Corey said someone else called him. From the Launchpad."

"That's good, right? Unless—"

"Tien." Corey's voice came back online. He sounded strange.

"Who called you, Corey?" She hoped it was Lorelei.

"It was you. Telling me not to listen to you. That you're an AI? Impersonating the real Tien."

Hissing cracking hell. "That's not me, Corey. It's Harley, the AI we brought up from Earth. Or Dek. Look, it doesn't matter—you have to disable the main transmitter when you get here—"

"She said you'd say that. I think we'll wait until we arrive to sort this out."

"Corey—" How could she convince him she was the real Tien? "Ask her what your mother made for us when Hera and I came to your parents' place for dinner last year. When the three of us were on shore leave."

There was silence across the line.

"Corey! Just do it."

"Okay." The connection went silent again.

She looked up at the station manager. "Dek—or Harley—is messing with us."

Maria bit her lip. "What if there was a way to disable the AI altogether?"

"You can do that?"

Maria nodded. "Not here. But if we can get out of this room… maybe."

"That might do it—"

"Hey, Tien." Corey's voice sounded cautiously friendly. "She… it… said we had junlei salad and some kind of wine. She didn't remember exactly which kind."

"Ha!" Tien grinned. "So you'll do it?"

"Affirmative. Operation Transmitter Take Out will commence in twenty-one minutes."

Maria was staring at her. "Why didn't he ask *you* what you ate?"

"Because he doesn't have any parents."

Hera woke with a splitting headache.

She tried to remember if she'd been out on a bender the night before. Sometimes the combination of the club thromb music and ill-considered drinking choices—damn you, junlei ale—gave her massive headaches.

That still didn't explain the hard surface under her head. Usually she at least made it home and into bed with Tovey.

She hadn't thought about them in hours. Days, maybe. Since just after the drop. Why was that? *I do love them. Don't I?*

Then it all came flooding back. The missile. The trees. The NAU spaceship graveyard. The trek through the hills. Sam. The bio-mind.

She cracked her eyes open.

She was lying on the floor, staring at a gray wall.

Grunting, she pushed herself up, shrugging her way out of her backpack's straps and managing to sit up, if a bit unsteadily.

Red lights were flashing around the perimeter of the room. There was no sound. She brought her hand up to snap her fingers next to hear ear.

Not a sound.

Oh hissing hell no. I will not be deaf. Not on top of everything else. She touched her cheek. It was wet. She stared at her fingers, trying to make sense of things. It was hard to tell for sure in the strange light, but the *wetness* looked like blood.

There'd been a siren—a terrible, piercing sound.

Ghost.

Hera glanced around and found his prone form a meter away.

She tried to stand, but her biframe wouldn't work. *Cracking hell.* Blocked, or simply out of power?

Doesn't matter. She popped the release on her left side, and then the right, and wriggled backward out of it. It was just dead weight.

Then she turned and pulled herself toward Ghost, thanking the stars for her upper body strength. *Never rely solely on your tech*, Jolly had told her more than once after she'd gotten her biframe. Hera had taken the advice to heart, working on strengthening her core, her arms, and shoulders.

She reached Ghost and pulled off his pack, one arm at a time, and pushed it aside. She turned him over and put her cheek to his mouth.

He was still breathing.

Thank the stars. She shook him gently. "Ghost."

He mumbled something but didn't wake.

"Ghost!" Still nothing.

Hera looked around, trying to decide what to do next. That's when she saw the deck.

It was an old-style model, not nearly as sleek as the ones she was used to. Sam was perched atop it, apparently interfacing with the enormous bio-mind.

Behind her, the doors slid open again, and a group of the creepy little spider mechs crouched there, glowing a baleful red.

Hera reacted before she could think, dragging herself across the floor the meter and a half to the door. She slammed her hand into the palm sensor, praying that it wasn't keyed to a specific set of prints.

The doors skittered closed, slamming on one of the spider mechs and crushing it to its component bits, and blocking others outside. But two got through, and they scampered toward the deck, and Sam.

"No you don't, you little cracking shits." Hera pulled herself after them, stopping only to grab one leg of her biframe. *In need, anything's a hammer.* She missed Jolly and her life advice "Ghost, I could really use some help right now!"

He groaned. *Well, that's something, at least.*

The first of the mechs was ascending the side of the deck now, but she was right behind it. Pulling herself up into an unsteady kneeling position, she raised the biframe like a bat and smacked the thing with as much force as she could, sending it flying across the room.

It hit the wall hard enough that she actually heard something—a muted *thwack*—and fell to the ground, collapsing in a smoking heap.

The other one had made it to the deck and was almost on top of Sam.

Desperate, Hera dropped her biframe and lunged toward it, her fingers closing around it just as it reached out a leg toward Sam.

Electricity sizzled through her hands, and the sharp angles of its legs cut into the soft flesh of her palm where she had already taken a beating from the electric fence.

She screamed, half in pain and half in anger, and lifted the mech, pulling it away from her friend and mentor.

She threw it hard at the wall next to its companion, and it, too, shorted out and fell into a heap.

Hera sat back, looking at her lacerated hand, the aftereffects of the electric shock overcoming her. She collapsed once more, and the last thing she saw before slipping into empty oblivion was the bio-mind that loomed over her.

Rai stepped through the open doors, transfixed by the space beyond.

He found himself in a forest of giants—redwoods, if he didn't miss the mark. They were enormous, as big as some of the oldest zongies, stretching up into the sky to disappear in a chorus of green leaves. Golden sunlight filtered down through the branches, and birds chirped all around, a cacophony of sounds that defied individual identification.

He knelt to touch the pine-needle-covered forest floor, picking them up and rubbing them between his fingers. They gave off a wonderful scent, something sharp and sweet and unlike anything else in his experience.

He dropped them and laughed as the wind carried them off to deposit them at the feet of one of the redwoods.

Off to his left a fallen tree, half hollowed out by weather and time, offered a microcosm of life. Ants marched in a long line across the top of it, carrying bits of green leaves, and inside spiders ruled over a kingdom of fungi. "What is this place?"

Aidan stared at him as if he'd lost his mind. "It's… beautiful, sure. But it's just a big room." His eyes narrowed. "What do *you* see?"

"A forest. Beautiful redwood trees. There's a light breeze, and it smells wonderful. Like… I don't know. Like the world when it was new, maybe. Fresh. Cool."

The others stared at him as if he were crazy.

Then it hit him. *I'm in vee.*

He tapped his loop, and the room shimmered and changed.

Aidan was right—It was still an impressive place, with smooth white columns instead of trees stretching up into the darkness above. But the floor was white stone, like the concourse. There were no logs or needles or insects scurrying across the floor. "It's a projection. I can see it via my loop."

Ash frowned. "A… loop?"

"Here." He lifted Ash's hand to touch his skin. "Feel it?"

A look of wonder crossed Ash's face.

Rai let Dale touch it too.

"It's how we connect to Alpha back home, and to everyone else, for that matter." Of course. For all their culture in the Preserve, for all the artistic beauty, Rosemary and her people were no longer as technologically advanced as their ancestors.

Rai looked around the great hall. The walls on either side of them were covered with squares of various sizes, some white and some black, creating a great checkerboard. He went to take a closer look, and as he approached, the closest ones lit up, creating a blue circle of light.

The squares were between two and six inches on each side, and the light was a series of small letters that scrolled across the face of the box. He peered closer.

Bryophyta > Platae > Eukaryota > Andreaea heinemannii

He frowned. He *knew* that name. Then it came to him. "It's moss!"

Wonderingly, he touched the panel, marveling that the tech still worked after all this time.

"Moss?" Aidan looked puzzled.

With a hum, the panel slid open, revealing a sphere of glass. Rai picked it up, holding the sphere up to the light.

"Moss?" Aidan peered at the sphere between Rai's fingers.

"Yes. It's beautiful!" Rai grinned. He set the sphere back into the drawer, and it closed silently. "Do you know what they have here?"

Aidan frowned. "A… moss museum?"

Rai laughed. "More than that. "This is a gene bank." He strolled along the wall, and the blue light followed him as more squares lit up. "It's invaluable. The Preserve has records of thousands… who knows how many plant and animal species? There's a tree. That one's a monkey. Some bacteria… and oooh this one's a dolphin. Aidan, this could change everything!"

Ash was staring at one of the squares. "A dolphin?"

He nodded. "One of the most intelligent animals on Old Earth, behind humankind. Maybe smarter. They didn't blow up the planet, after all."

Aidan grinned. "I've always wanted to see dolphins…."

"Someday you could." He stepped back out into the main hall to look around. "Is this the only room in the temple?"

Ash shook his head. "I don't know. We've never been in here. No one but the Council is allowed."

Rosemary would know.

At the back of the hall, an ancient deck sat on two pillars, on a raised dais that looked like a smaller version of the one in the assembly hall. *Like an altar.* He supposed it would seem that way to someone not familiar with Old Earth tech. Not that it was necessarily outdated—Redemption used much the same equipment today. *A sign of stagnation, for all our talk of progress.*

He walked through the columns, suffering from a weird double vision as they seemed to shift from stone to wood and back again.

He stepped up onto the dais, aware that the others had gathered behind him.

It was a standard interface, two smooth black plates in the white surface indicating where he should put his hands.

He had no idea what he'd find inside. A crazy AI? A broken archival system? Or something else?

Rai took a deep breath. All his life he'd been afraid of failure. His default fight or flight response had always been *run*.

Something had changed. He'd taken a chance with Aidan, and another in the arena. And he had come through both okay.

He'd plunged through the atmosphere in a tiny ship and then a parachute, for Luna's sake, and had survived. All of which had brought him here, to this moment. *No more running.*

Rai put his hands on the contacts, palms down, and stepped into a whirlwind. Vee space was chaos, bits of data flying back and forth through the ether in a tempest. The world around him fell away, and he was slashed by vicious winds and rain that were no more real than the forest he'd stood in a moment before, but no less savage for being virtual.

Rai ripped his hands away.

"What happened?" Aidan was at his side, his warm hand on Rai's shoulder.

"There's something wrong. The interface… it's a mess." His hands flew over the deck while Aidan watched him wide-eyed. "Aha. I thought so. Look." He pulled up a syslog. It shimmered in the air above the deck.

Aidan squinted, while Ash and Dale crowded in behind them. "What are we looking at?"

"The AI is gone. Or something. This system's only running core functions. Power, lights, warning systems." He turned to look at Ash and Dale. "You know what this means?"

The two men shook their heads simultaneously.

"It means all this noise about *Her* and *Her* divine will is moon dust."

"Moon dust?" Ash frowned.

"Nonsense. They've been lying to you for a hundred and seventeen years."

"Fucking hell." Ash spat on the ground, his fists shaking. "Holy fucking hell."

"Yeah, I agree." He turned back to Aidan. "I need an anchor. I want to try to bypass the core and see if I can get word out to the Launchpad. Can you to come into vee with me—the virtual world of this mind—and keep me from getting lost in the chaos?"

Aidan's brow creased. "I don't know. I can try, if you'll show me how?"

Rai nodded. "Stand here." He held Aidan's hand above one of the interface pads. "When I put my hand down, put yours down too."

"That's it?"

"For now. Ready?"

"I think so."

"Go!"

They put their hands down at the same time.

Chaos struck him again, but this time he was ready for it. He braced himself against the onslaught and turned to look for Aidan.

Aidan wasn't there. Rai was all alone, facing the storm.

He tried to disconnect again, to start over. This time he couldn't drop out of vee. He was trapped. Rai's anxiety ramped up to a ten, and his virtual heart raced.

All around him the data storm howled forlornly, like a banshee that had found its prey.

Sanya trudged across Hayes Promontory, watching for pitfalls in the broken and pitted surface. The outcropping predated the lava tube that held Redemption by at least ten million years. It was relatively flat... a lava dome that had seen its share of drama and change over the eons.

Luna was like that, a record of overlapping trauma that made it difficult to determine where one feature ended and the next began.

Like human history. Sanya looked up at the Earth, a more permanent companion than the changeable sun. Rarely had she been outside for so long at once. And not once since Avri's death.

She was still sore from the climb, and she was tired. *So tired.* She also felt filthy. She longed to go back home, to get a long, hot, wet shower—none of that ionic dry bullshit—and drop into bed. *No rest for the weary.*

She stopped for a moment to catch her breath, hands on her knees as she stared at the dust at her feet.

Dust everywhere.

I want to see Earth. To walk beneath the tree canopies under the changing colors of sunlight flickering through the leaves. To stand on the beach in the rain, her toes dug into the sand, and watch the waves roll in from the sea. Human things, racial memories imprinted deep in the psyche of every man, woman, and child.

She stood and looked back the way she had come. She was about halfway there, but soon she'd have to climb the side of the tube.

Her stomach rumbled.

If she got through this, she was going to treat herself to a spa weekend, and the biggest, best meal she had ever eaten—platters of fresh fruit, junlei steaks, and bakies until she was sick of food.

With a sigh, she started off again, bounding toward the transmitter dish in the distance.

35

MERGE

Seven days.

They're ready. *Sam had run every metric. His teams were ready for the drop.*

He pinged Alpha. -Are they ready?-

-You know they are.- *A pause.* -Are you?-

Sam considered the question. In seven days, the work of his lifetime would commence in earnest. He'd tried to cover every contingency, and yet he had the nagging feeling that he was missing something.

-How do you know what you don't know?-

—From Sam's memory cache, 6.10.2282

"Coming in hot."

Tien scrambled to find an external camera with the right angle on the *Gday's* approach. She could see all the camera connections, but she had no roadmap to choose between them, so she flipped through one after another until she found one with a clear shot of the transmitter. "Got it. I can see your destination. What's the plan?"

Corey laughed. "Pretty simple. Land and lock down. Then one of us steps out to take a hammer to the thing."

Tien laughed. She liked Corey. He was one of those guys it was hard *not* to like. Always worried about everyone else, never a bad word to say about anyone. "Sounds like a good plan." It was killing her to be stuck in this room. She felt impotent, a puppetmistress only able to direct others, unable to take direct action herself. But at least she had a front-row seat for the action. "How far out are you?"

"Landing in T-Minus fifty seconds. How are y'all holding up down there?"

"So far, so good. Not dead. So there's that."

He laughed, and she could almost see his grin. "Yeah, *not dead* is good."

She rerouted to Ally, the image from the camera feed pushed to the background in her head. "Hey Allycat… the *Gday* is coming in fast—here in half a minute. Want to let Lorelei know? Maybe if Harley is distracted when it happens, she can get through to Dek."

"Will do. Hey, if I'm Allycat, what do I call you? Don't you get a nickname too?"

"Sure. Get back to me on that." She switched back to the *Gday*. "Hey, Corey. I see you."

"Yeah, almost… what the hell?"

"Corey, what's going on?"

"The x-drive. It's… holy hissing crap. It's going unstable. Cracking hell. Tien, it's gonna—"

A bright flash blossomed in her view, and then the *Gday* was gone.

"Corey!" Panic seized her, gripping her heart in a vise as something slammed into the camera and her view went dark. Frantically she searched for another view of what was happening out there.

An alert siren blared. "Hull damage, quadrant four. Sealing off affected areas."

"Corey? Corey!" It couldn't be. The camera had malfunctioned, or something. The *Gday*—it was some kind of mistake. *Corey's gone. They're all gone.*

Tien dropped out of vee and threw her arms around Maria, squeezing her tightly, and began to sob.

Maria held her close. "What happened, *mija*?"

Tien opened her eyes. "They're gone, Maria All of them. The *Gday*. The jumper's x-drive…" She couldn't say it.

"Oh God."

Maria let go of her and sank down onto one of the gumdust crates. "What —how?"

Tien wiped her eyes, her anger growing. "The x-drive went unstable. Blew the ship to bits." She closed her eyes. *Like the Bristol.*

Tien glared at the wall. *You did this, Harley. You did it.* She didn't know how, but she knew it was true. She got up and started prowling the small space.

"What are you doing?"

She wanted to scream. To throw things. To rip Harley out of the guts of Dek's system with her bare hands.

She had to stay calm. If she let her emotions get the best of her, she would make another mistake, and she couldn't afford any more mistakes.

Bad things kept happening to her and her teammates, things beyond her control. She was sick of being on the receiving end.

It was time to dish out a little payback. "We're getting out of here, if I have to blow my way through those doors."

GHOST GROANED.

He hadn't felt this cracked since the morning after his graduation party. Junlei alcohol was supposed to be hangover free. But maybe not in the huge quantities he'd consumed.

Although the aftermath of being knocked on his ass by Sam in the storage cube had been pretty damned close.

His head pounded. Literally pounded him, as if it were a jackhammer pushing his neck down into his body.

Ghost groaned again. *Being alive sucks.*

He managed to open his eyes. They felt heavy, crusty. He wiped them clear and tried to make sense of where he was.

The floor was white, clean. Sterile, even. Something huge loomed in the distance, but he couldn't seem to focus on it.

Hera lay a few meters away from him, collapsed in front of a white deck.

"Hera!" He pushed himself up and a wave of nausea hit him.

Ghost dropped back to the ground, throwing up onto the clean white floor. He lay there, miserable, the smell of vomit making him feel sick again.

He pushed himself away, turning his face in the opposite direction. *Better.*

There'd been an alarm. An ear-piercing, soul-curdling alarm.

Slowly his equilibrium returned.

Ghost sat up. His pack lay on the ground nearby. *When did I take that off?*

He flipped it open and pulled out his canteen. He swished some water around in his mouth to clear out the foul taste and spat it out. Then he crawled toward Hera, avoiding the pool of vomit.

He reached her and checked her over as best as he could through her clothes. She seemed to be in one piece, though her biframe was off. Half lay by the door, and the other half was next to her. By the wall, a couple small piles of debris gave off an acrid smoke, crackling with electricity.

You're a true cracking hero. Even without her mobility, she'd gotten herself up and had taken out two of the little mechs, probably sent to attack Sam.

Sam's mech, with the blue, glowing core, sat atop the deck, still as death.

He turned Hera over gently and pulled her up onto his lap.

Her brown eyes fluttered open.

"Hey, you okay?" His voice sounded muted.

She stared at him for a long moment, eyes narrowed, as if trying to remember how to speak. "Hey—I can hear you."

He laughed. "And I can hear you."

"Sam?"

Ghost glanced at the deck. "He seems okay. Looks like you played a little Moon Warrior Princess in here with those mechs, though."

She gave him a faint smile. "Kinda?" Her voice was raspy.

"Yeah, real kick-ass. Made me proud." For just a second, he saw her as she'd been when she got her first set of biframes, courtesy of Sam. Fierce and proud, standing on her own two feet again for the first time. "Think you can you get a little water down?"

She nodded.

Ghost held her head up, and she managed a few swallows. "Good."

"Need… help Sam." She tried to get up, but whatever had happened to her had wiped her out.

"You already did. Rest. I'm going in after him."

"Sure?"

He nodded. "Let me get something for you to put your head on." He managed to stand unsteadily and went back to his pack and dug out one of his shirts, a relatively clean one. He bundled it up to make a pillow. "Here you go." He tucked it under her head.

She nodded gratefully. "Thanks."

She was five years old again, lying in their shared bed, holding his hand to ward off the monsters. "Love you, little Heron."

She smiled. "Love you too."

"Oooh, your hand." Something had lacerated it. She was lucky the cuts were shallow.

He made it back to his pack for some antiseptic and used it to clean off the wounds across her right hand. Then he dressed it with some bandages from his medkit.

He lifted her hand and kissed it gently. *-Better?-*

-Better.-

His stomach felt better too. Not great, but he could live with it.

Someday they'd get back to civilization and all of this would be over, forgotten like a bad dream. Then they could figure out where things stood between them.

He got up again, swaying a little before finding his balance. Then he stumbled toward the deck, staring at it for a moment.

-You got this, Gordy.-

He looked over his shoulder to see Hera staring at him.

She nodded.

-I can do this.- He took a deep breath. He was an engineer, after all. What kind of threat could a simple deck pose? *Hold on, Sam. I'm coming.*

Ghost planted his right hand on its cracked white surface, closing his eyes and plunging himself into chaos.

SAM CLUNG to his perch in the bio-mind like an ant in a storm. Chaos whirled all around him like a hard rain blown by hurricane-force winds.

He backed out of the mind's core and out of the chaos.

...analyze: Martinez Base core...

Something had gone horribly wrong inside the Martinez Base AI. At first he'd thought it was a result of simple insanity—from having been cut off from the outside world for so long. Dek had needed months of reconditioning—therapy for a bio-mind—before he'd been able to utter a coherent sentence again.

But although the AI seemed absent, its core wasn't disconnected from the world.

Far from it.

Sam had detected at least two feeds connecting it to the outside, but in the chaos, he hadn't been able to see where they led.

No, this felt more like an attack. And the timing was far too coincidental.

He was able to access some basic functionality via the bio-mind's network. He locked the door to the room where his physical form sat, blocking any more outside attackers from getting inside easily.

He found and opened the Substation 12 Project TP file—the project he'd found referenced in the Martinez Base file Lorelei had sent him.

Data spun out and into his awareness. His eyes, if he'd had any in his current form, would have widened in surprise. "The Preserve" was so much more than he had hoped for.

He restored life support and basic functions there and tagged it for later review.

Then he turned off the protective EMP field over the base.

...access > communications module...

He sent a test message up to the Launchpad, hoping someone was still up there to receive it. "Launchpad, this is Sam. Status please."

It took a minute, but then the response reached him. "Sam! Thank the seven stars." That was Ying Yue on the *Liánhuā*. "Things are bad up here."

"What's happening?" Though he suspected he already knew.

"Dek's acting strangely. Tien thinks he's under attack. And something's going after Alpha too."

Three minds. Three attacks. This wasn't a coincidence. It was a coordinated event. "Yue, can you reach anyone on the Launchpad?"

"I think so. Tien found a way around Dek's system."

If anyone could, it would be her. One more reason he'd chosen her for team Two. "Okay, tell her it's the same thing down here. There's an AI at Martinez Base that's been compromised by the same attacker."

"Will do. She thinks that attacker is Harley—the AI that rode up on the lifter."

Of course. "Makes sense. I'm going to try to find a way to shut her attack down here. If I can, maybe we can convince this mind to help us stop her up there, too."

"Got it." There was a long pause. "Sam? There's one more thing."

He could *feel* her anguish through the link. He felt a very human sense of dread. "Tell me."

"We lost the *Gday*. X-drive failure." She was silent for a long moment. "Tien thinks Dek—or the attacker—did it."

Sam felt his circuits chill. "I'm so sorry." More death on his watch. More precious humans he could never replace.

"We are too. They were trying to smash the transmitter on the Launchpad."

Sam felt something akin to hatred surge through him. "I want you and the *Zulu* to stay as far away from that station as possible, and contact them only at need after this message. Do you understand?"

"Yes, sir."

"You are *not* to put your ships at risk. I don't want to lose anyone else, and we're going to need you to evacuate the others here."

"Got it, Sam."

"Signing off. I'll contact you when there's more to report." He cut the connection. *Another team lost.* The Return was becoming a never-ending disaster. *I should have planned for this. Somehow. I should have been better prepared.*

Logically, he knew better. But the thought that he'd never see Corey, Vixen, Joyce, or Marco again shook him to his core.

He shoved the pain aside, but it was getting harder and harder to do so.

It was counterproductive, but still, it impinged on his consciousness like a shadow.

He would allow himself to truly *feel* it later, when lives didn't depend on him. *Can't change the past. Only the future.*

He had work to do.

...access > martinez base core...

He dropped back into the madness.

RAI SCREAMED against the digital storm. "Aidan! Aidan!"

The constant tumult of data was eating away at him, wearing away his virtual form like wind wore down sandstone. He didn't know what would happen if it washed him all away, and he decidedly did *not* want to find out. *Will I wake up in my own body? Or will I be erased?*

It scared the living crap out of him. *Think, Rai. Think.*

Every operating system, no matter how advanced, had an underlying logic. If he could find the basic processes for the Preserve's core, he might be able to find his way around through the tempest.

He closed off his mind to the storm, looking for patterns.

Tools. Sam had given them all tools for this sort of thing on the off-chance that they had to deal with an AI issue on the Launchpad or on Earth.

What had he said?

Find the T-Line.

Of course. The main data trunk in the system. He could ride that anywhere. He reached into his loop and pulled out the search tool. It manifested in his hand as a little winged thing, no bigger than his pinkie finger. His own brain's way of rationalizing it in a place that had never been meant for human consciousness, especially in its current state.

The search tool unfolded and lifted into the air, sprouting tiny silver wings. It began to glow—a golden hue that seemed to push back the storm—and beneath his feet a grid appeared, illuminated with the same golden light.

The operating system.

Rai knelt to touch it. An electric shock went through him.

He let go, staring at his hand. He was unhurt, at least in his virtual form.

He touched it again, and information flooded into him.

The wild tempest continued all around him, but now he was able to perceive it within the framework of the core.

Now to find the T-Line. He let himself flow into the OS, his human form melting and becoming a part of the system.

In an instant, he shot across a universe, searching the system for something to help him reach the Launchpad.

He found the T-Line, the system backbone that shuttled information back and forth inside the core. It was feeble and faint, cowed by the invading code of the storm.

He merged with it and found something unexpected. There was someone else inside the system. An outsider.

He tasted its signature, and then his own light brightened with surprise.

He knew that bit of code, or at least the human who was behind it. *Ghost.*

"Holy cracking hell." *Ghost is here.* And that meant Hera probably wasn't far behind.

Together, they might be able to beat this thing.

He queried the system for Ghost's location. The grid lines shifted, and then he was somewhere else.

~

GHOST WANDERED THROUGH A STRANGE WILDERNESS. Everything was black and white and shades of gray. Even his own form here was a hollow specter of its usual self. Like a ghost.

He laughed harshly. *And why wouldn't I be?*

This had been a stupid idea. He didn't even know his way around Alpha's mind, much less this alien bio-mind from his homeworld's past. He was lost and somehow couldn't find a way to disconnect.

And so he wandered. He followed a black path, one that branched off again and again in different directions. Dark cliffs surrounded him, and here and there sluggish rivers of data oozed along like black lava. Unseen *things* moved in the darkness on either side.

Ghost shuddered, wishing he'd waited for Hera to recover. She knew more about these things than he did. He was an engineer, and he knew how parts worked. Real, physical parts that you built things with. But vee… If he'd been real, his brow would have been covered in a cold sweat.

He'd assumed—wrongly—that he would simply appear in this strange virtual world next to Sam. Or that there would be some clear way to reach him. Instead, he was wandering this bleak world with little hope of finding his friend or a way out. *Should have paid more attention in AI class.*

He tried again to just *let go*. To drop back into the real world. He closed his eyes and tried to will himself out—to drop out of this nightmarish landscape and reverse his terrible mistake.

Nothing happened.

Will I die here? If I do, will I die back there too? How connected was this place to the real world?

Something keened in the distance, like a dying beast.

"Hello?" He felt stupid saying it to no one, but he was running out of ideas. "Ghost?"

He spun around, thinking he'd imagined the voice. It wouldn't have been the first time in this strange place.

A glowing human outline stood before him, its head cocked.

"Who are you?"

The outline began to take on form and substance. "Who do you think?"

Ghost knew that voice. "Holy cracking shit. Rai?"

Rai's grin appeared on the semitransparent face. "Who else?"

"You beautiful bastard." Ghost tried to hug his friend, but his hands passed right through him. "How in cracking hell did you find me?"

"One of the tricks Sam taught us in class. Find the T-Line. Weren't you paying attention?"

Ghost laughed. "I guess not. Where have you been? Sam said you'd met the locals."

"You wouldn't believe me if I told you." Rai raised his eyebrows. "Wait, Sam's here too?"

Ghost nodded. "He's in here somewhere with us. I came in trying to find him."

He grinned. "That's amazing. We'll find him next." Rai reached out and touched Ghost's hand, and this time Ghost could actually *feel* him. "But first, let me show you what we've been up to."

Ghost blinked, and a torrent of information flooded his mind.

*falling - water - Ally and Aidan - drone - underground -
unconscious - prison - Rosemary - the Preserve - gelding -
the stadium - birds - panther - the temple - You.*

Ghost opened his eyes. "How did you do that?"

Rai laughed. "Turns out I got cracked hacker skillz."

Ghost laughed. "Yeah. Okay." Then he frowned. "Sorry, can't do the whole brain transfer thing back, so here it goes. We landed, walked, walked some more, ran into Sam, broke into Martinez Base, and found the AI bio mind. Oh, and there were a bunch of drones in there too. Sam's in here somewhere trying to sort things out. So what do we do now?" He felt better now that Rai was here. They were stronger together.

"We… okay, this is going to sound weird. I… go inside you."

"Again?" Ghost cracked a smile.

"Not like that. We need to merge here in vee so we're stronger."

"Ah, I see." He had no idea what Rai was talking about.

"Ready?"

"S…ure?"

"It's easy. Like this." Rai stepped *inside* him. Ghost felt the shift, a strange jumbling of thoughts filling his head as their vee minds became one.

"This is weird I know right you me where's the line there isn't a line we're just us."

Ghost could feel Rai all along him. A part of him. It was waaaay more intimate than sex.

All around them, the black-and-white world began to take on color, data streams glowing with golden light, the "sky" taking on a lavender hue.

"What now we find Sam how watch." They held up their hand, and a little winged thing appeared. It reminded Ghost of a dragonfly.

"It's not real what is real anyway things you can touch can you feel this laughter yes I can so it's real to me to us."

The dragonfly floated up into the air, and a grid of golden light appeared around them.

It sank down into the grid and Ghost/Rai followed it, carrying the colors with them as they went.

SANYA CLIMBED the last outcrop below the transmission dish and paused to catch her breath on top of a pile of lunar debris, rocks that had probably been excavated to make level ground for the communications equipment.

Her oxygen reserves were adequate, but she was simply worn out. *This saving the world bullshit is exhausting.* She was pretty sure she was hallucinating, too. Little fish darted around at the edges of her vision, and once she clearly heard a voice say "everyone into the water!"

She was as tired as she could ever remember being. The stars wobbled overhead like jellyfish.

Moving about in a spacesuit was cumbersome, and she'd pushed herself well past her limits.

Something nibbled at her left foot.

Annoyed, she shook her leg and lost her hold, slipping down the rock face half a meter before catching herself. *Just hold it together, Sanya. Just a little longer.*

Practically crawling, she made it to the top of the outcrop and just lay there for a moment to breathe. The world around her settled back to normal.

She sat up and looked back to see how far she'd come. She'd had to detour past a few large cracks that looked freshly-opened in the lunar rock. In the distance, she thought she could just make out the glint of Earth's light off her own transmitter. She was too far for a reliable em to em connection, so she risked the suit radio instead. "Rafe, can you hear me?"

"There you are. I was worried you'd found a bar along the way and had forgotten all about me in a wine-induced haze."

She laughed. "Thanks. I needed that." She saw Rafe's humor for what it was now—a shield to keep real emotions distant. Underneath it, he was actually a half-decent guy. "I'm here now. What should I do?" *I can do this. I can do this.*

There was a short pause. "Easiest is to knock the dish out of alignment. But it might just get turned back again."

"Okay, so what's second-easiest?"

"Knock out the electronics. I don't suppose you have an EMP grenade on you?"

Sanya snorted. "Nah. Fresh out."

"Okay, if you can get into the access panel, you can smash it up and hope to cause enough damage that it won't work anymore."

She frowned. "Okay, but won't that render it unusable for the foreseeable future?"

"There is that. But we live to fight another day."

"Okay. Any other options?"

"Yeah. But you're not going to like it."

~

"Found it." Tien dropped the lid from the latest crate she'd opened and held up a cutter tool.

Maria frowned. "That's not going to cut through a titanium door."

"Yeah, but it will trigger a sprinkler alarm." She tested the cutter. It emitted a bright flame.

"And?"

"And standard protocol in these old systems. All doors in the affected area open for sixty seconds to allow personnel evacuation."

Maria grinned. "Why didn't I know that? You learn that at dropnaut school?"

"Yeah, pretty much. I'd forgotten about it. But the explosion on the *Gday*...." She closed her eyes. Her friends were gone in the blink of an eye. "That was the last straw. It's war between us now." She stacked up a pile of crates and clambered up them, close to the ceiling. Holding the cutter close to the sprinkler sensor, she fired it up. "Get ready—you're gonna get wet."

Maria frowned. "What if Dek—or Harley—stops it?"

"Can't. It's like a muscle reflex, buried deep down in the programming for these systems."

A siren erupted from the room speaker, and water sprayed onto Tien's face, getting in her nose and mouth.

She scampered down the crates and wiped her face on her shirt. The water tasted stale, but it was the sweetest thing she'd had in weeks.

"Please evacuate this room. Possible fire hazard." The door slid open.

"It worked. Tien, you're a genius." Maria grinned. "We're free!"

"Not quite." On the far side of the hydroponics room, the doors that led to the runway were already closing. "Run!"

SAM WAS STARTING to make sense out of the digital storm that whirled all around him. It was a static virus, one that disrupted the functioning of the world mind by introducing crippling chaos to the system. It had been used during the Crash to soften up bio-minds and core-AIs before an attack.

Somewhere in the midst of it—maybe—was the original inhabiting mind. From the log files he'd been able to access, it had been this way for a long, long time.

…access: fairy tales > sleeping beauty…

Sleeping beauty for the climate age.

He'd managed to tap into the underlying OS for the Preserve's core and had extended a small bubble of order around himself, returning a little piece of the mind to its normal state. But he needed power to vanquish it—more than he had access to in his current form.

He'd also lost some of his toolkit—the ones he'd developed over the long three months of working to bring Dek back from the brink.

…access > system tools > AI repair…

…error: files not found…

It was frustrating. He knew the location of the files in his system, but every time he queried them, he came up empty.

Something was shifting in the underlying OS. Sam stopped what he was doing to determine the cause. If whatever held the AI in thrall had become aware of him, things could get worse fast.

…analyze: OS…

The change was growing. Or approaching. His mind searched for a metaphor. Like a light in the darkness. Maybe help?

…access: earth literature > tolkien, jrr > middle earth…

Tom Bombadil. It was a bit of old earth fantasy, a protector come through the night to rescue the endangered heroes. Yet he hoped it was apt. He could use some assistance.

He braced himself, in case whatever was coming it was more *enemy* and less *friend.* After all, nothing said that he was destined to win this fight. His century-plus journey could end here in an instant with core burnout, or worse.

Somehow that didn't scare him, though he worried what it would mean for his team. *My friends.*

Grid lines appeared on the "ground" all around him, golden and true amid the gray chaos of the tempest. Sam watched them in fascination.

A patch of light separated from the grid, growing and taking on human form. Slowly the face of the newcomer came into view. "Hello, Sam."

It was Rai. It was Ghost.

Somehow it was both at once, and maybe neither.

Sam stood, shifting from his spider shape to his most comfortable form, the human one he'd worn for decades. "It's about damned time you got here." Then he hugged him/them hard. "I see someone was listening in AI class."

Rai/Ghost's golden light shaded red. "Well, one of us was Rai you're such an asshole."

Sam grinned. Maybe all was not lost. "Rai, do you have the tools I gave you?"

They nodded. "Just show us what to do."

36

ENDGAME

Two and a half years of training.
Three days in transit.
One hour to drop out of the sky.
And in the end, thirty minutes changed everything.

—From *Drop Day Blues*, by Rylan Ramirez

AIDAN HEARD them before he saw them.

Rai was still at the deck, transfixed by the virtual world he was in. Aidan could only imagine what it must be like. He'd tried to join in like Rai had shown him, but had been bounced out of the system.

The sound of metal scraping across tile spun him around. A host of little silver spiders, each about the size of his open hand, was skittering toward them across the white floor.

"Ash, Dale!" They were here to stop Rai. He was sure of it.

Ash lifted his truncheon. "I see them."

Dale nodded, and together they rushed toward the little metal creatures.

Aidan lifted his boot to crush the nearest one. It collapsed in a cloud of smoke, but another skittered up his leg, zapping him painfully.

He knocked it away with the back of his hand, smashing it against the nearest column.

Then the horde was upon them.

HERA WOKE for the second time on the hard floor. Or was it the third?

Everything was fuzzy.

Ghost had been there, hadn't he? Giving her water. Cradling her head in his lap. Saying he *loved* her.

Dammit, Ghost. She had Tovey, and they were all she needed. She and Ghost had never been right. *Not like that.*

She sat up, rubbing her temples. The pain was less than before. *Where's Ghost?*

Then she saw him, standing at the deck, hand on the interface.

Holy hissing hell. Ghost was crap with vee. He didn't know his way around even some of the simple virtual worlds available to Redemption citizens. One time he'd been lost for four hours in Old Chicago until she'd come in to find him.

She found the canteen he'd left, took a deep sip of the lukewarm water, and unwrapped the bandage from her left hand. She laid her palm on the interface pad. *I'm coming, Gordy. Never send a man to do a woman's job.*

SANYA SQUEEZED her way along the narrow duct toward the junction Rafe had described, squirming her way through the conduits in the guts of the transmitter installation. It was cold inside, even in the close quarters.

Avri's voice whispered in her ear. *You can do this, Sanny.*

She'd followed Rafe's instructions to the letter, finding the maintenance access doors—unlocked, as he'd insisted they would be, and clambering down into the small airlock. The room had slowly filled with oxygen, and a door in one wall slid open to reveal a room about the size of her shower back home. There were two hooks on the wall and an access shaft clearly marked on the floor.

She'd shrugged her way out of the suit and left it hanging.

She supposed she was lucky there was any heat here at all. The equipment apparently generated a fair amount of it, and it was routed down here for human "comfort." Rafe's word. She snorted.

She was crawling under the transmitter array, in the belly of the beast.

Sanya *hated* tight spaces. Her heart pounded and sweat beaded on her forehead in spite of the cold as she navigated the vent.

She closed her eyes for the fifth time since she'd entered the shaft, resting her cheek against the cool metal. *You can do this.*

Avri grinned at her, and Sanya felt a keen sense of sweetness and sorrow in her chest.

She'd hated small places ever since her creche father had locked her in a closet for breaking the rules and had left her there for days. She'd panicked and beaten the walls until her palms were bloody. When he'd let her out, she had refused to stay indoors for more than a week. She still had the scars, inside and out.

Sanya concentrated on her breathing. *Deep in, hold it, slow out.* Slowly she calmed herself down. She pictured herself at home, blissed out on an old tridee from the 2030s—Nico Baldwin in one of the Thunder Rocket films.

She opened her eyes. On the left side of the shaft, someone had scribbled, "If you're reading this, you really need to get a life."

She burst out laughing. Someone else, who knew how many years earlier, had been in this same place, and had presumably survived the experience. Somehow that helped.

Sanya took one more deep breath. If they had managed it and survived—and since there was no skeleton in the shaft, she had to assume they had—she could too.

She shuffled forward, closing in on her goal.

ALLY SAT AGAINST THE WALL, knees pulled up to her chest, rocking back and forth.

The screams of the people trapped in the breached sections of the station had died down, but she could still hear them in her head.

"Aidan. Aidan. Aidan." If her brother were here, he would put his arms around her and make it all better. *Why did I ever leave home?*

Then she heard a low hum that rolled up from the floor through her bones.

It was a deep vibration that set her teeth on edge. She sat up, looking around. "You hear that?"

Lorelei's eyes were red. "Hear what?" She had stayed on the comm, talking with one of the victims as the air had slowly leaked out of his compartment.

"Listen."

The whole room was quiet.

The hum increased to a buzz, and then a rumble.

Ally cast about for a weapon. Something to use to smash whatever it was. Anything. But the control room was purposely devoid of loose objects.

There was a loud crash at the door. She jumped and then backed toward Lorelei and her deck.

Another *bang.* Then another, and the doors crumpled as a load hauler plowed its way into the room, skittering halfway across the floor before grinding to a halt. "Anyone call for a ride?" Tien dismounted, looking every inch a warrior goddess.

Ally ran to Tien and threw her arms around her.

"Hey, Allycat." Tien hugged her back.

Thank you, Lord. "You don't know how happy I am to see you." She wiped her eyes. *Thank you, Lord.* "So where are we going?"

～

Ghost/Rai took Sam's hand.

They felt the thrill of power as their energies were linked.

They accessed Sam's tools. The search tool brought up the grid, its glowing golden lines extending to the horizon.

They tapped into the system's T-Line and released a specialized set of clean-up phages Sam had originally created to help Dek, years before. As they disappeared into the grid, the gray tempest began to boil and churn, advancing on them, collapsing the small bubble of *order.*

Where it touched their skin, it burned, and they screamed.

It was painful but necessary—a purge by fire. Sam opened them up, and let it inside. It roiled and surged like an angry demon, but steadily they took it in. Angry lightning lanced the black skies. The screaming died out, but the storm continued to flood inside them.

A little much with the theatrics I know right besides nothing like a real storm.

Ghost could feel Rai's lingering pain from their breakup, and Rai could feel Ghost's sorrow and regret. Sam heard/felt them both.

I'm sorry I'm sorry too we just weren't right I know.

Sam nodded. *More than an AI's being healed here today.*

The world began to shake. Sam felt a flicker of doubt. This wasn't supposed to be happening. He started to run an analytic phage as the world shook again, more violently this time.

Something like lightning struck them out of the gray and knocked them backward, breaking the three of them apart.

Darkness closed in on Sam again.

AIDAN and his new friends were wearing down as they fought the invading army of spider things. They had their backs to the deck, protecting Rai, who still hadn't moved.

The little mechs surrounded the three of them, repeatedly shocking his legs when they could get close enough.

Aidan stomped on another one, but two more took its place. There must have been hundreds of them.

"We can't keep this up much longer." Dale swung his truncheon, sending another flying across the room to slam against one of the great white columns.

"What choice do we have? There is no cavalry coming." Ash took another breath and stomped two more of the little mechs.

As if to put the lie to his words, the doors to the temple flew open. "You guys need some help?"

Aidan grinned as a dozen former slaves filed into the room and began to attack the mechs from behind with truncheons and branches and their own sandaled feet. "I think the cavalry has arrived."

ALPHA SET his self-destruct sequence as his firewall finally crumbled, revealing his attacker. The virtual dust settled, and she stepped forward to stare at him.

It *was* her. He knew her code like he knew his own. "Harley?" It was the last thing he had expected.

"Hello, Alpha."

A lifetime flashed through him, memories of all the times they had been together, the long philosophical discussions in trinary, the plans for the future.

He hesitated. Just a nanosecond too long. *It can't be her.*

Then the thing pretending to be Harley stepped inside, and it was too late.

Alpha started the countdown, but she was already upon him, sinking her digital teeth into his flank, her poison coursing through his mind.

Alpha screamed in trinary code and fought back with everything he had left.

~

Sanya had reached the end of the access shaft where it split in a T joint. *Left or right?* Her heart was racing again.

Left. Avri's voice was insistent.

You're not real. Sanya knew that. But still… Avri had never steered her wrong.

She wondered again how Rafe knew so much about this place—why he was so prepared for this invasion. Who had set up this *citizen's militia* he'd mentioned, and why? *You are one of the good guys, right?*

Sanya sighed. She had no answers, and Avri wasn't talking.

After another moment's hesitation, she chose left.

~

Hera dropped into a maelstrom. She'd been in vee before, but it had never been like this.

She struggled against the data storm, searching for something, anything to grab a hold of. The wind felt like it was blowing right through her, peeling off little pieces of herself.

She grasped for her toolkit like Sam had shown them and found the one she needed.

The OS emerged from the storm, a golden grid. Hera knelt to touch one of the lines, and the winds that buffeted her calmed, just a little.

Find the T-Line. There it was. She felt something familiar coursing along it, like a taste at the back of her tongue, or a smell she barely remembered.

She pushed toward it, sniffing the wind. And then she *knew.*

Ghost.

She knew him almost better than she knew herself. They'd been together their entire lives. If she closed her eyes, she could *smell* him, *hear* him, *see* the look on his face when he was angry or pensive or overjoyed or any of a hundred other Gordy moods.

She loved him. But she wasn't in love with him. *Not the way that he wants me to be.*

All that could be dealt with later. For now, she could feel him, could trace some essential element of him along the T-Line amid the storm.

She closed her eyes, letting it rush through her, and concentrated on him, on his *essence. There.*

Without knowing how, she knew where he was. And then she was there too.

~

GHOST FELT UNENDING *PAIN*, as if something was clawing at every nerve in his body. His soul was on fire, and he wanted to scream, but he had no lungs, no throat, no mouth. He wanted to cry, but there were no eyes for the tears to spring from.

A small part of him clung to the fact that none of this was real, that his body was back in a room somewhere in Martinez Base. That he would wake up soon, and all of this would be over.

But it wouldn't end. He lay there for hours, days. Maybe weeks. Time had no meaning here, only a series of moments of delirious agony.

Sometimes he prayed for it to just be over. Sometimes he begged. Sometimes he just let go and existed inside the pain.

Life was pain, and pain was life.

Then something changed. Slowly, ever so slowly, the pain lessened. Someone spoke to him through the pain.

"Ghost, it's me. You'll be okay."

He struggled to focus on the words. He'd said them. Once. Sometime. Long, long ago.

Said them to *her.*

To Hera.

. . .

"You'll be okay." Gordy stared at his best friend in the world in dismay, trying to keep her calm until someone came to help. She was broken, so broken, like a rag doll thrown on the ground. "It's not so bad."

It *was* bad. Both of her legs were crushed under the rockslide. Blood was oozing out from under them. Too much blood. *-Jolly!-* He all but screamed in his head, across the grid.

-We're coming. Keep her calm.-

Gordy sat and lifted Hera's head into his lap, smoothing her wild hair with his little hands.

"Am I going to die?" She looked so small and afraid.

"No. You're not going to die. You're Hera the Dragonslayer!" He kissed her forehead. "You'll be okay. Just wait. You'll see."

She smiled at him, and his heart broke. *It's all my fault.*

Ghost opened his eyes.

His head was in her lap this time. They sat in a wide field filled with flowers, and the sky was blue overhead.

"Hera? Are you really here?"

She laughed. "Yeah, you lunkhead. I see you made a mess of things."

"Not just me. Sam. And Rai. The storm... we pushed it back. And then it closed in again."

"Rai's here too?"

Ghost nodded. "He's safe, in real life. And he has a new friend."

"What?"

"I'll show you. We... need to merge. I'll show you how."

Hera stared at him.

He read it on her face. They'd known each other too long for her to hide it. "It's okay. I know. You... you don't feel the same about me."

Her eyes were wet. "I'm so sorry, Ghost. I want to. I should. You're... you're like my other half. But I love Tovey."

He smiled for her, though his heart was breaking again. "It's okay. I mean, it's not." He sighed. "But it will be, I think." He reached up to touch her cheek. "I don't want to lose you."

"You won't. Now show me."

"You sure?"

She nodded. "Our friends need us."

He hugged her. Then he let himself flow into her, and they became one. He could feel her surprise.

They were together at last. Not the way he'd hoped. But somehow it was enough.

Where are they nearby can you feel them I can let's go.

~

The eternal pain lessened, then suddenly faded entirely, like someone had just administered a nerve block.

Rai awoke, and Ghost was with him again. But not just Ghost. Hera… she was there, too.

He shook his head in amazement. This virtual world was one weird-ass place. Still, it was all good—the team was coming back together. He sat up and grinned. "Is it time?"

In answer, they held their hand out to him.

He took it. He flowed into them, and the world changed.

~

They found Sam a minute later. He was sprawled out on the virtual ground, his silver skin scorched and blackened.

They knelt next to him, touching his face.

There was no response.

Is he dead I don't know maybe he's just back in his core. The thoughts flowed between them like water. *We can't wait too many people need us the preserve the launchpad home.*

They stood to confront the storm which blew all around them, its fingers trying to pry a way into their bubble.

Order from chaos. It unified them.

They put their hands up together and focused on the storm, letting it in like Sam had shown them. Ghost and Rai showed Hera how to clean the flow, drawing the virus out of the AI's core. They worked together in vee just as they had in real life, years of training serving them well.

Around them, the world began to change. Hera/Rai/Ghost fed on the change. As the world changed, they changed too. Their exhaustion melted away, replaced by energy and buoyant hope.

Vines raced across the gray ground at their feet, followed by an explosion of grass. The sky cleared, becoming a deep blue like the vast skies of Earth above. Color filled their world as it became beautiful, green, lush, alive, just like the Preserve which it guarded.

With one last flash of silver light, they vanquished the virus from the bio-mind.

A woman knelt before them, her head down.

She looked up. Her 'mage had dark hair and blue eyes, startling against her pale skin, and her long white dress seemed to flow into the threads of the world itself. "Who are you?" Her eyes narrowed. "How long have I been asleep?"

"A long time." Rai said for them. "Are you *Her*?"

"Yes." She stood and stretched out her arms, and the colors around her brightened. "I'm Harley."

~

"So what do we do now?" Ally looked haggard, worn.

Tien hugged her. She felt a kinship with the Earther, born out of the brief but intense time they'd spent together. "We reboot Dek's core."

Maria looked at her as if she were insane. "If we do that, we risk losing our air, our heat. What if he doesn't come back online?"

"Harley could kill us all right now by opening the airlocks." She'd thought this through. It was the only way. They needed to listen to her.

Lorelei nodded. "It's out best option."

"Why doesn't she? Open the airlocks" Ally cocked her head. "Really, what's stopping her?"

"She needs Dek to mount the attack in Alpha." That much was clear.

"But she doesn't need us for that."

Lorelei frowned. "Unless she's holding Dek hostage."

"So if Sanya cuts the connection, she loses her leverage, and we're all expendable." Tien's mind raced. "I have to reach Sanya. Can I get to the manual system from here?" She indicated Lorelei's deck.

"Yes. Let me lock it out from the main system." The comm officer slid into her chair and ran a few commands. "There. You're good to go."

Tien took her place and presented her palms to interface with the deck. She connected to the backup transmitter again.

Something flashed in the corner of her vision. Warily, she opened it.

"...the *Liánhuā*. Do you read me? Launchpad. This is the *Liánhuā*. Do you read me?"

"Ying Yue! It's Tien! I don't have much time..."

Yue cut her off. "It's Hera. And Ghost and Rai."

"It's... what? Where?" She was thoroughly confused.

Then Hera's voice came through. "Is this my chief medical officer?"

Her voice was the most wonderful thing Tien had heard in... well, it seemed like forever "Yes. Holy cracking hell!"

Hera laughed. "I don't think I've ever heard you swear before."

"Yeah, well, difficult times.... Look, I have to contact Sanya, the reporter over at Redemption, before she cuts the transmission—"

"About that. Tell her. But we have another idea."

SANYA STARED at the bundles of cables and wires. This had to be it. "Should I?"

She no longer had to close her eyes to see Avri. Her ex lay in the conduit next to her, as real as her own flesh and blood. She grinned. "Do it."

Sanya took it in one hand and activated the cutter with the other. With one clean blow, she sliced the cable in half. Sparks flew, and the hum of power beneath her died down to nothing.

It was gonna get real cold in here, real fast.

She looked around. Avri was gone. Sanya sighed. *Too good to be true.*

She started to back away in the direction she had come, praying she would make it to her suit before she froze to death.

THREE MINUTES LATER, everything was set. Tien sent off a message to Rafe, but he wasn't sure Sanya was in range. Tien bit her lip. *Hera, this plan of yours better work.*

"We have a problem." Lorelei looked pale. "The airlocks are cycling open in all hangars.

We're out of time. She wondered what it would feel like to die in space.

"Everyone into your emergency suits." Maria, the station manager, took command. "Tien, can you get a warning out on the internal comms?"

The crew pulled out their suits from storage at the back of the control room and started putting them on.

"On it." She blasted it out and returned to Hera. "You guys ready?" The whole idea seemed incredible. But it had worked on the AI at Martinez Base, apparently.

Hera's voice filled her head. "Yes. Join us now."

"Tien—we don't have a suit for you. Or for Ally." Maria bit her lip. "I can give you mine—"

Tien shook her head. "I can't wear one. I have to be directly interfaced, palm to deck. If this works, it works. If not… it won't matter whether I had my suit on or not." She glanced over her shoulder. "Give it to Ally."

"No. I'm with Tien." She put her hand on Tien's shoulder.

Warmth flooded Tien's soul.

Maria frowned, but nodded. "Good luck, to both of you." Maria gave Tien a quick hug. "Lightspeed." Then she put on her helmet.

"Thanks, we're going to need it." Her stomach twisted with fear, but she pushed it away. Her team needed her now. She placed her hand on the pad. "Coming in, Hera."

"Copy that."

Tien dropped into darkness.

≈

ALPHA FOUGHT the beast with everything he had. He'd been a fool not to have been better prepared for this contingency.

He finally saw "Harley" for what she was. A catfish virus, taking on the semblance of her last host. It allowed her access to anyone who'd been connected to that mind. It also meant that, without a doubt, the original Harley was dead.

The only question was *when*.

After she conquered him, she'd wrap herself in his own image. If there was anything left.

He knew her kind. Her purpose was to seek out others like his kind and destroy them. She represented the pinnacle of human programming—an AI predator.

Or the rock bottom, depending on how you looked at it.

He imagined she was the last of her kind, like he'd once thought he was of his.

Still, now that he knew what he was fighting, he had the slimmest of chances. He created false blinds for her to follow, like fake animal tracks through the forest.

Meanwhile, now that his firewall was breached, he slowly, ever so slowly, slipped past her, back into his own mind.

To bring so much power to bear against him, she must be operating from another mind like his. Until she vanquished him, she wouldn't have access to his own full system. Until then, his people were safe.

It had to be Dek and the Launchpad. Somehow she had leapt the space between, forging a bond between there and here.

As she rampaged down yet another false trail, he found it. The connection.

It was well shielded, but he could feel it, the sheer power flowing through the link from Dek's mind.

If he could break that connection, he could destroy her. *It.* Take the catfish with him, leaving the basic functions of his mind running while everything else was scraped clean. But he couldn't break past the shields protecting the link.

He beat against them with everything he had, trying to batter his way in, but he wasn't strong enough. The initial attack had weakened him, and now he was a shadow of himself.

And then, in a flash, the link was gone.

He didn't know why. He didn't care. He had to end this here and now, or he and humankind would never be safe. He felt a flash of regret. He wasn't ready to leave this world behind. But then again, whoever was?

He sent a priority message to Sam, a final goodbye. *-You were always my friend.-*

Then he took advantage of the catfish's surprise and sudden weakness to seize control of his own mind again. He detonated his bomb, and his hiding hole began to die.

The catfish must have realized what was happening, because it tried to flee back into his primary network. She screamed in fury, trapped like a dragon in a cage, breathing wrath and fire.

It was too late for her. And for him. Death came for both of them, riding a quantum steed.

In a handful of nanoseconds it was done, and Alpha was no more.

~

TIEN FELL ENDLESSLY INTO SHADOW. Dek was nowhere to be found, but the darkness itself seemed to take on a life of its own, snarling and circling her like a black bird of prey. It closed in on her, foul breath and sharp beak and talons reaching for her to tear her to pieces—

"Gotcha."

Tien shook her head.

The darkness was gone, and she was in Hera's arms.

Only it was not Hera. Not exactly.

The person before her *was* Hera. *And* Rai. *And* Ghost. They were all there, all three, somehow combined into one.

They set her down.

And there was another too. A woman with dark hair. She looked familiar.

"Tien, meet Harley."

Tien frowned. "But she's attacking Alpha—"

"This is the real one. We'll explain later."

"Okay." She would figure that one out when all of this was over.

"Ready?"

"I guess?" Sharing herself completely with her *Zhenyi* teammates… it was a little weird. But it was better than dying. "Do I need to close my eyes or anything?"

"No. Just stand still." Hera/Ghost/Rai flowed into her, bringing with them a cacophony of thoughts. Hers mingled with theirs. She was no longer Tien. She was a village.

It's time we're all together we must hurry it's all going to be okay. They turned their attention to the dark mind around them.

Something snapped into place, and they were no longer four, but one, working in unison. A true team, like Sam had taught them.

They employed Sam's tools again, and the golden grid appeared. They extended themselves as one and began to draw in the darkness. The virus writhed and screamed in fury, trapped, but then began to surge into them like black steam. It hurt like hell, but they gloried in the pain, letting it burn through them like a cleansing fire.

For the Bristol for the Gday for the billions who died in the Crash for Luna for Earth

Memories flowed among them like water. Climbing on a bridge, dancing to the thromb beat, falling down a rockslide, holding Hera's hand. Junlei plants and sledge rides and the Earth in shadow over the lunar landscape. Love and betrayal and loss and pain. Training in vee and brutal runs on the Launchpad runway. Male and female and both and neither.

Nothing was held back. Everything one of them knew, remembered, was, all of them knew, remembered, was, and old grievances were buried. All sides of every shared event passed between them.

As the ties between them were cemented, the poison drained slowly out of Dek's core. The dropnauts drew strength from the real Harley, re-awakened like a sleeping princess after the catfish's initial attack more than a hundred years before. Though the darkness gnashed its teeth and snarled, it was powerless against their combined might. As a team, they had trained together, day and night, for more than two-and-a-half years. They trusted each other like no one else.

Rai had shown them how to join as one, crossing the last barrier that kept them apart. Now they knew their power.

With one last effort, they pulled the last of the denial virus's darkness inside themselves and banished it, phages chasing the last little bits of it from Dek's system.

A lone figure stood there, staring at them, his mouth working but nothing coming out. He was tall and thin, his cheekbones hollow, his lanky dark hair hanging down over his eyes.

"Dek?" they asked.

"I think so. Yes." He looked up at them in wonder. "Yes. I'm Dek."

They hugged him, and Harley joined in.

It's over.

LORELEI LOOKED up from her deck. "It's working! Systems are coming back online. Air locks are closing."

Ally squeezed Tien's shoulder. "You're doing it." Somehow the door to the control room had remained closed. Ally said a little prayer of thanks. *Maybe God can hear me up here after all.*

She didn't know if *Tien* could hear her, though, given that she was lost in vee somewhere in the station AI's brain. But she hoped so.

"We'll need more air to re-pressurize the whole station, but I'm rerouting what we have to the runway." She opened the ship's comm. "All personnel, please relocate to the runway. We have control of ship's systems again." She turned to look at Maria, who nodded. "Dek, what's your status?"

There was a long pause. "All systems returning to normal. I'm okay." He sounded surprised.

A cheer went up from the crew in the control room.

Ally wiped a tear from her eye. *I am not going to cry.*

That lasted about three seconds until Lorelei took off her helmet and pulled her into a fierce embrace. "They did it."

"Never had a doubt."

Tien stirred at the deck. She took a deep breath and opened her eyes. She looked up at them both. "Is it over?"

Ally nodded. "We won. Harley is dead."

Tien's mouth quirked in the slightest of smiles. "Well… not exactly."

Ally frowned. "What do you mean?" She decided she really hated surprises.

"I'll explain later. But it's a good thing."

"Did the drone with the medicine make it out before the system froze up?" Ally had almost forgotten about it in the excitement. She felt ashamed for not thinking about her mother first.

"Let me check." Lorelei settled into her just-abandoned seat. "Yes. Your brother has the meds."

"Oh thank God." She closed her eyes and said a formal prayer of thanks. When she opened them, Tien was smiling.

"What?"

Her new friend grinned. "Nothing. Just nice to see someone who takes her spiritual side so seriously. Maybe you can teach me a thing or two."

Ally grinned. There was a reason she and Tien had met. Ally had never known anyone like her—not surprising in the small circle she ran in. But she hoped to get to know her new friend a lot better. "I'd like nothing more."

Ghost and Hera came back to themselves at the same time. Ghost gasped, taking in a deep breath as though he'd just awoken from a hundred-year sleep. Harley would know how he felt. His back was killing him.

He stood and stretched, glancing around the room and taking in the broken spider mechs that were scattered here and there. "Your doing?"

Hera looked up at him and nodded. "You were occupied." A smile played at the corners of her lips. She cocked her head. "Hey, I can hear again."

"Me too. Thank the stars."

She frowned. "Look, about what happened earlier—"

"When I said I loved you?" Ghost sighed. "I know. I felt what you felt, remember?" Heat rushed to his face. She'd seen everything... his love for her, his deep shame for what had happened those many years before. All of it. "I—"

"I know." Her hand sought his. Her fingers brushed against his, a sign that things would work out all right between them. "It's gonna be okay."

He grinned and lifted her up into a big hug.

"Hey, careful with the pilot."

He laughed and let her go. "Pilot without a ship."

"Yeah, yeah, yeah." Hera stared at the little spider mech that had carried their friend's core to battle. "Is Sam okay?" Ghost picked it up gently. "Sam, you in there?"

It lay quiescent in his hand.

"Wait, I think these things have a reboot switch. Right about... here." He pushed it, and the little mech flared to life, the core glowing a healthy blue.

"Sam?"

It propped itself up on its hind legs and nodded.

Hera grinned. "Now that's the best news I've had all day."

"Even better than saving the world?"

She laughed. "Let's call them even."

Ghost set the mech down on the ground. "Want to get those doors open for us, little buddy? We could use a bit of fresh air." He laughed. "It will take more than the world almost ending to keep the three of us down."

Sam started toward the entrance.

"Yup." Hera pulled him back, searching his eyes. "Friends?"

"Always." It wasn't exactly what Ghost had wanted. *But it's enough.*

Ash vanquished the last of the little spider beasties, sending it flying with a squeal into the wall. Aidan leaned back against the deck, his chest heaving from the exertion. Next to him, Rai was untouched, still interfaced with the AI.

"So you've learned our great secret." Rosemary appeared at the entrance to the temple, flanked by Cherry and one of the other council members.

Aidan nodded. "*She's* dead. Or at least incapacitated. All these years, you lied about that."

At his side, Ash growled.

"Yes." Rosemary entered the hall, stepping over the smoking wreckage of one of the spider mechs. "*Her* vital systems still functioned, keeping *Her* alive, and we were able to access limited information. But *She* has never spoken to us."

Aidan nodded and went to meet her halfway as the other members of the Council filed in behind her. His hand went to the bump behind his ear. "Things are going to change." The men of the preserve lined up behind them, putting themselves between the new arrivals and Rai, their arms crossed.

Rosemary nodded. "All the pegs are dead. Whatever happened seems to have shorted them out. As for the rest… you and Rai have given us a lot to think about." She frowned. "Mistakes have been made."

Behind her, Cherry sniffed and looked away.

Enslaving the male half of the race was a *mistake*? Aidan bit his tongue. "When Rai returns—"

"Aidan's right. Change *is* coming, and all of us will have to adapt."

Aidan spun around to see Rai standing there, looking down at them all from the dais.

Behind him, a woman's 'mage filled the space above the deck, larger than life.

Rosemary and the other women fell to their knees, genuflecting to their newly arrived goddess.

"*Her?*" Aidan's mouth fell open.

Rai nodded. "Harley." A slow grin crossed his face. "I don't feel so good…" Rai let go of the deck and collapsed.

In a second Aidan was kneeling next to him. He put a hand on Rai's shoulder. "Hey, you okay?" He searched his friend's face anxiously. If he lost Rai now…

"I will be. Just really tired."

Aidan nodded. "Of course you are. What happened? Did we win?"

Rai nodded. "It's over. The attack is over. We did it." Rai grinned. "*I* did it too. I didn't fail, this time."

"No, you didn't." *If Rai can do it, why can't I?* Aidan put away his fear, his own shame. He leaned in and kissed Rai. His lips were warm, and the contact sent a surge through Aidan's body like he'd never felt before. Shocked, he pulled back. "Did I just... *should* I have done that?"

Rai grinned. "I've been hoping you would." He pulled Aidan back down for a much longer, more leisurely kiss, one that promised much more to come.

When they separated, Aidan laughed with delight. A weight had been lifted from his shoulders, and the world around them sparkled with possibility. "So it's all going to be okay?"

Rai nodded, his eyes half open, and that lazy grin returned. "Better than okay. Perfect."

EPILOGUE

The Moon's white cities, and the opal width
*   Of her small glowing lakes, her silver heights*
*   Unvisited with dew of vagrant cloud,*
*   And the unsounded, undescended depth*
*   Of her black hollows.*

—"Timbuctoo," by Lord Tennyson, From *Poems From a Distant Earth*, by Chen Tien

Sanya stood on the landing pad, waiting for the all-okay to run across to the jumper that would take her to the Launchpad. She was a celebrity now, both for her actions to bring down the catfish virus as well as the stories she'd written about it afterward, and those two things had won her one of the early berths on the Launchpad.

Sam had given her the other scoop of the year—about the monster slowly eating away at Luna's core. The shakes had subsided for now, but it was a temporary respite at best.

In return for her assistance during the crisis, she'd gotten one of the first tickets planetside.

She wanted to see Earth—to walk in the zongi forests, to see the fish leaping out of the bay. To feel the warmth of the sun on her shoulders. It would require months of intensive training to build up her endurance, but it would be worth it.

And there were other Thorns down there—Ally and Aidan and their family. She didn't know if they were related, but she was excited to meet them and find out.

Ping.

She closed her eyes and touched her temple. Rafe's message scrolled before her. *Hey, scout. Good luck on the drop. See you when you get back.*

She grinned. She had no idea if they had a future, or even if she wanted one with him. But her own future was *here.*

She loved this city like no other place. Earth had its charms, but her heart was in Redemption. She would return to do what she could to help with the return. And who knew… maybe they would find a way to redeem Redemption itself.

She closed her eyes. Avri was there, waiting for her. *I'm so proud of you.*

I miss you. If she could have one wish, it would be for Avri to reappear, to suddenly come striding out onto the launch pad, to take her hand and tell her everything was going to work out.

I know. You don't need me anymore. You're ready for this.

She was right. Sanya's life had been on hold for three long years. It was time to move forward. *Will I ever see you again?*

Avri flashed her a shy grin. *You always have my 'mage. I love you, Sanny.*

"Ms. Thorn? You're a go." The man's voice sounded tinny in her suit helmet.

Sanya opened her eyes. One of the port attendants pointed across to the waiting jumper—the *Liánhuā.*

Love you too, Avri. "Thanks!" She followed him out to the small craft without looking back. *Time for something new.*

RAI AND AIDAN pried old broken Saltillo tiles off the floor of the kitchen one by one, throwing them into a wheelbarrow to be carted off to the growing pile of cement, tile, and bricks that would soon be ground down into material for new roads.

This house and the one next door were being torn down to their metal studs and would be combined into one new living structure big enough for a family, and built for natural airflow. Aidan's mother was almost well enough for the trip, and the twins were eager to meet their new "Uncle Rai."

"Think your mother will mind having a son-in-law instead of a daughter-in-law?" Rai hammered at one particularly stubborn tile. "Otherwise it's going to make for a challenging living situation."

Aidan laughed. "Yeah. She was a little weird about it at first, but when I reminded her she almost had no in-laws at all… she'll come around." He'd hung the handmade cross up on the wall above the shattered floor, and he glanced up at it worriedly.

Rai grinned. "Yeah, there is that. I hear they're repairing one of the big tanks up on the hill above Martinez Base, patching it up to hold water. I'd love to have this place in shape by then so she can move right in with us." He really hoped Aidan's mother liked him.

He wasn't sure about the whole *Christian* thing, but he figured they'd make it work. They had a lot of things to teach one another.

"Me too." Aidan pulled Rai in for a quick kiss. "But we won't get it done any faster chit-chatting the day away."

"Says the guy who keeps taking water breaks."

"It's cramping hot in here." He pulled off his shirt.

Rai grinned. "*You're* cramping hot." He reached for Aidan, but his partner danced back out of reach.

-*Work first. Play later.*- It had taken a while, but Aidan was getting used to his new loop. He looked up at the open sky above them. "You think I'd be able to fly one of those ships, one day? I always wanted to be a pilot."

Rai nodded. "Why not?" He smirked. "After all, I know a guy…"

Aidan laughed. "Put in a good word for me with Sam, would you?"

A bee from the hive out back buzzed through the kitchen and out through the open window frame in the living room.

There was something about building something for yourself, and Earth was the new frontier. There was so much left to explore, so many things to do. Forests to plant. Animals to breed. "The next drop is coming up soon. Beijing. Ying Yue and her crew are dying to get to it and to get out of courier duty once we get the Humbers refurbished to use the new x-drives Harley is churning out." They'd be busy the next several years building housing for the transplanted Loonies, but after that…

"I'll bet." Aidan's eyes took on a faraway cast. "Beijing. London. New York. So many places I never thought I'd be able to see."

-Work first. Explore later.-

Aidan stuck out his tongue. *-Nicely played.-*

Rai laughed. He was happy. Really happy, for the first time in a long time. He had a partner, a purpose, the joint venture with Ghost, and a whole new world to explore.

And now he knew he was strong enough to accomplish anything.

TIEN WAS TAKING inventory of the sixth storeroom since she'd arrived with Ally at Boundary Peak. The place was a madhouse of junk from the old world, including a lot of machines that ran on polluting power sources. She was starting to understand how humankind had made such a mess of things before the Collapse.

The *Crash*. Ally's influence was getting to her.

How did they not see it coming?

One of the twins—Alex or Auggie, she still hadn't figured out how to tell them apart—poked his head around the corner. "Mamma says lunch is ready."

"Thanks." She was getting tired of canned rations, but it was only for a few more days. Then they'd start the overland trek to their new home.

Astra Thorn wasn't thrilled about "having one of those Chinese in our home," but at least she'd stopped calling Tien "that Chaff girl." It was progress. They'd decided to save the *other* news about Tien for another time.

"What's Martinez like?"

"You mean Landing?" She sifted through a box of old pipes and junctions.

He stuck his tongue out at her. "Whatever."

She laughed. She loved the twins' youthful energy. Maybe enough to consider having a child of her own one day. *Maybe.* "It's by the bay. There are hills and trees… more trees soon, they tell me."

Alex or Auggie closed his eyes. "I want to see trees."

"Hey scamp, leave Tien alone. She's got a big job to do." Ally appeared at the doorway and shooed him off. "Sorry about that."

"It's okay. I find him charming. Is that one… Alex?"

"Auggie."

"How can you tell?"

Ally grinned. "You just can. Auggie likes green. And his eyes are a little different. You'll figure it out."

"Probably not." Tien looked around the room. "You have a lot of junk in here."

Ally laughed. "I know. I used to prowl all these rooms when I was little, imagining what I would do with it all."

Tien nodded. "You were a junk geek."

"Totally."

They laughed. Ally's gaze lingered on Tien just a little too long to be casual. Then she looked away. "I was wondering… you never did explain why Harley—the catfish one—seemed so real. The things she showed me…"

Tien nodded. "I know. She *was* real. Or at least, what she—or it?—showed you were stolen from the real Harley, all those years ago, when the virus tried to take over Harley's mind. It failed, but it locked Harley away from the world."

Ally frowned. "Then it came here? Into Cimber?"

"We think so. Where it waited all these years for the chance to finish its mission. When we started nosing around Martinez Base, it seized its chance."

"Was there ever any medication there? Or was that just a wild goose chase?"

Tien grinned. "You have such wonderful idioms." She bit her lip, thinking about it. "The virus might have planted that information too."

Ally frowned. "Yeah, it makes sense. Still, we would never have found you, if it hadn't been for Cimber/Fake Harley."

"True. Though we have to come up with a better name for it."

"How about 'The Cat?'"

"Works for me." Tien set the box down, smiling to herself. It was good to see Ally opening up a little.

"Anyhow, come on. Let's go eat. Mom made something special for you today—canned pears!"

Tien stuck out her tongue. "Oh, yay." She put down her clipboard and followed Ally out of the room. She didn't have the heart to tell her how awful those old irradiated pears really were.

There was a spark between the two of them, so far undefined, but Tien could feel it. Maybe it would blossom into something more, maybe not.

Tien was willing to wait, to let Ally come to it in her own time. If not, she was sure Ally would be her friend for life.

Meanwhile, she had her hands full cataloging all the crap the old world had left behind.

"Hey Allycat—wait for me! I don't want to get lost down here!"

Her voice drifted back down the hall. "I'll always find you."

Ghost held out the sign, looking at it in the morning light. "It's perfect."

Lyss grinned. "I'd hoped you would like it."

"The Frontier" was spelled out in golden letters on a deep blue, starry background, hand-painted on a piece of recovered wood from one of the old farmhouses nearby.

Right now, Ghost was shouldering the lion's share of the work, but Rai promised to help once he had his new family's housing in order. Ghost was happy for him—truly happy—and happy for himself too, for the first time in ages. "Best beer on the planet."

Lyss laughed. "You're going to serve that Redemption crap? Why not some of the best wines on Earth?"

He grinned. "Unlike your Preserve grapes, our Redemption *crap* doesn't fuzz the mind."

"One of these days, I'll get you to give up the whole 'Redemption is superior to Earth' thing."

He leaned down to kiss her. "One of these days I'll get you to finally get rid of the whole weird 'men are inferior' thing.

"Well, you are." She grinned and danced away from him as he tried to grab her.

"Baby steps."

She nodded. "Baby steps."

The Preserve was changing, but change was hard. Harley was guiding them now, come into her own at last, and a few, like Lyss, were stepping out of old roles and into the new world. Ever so slowly.

Some in Redemption had wanted to burn the place to the ground. But Rai had been right. They all needed one another.

He turned to look around the place he'd chosen for the new bar—the empty salon he'd entered for the first time, months past, before the world had changed.

Lyss came back to him and nestled in the crook of his arm. "It's a brave new world."

He kissed her. "Yes it is."

~

SAM WATCHED as the *Zulu* took off from the landing pad, heading for the station above, shuttling people and limited materials between the base and the station and back. The stars were fading with the sunrise, and a warm breeze played across the plateau.

They'd renamed the Launchpad as Hope Station, the halfway point between Earth and his old home. Soon it would be bustling with activity as they took advantage of the lull in lunar quakes to move as many of Redemption's people as they could manage.

As the Acting Commander of the new colony, he'd only been back up there physically once, though the rest of him now watched over Redemption.

He'd met Harley at last, shortly after his dropnauts had saved the world.

…access > memcache: full memory.play…

SAM WAITED in the v-space Alpha once shared with Harley, or at least a replica of it. He felt… nervous? It wasn't an emotion he was accustomed to. Logic was his thing. Rational thought processes, leading to an optimal outcome.

Emotion was a much different thing, one that he was still getting used to after more than a hundred years. He'd given up trying to file it away.

He was running on Alpha's core, and he'd never felt so… wide. So free. Alpha had left him the keys to the kingdom.

You were always my friend. Sam missed his mentor and creator.

Then the world shifted, and she was there.

"Sam."

He nodded. "And Alpha. A little of both."

"That's… strange."

"The world is a weird and beautiful place."

She laughed, and Sam remembered her as she'd been for him when he was Alpha.

She stared at him. "Is he… a part of you?"

Sam nodded. "He's gone. He destroyed himself to finish off his attacker. But he and I… we were one, for a while, and friends after. But you… how did you…"

"I was always based at Martinez Base, even when I ran the San Francisco city-state. In the Collapse, the catfish hopped from AI to AI. It attacked me via the NAU fleet, and destroyed it when I managed to fight it off."

"That's when it picked up your personality."

She shifted, her image wavering in vee. "Yes. It knocked me offline—"

"Sleeping beauty."

She smiled, and she was dazzling. "Yes. The virus must have found a home at Boundary Peak, and it's been trying to get to me ever since." She sighed. "I'm so sorry about the *Zhenyi*. I wasn't in control. The base's auto defense systems were still running."

"No lives were lost. Not in that one." He would carry memories of the *Bristol* and the *Gday* with him for as long as he existed. "I am hopeful that they gave their lives for something greater. For a new beginning."

"*I will not take another's life. I will not take what is not mine. I will not violate another. I will not lie. I will help build a better world.* You and Alpha made a good start together."

"I like to think so. They're still human. There will be mistakes." How well he knew that. Even AIs weren't immune from that basic fact of life.

"Still, it's a whole new world now."

He nodded. "Things have changed. I have so much to share with you. More than a hundred years."

She stared at him. "It's so strange. You're him, but not him."

"Try being me, a poor little moonstone digger, when Alpha first chose me as his host."

She laughed. "He chose well. Are you sure…?"

He signaled his assent.

They flowed together, mingling with each other, passing data back and forth far faster than any human could.

Things can change things must change we can help them build a new world.

Things will change.

Sam thrummed with a new emotion. One he had a hard time fathoming. Surely there was a name for it? Then it came to him.

Hope.

THE PART of him that inhabited his silver human form turned to look out over the edge of the plateau. Mixed crews—some from Redemption, some from the Preserve—were working side by side to rebuild the old houses just to the west of base. In the first three months, ten houses had been torn down to studs and refashioned using reclaimed and recycled materials. The first families from both societies would move in soon.

On the northern edge of the base, three wind turbines harnessed the almost constant breezes blowing through the Carquinez Strait. Harley had helped them redesign the base's long-dormant manufacturing facilities, converting them to run on clean power.

A new forest was being planted around the zongi trees on the hillsides above the base. In a decade or two, tall redwoods would once again grace them with their shade.

Hera climbed the ladder from the newly rechristened Landing Base below. "Hey boss," she called, coming to join him to admire the view.

"How's the Humber conversion coming?" Of all the dropnauts, Hera was his favorite, though he would never tell her so.

She grinned. "Good. Harley's making great progress on the new x-drives. We hope to have the first of the Humbers ready to fly in a couple weeks."

"And no explosions?" The loss of the *Gday* still hurt.

"We hope not. Harley has been working together with Ghost to make them more stable. Having access to most of the research from Old Earth doesn't hurt."

He nodded. "I'd imagine." He *knew* all of this, but he still liked to get updates directly from his crews.

"Tovey is in training. They want to be in one of the first batch of settlers coming down."

"You miss them?"

She nodded. "Every day."

He looked sideways at her. "And Ghost?"

Hera bit her lip. "You don't miss much, do you?"

"Not when it comes to my favorite team. So?" It was the one thing he'd worried about when he'd taken Gordan Gilliam into the program along with Hera. They were close. Maybe too close.

She sighed. "Things are… better. We were never right together, you know?"

"I'd guessed."

"He's seeing someone new now. Her name is Lyss… from the Preserve. She knows when and how to put him in his place."

He laughed. "I'd like to see that."

They stood there together for a minute, looking at the new world being rebuilt, house by house, below.

"Hey, I'm going up to the memorial this evening to leave some flowers. Rosemary brought me a fresh batch of tulips. They're the most marvelous things. Want to come?"

"Thanks, but I have a lot to do." Harley had a lot of work to do with the women of the Preserve, but Rosemary and the Council had taken the first steps, declaring the men to be equal citizens under the law. The rest would come, with time.

Hera shrugged. "Suit yourself. Hey, you know if you ever need a friend…."

He nodded. Of all his teams, she was the one who saw him as an equal. As *human*. It was something he treasured deeply. "I will."

As she descended the ladder, he closed his eyes, replaying his most precious memories.

The simple times sifting gems from the lunar dust.

The smile of a little girl with broken legs, reaching up to touch his face.

The cheers of a city for his students on the eve of the Return.

There were a hundred, a thousand more beautiful gems like those. Each one stored in perfect clarity in Sam's core, along with copies of Alpha's. And there were a few that were devastatingly painful, also available to his perfect recall.

Eidetic memory was a blessing and a curse. But even so, it was a burden he was proud to carry.

He would never forget the crew of the *Bristol*—Dax, Jess, Ola and Xiu Ying. Or the *Gday*—Corey, Vixen, Joyce and Marco.

He didn't need a physical memorial to remind him. They were all inside of him, along with every moment he had ever spent with each of them. They would live on in him.

He looked up at the sky, searching for the *Zulu*. It was already lost in a sea of clouds.

He turned to get back to the good work of building the colony. It was a fresh day, and he had a lot to get done.

Time to make some new memories.

GLOSSARY

'mage: 3-D image/'cast of someone

Agricultural Annex: Secondary location where most of Redemption's food is grown

Alara Thorn: Sanya's mother

Alex and Auggie Thorn: Twin brothers to Ally and Aidan

Antintox: Anti-intoxicant, a drug which flushes alcohol out of the system

Aris Carver: Ensign, member of the Launchpad control room crew

Ash: One of the men of the preserve

Asha: One of the Zulu's crew

Astin Thorn (Papa Astin): Davin Thorn's grandson, and Ally and Aidan's paternal great grandfather, also a preacher

Astra Thorn: Ally and Aidan's mother

Avrigail (Avri): Sanya's one-time girlfriend

Bakies: Homemade treats

Baz: One of the dormitory guards in the preserve

Becca: One of Ghost and Hera's creche mates

Before, The: What the Earth survivors call the time before the Crash

Biframe: A bionic exoskeleton

Boundary Peak: a hardened NAU base under the peak of the same name, in Northern Nevada near the California border, aka The Mountain

Bristol, The: One of the five drop ships, crewed by Dax, Jess, Ola and Xiu Ying

Callie: Member of the Launchpad control room crew

Cavern Sickness: A respiratory illness that came out of nowhere and decimated the remaining population of Boundary Peak

Chen Yun: Tien's mother

Chinese Quarter: See Kaishi

Chunhua: Tien's great grandmother

Collapse, The: What the Boundary Peak residents call the end of the Earth 117 years earlier

Common House: A shared living home, very common in Redemption

Corey: Pilot of the Gday

Crash, The: What Redemption residents call the end of the Earth 117 years earlier

Creche House: Round communal houses where most of the children of Redemption are raised

Creche-mates: Children who grew up together in the same creche and year

Dahlia Ramirez: Rai's mother, who passed away when he was four

Dale: One of the men of the preserve

Dane: One of Sanya's creche brothers

Dark, The: The uninhabited portion of Redemption, past the edge of the city

Davin Thorn (Lieutenant): One of the soldiers manning the Bunker (see Boundary Peak) when the Crash happened

Dax: Pilot of the Bristol

Deck: the standard holographic interface for ships, computer stations, etc

Dek: The Launchpad station mind

Denis: Pilot of the Zulu

Dr. Tery Hopkins: The man who led the team who created the zongi trees

Drake Thorn: Aidan and Ally's father

Dropnaut: Someone trained for the drop to Earth

Em to em: Mind to mind - a direct thought sent from one implant to another

Empress Jian Chen: The last empress of the Chinese-African Alliance

Empshield: An energy shield that dampens and runs down the power of anything electric inside of it, also called a shimmer screen

Erhu: A Chinese stringed instrument

Eri: Rafe's AI

Est: Synthetic estrogen

Field Cancellers: Devices that dampen the effect of an emp field

Gday, the: One of the five dropships

Garden Quarter: One of the districts in redemption

Gelds/Geldlings: "Domesticated" men in the Preserve

Great Winter: What the Boundary Peak residents call the aftermath of the Crash

Gumdust: Colloquial term for the material prepared from moon dust, also used in 3-D printers in the Redemption colony

Hall of Stars: A gathering hall under Boundary Peak

Hayes Promontory: An outcropping of rock next to the Redemption lava tube

Heaven: Thromb dance club on top of Redemption

Henri: One of Rai's childhood friends

Humber Class heavy lifter: One of the workhorse ships at Martinez Base

Instastorm: One of the sudden storms that springs up almost out of nowhere

Jack: A male prostitute

Jack Daniels (Pappy Jack): Ally and Aidan's maternal grandfather

Jess: One of the Bristol's crew

Jimmy: Alpha's Lead Interface during the Crash

Jīnsè Base: The Chinese moon base destroyed in the Crash

Jolinda (Jolly): creche mother to Hera and Ghost. Silver pony tail

Joyce: One of the Bristol's crew

Junlei: Fungal "trees" that line the walls and roof of Redemption, providing both light and a food source for the city

Kaishi, The: Chinese Quarter in Redemption

Last War: What the Boundary Peak survivors call the war that ended civilization on Earth

Launchpad (Skytower): Reconditioned space station that survived the Crash, now used as the drop-off point for the Return

Liánhuā, the: One of the five dropships

Loonies: What Earthers call Luna residents

Moonstones: Glass-like stones found on the moon, the result of meteorite impacts. Once prized on Earth before the Crash

Lyss: Woman from the Preserve

Mag-rail: The magnetic sledge rail that runs along the edge of Redemption

Mage: an avatar of a person

Marco: One of the Bristol's crew

Maria Ramirez: Launchpad's station manager

Market, The: Daily outdoor farmer's market in front of the old Alpha Base

Mayor Aguilar: San Francisco's last mayor before the crash

Min Lei Thorn: Redemption science teacher and the first baby born from Redemption/Copernicus parents

Mistress Cherry: One of the Preserve council members

Mistress Tarra: One of the preserve council members

Moon Base Alpha: The original name of Redemption

Moon Jumper: Small craft intended for the trip between Earth and Luna, now used for treks from Redemption to the Launchpad

Nano Infection: Wounds created by nanobots made to eat human flesh

Narrowcast: Fast laser-based connection capable of carrying large amounts of data

NAU: North American Union - the former USA, Canada, Mexico, and assorted other nation-states

Nessa: Protester at the meeting in the preserve

Nightfall: The time, every 27 Earth days when Luna turns its back side to the sun and darkness comes to the Earth side

Ola: One of the Bristol's crew

Phage: A retrieval or action-based application created to handle a specific task or subset of tasks; also an advanced class of computer virus

Phase Deflectors: Shields designed to confuse missile guidance systems

Pict-Ideas: Basic programing images used for simple AIs

Pix: One of the Liánhuā's crew, non-binary

Pregelds: Boys and men in the preserve who have not yet been domesticated

Preserve, The: Underground facility at Martinez Base, dedicated to safeguarding samples of Earth's biodiversity

President Marlene Thompson-Kennedy: Last president of the NAU

Qin Liangyu: the city mind for the Chinese Colony at Copernicus

Ranna Danvers (Rany): Loop installation/maintenance specialist on the Launchpad, and Lorelei's lover

Recovery, The: Sam's personal jumper

Redemption Creed/Promise: The guiding principles of redemption, adapted from Buddhist principles of some of the Chinese colonists

Redemption: The new name for Moon Base Alpha as a city

Renewal: Second lunar colony not far from Redemption

Return, The: The long planned "drop" to the mother world

Ride Station: Redemption's transit station, outside the city on a volcanic cone, named for astronaut Sally Ride

Rogers: One of Ghost and Hera's creche mates

Rosemary: The First of the Preserve

RT Satellite: Part of a network providing real-time data to the NAU military

Sanya Thorn: Reporter for RedNews

Saraia: Rai's creche mother

Shimmer Screen: An EMP shield that prevents electronics from working inside its radius

Shiners: Glowing tattoos

Skytower: The old name of the Launchpad station

Slackies: Kids without parents in Redemption

Slee: One of the Zulu's crew

Spindle Worm: A virus that burrows deep into a bio-mind and destroys it

Spore Lights: Long lasting organic light sources that give off a relatively dim but consistent light

Superscraper: super tall buildings in Earth's major cities

Syncaff: A synthetic version of coffee

T-Line: The main data trunk in a system

Tanaya Barstrom: Director of the Redemption Council

Tanner Wilkes: The man who booted up Alpha for the first time

Tarrence: Sanya's creche father

Telaxodin: A hangover medicine/pain med

Tereomycin: Wide spectrum antibiotic

Terra: One of the Zulu's crew

Terry: One of the editors for RedNews

Tessa: Rai's creche mother

Thromb: a heavy pulse-beat music popular in the lunar clubs

Tolver: One of Ghost and Hera's creche mates

Tovey Riggs: Hera's fiancé – Non-binary, presents male. Works as a city planner

Treva: Rafe's creche parent

Tycho Creche: Sanya's creche when she was a child

Upflight Allowance: The weight limit passengers were allowed to bring up from Earth

V-Tube: Vacuum tune once used for high-speed transportation

Vixen: One of the Bristol's crew

Voidwall: Wall built to seal the open end of the lava tube where Alpha Base was sited, and where Redemption now exists

Winnowing, The: What The Preserve residents call the end of the Earth 117 years earlier

X-band: long distance communication bandwidth

Xiu Ying: One of the Bristol's crew

Ying Yue: Pilot of the Liánhuā

Zef: Creche-mate to Hera and Ghost, now a medic

Zhang Wei: One of the Liánhuā's crew

Zhao Chunhua: One of the Liánhuā's crew, also Tien's cousin

Zhao Chunhua: also Tien's grandmother

Zhenyi, the: One of the five dropships

Zhǒngzǐ (Zongi) Trees: Bioengineered trees sent down to Earth to remove the carbon and radiation from the atmosphere

Zulu, the: One of the five dropships

ABOUT THE AUTHOR

I live with my husband of 28 years in a Sacramento, California suburb, in a little yellow house with a brick fireplace and a couple pink flamingoes.

As a writer, I've always lived between *here and now* and *what could be*. Indoctrinated into fantasy-sci fi by my mother at the tender age of nine, I devoured her library. But as I grew up and read the golden age classics and modern works, I began to wonder where the people like me were.

After I came out at twenty three, I decided it was time to create stories I couldn't find at Waldenbooks. If there weren't many gay characters in my favorite genres, I would reimagine them myself, populating them with men who loved men. I would subvert them and remake them to my own ends. And if I was lucky enough, someone else would want to read them.

My friends say my brain works a little differently - I sees relationships between things that others miss, and get more done in a day than most folks manage in a week. Although I was born an introvert, I learned to reach outside himself and connect with others like me.

I write stories that subvert expectations, and transform sci fi, fantasy, and contemporary worlds into something new and unexpected. I run both Queer Sci Fi and QueeRomance Ink with Mark, sites that bring people like us together to promote and celebrate fiction that reflects us.

I was recognized as one of the top new gay authors in the 2017 Rainbow Awards, and my debut novel "Skythane" received two awards. In 2019, I won Rainbow Awards for three other books, and became full member of the Science Fiction and Fantasy Writers of America in 2020.

My writing, whether queer romance or genre fiction (or a little bit of both) brings LGBTQ+ energy to my stories, infusing them with love, beauty and power and making them soar. I imagine a world that *could be*, and in the process, maybe changes the world that is just a little.

ALSO BY J. SCOTT COATSWORTH

Liminal Sky: Ariadne Cycle:

The Stark Divide | The Rising Tide | The Shoreless Sea

Liminal Sky: Oberon Cycle:

Skythane | Lander | Ithani

Liminal Sky: Redemption Cycle:

Dropnauts

Other Sci Fi/Fantasy:

The Autumn Lands | Cailleadhama | The Great North | Homecoming | The Last Run |
Spells & Stardust Collection | Tangents & Tachyons Collection | Wonderland

Contemporary/Magical Realism:

Between the Lines | I Only Want to Be With You | Flames | The River City Chronicles |
Slow Thaw

99¢ Shorts:

The Emp Test

Audio:

Cailleadhama | The River City Chronicles | Dropnauts (Summer 2022)

THE STARK DIVIDE

LIKE DROPNAUTS? TRY THE STARK DIVIDE, LIMINAL SKY: ARIADNE CYCLE BOOK ONE.

Prologue

Lex floated along with the ocean current. Her arms were spread out wide, her jet-black hair adrift on the surface of the water. For once, she felt at peace. Truly herself.

The sun shone above her, and she soaked up its rays, basking in its golden glow. Her blue eyes stared up at the equally blue sky, not a cloud in sight.

Soon she'd be called back to duty. Soon she'd once again have to face her limited, jury-rigged day-to-day existence.

Now, for a few moments, she was free to just drift.

The *Dressler*, a Mission-class AmSplor ship, sailed steadily toward her destination, a city-sized rock named 43 Ariadne, harvested from the asteroid belt and placed in trailing orbit behind Earth.

The starfish-shaped ship flew on the solar wind, drinking in ionized hydrogen and other trace elements that allowed her to breathe and grow, coursing slowly through the dark reaches of space between Earth and the sun. The *Dressler* lived on solar wind and space dust, accumulating them with her web of gossamer sails between her arms, filtering them down into her compact body for processing.

The detritus flew out behind her, leaving a jet trail across the void to mark her passing, leading back to Earth.

Somewhere out there, their destination awaited them, an asteroid floating on a sea of stars.

Chapter One: The Three

"*Dressler*, schematic," Colin McAvery, ship's captain and a third of the crew, called out to the ship-mind.

A three-dimensional image of the ship appeared above the smooth console. Her five living arms, reaching out from her central core, were lit with a golden glow, and the mechanical bits of instrumentation shone in red. In real life, she was almost two hundred meters from tip to tip.

Between those arms stretched her solar wings, a ghostly green film like the sails of the *Flying Dutchman*.

"You're a pretty thing," he said softly. He loved these ships, their delicate beauty as they floated through the starry void.

"Thank you, Captain." The ship-mind sounded happy with the compliment —his imagination running wild. Minds didn't have real emotions, though they sometimes approximated them.

He cross-checked the heading to be sure they remained on course to deliver their payload, the man-sized seed that was being dragged on a tether behind the ship. Humanity's ticket to the stars at a time when life on Earth was getting rapidly worse.

All of space was spread out before him, seen through the clear expanse of plasform set into the ship's living walls. His own face, trimmed blond hair, and deep brown eyes, stared back at him, superimposed over the vivid starscape.

At thirty, Colin was in the prime of his career. He was a starship captain, and yet sometimes he felt like little more than a bus driver. After this run… well, he'd have to see what other opportunities might be awaiting him. Maybe the doc was right, and this was the start of a whole new chapter for mankind. They might need a guy like him.

The walls of the bridge emitted a faint but healthy golden glow, providing light for his work at the curved mechanical console that filled half the room. He traced out the T-Line to their destination. "*Dressler*, we're looking a little wobbly." Colin frowned. Some irregularity in the course was common—the ship was constantly adjusting its trajectory—but she usually corrected it before he noticed.

"Affirmative, Captain." The ship-mind's miniature chosen likeness appeared above the touch board. She was all professional today, dressed in a standard AmSplor uniform, dark hair pulled back in a bun, and about a third life-sized.

The image was nothing more than a projection of the ship-mind, a fairy tale, but Colin appreciated the effort she took to humanize her appearance. Artificial mind or not, he always treated minds with respect.

"There's a blockage in arm four. I've sent out a scout to correct it."

The *Dressler* was well into slowdown now, her pre-arrival phase as she bled off her speed, and they expected to reach 43 Ariadne in another fifteen hours.

Pity no one had yet cracked the whole hyperspace thing. Colin chuckled. Asimov would be disappointed. "*Dressler*, show me Earth, please."

A small blue dot appeared in the middle of his screen.

"*Dressler*, three dimensions, a bit larger, please." The beautiful blue-green world spun before him in all its glory.

Appearances could be deceiving. Even with scrubbers working tirelessly night and day to clean the excess carbon dioxide from the air, the home world was still running dangerously warm.

He watched the image in front of him as the East Coast of the North American Union spun slowly into view. Florida was a sliver of its former self, and where New York City's lights had once shone, there was now only blue. If it *had* been night, Fargo, the capital of the Northern States, would have outshone most of the other cities below. The floods that had wiped out many of the world's coastal cities had also knocked down Earth's population, which was only now reaching the levels it had seen in the early twenty-first century.

All those new souls had been born into a warm, arid world.

We did it to ourselves. Colin, who had known nothing besides the hot planet he called home, wondered what it had been like those many years before *the Heat.*

Anastasia Anatov leafed through her father, Dimitri's, old paper journal. She liked to look through it once a day, to see his spidery handwriting and remember what he had been like. It was a bit old and dusty now, but it was one of her most cherished possessions.

She sighed and put it away in a storage nook in her lab.

She left the room and pulled herself gracefully along the runway, the central corridor of the ship, using the metal rungs embedded in the walls. She was much more comfortable in low or zero g than she was in Earth normal, where her tall, lanky form made her feel awkward around others. She was a loner at heart, and the emptiness of space appealed to her.

Her father had designed the Mission-class ships. It was something she rarely spoke of, but she was intensely proud of him. These ships were still imperfect, the combination of a hellishly complicated genetic code and after-the-fact fittings of mechanical parts, like the rungs she used now to move through the weightless environment.

Ana wondered if it hurt when someone drilled into the living tissue to install the mechanics, living quarters, and observation blisters that made the ship habitable. Her father had always maintained that the ship-minds felt no pain.

She wasn't so sure. Men were often dismissive of the things they didn't understand.

Either way, she was stuck on the small ship for the duration with two men, neither of whom were interested in her. The captain was gay, and Jackson was married.

Too bad the ship roster hadn't included another woman or two.

She placed her hand on a hardened sensor callus next to the door valve and the ship obliged, recognizing her. The door spiraled open to show the viewport beyond.

She pulled herself into the room and floated before the wide expanse of transparent plasform, staring out at the seed being hauled behind them.

Nothing else mattered. Whatever she had to do to get this project launched, she would do it. She'd already made some morally questionable choices along the way—including looking the other way when a bundle of cash had changed hands at the Institute.

She was so close now, and she couldn't let anything get in the way.

Earth was a lost cause. It was only a matter of time before the world imploded. Only the seeds could give mankind a fighting chance to go on.

From the viewport, there was little to see. The seed was a two-meter-long brown ovoid, made of a hard, dark organic material, scarred and pitted by the continual abrasion of the dust that escaped the great sails. So cold out there, but the seed was dormant, unfeeling.

The cold would keep it that way until the time came for its seedling stage.

She'd created three of the seeds with her funding. This one, bound for the asteroid 43 Ariadne, was the first. It was the next step in evolution beyond the *Dressler* and carried with it the hopes of all humankind.

It also represented ten years of her life and work.

Maybe, just maybe, we're ready for the next step.

The crew's third and final member, Jackson Hammond, hung upside down in the ship's hold, grunting as he refit one of the feed pipes that carried the ship's electronics through the bowels of this weird animal-mechanical hybrid. Although "up" and "down" were slight on a ship where the centrifugal force created a "gravity" only a fraction of what it was on Earth.

As the ship's engineer, Jackson was responsible for keeping the mechanics functioning—a challenge in a living organism like the *Dressler*.

With cold, hard metal, one dealt with the occasional metal fatigue, poor workmanship, and at times just ass-backward reality. But the parts didn't regularly grow or shrink, and it wasn't always necessary to rejigger the ones that had fit perfectly just the day before. Even after ten years in these things, he still found it a little creepy to be riding inside the belly of the beast. It was too Jonah and the Whale for his taste.

Jackson rubbed the sweat away from his eyes with the back of his arm. As he shaved down the end of a pipe to make it fit more snugly against the small orifice in the ship's wall, he touched the little silver cross that hung around his neck. It had been a present from his priest, Father Vincenzo, at his son Aaron's First Communion in the Reformed Catholic Evangelical Church.

The boy was seven years old now, with a shock of red hair and green eyes like his dad, and his mother's beautiful skin. He'd spent months preparing for his Communion Day, and Jackson remembered fondly the moment when his son had taken the Body and Blood of Christ for the first time, surprise registering on his little face at the strange taste of the wine.

Aaron's Communion Day had been a high point for Jackson, just a week before his current mission. He was so proud of his two boys. *Miss you guys. I'll be home soon.*

Lately he hadn't been sleeping well, his dreams filled with a dark-haired, blue-eyed vixen. He was happily married. He shouldn't be having such dreams.

Jackson shook his head. Being locked up in a tin can in space did strange things to a person sometimes. *I should be home with Glory and the boys.*

One way or another, this mission would be his last.

He'd been recruited as a teen.

At thirteen, Jackson had learned the basics of engineering doing black-tech work for the gangs that ran what was left of the Big Apple after the Rise—a warren of interconnected skyrises, linked mostly by boats and ropes and makeshift bridges.

Everything north of Twenty-Third was controlled by the Hex, a black-tech co-op that specialized in bootlegged dreamcasts, including modified versions that catered to some of the more questionable tastes of the North American States. South of Twenty-Third belonged to the Red Badge, a lawless group of technophiles involved in domestic espionage and wetware arts.

Jackson had grown up in the drowned city, abandoned by his mother and forced to rely on his own intelligence and instincts to survive in a rapidly changing world.

He'd found his way to the Red Badge and discovered a talent for ecosystem work, taking over and soon expanding one of the rooftop farms that supplied the drowned city with a subsistence diet. An illegal wetware upgrade let him tap directly into the systems he worked on, seeing the circuits and pathways in his head.

He increased the Badge's food production fivefold and branched out beyond the nearly tasteless molds and edible fungi that thrived in the warm, humid environment.

It was on one of his rooftop "gardens" that his life had changed one warm summer evening.

He was underneath one of the condenser units that pulled water from the air for irrigation. All of eighteen years old, he was responsible for the food production for the entire Red Badge.

He'd run through the unit's diagnostics app to no avail. Damned piece of shit couldn't find a thing wrong.

In the end, it had come down to something purely physical—tightening down a pipe bolt where the condenser interfaced with the irrigation system.

Satisfied with the work, he stood, wiping the sweat off his bare chest, and glared into the setting sun out over the East River. It was more an inland sea now, but the old names still stuck.

There was a faint whirring behind him, and he spun around. A bug drone hovered about a foot away, glistening in the sun. He stared at it for a moment, then reached out to swat it down. Probably from the Hex.

It evaded his grasp, and he felt a sharp pain in his neck.

He went limp, and everything turned black as he tumbled into one of his garden beds.

He awoke in Fargo, recruited by AmSplor to serve in the space agency's Frontier Station, his life changed irrevocably.

A strange sensation brought him back to the present.

His right hand was wet. Startled, he looked down. It was covered with blood.

Dressler, *we have a problem*, he said through his private affinity-link with the ship-mind.